MERCILESS REACH

HOUSE GLUTTONY

ROOTS AND REMEDIES

OX & RAVEN TAVERN

OX & RAVEN

PÂTISSERIE

F SECRETS

THRONE OF
SECRETS

ALSO BY KERRI MANISCALCO

PRINCE OF SIN

Throne of the Fallen

STALKING JACK THE RIPPER

Stalking Jack the Ripper

Hunting Prince Dracula

Escaping from Houdini

Becoming the Dark Prince

Capturing the Devil

KINGDOM OF THE WICKED

Kingdom of the Wicked

Kingdom of the Cursed

Kingdom of the Feared

THRONE OF
SECRETS

A Prince of Sin Novel

KERRI
MANISCALCO

LITTLE, BROWN AND COMPANY
New York | Boston | London

The characters and events in this book are fictitious. Any similarity to real persons, living or dead, is coincidental and not intended by the author.

Copyright © 2024 by Kerri Maniscalco

Hachette Book Group supports the right to free expression and the value of copyright. The purpose of copyright is to encourage writers and artists to produce the creative works that enrich our culture.

The scanning, uploading, and distribution of this book without permission is a theft of the author's intellectual property. If you would like permission to use material from the book (other than for review purposes), please contact permissions@hbgusa.com. Thank you for your support of the author's rights.

Little, Brown and Company
Hachette Book Group
1290 Avenue of the Americas, New York, NY 10104
littlebrown.com

First Edition: October 2024

Little, Brown and Company is a division of Hachette Book Group, Inc. The Little, Brown name and logo are trademarks of Hachette Book Group, Inc.

The publisher is not responsible for websites (or their content) that are not owned by the publisher.

The Hachette Speakers Bureau provides a wide range of authors for speaking events. To find out more, go to hachettespeakersbureau.com or email hachettespeakers@hbgusa.com.

Little, Brown and Company books may be purchased in bulk for business, educational, or promotional use. For information, please contact your local bookseller or the Hachette Book Group Special Markets Department at special.markets@hbgusa.com.

Print book interior design by Taylor Navis

Map by Virginia Allyn

Interior art: Dragon © Gaspar Costa/Shutterstock.com

ISBN 978-0-316-55754-2 (HC); 978-0-316-58237-7 (international tpb); 978-0-316-58094-6 (HC Barnes & Noble exclusive edition); 978-0-316-58309-1 (HC Target exclusive edition)

LCCN is available at the Library of Congress

Printing 1, 2024

LSC-C

Printed in the United States of America

For my Bella baby, you're mommy's girl. Always.

And for my Gage man, who's undoubtedly transfixed by that magical, babbling brook in the Great Beyond.

I miss you both more than words can say.

If Cinderella considered her prince more wicked than charming at first,
and wanted to unravel his darkest secrets and ruin him,
this would be their twisted fairy tale...

Gentlemen of vice are especially nice,
since their filthy tales contain an abundance of spice.

POEMS FOR THE WICKED, VOLUME TWO

THRONE OF
SECRETS

In an Underworld realm known as the Seven Circles, seven immortal princes rule their wicked courts through sin and debauchery.

Each circle relies on its citizens and other mythical creatures to fuel the prince's power by indulging in their sin of choice: wrath, envy, greed, lust, sloth, pride, or gluttony.

Power is each prince's greatest currency, and an overarching curse that recently broke threatened to weaken them, leaving them open to attack from other wicked beings that call the underworld home—witches, Fae, shape-shifters, goddesses, and the ever-scheming vampires in the south. Now each House of Sin is secretly fighting to regain its full might and save its court from the curse's lingering effects.

This story takes place in the blustery, northernmost circle, and follows the Prince of Gluttony, whose sin is not simply gorging on the finest foods and drinks but seeking adventure and thrills. Like hunting ice dragons that roam the unforgiving terrain, or maybe fighting his biggest battle to date: trying not to fall for someone he hates...

As mortal poets and playwrights have said: all is fair in love and war.

May the old gods have mercy on the Prince of Gluttony.

A storm named Adriana is coming and she is merciless. At least where he is concerned.

ONE
Prince Gluttony

A STRONG GUST OF wind raced down the snowcapped mountains, screaming through the pass, the sound almost as chilling as the winter air itself.

This far north of the Seven Circles, beyond any of the royal Houses of Sin, where nightmares and lesser demons stalked the forest's edge, even the elements gave in to fear.

Fainter, another noise emerged above the tree line. One we'd been waiting for.

I paused, holding a hand in the air, a silent signal for my hunters to halt.

Leather snapped in time with the breeze, the familiar sound muffled only slightly by what I knew was an outer layer of angelic-looking white feathers.

Like most things in the Underworld, that unexpected plumage was a beautiful deception hiding a sinister purpose. Those downy wings in conjunction with the iridescent scales of their bodies helped to conceal the unholy beasts as they slowly flew through snow-laden skies, circling us—their prey—below.

I gripped my House dagger in my fist, heart pumping fast as I peered up through the trees, blinking ice from my lashes, waiting for that first glimpse of Death made flesh.

Immortality would keep me breathing no matter what, but not everyone in our hunting party had that luxury. Like me they fought for the thrill of it, but it also was one of the greatest sources of fuel for my power. The hunt fed my sin more than anything else. Since my circle's sin was gluttony, most outside the Underworld believed that meant overindulging in food and drink. We did that too, along with fucking and fighting, but most of my sinners took after me—preferring to overindulge in adventure and danger.

That fear, the possibility of failure mixed with a fierce desire to indulge in adventure at any cost, drove the hunters forward through the narrow, unforgiving pass with me, gazes locked on the overcast sky, bodies tensed and ready for battle.

I glanced over my shoulder at the line of elite fighters who'd braved Merciless Reach, the walled outpost I'd built a century before to monitor the savage northern lands just beyond my territory, House Gluttony.

All except one had my royal crest stitched onto their battle leathers, searching for dragons and glory.

I motioned for everyone to remain silent, to be vigilant. It wouldn't be long now.

We'd been tracking the dragons for hours, playing a cat-and-mouse game, both parties eager to pounce. The dragons had known we were close, but thanks to a smattering of evergreens lining each side of the pass, they didn't have a clear visual.

Some hunters bit down on a leather strap to silence the sound of their chattering teeth. They wouldn't last another hour out here, no matter how brave they were.

We needed to start moving again.

I scanned the line until I spotted who I'd been looking for bringing up the back of our group. Gold eyes glinted in the sliver of sunlight shouldering its way through the storm.

My brother Wrath, the general of war, was the only one who looked as thrilled as I was by the approaching sound. He was made for battle just as I was built for danger; a combination that made for poor decisions but great stories.

Out here, where only monsters dwelled, ice dragons were the worst predators.

Which meant they were the best opponents for us wicked Princes of Hell.

Tonight's hunt promised to be a memorable one. Violence simmered in the air, so close I could practically taste the impending battle, my mouth watering in anticipation.

For hours, we'd ruthlessly tracked this particular pack of ice dragons north, far beyond hospitable land. There were seven known dragon packs spread throughout the region; this one happened to claim the territory closest to my House of Sin.

The terrain was milder than that of the far north, but it was still brutal.

Several members of the hunt had been forced to retreat, the harsh winter elements too deadly to contend with. The few who remained were the fiercest, or the most foolish.

Jackson Rose, one of the newest initiates of the royal hunting guild, tripped over an ice-coated root, cursing as he landed face-first in the snow. Felix, a seasoned veteran, shot me a look of apology and grumbled as he hoisted the younger hunter up by his straps.

My skin prickled with sudden awareness.

That one sign of exhaustion was the spark needed for violence to ignite. If the dragons had been unsure of our precise location, that element of surprise was gone now.

"On alert!" I shouted, dagger aimed skyward as I stepped off the path, pausing under the nearest evergreen to avoid what was certain to be an aerial attack.

I silently counted, pulse drumming madly.

The sound of beating wings ceased.

"Be ready!"

All at once the great beasts dove at us like comets falling from the skies.

Majestic wings tucked against their big, scaled bodies, they plummeted to the earth one after another, their numbers taking our party by surprise.

Wind howled around their massive forms, the sound raising the fine hair along my arms.

The largest thundered to the ground before me, snarling as its impact made a crater that displaced several feet of snow and frozen earth, missing me by inches. Iridescent scales shone like diamonds, its jaws filled with rows of snapping teeth that were as deadly as daggers.

A single jagged scar glinted across its chest.

I bared my teeth in a feral grin. It was Silvanus, a dragon I'd sparred with for nearly a century and one I'd hand-raised from a hatchling.

That bond meant little on the battlefield, though.

Our skirmishes were well matched, neither of us willing to be defeated easily.

Silvanus had the temperament of an ornery house cat. Which meant he was similar to my brother Sloth; he only sparred when the mood struck and couldn't be bothered otherwise.

I stole a quick glance at the hunters; almost everyone had their own dragon to battle, and all wore the same wolfish grin as they took turns striking at their opponents.

I focused on my fight again, allowing the thrill to take over as I tuned everything else out.

"Ready to waltz, old boy?" I taunted, trying to spot any opening to strike.

Whoever drew first blood won. With two giant barrels of spiced ale waiting for me back at my warm castle, I felt like celebrating victory tonight, far from the miserable cold that gripped my balls in its icy fist.

Silvanus spewed a stream of white flame at my left foot, forcing me to dance backward. The bastard almost destroyed my favorite hunting boots.

I aimed my dagger at my feet. "Have some respect for fine leather, you scaled heathen."

Pointed teeth gleamed in the waning light, the dragon's version of a grin.

I laughed softly as he unleashed the next stream of icy fire, this time aiming for my other leg. I'd offered to waltz with him, and the prick was making me dance.

"Well played."

My grin faded. The need to hunt, to win, was taking over.

I stalked forward, gaze narrowed, plan whirling into motion. I'd feint to the left, then catch him with a jab on the right, nicking him under his snout. He was broad, and agility wasn't his strong suit, an advantage I'd press until I claimed victory.

Instead of charging me, Silvanus held his ground, a warning growl sounding low in his chest. His attention was fixed to some point above my shoulder. Given my nearly six-and-a-half-foot frame, he wasn't looking at one of the hunters.

The dragon was warning me about some*thing* else.

I spun around, narrowly avoiding a blow from a second dragon that would have taken my head off had I been mortal.

All levity vanished at once. A death blow was forbidden in our little games, the fact I couldn't be killed notwithstanding. There were several other hunters here who *could* die.

"Need I remind you of the pact?" I seethed, keeping both dragons in sight.

Silvanus might have warned me once, but I couldn't trust he'd do it again. Like wolves, dragons were pack creatures. They'd fall in line with their alpha.

Silvanus inclined his head, acknowledging the pact.

The other dragon simply snarled.

Once upon a time, ice dragons had freely roamed the Seven Circles, hunting demons and whatever other creatures they desired.

During one of the darkest hours in our history, the seven alphas from each pack planned a coordinated attack, carving a blood-drenched swath across the realm, terrorizing all.

Unlike most creatures, ice dragons didn't always hunt to eat. They *liked* killing. And they'd unleashed all their darkest desires on each House of Sin. The loss of life had been staggering.

So, more than a hundred years ago, I'd negotiated the first peace treaty between the dragons and my brothers. Aided by the right spell, we could communicate clearly with the dragons and had come to terms all agreed upon.

Unless I invited them into my circle for a particular event, the pact kept them sequestered in the far north, on the brutal, almost entirely wild land just above my territory.

They'd divided their territory into seven regions, each run by a different alpha. They kept the identities of their alphas from us, unwilling to share pack secrets, though I strongly believed Silvanus led the pack we interacted with the most.

The dragons simply stated "the alpha" when discussing the lead dragon.

We agreed to leave them to their private politics, so long as they didn't cause serious harm or damage to one another.

In exchange for their acceptance of the pact, I had agreed that my hunters and I would arrange hunts to battle them for sport each month, keeping their minds properly engaged. My brothers were free to join us whenever they submitted a request to my House of Sin.

None of us were permitted to kill.

The new dragon—Aloysius, judging by the slightly darker silvery blue coloring along his tail—took a threatening step closer, his iridescent eyes flaring.

His talons clawed at the ground, churning the snow.

There was an almost wild gleam in his eyes.

I tuned in to my surroundings, becoming aware of the familiar sounds of fighting. I spared a quick glance around—other dragons were behaving normally, if not a bit savagely. The other hunters were flushed from adrenaline surges, their eyes sparkling with each hit.

Still, an uncomfortable feeling prickled in warning.

"Halt!" I called out, my voice laced with the magical command of a Prince of Hell.

My brother stopped fighting, shooting an incredulous look in my direction, his dagger mere inches from his target's throat. He would have won. Instead, I'd make him forfeit.

And the demon of war was not one to easily give up a fight.

Wrath looked ready to argue but eventually pressed his mouth into a firm line. He clearly didn't agree with my assessment. But it wasn't his call to make; I ruled the hunt out here.

And my gut said to retreat.

I'd learned to never screw with that innate warning system, knowing it'd fuck me back twice as hard for my arrogance and it wouldn't be an enjoyable time.

After tracking the dragons through the blizzard all day, I was just as disappointed as everyone else to end our game so soon. But for now, I had to get us out of here before something went horribly wrong.

"Hunters, dragons." I nodded to each side, then hit my chest twice with a closed fist, a sign of respect and the signal the hunt was indeed over. "Good fight."

I gave Silvanus a long look, ensuring the dragon knew he'd be called forth soon to discuss what had almost happened. Part of the pact ensured he'd heed my royal summons.

His slitted pupils dilated rapidly, his serpentine head shaking almost imperceptibly before he finally gave the signal of understanding.

I had no time to consider Silvanus's odd reaction, as a feral shriek pierced the silence, sending ice rushing through my veins.

I turned just as Wrath's ice dragon lunged forward, its jaws opened wide, latching onto his throat.

My brother was brutally fast, but even his hands found their way to the dragon's mouth seconds too late. Its teeth sank deeper, its eyes rolling back as bloodlust took over.

Ichor spurted from dozens of puncture wounds as it shook my brother, then tore his throat out in one violent motion.

For a long and horribly taut moment, silence reigned as Wrath slowly dropped to his knees, blood pouring from his wound in torrents, the hunters staring, frozen in horror, at the place where his throat should have been.

It happened from one blink to the next. There was no time to react, even with my supernatural strength and speed.

I inhaled, my inner demon rattling its cage. My brother was not a small male by any means. Nothing could be done to stop the bleeding; the attack was far more than simply drawing first blood as rules dictated. And it would not go unpunished.

But first I had to make sure my demons lived through what came next.

The hunters stood motionless, the pungent scent of piss perfuming the air. These were some of the bravest members of my circle and they were terrified. If a prince could be cut down so brutally, they knew they stood little chance of surviving.

Up until now, during our games, the dragons had held back. The hunters never faced the full might of the creatures, and everyone knew this was suddenly no game.

My brother shot me a furious look, his expression telling me all I needed to know as the light slowly faded from his eyes.

I nodded at him, signaling I understood. I was ready.

I gripped my dagger, waiting.

The second my brother fell, chaos erupted.

As if some invisible tether snapped, the dragons all turned on us as one. And attacked.

TWO
Adriana

"You really should smile more, Adriana, my love."

Given Jackson's words were a soft slur, and his steps were almost as heavy as the hand he'd been inching lower on my hip, it was mildly impressive he recalled my name.

As an initiate hunter in House Gluttony's elite tracking forces known as the royal hunting guild, Jackson was my assignment tonight, which meant I needed to play nice to unravel the secrets of his last mission.

Rumor had it the ice dragons were growing restless in the north.

If proven true, it would be *the* story of the century. Breaking a story like that first could generate a lot of public interest, completely changing my family's circumstances.

Not because dragons were both feared and revered in our circle, but because public safety would be at stake.

I couldn't just let the story go and hope for the best. My family lived here. My friends. And all the citizens who deserved to know the truth before something terrible happened.

If the peace treaty was no longer being honored, there had to be a reason for it.

And I fully intended to discover what that reason was.

Jackson waltzed us around the ballroom, his hand continuing its downward path, his drunkenness becoming painfully apparent with each misstep and stumble.

We were drawing unwanted attention.

And not simply because we were waltzing during a minuet.

We bumped into several lords and ladies, earning glares and harsh whispers. When we careened into dowager duchess Oleander, I worried she'd have us tossed from the party. Her icy glare followed us as we continued to spin across the floor.

I grimaced as she leaned into her companion, Lady Violet Gunner, the host of the event, and undoubtedly demanded justice for her crushed toes.

The idea of accidentally knocking Jackson into the hot chocolate station warred with my need to draw him closer, my jaws clamped so tightly they ached.

I'd made two mistakes tonight.

The first was listening to Miss Ryleigh Hughes. My best friend and coworker had instructed me to use our circle's sin of choice to my advantage and encourage overindulgence.

"Loose lips cause delightful slips" was a motto she lived by.

Now I had a drunken hunter causing a scene, a headache starting at my temples, and I was no closer to unraveling his secrets before my next article was due.

I couldn't afford to miss turning in a column. If I didn't get information on the ice dragons soon, I'd need to embellish another rumor involving my nemesis. But if I reported on it first, the ice dragon story would catapult my career—and in turn my salary—more than another scandal sheet would, so I wasn't admitting defeat just yet.

My second mistake was attempting to use my feminine charm to wheedle information out of Jackson. Holding my tongue often proved difficult, and with the clock ticking ever closer to my deadline, my patience was quickly fraying.

Flirting was hard for me under the best circumstances.

And these were *not* the best circumstances.

All at once, I remembered a porcelain doll from my childhood.

Eden, my younger sister, had wanted it desperately, the bright pink dress sparkling in the rare sunny afternoon, catching her fancy.

As the eldest by ten years and already painfully aware of our circumstances, I'd been suspicious of the doll. The dull expression it wore like a shield made me wonder what it was hiding.

Perhaps I should have considered the possibility that the toymaker had been baring their soul and the doll simply represented society's cage for young women.

Be agreeable, pleasant, and beautiful, even if it drains the life from you.

Against my quiet warnings, my stepmother used the coins we'd saved for food to buy the doll, leaving our bellies empty that week.

Eden had cried every night, the doll all but forgotten as the harsh truth settled in: the fortune our father had saved before he died was gone. Spent in its entirety by my stepmother, on one useless indulgence after another. Not that a doll for a child was frivolous. I never scorned my sister for wanting a toy; even then I wished to give her the moon.

Sophie Everhart, my stepmother, was the only one who wouldn't accept our fate, as if her refusal to acknowledge our change in circumstances would prevent it from happening.

Even when we'd been forced to give our town house to debt collectors and moved into the crumbling building we now called home, Sophie Everhart found ways to spend coin we didn't have. Her sin was gluttony and her need to overindulge surpassed common sense.

I'd vowed then and there to make sure we'd be taken care of and would never fall prey to those same sins. Gluttony wasn't simply overindulgence in material things.

Sinners like me often indulged in adventure. And I found no greater thrill than solving a mystery and reporting on it first.

Which made dancing with Jackson and his straying hands tolerable.

Somehow, I managed to muster up the same bland smile the doll had worn, determined to encourage him into carrying on a decent conversation about the dragons.

He gave me a lopsided grin, his attention dropping southward, just like his cursed hands.

Normally, I preferred my romantic partners to take a direct approach rather than bore me with false declarations of love, but *some* attempt at conversation was necessary.

If someone didn't try to seduce my brain, they didn't make it to my bedchamber. Not that I'd entertained a lover in the last two Seasons. Much to my dismay.

"Elite hunters such as myself prefer a female who simpers. Can you simper?"

No better than he could use proper grammar. "No, my lord. I daresay I can't."

"Shame. You're rather pretty when you're not scowling. That ice-blue hair..."

I drew back in time with the crescendo of the string quartet, narrowly avoiding another unwanted touch, his fingers sliding through empty space instead of my unbound hair.

Jackson's gaze turned hot and hungry.

Initiate or not, he was like most members of the royal special forces: he enjoyed the thrill of the hunt.

"You were telling me of the north, my lord. The ice dragons that roam just outside House Gluttony's territory. I've heard there was an attack."

"Mm. Was I? I can't recall."

I couldn't tell if he was stealthily dodging the question or if he was so caught up in trying to seduce me, he didn't particularly care to listen to a single word that came out of my mouth.

"What were the specifics of your assignment?" I asked, hoping his inexperience with the guild would benefit my investigation. "I can't imagine being stationed up there for long. I've heard it's quite isolated."

"Ah. Merciless Reach. The end of the civilized continent and the Seven Circles. Best known as the outpost of nightmares because of how far from here it is. Until the sweetest sinners sneak into the barracks. After that, acting civilized is the furthest thing from anyone's mind."

Internally, I screamed. "Did His Highness travel with your hunting party? Reports suggest another Prince of Sin was involved in the incident."

Surely I could steer this conversation back to safer ground.

"Everyone always wishes to gossip about the princes. But there are more interesting things to discuss. Did I tell you how we keep warm during those frigid borderland nights?"

His attention dropped to my bodice. Where it remained. Apparently, he was under the impression my breasts would magically answer his question if he stared at them long enough.

"By carving open your enemies and sleeping inside their steaming innards?" I asked sweetly, batting my lashes.

His gaze shot upward, the fire in his dark eyes banking at once. "Pardon?"

"No steaming innards." I sighed dramatically. "I rather liked the idea of brutal savagery. Lust and violence. Such a sinful combination to indulge in, isn't it?"

He slowly blinked down at me. Part of him was clearly still interested, if only for the wild, untamed bedroom antics I might provide, but part of him also looked wary.

I suppose I looked like the sort of female who could just as easily carve him open as give him an intense orgasm; he appeared to be weighing the risk.

Blessedly, the music came to an end and so did our time together. My mission failed, but at least Jackson wouldn't have to struggle any longer with deciding which head to listen to.

I gave a polite curtsy, then made my way toward the far side of the ballroom. Unsurprisingly, Jackson didn't follow. He turned his sights on a beautifully coiffed noblewoman.

Ryleigh leaned against the wall, mirth sparkling in her amber eyes as I joined her in the shadows. We were both commoners, only invited to these events to report on them, though most nobles forgot our station since we did our best to blend in.

"Jackson looks half in love and half terrified. You really need to work on honing your flirtation, Miss Saint Lucent," Ryleigh teased. "Practice will do you a world of good."

"He's either too drunk to focus on my questions or won't talk unless I take him to my bed." With his new partner, Jackson trampled another unsuspecting couple. Completely drunk, then. "And why is my flirtation always to blame?"

Ryleigh gave me a long, lingering look. "Did you get anything useful from him?"

I swiped a flute of demonberry wine from a passing tray, downing it by half. The sparkling demonberries caught the light, looking like miniature stars.

"Nothing that will help tear down Axton or prove the ice dragons are a threat."

"It's Axton today, is it?" Ryleigh said playfully. "Prince Gluttony would be flattered you're finally using that moniker."

Gabriel blasted Axton, Prince of Sin.

His preferred alias, though not his full true name or else the witch I'd scrimped and saved to pay would have successfully hexed him long ago. "Gabriel" was known the realm over as the Prince of Gluttony, one of the seven wicked princes of the Underworld.

I knew mortals had myths and legends of all the gods and goddesses who ruled the expanse known as the Underworld—my contacts who'd been granted entry to our kingdom told me as much. Although even they had only made it as far as the Shifting Isles.

In truth, the Underworld was broken down into seven circles, each governed by a different Prince of Sin. There was an eighth circle that spanned closer to the southern edge of our realm, but it was forbidden and often ignored by denizens of the Underworld.

On a larger island, due west, were the Fae lands. And near the southern tip of our realm was Malice Isle—home to the vampires. House Gluttony, where I resided, was the northernmost territory, bordered above by wild land inhabited by dragons, lesser demons, and other creatures too dark and twisted or solitary to choose a House of Sin.

Within the Seven Circles, demon princes needed sinners to stoke their sin of choice and thus their power, ensuring they remained strong enough to protect us from outside threats, so denizens were sorted into the House they best aligned with.

Unlike most in the realm, who were utterly charmed by Axton, I despised the prince.

There was no rule stating that just because I aligned with his sin I needed to *like* him personally. Which meant at least one of the old, major gods was indeed petty.

Not many other circles believed in the old gods, who mostly ruled the seasons, but in the north, some still paid tribute to them. I'd need to figure out who to bribe to take down the prince.

I refused to call him Prince Gluttony in private, and "Gabriel" was too regal sounding for the rake. Axton might be his preferred alias, but that made little difference since it reminded me of a weapon. The prince was far too charming in public to be believable, and everyone ought to associate him with an ax. He'd certainly hacked apart enough hearts throughout the years.

"He's not attended a party in nearly a week, which coincides perfectly with the first rumored dragon attack to have taken place in over a century," I said. "Have you known him to miss any opportunity to feed his sin?"

"Please don't tell me you've been marking the events he's missed in a calendar, Adriana."

I didn't deign to respond. The music ended and dancers exchanged partners as the next song began. We watched silently for any hint of scandal, any refusal or snub.

Men twirled their companions across the polished marble, the noblewomen's skirts unfurling like colorful blossoms. I made a quick note of who was dancing with whom, who stole onto the balcony, and who returned from the gardens looking tousled.

Dowager duchess Oleander continued to glare in our direction, clearly holding a grudge over the accidental toe stomping. Her hair was a deep plum that looked pretty with her complexion but did nothing for her sour disposition.

She was young for a dowager duchess, not too many suns older than me and Ryleigh. Everyone knew she'd married the Duke of Oleander for his title, not his heart. A depressing but common practice among the nobles in both our world and the mortal land.

Her attention shifted to Ryleigh and turned colder. Years back there were hints of scandal involving my friend and the former duke. It would have been the type of news splattered across every gossip column if another more scandalous event had not taken place shortly after.

I quickly averted my gaze.

I spotted Anderson Anders, a journalist from one of our rival papers with a ridiculously haughty nom de plume, lurking on the opposite end of the room, watching everyone with a hawklike gaze. He liked to believe his pieces were destined to win awards.

"Why aren't you concerned about the implications of a dragon attack?" I finally asked.

Ryleigh heaved a sigh. "Your source was unreliable at best. If he had proof, he would have gone to the highest-paying scandal sheet by now. Instead, he disappeared."

"He didn't feign the terror I saw, Ry."

"Perhaps not, but there are plenty of other explanations for his fear."

"Such as?"

"Hexes. Curses. Dark magic. Glamour." Ryleigh ticked each one off. "Hells, someone could have used the Hexed Quill and rewritten his memory. Shall I go on?"

I hadn't heard any whispers of the Hexed Quill aside from rumors Ryleigh uncovered during one of her earliest investigations centered on it, but I knew objects of untold power existed in the dark markets and personal collections across the realm.

My friend had a valid point, but I couldn't rid myself of the feeling that the informant had encountered something that terrified him. Something more powerful than glamour.

Ryleigh didn't agree—she felt it was a nefarious plot devised by a rival paper. But there was no need to rehash my theories again tonight. The ball was almost over, and I had much to do before turning in for the night.

I scanned the room again. No scandal in the making other than Jackson's two left feet and too-bold hands.

"Did you get what you need for your article?" I asked. Ryleigh nodded. "Wonderful. Let's go, then. I want to go home and crawl into bed and stay there forever."

Ryleigh sighed but looped her arm through mine and started for the door. "If you're not careful, your eulogy will be 'she whittled away her days with work and sleep, boring her friends to untimely deaths.' I'm destined for much more than 'death by boredom.'"

I couldn't help but snort. "You poor thing. Your reputation will be destroyed by my need to provide food and shelter for my family. However will you carry on, being tarnished so?"

"Precisely, so you should come to the night district with me. Let's get a drink and gossip about Jackson."

"I'd rather offer myself up for a lobotomy."

"You know, it wouldn't be the worst thing for you to come out with me. We could go dancing. Flirt. Make terrible decisions we'll regret in the morning. Maybe you'll even meet a mysterious stranger and receive an invitation to the Seven Sins."

That was as likely as me publicly professing my love for our prince, but my friend was ever hopeful.

"Maybe another time."

Ryleigh didn't press the issue, though I knew she was disappointed.

I *wanted* to indulge in fun but couldn't. I saw what happened when my stepmother put herself above our family's well-being. My focus was on work and providing, and it was...not adventurous or exciting, but it was enough. Because it had to be.

As we worked our way toward the exit, the rake of rakes at last made his grand appearance on the opposite end of the ballroom, a buxom lover tucked beneath each arm.

The Prince of Gluttony tossed his head back, laughing in that bold, annoying way that crinkled the corners of his eyes at whatever the lover on the right whispered in his ear.

Watching the nip he gave her neck, I could only hope she'd admitted to genital pox.

I didn't realize I'd stopped walking until Ryleigh snapped her fingers in front of me.

"See?" she said, nodding to the prince. "Does he look like he was recently attacked by dragons?"

No. He did not. But that little voice named Intuition told me to dig deeper.

❅ ❅ ❅

After a long, cold trek through the city, with my gown and fur-trimmed cape hiked up to my knees to avoid ruining the hems, I slipped into our small home and closed the exterior door as quietly as I could manage, taking a moment to orient myself in the dark.

We'd run out of oil for the main room's lanterns days before.

A problem I needed to rectify soon, as my livelihood depended on it. Writing my articles in darkness was difficult at best, and any moonlight was almost always obscured by the heavy snowfall this time of year. The *Wicked Daily* was miserly with supplies and only granted us one piece of parchment per article, so any mistakes I made that caused me to use a second sheet came out of my nearly empty pockets. Drafting in the dark usually stole any spare change I might save if my stepmother or informants didn't take it all first.

"I need money for a new gown."

My stepmother's voice startled me.

I turned the key in the lock and slowly pivoted to face her. She sat on a threadbare settee we'd taken from our former life, spine straight, chin notched up to stare down her nose at me. Her pale blond hair was plaited and pinned as if she'd come from some grand event.

Even in the shadowy room I knew the expression she wore: disdain.

As if I were responsible for her poor choices.

I felt her attention drift over me as I took off my best cloak, and the tension in the small room grew.

She despised when I attended a ball, even knowing I only did so to report on them. Sophie Everhart felt it ought to be *her* waltzing and drinking with her former peers.

Demons aged much more slowly than humans, so Sophie still very much looked to be no older than thirty. I knew she was at least twice that. And, unfortunately, none the wiser.

When she'd met my father, I was just eight and my mother had only been gone for a month and he'd been in deep mourning. Sophie had loved his wealth, liked him, and barely tolerated me for reasons I'd never gleaned. Perhaps it was simply because I reminded her that she always came second in my father's heart, and Sophie didn't like losing to a commoner.

"We don't have any more coins to spare," I said, mindful to keep my tone pleasant. "I need to pay our rent this week. And we need oil. I can't afford to keep going through so many pieces of parchment and put food on the table."

I didn't bother pointing out that we'd be fortunate if we could purchase potatoes at the market this week; most everything else was out of the question.

Though I supposed Sophie didn't care much about that—when it came down to it, she knew I'd give up my rations for her and Eden, like always.

"You'll give me the coin for the gown, dearest. Or I'll have to sell off more of your father's trinkets."

Anger burned deep within me, but I swallowed it down. My father's belongings were my most prized possessions.

Really, all that was left was a small journal he'd used to tally items he'd sold, worthless aside from the sentimental value of his handwriting. And an earring and bracelet set he'd given my mother upon their betrothal, then passed on to me. Of which I'd had the misfortune of losing the bracelet years before. Plus a few other items that held little value to anyone but me.

I tried a new approach, one that had the only chance at breaking her selfishness.

"Eden needs shoes. I thought we agreed that after our rent and basic needs were met, that would be our one indulgence this month."

My stepmother slowly rose from her seat, looking far too innocent as she fingered the diamond necklace at her throat. I tried to keep my gaze from lingering on the enormous stone.

She could sell the necklace and earn us enough coin to not worry about food or shelter for the entire year. We'd probably have enough to even purchase a small house of our own outright, and we would no longer be indebted to any landlord.

But that would require sacrifice on her part.

Instead, she wore the diamonds around our home, showing them off to the mice and other vermin that chewed through our walls, only to quickly scurry away, disappointed by the lack of crumbs in the pantry.

She caught me staring at the diamond and her lips curled up in a poor imitation of a grin.

"You misunderstood, dearest. The gown has already been ordered. Come up with the money this week, or I will. And it won't be my trinkets that get sold."

THREE
Prince Gluttony

*A*N INCESSANT POUNDING at my bedroom door roused me from the most sinful nightmare I'd ever had. I rolled onto my back, breathing hard, cock standing painfully erect as I stared at the silk-covered ceiling, trying to orient myself.

I couldn't decide if I was relieved by the interruption or annoyed to wake up right as I'd tied my lover to my bedposts and spread her milky thighs wide.

A shiver rolled down my spine. The things I'd do to punish that sweet, tight —

"Your Highness?"

Val, my second-in-command, knocked louder. As if I'd missed the first small seismic event she'd unleashed on my poor bedchamber door. Her tone was curt, annoyed. Which meant she'd had to track me down and was losing patience.

I glanced at the decadent cobalt silk covering the walls, the excessive number of silver pillows spilling onto the floor, the plush fur blankets. *Not* my chamber.

A foggy memory came back; I'd tumbled into the guest suite I reserved for lovers sometime after the Gunners' ball and before sunrise.

But not before I'd indulged in one too many bottles of demonberry wine, giving the demons of my circle the debauched prince they craved. It was best, I had decided after secretly visiting Wrath's circle to monitor his recovery, for me to make a public appearance to quell any more rumors before they spread. My best spy, known simply as Shayde, reported whispers had somehow flitted past the almost impenetrable walls of Merciless Reach.

One of my hunters had been careless with who he or she had spoken to. It was a problem I needed to solve before any other whispers found their way to a certain gossip columnist.

I smiled at the memory of the night before. I'd taken my task to distract my circle very seriously. Aside from the issue of the hunter who talked too much, my brother was healing nicely, the dragon attack—brutal as it had been, no one was killed—seemed to be an isolated event, and it had been too long since I'd fed my sin through other means. They weren't nearly as potent as when I hunted an ice dragon, but they were sufficient for now.

Last night had certainly indulged my appetites.

A warm hand stroked along my bare chest, tracing the lines of my tattoo.

I'd forgotten I wasn't alone.

Crimson hair spilled across the lithe body of . . .

Callie? Cassie?

My head ached too much to recall many details. She slowly worked her way down the hard ridges of my stomach, her intention clear from her downward path.

If I closed my eyes, I could easily fall back into my dream.

Nightmare, I reminded myself. It was clearly a nightmare. One that started the moment I walked in and saw *her* at the ball, her gaze locking onto me like I was the scourge of the realm and she wanted nothing more than to rid our world of me.

It'd been almost an entire blessed week of avoiding the bane of the Seven Circles and her ruthless reporting. And then there she was. Miss Adriana Saint Lucent, in all her blue-haired, blue-eyed, hellion glory, scowling. I'd purposely brought two lovers with me, feeding into her distaste as I swept into the party, all arrogant, devil-may-care demon prince, and pretended not to notice the dark look she aimed at me from across the chamber.

Knowing how much she despised my public displays gave me a perverse sense of elation.

There was nothing quite as satisfying as ruining your enemy's night.

I gently clasped Cassie/Callie's wrist before she reached her target, then rolled out of bed, thankful I'd kept the low-slung trousers on.

I cursed softly at my body's refusal to relinquish its twisted fantasy as I padded barefoot across the overly plush woven rug to the source of my annoyance.

The door nearly rattled off its hinges from Val's next thrashing.

I yanked it open, giving her my most innocent look as my raging hard-on persisted. You'd need to be barred from your senses to miss it, and Val was never out of her senses.

Most unfortunate for her in this instance.

Val cursed under her breath, then narrowed her eyes on my drowsy-eyed bedmate. Probably checking to see if she was decent under the furs. Which she was not.

I twisted just in time to see Callie/Cassie drop the blanket, exposing the globe of her generous breast and the taut bud at its tip, clearly trying to entice my second into indulging her in a morning tryst. I raised my brows in question, mostly to needle her.

Val rolled her eyes at the predictability.

"Rough night, Your Highness?"

Her white-blond hair was braided back from her angular face, her eyes the gleaming blue of most in the north. She had little use for my theatrics, which was ironic since she helped craft my image through her over-the-top parties and events that were designed to fuel my power.

"Waking your prince before the sun rises is poor form."

"Considering it's an hour *after* sunset, and you have a royal matter to attend to in the north tower, I figured you wouldn't mind the interruption."

"North tower" was our code for issues relating to ice dragons and all things north of Merciless Reach, including my hunters. Jackson was here for his debriefing.

Any lingering arousal from my nightmare vanished.

I grabbed my shirt from the chair I'd tossed it on, stepped into my boots, then flashed Cassie/Callie a wicked grin. "A pleasure, as always."

There was only a slight furrow between her brows. One I doubted even Val picked up on.

I swept from the room before she could reveal one of my most closely guarded secrets.

I had a reputation to uphold, and if she blurted out the truth, everything I'd cultivated over the last few years would be ruined.

❄ ❄ ❄

Val kept pace with me as we strode through the east wing and turned down the wide, brightly lit corridor leading to the north tower. Marble gleamed under our boots, the sound muffled by the cobalt-and-silver runner that spanned the center of the whole hall.

I barely registered the colorful collection of art in gilded frames we passed, the bouquets of freshly cut flowers, the scented candles, or the intricate sculptures displayed on top of columns evenly spaced on either side of the corridor. Every few feet platters and trays of decadent tarts and chocolates and other pastries tempted all who passed by to stop and sample them.

Almost every inch of House Gluttony was a feast for the senses, should any guest or servant wander down the expansive interior and wish to indulge.

Normally, my second snagged a flute of sparkling wine and filled me in on any reports that came in after a public appearance.

Today she fingered the knives strapped to her hip belt.

"Go on, then." I glanced sideways at her. "What sage advice are you dying to impart?"

Her hand stilled on the hilt of one knife. Knowing Val, either she was considering stabbing me or she was trying to hide the fact that she was mulling something over.

Something she knew I wouldn't like.

"Miss Saint Lucent published another gossip column about you this morning."

"Did she at least wax poetic on how handsome I am?"

Without breaking her stride, Val flashed an incredulous look my way. We both knew there was no way in any of the hells that Adriana Saint Lucent would write something nice about me.

"Among other colorful terms, she called you an overconfident, ruthless rake."

My lips twitched. "At last. An acknowledgment of my finer qualities."

"Were you even aware that the two ladies you attended the ball with were sisters?"

"I don't recall much talking."

Val pressed her lips into a firm line. "She also said you were more slothlike than your brother. With all due respect, one day the circle might truly listen to her scathing commentary, and some will grow tired of your antics, even if they need your sin."

I exhaled. It was a fine line on which to balance—overindulging to feed my sinners, who in turn fed my power, without tipping them into another House of Sin, like envy.

I understood why Val worried about Adriana's thinly veiled disapproval; it could eventually impact the strength of my House. But, at present, I had other things to worry about.

Like whoever had been telling quite the thrilling tale of ice dragon attacks.

At the end of the corridor, we climbed the winding staircase leading to the tower in silence, the tension building with each step. Halfway up, Val finally said what I'd suspected had been on her mind all day.

"My advice remains. Either completely banish the reporter from your circle or bind her into a magical bargain to keep her silent. She's a liability."

It was a familiar debate between us, and one of the only times we didn't agree on how to proceed. I took her opinion under advisement but would handle the reporter how I saw fit.

Once we reached the top of the stairs, Val waited in the corridor outside the war room tower, spinning her throwing knives, ensuring no one got close enough to spy.

I entered the spartanly appointed chamber without preamble, the door slamming shut behind me hard enough to rattle the leaded-glass windowpane on the opposite end of the room. It was one of the few places in the castle that wasn't lavishly decorated; the tower room was designed for plotting and planning; there was no need for excessive frills here.

Jackson nearly tumbled out of his seat. He'd been leaning back, boots kicked onto my battered wooden table, arms crossed behind his head, humming a popular tavern song.

I hadn't snuck up the stairs; his instincts should have been sharper, honed. He had much to learn about remaining alert to his surroundings if he was to advance in the guild.

I'd put Felix in charge of testing all hopeful hunters in the field as part of the second phase of initiation, so Jackson still had time to learn.

In an odd, almost endearing way, he reminded me of a puppy, overexcited to be near you, big hopeful eyes, yet completely unaware that pissing on the floor was frowned upon.

He blinked slowly, as if coming out of some daydream.

He kept staring as if I was some figment of his imagination and not his prince. "Well?" I arched a brow, waiting.

Jackson's boots slapped against the limestone as he righted himself, jumping to his feet to offer a deep bow.

"Rise and report." My voice was steely, hard. It had the initiate hunter straightening at once.

"She was asking a lot of questions about the hunt."

I fought the urge to pinch the bridge of my nose. "I assume you mean Miss Saint Lucent. When you give a report, always start with the subject, then move on from there. What, *specifically,* was she asking about the hunt?"

"She knew there was an attack, that a prince was involved. Wanted to know what I knew, but I deflected like we're trained."

"Miss Saint Lucent specifically said a prince was attacked?"

Jackson nodded enthusiastically. "Pretty girl, horrendous flirt. She started talking about steaming innards when I told her about the barracks at night. Nearly killed my arousal."

A smile *almost* twitched at the corners of my lips. It wasn't meant to be friendly. And Jackson seemed to pick up on the nuance.

He blinked up at me, unsure about the tension building as I towered over him.

He'd made an error.

"What happens in Merciless Reach is supposed to remain there," I said, voice pitched low. "How did that topic come about?"

"I can't recall." Crimson spread across his face. "But I do remember her bottom is firm."

Maybe he wasn't as astute as I thought.

"You groped her?"

He swallowed audibly. "We were dancing…"

"And? She suddenly asked you to grab her right there in the ballroom?"

"Not exactly, Your Highness."

I stared until he dropped his gaze, the temperature in the room chilling by several degrees. All Princes of Sin could impact the environment around them with their displeasure. Jackson might have misread my expression, but no one misinterpreted what an icy room meant.

"Need I remind you that the royal hunting guild is a direct reflection of me? *Never* touch Miss Saint Lucent or any assignment again. As a matter of fact, never touch *anyone* without their permission again. Or I will be the one talking about steaming innards. And I promise I will do much more than simply talk about them, initiate hunter. Understood?"

"It won't happen again, Your Highness."

Given the trembling of his limbs and the stench of sweat permeating the small, circular room, I believed him. I eased back a step. "What else did Miss Saint Lucent ask?"

Jackson reported each of her questions, his deflections, an unnecessary but semi-entertaining commentary of the way she carried herself on the dance floor, and an entire monologue about the spiked hot chocolate station's lack of brandy-flavored marshmallows.

"If you were to advance in the guild, I expect discretion. No more storytelling to impress your friends. No discussing a hunt outside of the warded walls of Merciless Reach. If you ever start another rumor, accidentally or not, you will be banished from the guild and stripped of all memory of it. I will not tolerate any breach of rank."

I stared until he seemed to shrink in on himself. I had a strong suspicion Jackson had been the one to start the rumors.

As soon as he finished promising he'd never speak of the hunt again, I dismissed him and strode over to the arched window in the tower, glancing down at the city below.

Snow fell in heavy drifts, covering the tiled roofs and cobblestone streets.

My gaze traced the closest avenue at the base of the mountain where House Gluttony sat, skimming over my favorite tavern, then drifted along the night district, before finally settling on printers' row. The section of the city that housed each of the scandal sheets and bordered the working-class town houses.

The location of my sweet nemesis.

Val was right. Adriana Saint Lucent was a problem. Jackson might have boasted to his friends, his family, or his favorite bartender, but how Adriana found an informant who knew details of the hunt and the subsequent attack on Wrath so quickly was impressive.

And dangerous.

I needed to plot my next move carefully. Removing her from the playing board was priority number one.

"Your Highness?" Val cracked the door, popping her head inside. "Silvanus is here."

❄   ❄   ❄

Behind the stables of House Gluttony, isolated from the many eyes of my courtiers, an unmarked carriage rolled to a stop. Despite the long cobblestone drive, the wheels hadn't made a sound as they clattered up the hill, nor had the horses. The whites of their eyes flashed as they stamped the ground, nostrils flaring; they were no doubt unsettled by the unnatural silence.

Even my skin prickled in discomfort.

I waited until the magic that cloaked the vehicle dropped away, then pushed off the fence I'd been leaning against. I plucked up the lantern at my feet and made my way to the coach, my boots crunching over the hard-packed snow. The coachman jolted in his seat, his muscles taut as I emerged from the shadows. He remained that way until I lit the lantern and held it up.

With my hood tugged low over my brow and the quiet menace that radiated around me from waiting in the storm for nearly an hour, I understood the driver's fear.

But he hadn't drawn my ire. That honor belonged solely to his passenger.

The warm glow from the lantern defused the remaining tension as I stepped up alongside the carriage and flashed a robust coin purse his way.

"For your continued discretion, Niles."

"Always, Yer Highness."

I tossed the money to the driver and motioned to where Val still lingered in the shadows to grab our esteemed guest so we could get on with this already.

Before she reached the handle on the coach, Sascha stepped from the conveyance, flipping back the hood of her midnight-hued cloak, and glanced around to ensure we were alone. Snowflakes melted into her equally dark locks, but she didn't seem put off by the frigid weather.

She ran an unsettling gaze over me, her lips twisting up on one side. Tonight, I looked more assassin than prince, my crown was nowhere to be seen, but my dagger glinted in the silvery wash of moonlight breaking through the storm clouds.

I set the lantern down.

"Forgetting something?"

The witch's eyes glimmered with annoyance, but she dropped a deep curtsy and held it.

"Your Highness."

"Next time you're late, I'll personally hunt you down, Sascha."

The column of her throat moved as she swallowed.

"Apologies, Your Highness. It won't happen again." She held a gloved hand out, palm up. "Half up front, same as always."

Val's fingers grazed the hilt of her favorite throwing knife, not liking Sascha's impertinent tone. Demons and witches were mortal enemies and tempers flared easily at any perceived slight.

I casually stepped between them.

I paid an obscene amount of coin for Sascha to forget how much our species hated each other, and to sweeten the deal of our association, I also permitted her to keep a permanent apothecary shoppe in the heart of my circle. Most witches lived in the Shifting Isles, but Sascha either had been banished from the coven, or chose to leave for reasons she hadn't shared.

Like all Princes of Sin, I detected lies, so I knew she'd been sincere when she'd requested to stay in my circle and vowed to not be plotting any revenge.

I'd been dealing with this particular witch for decades and knew how to needle her the most without inciting a war.

I gave her a lazy grin that had her teeth grinding together. "Val? Hand the first coin purse to the lady."

While the money exchange took place, I glanced toward the tree line where the hulking dragon waited. At my direction, Silvanus had flown in low, then walked the rest of the way to our meeting location to avoid anyone seeing him.

Since I sometimes hosted hunts here, dragons weren't entirely uncommon on my grounds, but with the current rumor flitting through the shadows, I wanted to avoid any unnecessary sightings. My stables were far enough from the castle proper and high enough on the hill to keep us hidden from any drunken courtiers who might have spilled from the current party into the gardens or terraces for clandestine trysts.

"Ready?" the witch asked, tying off the coin purse.

I nodded. "Sil. Care to join us?"

The dragon snuffed at my tone but lumbered into the clearing, the air chilling with his arrival. Both Val and the witch shuddered from the proximity to the creature.

Sascha stuffed the coins down her bodice, then whispered a phrase in Latin while making sharp motions with her hands that I swore were simply colorful curses in her native tongue.

She briskly walked over to where Silvanus watched with slitted eyes and repeated the motions, hurrying as her teeth began to chatter. Ice dragons were formidable even when they weren't actively trying to be. Their very presence was harsh to anyone who wasn't immortal.

Once Sascha finished, she burned an herb bundle and waved it from head to toe, a dewy sweat breaking across her brow.

"Done?" I asked, picking my nails with my dagger.

She held an ageless hand out, palm up again. I noted the slight tremble in her arm. Whether it was fear or simply the icy chill, I couldn't quite tell.

"You've got a quarter of an hour."

"For your spell and your silence," I reminded her, then dropped the coin purse into her grasp. Val escorted her back to her carriage, leaving me and Silvanus to our meeting.

I eyed him for a moment, searching for any sign of aggression.

He huffed an annoyed snort at me.

If you wished to gaze upon my splendor, the coin you paid the magic leech was unnecessarily excessive, though unsurprising, given your sin.

"Witch. And don't sass me. You know why you're here."

The attack.

"No, the masquerade I invited you to. Of course I'm talking about the attack. Wrath is still recovering, and you better pray to your scaled gods that he doesn't demand retribution."

Your brother's temper does not concern me.

My mouth curved wickedly, showing a hint of teeth. It was not something dragons appreciated. Showing your teeth was akin to drawing a sword.

"When he skins you alive and sews your hide into pretty boots for his wife, you might feel differently."

At least you think they'll be pretty.

"You're in a mood, aren't you?"

He huffed again, the arctic puff sending shards of ice into the air, but remained silent. Stubborn, gods-damned creature. When he was a hatchling, he'd dig in his little claws much the same way. One hundred years later, not much had changed.

"Explain why Hectaurus attacked, or I'll be forced to turn you over to House Wrath."

As if I'd permit that, demon. The alpha believes he was infected by another creature he'd battled several moons before. One of the abominations that roam the northern woods. What happened with the rest of the pack was instinct.

There were many beasts and lesser demons who braved the brutal landscape. Getting a good description about any creature a dragon wanted to fight or kill was often a fruitless venture; they were almost entirely focused on the takedown, but it was still worth trying.

"What creature did he battle? Demon? Hell beast? Shape-shifter? Fae?"

Silvanus's tail swished across the snow. *One with claws and teeth.*

"Which narrows it down so nicely."

Silvanus ignored the sarcasm. *It matters not. The creature was destroyed in battle.*

A fact that was unsurprising. Most creatures didn't survive a true fight with a dragon. We'd been lucky. Shortly after Wrath had been taken down, they took to the skies. My hunters had walked away with injuries, but all had come through it.

"Does your alpha believe this is an isolated incident or something we need to address?" I thought back to the fight. "Your eyes dilated strangely. Aloysius was rather aggressive too."

The dragon batted his lashes at me dramatically.

What of my eyes now, great prince? Do they still frighten you?

I gave him a flat, unamused look that had him huffing. He was in rare form tonight.

Aloysius has a temper. And as for Hectaurus, it has been dealt with.

My eyes narrowed on the giant beast. "Exile?"

Silvanus gave a sharp negation of his pointed head, the diamond-like scales sending prisms of light across the snow.

By acting against the treaty, Hectaurus threatened the entire pack's safety. Our alpha tore out his throat and fed until nothing but bones remained.

I kept my emotions from my face as that savagery sank in. Nature, I reminded myself, had its own laws. Predator or prey. Kill or be killed. One weak link threatened all. Mercy wasn't in their frame of reference; the very concept of it threatened their survival.

"And what if the alpha is now infected or exposed to what Hectaurus had?"

Silvanus spewed a frosty breath.

The alpha is unchanged, protected by the healing magic of the alpha, and the move was justified.

It was a warning to us all. His law was broken, his punishment swift. An alpha cannot show weakness. Or mercy.

He sent this.

Silvanus stepped aside, beating his feather-covered wings once before revealing what he'd been hiding. *For the love of all things corrupt and unholy,* I thought, hiding my revulsion. An enormous dragon skull jutted up from the snow, the silver bone scarred from teeth marks.

A chill descended down my back.

It was gruesome. Hectaurus had been another hatchling I'd helped socialize. I hated how he'd turned on my brother, but to see his bones picked clean...

I yanked my attention back to Silvanus, who'd been watching me closely.

"I accept the peace offering. But the upcoming hunt will be postponed until the following full moon. I expect the pack will follow all pact rules from here on out."

It would weaken me slightly, but it was only for a month. I'd feed my sin elsewhere.

I will tell the alpha you are pleased. We look forward to sparring at the next full moon.

I dismissed the ice dragon and stared at the grisly gift his alpha had given me, mulling the information over. For all intents and purposes, it pointed to an isolated incident.

However, relief was not the foremost emotion I felt, given the reasonable explanation for the attack. If there was a creature brave or stupid enough to battle dragons on its own, and it was infected with some madness, there was no telling who or what it might have attacked before it met its end. Just because the creature was dead, didn't mean the threat was over.

I'd have Felix send a patrol into the woods to search for any creatures who seemed ill.

A shiver rolled down my spine. I decided that was due in part to the dragon skull gazing up at me, empty-eyed and brutalized. As soon as I got back to the castle, I'd call for him to be placed in the royal mausoleum, in a crypt to honor him.

My unease didn't cease with the plan to lay the dragon bones to rest. I had a feeling it was also due to the little issue of Miss Adriana Saint Lucent that I still needed to address.

First order of business: while Felix searched the north, I'd also set a select group of scholars on the hunt for any illnesses or diseases that could impact ice dragons, just to confirm that was the cause of the attack. Then I'd ensure my circle remained blissfully unaware of the incident to avoid any unnecessary panic.

The immediate threat might indeed be over, but it would only take one article to tear away the feeling of safety I'd worked hard to instill in my circle and create hysteria.

As I made my way back to the castle, I thought about what Jackson had said regarding the meddlesome reporter, and a plan slowly began to form.

It would take a few days to set up, but I knew exactly how to keep Adriana from spreading any gossip about dragons or looking into the story.

And best of all?

She'd positively *hate* it.

FOUR
Adriana

"Do you know what this is, Miss Saint Lucent?"

A very red-faced Mr. Gray, one nearly bald and entirely without humor editor in chief of the *Wicked Daily,* slapped the envelope down hard enough to jolt me from the first draft of my latest scandal report, a particularly scathing article I'd written on my favorite nemesis.

Technically, my *only* nemesis, but still. He'd positively hate it, which suffused me with *such* a warm, radiant joy on this blustery afternoon.

It was a welcome relief after a difficult week of reporting. No more rumors of ice dragons attacking circulated, so I had to set that story aside for now. I'd still dig into it in my spare time, though, if only to quell my own curiosity.

Ryleigh was probably right; the informant could have been glamoured by a rival paper, hoping to discredit me. It wouldn't be the first time another paper went to such lengths to boost their credibility while taking down the competition. Our paper had been doing quite well as of late, thanks in part to my ongoing antagonization of Prince Gluttony.

I glanced up, tucking a strand of pale blue hair behind my ear, wondering if Mr. Gray had hit his head, or if the question was meant to be rhetorical.

Unfortunately, my editor wasn't known for engaging in intellectual debate and his brows remained stubbornly raised while he waited for my response.

I decided if one asked a stupid question, one surely expected a stupid answer in return. I set my quill down, giving him my full attention.

"It's an envelope, sir."

Impossibly, Mr. Gray's face darkened to an unnatural shade of burgundy, his nostrils flaring at my—admittedly—impertinent response.

If he wasn't careful, he'd have an embolism right there on the reporting room floor. Though given the nature of our business, one of the staff writers would put a scintillating spin on the tale, driving sales of the *Wicked Daily* to new heights across the realm.

Nothing sold quite as well as stories involving murder or sex or scandal, or better yet, tales containing all three. And if a Prince of Sin was involved? All the better.

It didn't matter if the stories were entirely true; perception was all that counted.

Sounds of quills scratching on fresh parchment ceased, the five other staff reporters pausing at their desks, wooden chairs creaking like swaying trees in a forest as they leaned closer, always primed for potential gossip.

Julian Wren was the worst; he looked ready to sink his teeth into the growing tension and gorge himself on it. I half expected drool to dribble down his pointed chin. I subtly gave him a crude hand gesture, causing Ryleigh to stifle a laugh and the other reporters to snort.

Our office was a small three-room rental on the lower level of a two-story row house.

We had access to a basement that I was convinced was the chosen habitat of ghouls and refused to set foot down there lest I attract the undead and invite them home.

I had enough mouths to feed without adding any invisible interlopers.

The top floor was rented by a rival paper, making for interesting and hostile meetings in the shared stairwell. Our main room had six desks, all scarred, ancient, mismatched things collected when others tossed them out for trash.

The small back room held Mr. Gray's office, and the final space was a tiny water closet that always perfumed the air with a foul odor. The stench was suspiciously worse after Mr. Gray brought his newspaper in and shut the door for an obscenely long hour after a dairy-rich lunch.

No one had the intestinal fortitude to tell him *his* intestines clearly revolted against cheese. But I was getting closer to letting him in on that poorly kept office secret.

Though, given the steam practically coming from each of his orifices, today wouldn't be that day.

"It's much more than an envelope, Miss Saint Lucent," Mr. Gray gritted out. "Until further notice, you're off the gossip rags."

My ears began ringing. *Surely* I wasn't being fired. From a scandal sheet.

Brazen as I normally behaved, I *couldn't* lose this job. My sister and stepmother depended on my meager earnings to keep the roof over our heads.

Our landlord would toss us out without a second thought if I missed a payment. Out of necessity, not malice. Times were still difficult for a great many, not just my family. Sinners in our circle overindulged in various vices, which led to spending more than we saved. No one regretted their choices; it simply made day-to-day living a struggle for the majority.

"On what grounds am I being let go?"

"Why else? Your rivalry with the prince."

"It's a few unflattering gossip columns; they're hardly serious enough to create a rivalry, sir."

"Perhaps not to you, but His Highness is threatening to burn us to the ground."

Mr. Gray wrenched open the letter and pointed a meaty finger at the House Gluttony crest. I glared at the serpentine dragon winding itself around the stem of the chalice overflowing with grapes, its jeweled eyes slitted from overindulging.

"His Highness alleges your *egregiously* false reports are tarnishing not only his reputation, but his House of Sin, and demands immediate action be taken, or else he'll hold the paper liable. We can't afford to keep our doors open if the prince makes good on his threats. I warned you to stop antagonizing him."

It was surprising that Axton at least knew the word *egregious*. Too bad the damned prince was ruining my life once again, it seemed.

Maybe *I* was the true glutton for punishment, a fact that irked me to no end.

I wanted nothing to do with the spoiled, self-absorbed prince aside from watching—or better yet, sparking—*his* downfall in the Seven Circles.

A feat that was proving to be harder than I'd expected.

Apparently, everyone in the realm adored his rakish antics and lavish parties, finding him completely charming and aloof.

Prince Gluttony was touted as "the perfect, unattainable bachelor." One who didn't care how often he wasted riches others dreamed of having, all in the name of feeding his sin.

He was the epitome of decadence and frivolity, of overindulging.

And I despised all he stood for.

One of his parties could feed my entire neighborhood for a month. And yet his guests hardly noticed the delicacies being served.

Not everyone in the Seven Circles came from wealth, but most of the working-class citizens in my neighborhood believed in impossible fairy tales. Stories of hope.

Rags to riches and the unrelenting idea that true love could overcome class, station, rank, and other societal barriers. As if those were simply small hurdles to jump over and not massive walls erected to keep the rich together in their own private world.

Once upon a time, I'd gotten swept up in that fantasy too.

A mistake I wasn't foolish enough to repeat.

My sister called me a cynic, but I saw it as being logical and not prone to delusion.

Prince Gluttony had divested me of any daydreams I might have secretly had nearly ten years prior, when I was just nineteen and only partly cynical.

Not that he knew or cared. His prospects were unending, his immortal life charmed.

Ryleigh had informed me and two other reporters just this morning there were *eight* new petitions circulating that called for the prince to host a competition to find a bride, for saints' sakes. Even Prince Lust, the premier prince of pleasure, hadn't drawn such notice among the matchmaking mothers in the Seven Circles. Prince Gluttony was all anyone seemed to discuss.

As if he were the prize of the century.

The whole damned realm was under his spell; even noble families from other circles wished to make an advantageous match for their heirs with him, regardless of whether their sins aligned.

Gabriel Axton didn't even have the decency to recall the role he'd played in my fall from grace all those years ago. But I would *never* forget.

"Since when is reporting on truth punished?" I challenged my editor.

Mr. Gray leveled me with an icy stare as he quoted, most impressively, " 'That the prince would attempt to play coy and fail spectacularly is unsurprising. Gluttony is the least clever of his brothers.' Sound familiar?"

Of all the things I'd written, that *was the most offensive?* What of the newest article claiming he was more slothful than the Prince of Sloth? *That* was the highest insult I could sling, claiming Axton's sin was more like his brother's than his own.

The old door clattered open behind us, letting in a burst of frigid air that unsettled the papers on my desk, but I didn't remove my attention from my boss.

I waited for Mr. Gray to crack a smile or break into laughter at the absurdity, to tell me it was all in jest and to carry on with my latest draft. My articles might not be award-winning pieces, but they were entertaining and often helped sell our paper to keep us afloat.

When he didn't smile, I drew myself up so I was almost eye level with him.

"Where is the lie? He *did* fail at playing coy and, in my opinion, Gluttony is the least clever of the seven princes."

Ryleigh coughed into her fist, but I was too annoyed to glance her way.

"Gluttony doesn't have Wrath's mind for war or strategy, or Envy's cunning for games, or Pride's exceptional focus. All he does is indulge his sin by raking and ravishing. Those are hardly qualities to boast about."

"No one's perfect, darling," a deep voice interrupted from behind me. "But your opinion is personal, not factual."

It was the sort of low timbre that teased and seduced, eliciting all sorts of dark fantasies.

I would know; it often fueled my fantasies of murder and dismemberment.

I stiffened for only a beat before my temper flared, my gaze clashing with Ryleigh's across the aisle. *A cough?* I thought at her, knowing she'd read the incredulous look in my expression.

Ryleigh had the good grace to glance away, finding her own article suddenly *very* interesting as she fiddled with her inkpot and avoided my accusing stare.

I shot another withering look around the room. None of my wretched coworkers had warned me the bane of my existence had entered our small office. Not that they would. We were all in slight competition with one another to earn the most coin for the paper, which made for a rather hostile work environment. Ryleigh and I never competed, though.

My coworkers all bowed their heads in deference, my editor included.

I drew in a deep breath, resigned to what I had to do for the sake of propriety.

I slowly pivoted to face the saints-forsaken prince in question, hating that victorious grin curving his lips as my attention swept over him in cool assessment.

All six feet whatever inches of him lazily leaned against the doorframe, toned arms crossed in his fine suit, hazel gaze running over me in triumph, his wretched golden-brown hair mussed in a way that suggested he'd just come from someone's bed.

The perfect image of royal debauchery and indulgence.

A legendary lover, if only in his own mind.

If he thought he'd won, he was sorely mistaken.

Our little war was only just beginning.

Out of protocol for his rank, I offered him a slight curtsy, standing again before he'd acknowledged it.

Wry amusement tugged at the corners of his mouth.

"We report on rumors and gossip, Your Highness. With all due respect, it's *all* hearsay and opinion."

"Yet your *opinion* is almost entirely fiction these days, Miss Saint Lucent."

"Are you claiming that other gossip columnists don't embellish their stories?"

"We're not discussing other columnists. Just you."

"Precisely the point, Your Highness. I'm the only one being sought out and punished for doing my job."

"So you admit your job has devolved into writing fiction, not fact."

"My job is to take the truth and make it entertaining. And yes, I'd argue that my opinion is perfectly valid for doing just that."

"Except when it's printed for the world to see and is not based in fact yet claimed as such. *That,* Miss Saint Lucent, is delving into the realm of libel."

The self-satisfied ass looked entirely too pleased with his argument. My coworkers and editor, however, appeared ready to launch themselves out of the line of fire.

Except, of course, for drooling Julian. The salivating leech furiously scribbled notes in his journal. I made a mental note to snatch it from his desk and burn it before the office closed.

I focused on the matter at hand, silently counting until the urge to throttle Prince Gluttony passed.

"If I may speak plainly—"

He snorted. "As if you've ever held your tongue. Don't start now, darling."

I drew in a deep breath, ignoring his antagonistic term of endearment.

"As I was saying, you've yet to prove me wrong in any of my assumptions. I do not believe you succeeded in playing coy. Please educate me on how that's fiction."

I crossed my arms, waiting.

A muscle in the prince's jaw ticked but he remained quiet.

Victory had never felt more satisfying. I ought to have quit while I was ahead, but I couldn't stop myself from twisting the knife a bit deeper.

"It sounds as if the true issue is that I've struck a nerve, Your Highness. Though I can't say I'm surprised. The male ego is one of the most fragile things in the universe. One teeny, tiny hit and it shatters like glass. Maybe it's not my fiction, but the truth you abhor. I doubt anyone tells you how they actually feel. In any aspect relating to your public or . . . private life."

The devil-may-care smile didn't falter, but the glint in his eyes darkened to something dangerous. He'd certainly understood the subtle jab at his lovemaking.

Gabriel Axton, Prince Gluttony, was well and truly annoyed now.

At least that was one emotion we grudgingly shared.

And to think it was often said that enemies couldn't find commonality.

My lips twitched upward, his gaze narrowing on the movement. Axton was at least wise enough to note the action meant his battle was far from won.

As much as I would have loved to keep needling him for my own personal satisfaction, it was time to keep my mouth shut. There were too many important factors at stake, none of which included my pride, so I vowed to bite my tongue. For now.

Surely we could be in the same room for five minutes and not kill each other.

The prince seemed to feel differently. He straightened from where he'd been leaning, his body tensed like a predator ready to strike. Gone was any pretense of indifference.

He was all fire now, no ice.

"The truth is I couldn't care less about your boring opinion pieces, Miss Saint Lucent. Libel is another matter altogether. I won't tolerate outright lies being printed, especially when they negatively impact my House of Sin."

"I—"

"Your opinion on what you believe I've done is just that, *an opinion,*" he continued, not waiting for my response. "Unless you interview me or are physically present and I'm explaining every last action aloud, you ultimately don't know the first thing about the truth. Claiming you do is where you're wrong. Writing '*I believe* he is the least clever of the princes' wouldn't have been libelous. That would have alerted readers that you were speaking on opinion. Instead, you framed it as fact. And *that* is what I take issue with."

I wanted to argue but couldn't. He was damnably correct.

For once.

He gave me a cool once-over, his attention passing over my drab woolen dress, falling to my scuffed black boots, then flicking back up, his expression now unreadable.

The prince had never sought me out outside of any royal parties I'd attended for work before and clearly wasn't used to seeing me dress like the commoner I was.

I'd heard rumors over the years, whispers of my being from the Shifting Isles, or distantly related to witches—which was especially damaging to my reputation and career since witches and demons were sworn enemies and the nobles would trust me even less to openly share gossip—so I'd gone out of my way to present myself as a member of the nobility, often fooling others into believing I'd grown up as privileged as they had.

It was necessary to gain entry to their world and secrets.

Times like this, however, revealed who I really was. And Axton seemed less than impressed—one more blasted sentiment we shared about each other.

I locked my jaw, remembering what was at stake: my family's security. That was worth more to me than engaging in another disagreement.

"Perhaps you ought to think about joining House Envy," he said, far too casually.

He was baiting me.

I knew it.

The office of nosy reporters who drew in a sharp breath knew it. And yet...

"Why would I do that?" I asked.

As if my question granted him permission to cross the room, the prince was suddenly before me, his lips almost touching the shell of my ear as he leaned in and dropped his voice.

"You're clearly jealous, Miss Saint Lucent. If you'd like to visit my bed, say the word. I'd hate to leave you in such a distressed state when I can indulge your obvious desire."

A fresh wave of annoyance crashed through me. Each time he opened his mouth, the prince only proved my assumptions of him being a self-absorbed ass correct.

He stepped back, turning his attention to Mr. Gray before I could do something foolish like step on his boot. Or drop him to his knees.

"Keep Miss Saint Lucent on staff—I imagine she'd do well with any subject aside from gossip. Perhaps an advice column since she has so many opinions to share." He paused for a moment, immediately putting me on edge. "Romance might be her strong suit."

I quickly wiped any horror from my expression, my pulse ticking faster as my editor flashed a look of interest my way, his bushy brows raised in thought.

An advice column on romance was the worst thing I could imagine writing each week.

I felt the unmistakable heat of attention on me and glanced Axton's way. The cursed prince had been watching me carefully, his smile growing more wicked by the second.

All at once I understood.

Axton knew I'd hate that; he'd chosen his return fire carefully. He didn't march in here today with the hope of taking my job; he'd come with a much more cunning plan to destroy me. Proving he was far more strategic than I'd believed. Saints curse him.

I'd burn at the stake before I ever gave him credit for the clever move.

I had wondered why he'd come all the way to printers' row to deliver the message himself, when as far as I knew he'd never so much as stepped foot below the night district.

Now I understood with stark clarity. It was to see his plot unfold in real time. Probably so he could stroke himself later to the memory of his one great act of cleverness.

I immediately banished the image that came on the heels of that thought.

"In fact, Mr. Gray," he went on, eyes sparkling with silent laughter the madder I became, "I rather like the idea of citizens of my circle writing in to Miss Match. Or Lady Lovestruck. I'll leave the details to you. And Miss Saint Lucent, of course. She *is* the one with the wildly creative imagination, after all."

"Your Highness, I promise my imagination is hardly worthy of note."

"Don't be coy, Miss Saint Lucent. Just last week Jackson Rose was telling me all about your time together; you made *quite* the impression on him at the Gunners' ball."

My face heated. I was going to borrow a shovel and bury Jackson in a deep, dark hole.

"Well, it looks like we're done here." He flashed another victorious grin my way. "Have a *wonderful* evening, Miss Saint Lucent. I so look forward to reading your romantic advice. It might come in handy. What with all my ravishing and raking and all."

Prince Gluttony winked at me, then swept from our office as quickly as he'd come, leaving me quietly fuming.

I stared after him, mind racing. Of all the nefarious plots he could devise, the devil had chosen my personal hell with devious precision.

I wasn't sure if I should be impressed or run screaming into the abyss.

Unless I could think of a better alternative right away, I was well and truly trapped.

"That's settled, then," Mr. Gray said, striding toward his office at the end of the room. "We'll collect some questions from staff shortly and print the first Miss Match article in two days."

I rushed after my editor.

"With all due respect, I know nothing of giving relationship advice, sir."

Mr. Gray paused outside his door, glancing over his shoulder at me.

"Then I suggest you sort that out before we go to print. You did have hopes of being a novelist, did you not?" he asked. "That skill might be useful. Pretend they're characters."

Once, I'd imagined myself creating thrilling mysteries to escape to, sharing them with the world. Now my time was devoted entirely to keeping my family fed and sheltered, not indulging in fanciful dreams that might never come true.

When I remained silent, my editor shook his head, disappointment plain on his face.

"I expect the first draft on my desk tomorrow afternoon, Miss Saint Lucent. If you miss the deadline, don't bother coming to work."

FIVE
Prince Gluttony

*Y*OU'RE EITHER GOING to have the most intense hate sex in the history of the realm," the Prince of Lust drawled from the seat across from me, "or—"

"She's going to castrate him," Prince Envy said, swirling his signature cocktail, a Dark and Sinful, his expression one of mock contemplation as he sipped his blackberries and bourbon.

"My coin's on the castration." Lust's charcoal eyes lit with dark amusement. "Especially after today."

My good mood couldn't be tarnished by my brothers' jabs.

We were in my favorite pub—the Ox & Raven, a dark, ancient place with rustic beams, scarred tables, surly patrons, broad floorboards that hadn't been mopped in an age, and the best food in the whole gods-damned realm.

No one treated me like royalty at the Ox & Raven; I was just Gabriel Axton here, Axton to most, not Prince Gluttony. Which was how I preferred things outside of my courtly duties.

The pub was close enough to the castle proper that I often slipped away to luxuriate in the crowded space, frequently eavesdropping on the other patrons to learn how my court was really faring these days.

For several long years provisions had been almost impossible to come by thanks to a realm-wide curse that recently broke. Each of the Seven Circles of sin had been impacted by it, but, as time wore on and not all had been restored, it seemed we all had different spells to break on our own too.

Envy recently participated in a deadly game to end his circle's private curse, but I only knew the smallest details of how he'd accomplish that from my spies.

My brothers and I kept certain House secrets from one another, which meant I had to solve my territory's issue on my own.

And, truth be told, I wasn't sure where to start.

With the main curse over our world broken, things had slightly improved, but my circle wasn't operating as well as it should be, so I gorged on my sin, using the excess power to help those who'd been impacted the most in hopes of relieving some ill effects.

But I'd never admit to any altruistic acts.

I was one of the Wicked, the great villains and monsters of mortal lore. Dark princes who embraced sin, debauchery, and wicked games, tempting and teasing mortals to our beds so they'd sell their souls to be ours.

Or so the stories claimed.

But those were tales for another day.

Today was a day to enjoy a distraction.

When I arrived at the Ox & Raven tonight, Envy and Lust were already waiting.

I could have declared war on their circles since they'd showed up in my territory unannounced and it was technically an act of war, but I hadn't seen them since Envy's betrothal ball last month, and I enjoyed their banter.

The lovable pricks.

"You should have seen her face." I grinned at my brothers across the worn leather booth, my goblet filled to almost spilling with demonberry wine. "It was a *brilliant* move. I only wish Camilla had been there to immortalize my victory in a painting."

"Victory." Envy snorted. "Your idiocy is astounding, but entertaining."

"You know what'll be entertaining? Watching that abysmal reporter attempt to offer relationship advice. She doesn't know the first thing about indulging in romance or building any meaningful bonds."

"And you do?" Lust's grin grew wider. "When was the last time you courted someone and met their family?"

"The triplets you bedded don't count as building meaningful familial bonds," Envy said.

Lust almost choked on his drink.

"You're both hilarious," I said, ignoring Lust's wheeze.

Envy pounded his fist into our brother's back, a bit harder than necessary, laughing darkly when Lust slammed his House dagger into the table between them.

House daggers couldn't actually kill a Prince of Hell, but a well-placed stab sent us back to our own House of Sin, even if we didn't want to go.

Envy's smile turned into a dare the longer Lust seethed.

The idiots would brawl before our meal if I didn't intervene.

"I'll wager ten of Greed's gaming hells that she'll be banging on my door," I said, breaking the tension, "asking for forgiveness by week's end."

"You're bloody ridiculous." Lust finally tore his attention away from Envy and settled it on me. "And looking to lose some serious coin."

"I'm confident. And you sound like you've been hanging around him too long." I jerked my chin toward Envy. My brothers bared their teeth in a menacing sneer, but I didn't care.

My elation grew with each memory of Miss Saint Lucent's abject horror over her new assignment. Despite my brothers' constant teasing over the years that I'd end up with the hellion, I harbored no secret affection for her. I simply wished to win our private war.

Adriana had been publicly slaughtering my reputation for years and I'd plotted this moment for a small eternity. I was going to enjoy every second of finally besting my rival.

And this victory was especially sweet since it was twofold.

When Jackson reported her horrendous attempt at flirtation along with her fascination with the ice dragons, I knew exactly what to do to solve both issues at once.

"Seeing Miss Saint Lucent on her knees, with all that hate glittering in her eyes as she begs…" I sighed. "Nothing will feel quite as good, I promise you that."

"Except if she was on her knees under much different circumstances and you were the one begging," Lust joked.

"Contrary to your misplaced belief that 'hate sex is best,' dear brother, I wouldn't let her near my cock."

"She'd definitely bite it off." Envy's emerald gaze tracked the platter of food heading our way along with mugs of winter ale. It was a spiced lager only found in this tavern, and my brothers all found excuses to visit the Ox & Raven almost weekly to drink their fill.

Even Wrath, the least tolerant of our antics, graced the pub whenever he could.

The owner—and cook—set the steaming plates before us along with the spiced lagers.

"Did ya need anything else, Axton?" she asked, wiping her hands with a rag she'd pulled from the waistband of her apron.

"No, thank you, Shirlee."

I gave her more coin than the food and drink cost by triple, knowing she had children at home in need of extra care since her husband had broken his foot last week. I'd offered the royal healer, but they'd declined.

Shirlee pursed her lips at the abundance of coins but gave me a grateful nod.

"Holler if ya need anything else. I'll have Barn open a tab."

When we ordered more winter ale, I'd leave more coin, but I dutifully pretended otherwise, then turned my attention to the pub fare before me, inhaling deeply.

If I could propose to this dish, I would.

"Gods' bones." Envy grabbed his fork. "What kind of magic do they use in that kitchen?"

"No magic. Just a northern recipe passed down through the generations," I said. "Emilia visited a few weeks ago and loved it."

Envy snorted. "Did our sister-in-law persuade Shirlee to give up the recipe?"

"Not even close. Shirlee laughed all the way back to the kitchen."

Envy's grin widened; his fondness for our sister-in-law always broke through the mask of indifference he wore like armor. "I imagine Emilia took that well."

Emilia had. She'd dug into the food and immediately tried to identify the ingredients, wanting to re-create the dish once they'd returned to House Wrath. I'd watched, almost as amused as her husband, but kept silent to enjoy the moment.

The savory potpies with flaky golden crusts were honestly the best food in the realm. The food was simple, straightforward, and delicious. Just chicken, diced onions, carrots, and celery, minced garlic, sprigs of fresh thyme, salt, pepper, and a splash of white wine.

It took years of constant persuading and cajoling, but I was finally allowed into the kitchen to help prep for dinner service and discovered the secret was the chicken thighs fried with rosemary butter Shirlee used instead of chicken breasts. It added a richness to the gravy that couldn't be beat.

I'd take the pub food over any of the more extravagant meals that were served in my castle any day. I'd asked Shirlee once if she'd want to work for my House of Sin and she'd laughed in my face, too, saying to marry her eldest and we'd talk then. I knew she had been joking about marrying into the family, but it wouldn't be the worst fate.

In a way, I was relieved she'd turned me down. I enjoyed this old tavern, and it wouldn't be the same without its colorful owner and chef.

After I'd eaten half my meal, I took a deep pull of winter ale. I'd been keeping the conversation light but suspected my brothers were here for more than just the ale and food. We all had spies stationed around the realm. I wanted to know what theirs had heard.

"I'm surprised you tore yourself away from Camilla," I said. "Trouble at home already, brother?"

Envy's expression shuttered. "My fiancée is tending to her gallery in Waverly Green."

Lust's smile turned wicked.

He loved sharing gossip, especially when it needled one of us. Which meant this ought to be good. "He's pissy because Wolf went with her."

"Ah. Jealousy," I mocked softly. "So necessary to stoke your sin, but gods' blood you look ready to put your fist through a wall. Camilla really knows how to work you up."

Envy's grip on his tankard tightened, but he showed no other outward sign of being annoyed.

I knew him well enough to know he was probably envisioning all the ways he'd slaughter the Fae male who'd been Camilla's first lover.

From what my spies had gathered, Wolf had stayed at House Envy for the last month. That Envy hadn't murdered him in his sleep was a testament to how much he adored his soon-to-be wife. But Envy only played nicely for so long. Even we knew not to test him too much.

"Playing the game is only fun when you're the one making the rules. Isn't that right, dear brother?" Lust dodged Envy's blow, laughing harder than he had before.

"Bullshit aside," Envy said, teeth gritted, "we're here because of a rumor."

"Oh?" I lazily traced a line of condensation on my mug. That my brothers came to deliver the news in person didn't bode well. "No, I'm not hosting a competition to find a consort. Much to the *constant* dismay of the realm."

Envy and Lust exchanged serious looks.

"It's about the ice dragons."

My pulse roared through my veins. Wrath and I had been careful with our cover-up.

"What about them?"

For the second time tonight Envy's mask of indifference slipped.

"They've been gathering in larger groups."

"How highly unusual." I leaned forward, my tone dripping with sarcasm. "Maybe they're brewing tea and making scones. The weather has turned frigid."

"You know as well as I do they're not sitting down to sip some bloody tea," Envy snapped. "There's talk of the alpha recently killing off a member."

I didn't stop tracing the line of condensation on my mug, but inside I stilled.

"Rumor claims it was a punishment," Lust said, watching me carefully. "Have the dragons broken the treaty?"

"Aren't you both above listening to gossip?" I asked.

"Answer the question, Gabriellis." Envy's gaze was as hard as his tone.

"You're in *my* circle," I said quietly. "I take orders from no one."

A tense moment passed between us as I held my brother's stare.

I hadn't pulled my House dagger on him, but I would without hesitation, and Envy knew it. I'd permitted my brothers to stay here only because it served my needs.

My hospitality was fleeting, though. Especially when my House secrets were at stake.

The air around us chilled with our mutual displeasure, the other tavern patrons giving us sideways glances, their hands creeping toward their own weapons in case a brawl broke out.

Finally, Envy settled back against his seat, easing some of the tension with the movement.

"Where did you hear these rumors?" I asked, unwilling to alert my brothers to a lie if I answered their question. A Prince of Sin couldn't exactly lie, but we found ways to omit truths. Word in the shadows claimed that Envy had actually found a way around that rule but hadn't given up that secret to anyone.

Lust's expression turned uncharacteristically somber. "Our spies."

"Do either of you have proof?" I demanded.

"Not yet." Envy pushed to his feet, tossing an extra coin into the center of the table for the staff. "But if you won't tell us the truth, we'll hunt it down on our own."

"And?" I said, tone hard. "Once you go off on your little adventure, do you think I should welcome you back to my circle with open arms?"

Envy and Lust exchanged another charged look.

"If the rumor proves true and the treaty was violated," Envy said, "then you'll have little choice. You might be the one tasked with enforcing compliance, but we all signed the pact."

I cursed that one clause I'd included. It granted my brothers a meeting of their choosing if there was ever a breach of conduct or break in the treaty, since it would signal an issue for the entire Seven Circles. It had seemed wise all those years ago, and a bit unnecessary. After the dragons' massacre of our people and the signing of the treaty, we all thought peace would reign.

Now it meant I had to be even more vigilant against surprise visits.

I finished the rest of my winter ale and stood. "Have fun on your fruitless quest, dear brothers. I have much more stimulating entertainment planned for this evening."

SIX
Adriana

"CHEER UP, LOVE," Ryleigh said several hours later, judging by the wan light giving way to shadows crawling across the dusty office floor. "You're still employed."

I made a noncommittal sound and stared at the blank sheet before me, the unblemished parchment mocking me in all its perfect, unmarked glory.

No matter how hard I tried to place quill to paper, no words magically appeared.

Technically, I should be able to create *some* advice. Even if it was fiction. And yet I kept hitting a wall a million miles wide each time I tried to draft something.

Normally, whenever writer's block struck, I'd jot down the most outlandish sentences to unlock any words that had been trapped. It was far better to revise what had been written than battle the blank page. But that trick wasn't working now.

All I could see when I squinted at the parchment was Axton's smug face. I considered stabbing the paper until the growing need to scream passed. Which wouldn't do a thing for my work problem but would at least make me feel better, if only fleetingly.

"I wish I had the damned Hexed Quill," I muttered, still glaring at the sheet. "Perhaps I could manifest some relationship advice into being. You wouldn't happen to know where I could find it, would you?"

"Adriana."

Ryleigh pressed closer to my desk until she drew my attention away from my stare-off with my new mortal enemy, the blank page. She'd tried to hunt down the Hexed Quill ten years ago, obsessed with the idea of rewriting an event. Nothing ever came to pass, but my friend certainly loved learning about hexed objects as much as I loved mysteries.

"You wouldn't want to use a hexed object. Look at the rumors circulating around Prince Envy's game. And you *can* do this. You simply need to trust in yourself."

"Why are you always so reasonable?" I quipped, slowly dragging my focus upward to settle it on my friend.

"I'm only reasonable during the day so I can indulge in the proper amount of debauchery at night. Just as you should do."

"I can't afford to have fun, especially with this new deadline."

"Nonsense. If you took a little break, you'd write twice as fast."

Ryleigh stood over me, thick winter cloak in hand, giving me the sort of dazzling smile that won her lovers and all their secrets.

Ryleigh was classically beautiful, with warm bronze skin, pale amber eyes, and thick dark hair that was long enough to spark jealousy in denizens living outside House Envy.

It was that grin, though, that undid even the most jaded soul. She'd tried to teach me her charming ways, but I was a terrible student and she'd eventually given up.

Ryleigh had started out with the same lack of means but had amassed a small fortune since she didn't have a stepmother who spent all her coins and she used her talents to finagle exquisitely tasty gossip from nobles.

"You're still employed," she repeated. "Silver lining."

"Not for long."

I sighed and rolled my neck, trying to loosen the muscles that had grown tense throughout the afternoon. Earlier, my coworkers had all anonymously submitted several questions for the first Miss Match column so I'd have something to start with.

And they were good questions, excellent even; the problem was me.

Almost all my time was spent writing or researching for my column, speaking with informants in seedy places, then making sure my sister and stepmother were taken care of.

With her nineteenth birthday coming up, Eden was certainly old enough to work now too, but my stepmother had refused to allow her daughter to "toil away the day like a commoner."

She was holding out hope of securing an advantageous match for Eden and claimed Eden needed to behave as if she were a gently bred lady.

By nineteen I'd been forced to earn enough coin for a household of three. My stepmother claimed it was because my father was a merchant and *she'd* been born into the peerage; therefore, it was my duty to step into my father's shoes.

It didn't matter that Eden also shared the same merchant blood. Not that I blamed her for her mother's beliefs. I loved my sister immensely and she was only nine when Father died.

Sophie ought to have done whatever it took to provide for her young daughter. It only took a few weeks to see that would never happen. Our pantry dwindled down to crumbs and stayed that way for days.

One of us needed to provide for our family. So I applied to every scandal sheet and journal in the realm until landing the position I held now.

Researching gossip left very little time for any leisure activities, namely, courting or romance, since every event I attended was work based. I'd taken lovers, but it was always a fun distraction, nothing more serious than one or two nights, and none of them snared my attention for very long. To be fair, that was partly my fault for choosing lovers I knew weren't right for long-term relationships. It was much safer that way to avoid heartbreak.

Giving advice on something I painfully lacked knowledge in was forcing me to remember the evening I'd spent years trying to forget.

After *that* emotional disaster, I'd built a wall around my heart brick by brick, never wanting to be vulnerable again. Now I had to tear that protective barrier down in order to help others, and it terrified me more than I cared to admit.

Writing scandal sheets was one thing, but helping someone through an emotional crisis was entirely different. One wrong bit of advice could destroy someone else's happiness.

It was an enormous amount of pressure to be under. Aside from Axton, for very personal reasons, I only wished the best for others.

"I know nothing of love. Only hate and occasional lust. Look at this." I handed Ryleigh the slip of paper.

"'How do I move on from my last heartbreak?'" she read aloud. "That's simple."

"If it was so simple, the article would be written, and I'd be home."

"Lucky for you, I happen to have a plan."

She flourished a beautiful silver key in the shape of a seven. Runes had been engraved onto its entire surface, glittering with invitation.

I exhaled. My day was going from bad to worse.

"I'm not sure how visiting *that* club will teach me anything of love, Ry."

That club was the Seven Sins, a mysterious invitation-only club of vice where the only rules were: despite being glamoured upon entry, patrons must also *always* be masked, and no one could ever give their true names or speak of the club's secrets outside its walls.

No one knew who owned it or who gave out the magic keys.

The scandal wasn't the sex taking place—the whole realm openly thrived on passion—but any of the seven sins that could be indulged there.

Each sin was typically only celebrated within its own circle. House Envy exuded envy in all its forms. House Wrath aligned with wrath and so on. It was considered taboo to openly enjoy a sin that related to any rival House of Sin.

The Seven Sins was secretive and legendary, and not just because the club itself glamoured anyone who entered, disguising voices as well as physical appearances to ensure anonymity remained for guests. Only the lucky were admitted into its doors, the runes on the keys changing each night to ensure the list remained exclusive.

One night you could be on the list, the next left off. No explanations given.

Unlike other popular clubs and gaming hells, it wasn't restricted to the wealthy. Anyone could be given a secret key and bring one guest, though it wasn't guaranteed that the club would permit the guest entry, making it even more exciting.

There was no discernible pattern for the guest list, but I suspected it was based on intrigue and interest. And, of course, a burning desire to indulge in all manner of sin and debauchery.

It was infuriatingly perfect for a circle of sinners who overindulged.

I had never been. Ryleigh had. She'd been a guest on several occasions, though to my knowledge this was the first true invitation of her own.

"We'll go, have some fun, ask some questions." She grabbed my cloak from the back of my chair and flourished it in front of me like a gallant storybook knight. "Indulge in some dirty, sweaty sex, drink copious amounts of demonberry wine, and write the best relationship advice column the realm has ever read."

"My family—"

"Arrangements have already been made with your neighbor to help cook dinner. She's making stew with them now."

I'd need to pay Lily a visit this week to return her kindness. Eden would attempt to help, and Sophie would pitch a fit. "Making stew *with* them" meant Lily would be playing the role of private chef for my family. And I knew how much she disliked my stepmother ordering her around, then complaining about the food.

"Well?" Ryleigh asked. "What do you say?"

It was tempting, but...

"I really need to focus on work, Ry."

"This is absolutely work related. You need to research. And I guarantee almost everyone there will have romance on their mind. It's really the perfect place for your column and you know it. Stop being stubborn and put your cloak on."

I couldn't decide if I wanted to hug her or switch out the sugar she used for her morning tea with salt. I *did* need to do research. And the club would provide lots of opportunity for discussions on romance. Since dinner was taken care of, I could stay out later for work.

I glanced at my scuffed boots, my heavy wool skirts. Both drab and dreary, but practical.

This morning I'd picked something to wear that would be warm as I trudged through the slush-filled streets, not fashionable. And while the club could be fun as well as helpful for my column, I really *should* check in with some of my informants, let them know my job title had shifted but I still planned to carry on in secret.

Axton might have temporarily won this round, but it would take more than an advice column to clip my reporting wings for good. I wasn't entirely sure how I'd proceed just yet, but I'd figure it out soon enough. If the ice dragon rumors proved true, I could sell my story to a different publication, bypassing the *Wicked Daily* if I must.

"Well? Are you coming with me or not? I'm practically aging before your very eyes."

I glanced at the blank page again. I'd need to turn my column in to get paid, which meant I had no spare coins to pay my informants tonight anyway. And yet...

"I'm not dressed for the Seven Sins."

Ryleigh's smile widened; she knew she'd won. "Not yet."

❄ ❄ ❄

"Up, up, up!" Carlo punctuated each demand with a loud clap, his expression pinched as he looked me over. "There's much to do and not a lot of time to do it."

I expelled a long breath and stood from the copper tub, wincing only slightly at the chill bite in the air as warm water traveled in rivulets along my body, pebbling my skin from the sudden temperature shift.

We were backstage at the Scene Stealer, the most celebrated theater in the circle. Thankfully tonight's rehearsal was over, and all the performers were already home.

I didn't bother hiding myself while Carlo quickly toweled me off with a long swath of linen; I'd just been scrubbed from head to toe in the scalding water until my skin felt raw.

Carlo snapped a thin dressing robe at me, motioning for me to put it on. Swiftly.

I did as he beckoned and cinched the sash before dropping onto the stool he'd pulled out before a lit mirror.

The tabletop was cluttered with all manner of makeup: a candy-colored assortment of powders in every color of the rainbow, with brushes in all shapes and sizes, false fur lashes, and other costume pieces I'd never seen before.

"You're certain you want to wear a wig?" Carlo asked, giving me a doubtful look as he brushed my hair out where he styled each actor and singer to perfection.

Carlo had been one of Ryleigh's first relationships after we became friends, so Carlo shot his former lover a look that begged Ryleigh to talk sense into me.

"Nope." Ryleigh held her hands up as she backed away. "Not getting involved."

She swiped a piece of cheese off a tray, then leaned back, watching with dark amusement as I submitted to Carlo's demands.

I stared at my reflection in the lit mirror. Unbound, my pale blue locks fell past my shoulders in loose waves, nearly matching the same light hue of my eyes.

"Your natural color is so flattering against your skin," Carlo said.

My complexion was pale, often described by others like moonlight on water. Ethereal, otherworldly. And it couldn't be further from the mundane, very common life I led.

My stepmother made sure to remind me that it was most unflattering. Especially compared to the golden hair of my sister and her shimmering golden skin. She'd been trying to force a wedge between us for years, but my sister and I loved each other fiercely.

"I don't want to be recognized," I reminded him. "A mask is one thing, and I know the club glamours its guests upon entry, but I want to ensure my identity remains secret no matter what. We still need to walk to the club, and anyone might see us arriving or leaving."

I wasn't the only demon in our circle with pale blue hair, but it wasn't as common as the paler blonds, rich browns, plums, and darker blues.

Carlo set the brush aside, mumbling about wasted potential, and fetched a trunk full of wigs. He dug around, gingerly pulling one out of a sack.

It was a lovely dark cobalt that had strands of silver glitter woven throughout. Despite it being Prince Gluttony's House colors, it was beautiful.

"We'll stay in the same tonal family as your natural shade," he said, his expression telling me this was not up for debate. "A good dramatic kohl-lined eye and bold lip will be perfect. Perhaps a bit of silver dust along your cheekbones to tie in the glitter highlights of the wig."

"I'll be wearing a mask."

"You'll also be wearing the makeup underneath," Carlo said. "Contouring and enhancing will help disguise your features. If only to slightly adjust the pout of your lips. Since you're concerned about being recognized on the way in or out of the club, this will solve that."

He looked me over as he brushed powder along my brow bone and cheeks.

"We're going for an ice queen approach, which should suit you well."

I bit my tongue, certain I'd been insulted. Ryleigh shot a sympathetic look my way.

I wasn't an ice queen. At the root of everything, I was deeply careful about who I let in for fear of heartbreak. My caution was often misinterpreted as indifference, which often alienated me more.

"Now hold still. This will likely hurt."

After a lot of twisting and pinning of my natural hair, Carlo finally threaded the wig into place, his gaze tracking over me critically.

"Good." He ran his fingers through the locks, tugging gently at the scalp, clucking his tongue in approval. "It will survive a night of debauchery at the Seven Sins."

I had no plans of taking a lover at the club, no matter how welcome the distraction might be. Tonight was strictly for research purposes.

If I didn't turn a draft in for the first Miss Match article...

I wouldn't allow myself to consider failure. I hadn't entirely given up on the ice dragon story, but until I could run down any new leads on that, I couldn't risk another financial loss. Especially with my stepmother demanding a new dress and my father's belongings at stake.

"Now for the gown." Carlo disappeared behind several rolling racks filled with gorgeous costumes. Beaded gowns, sequined lace, frothy tulle, silk. Each more luxurious than the last.

He emerged a moment later, brandishing a garment that would make even the most debauched sinner blush. I loved it but wondered if it would aid or hinder my mission of luring members into discussions on lasting relationships and romance.

This dress would certainly inspire lust.

I fingered the silver chains that reminded me of dragon scales holding the sides of the snowy-white gown together. Though *gown* felt like a pedestrian term for such a magnificent costume. If I decided to wear it, it would be by far the most luxurious thing I'd ever worn.

The soft fabric of the skirt was made of glitter—eliciting images of freshly fallen snow or ice illuminated by morning's light every time it moved.

And it was scandalously short, hitting well above my knee. The corset top was crafted of nude mesh with sequins and gemstones sewn across the bust.

Ice queen indeed.

The irony being if I wore this to the Seven Sins, there would be no ice, only fire left in my wake. It was tempting. So very tempting to step into the role of someone else, if only for one night. Perhaps I could pretend I was a character in a story. One who took risks and dreamed.

Once upon a time, ten years ago, I *had* taken a risk. I'd stepped out of my comfort zone and put myself out there for the world, allowing hope to be my guiding light and North Star.

It ended badly, but I'd survived.

Almost entirely intact, if the invisible scar I bore across my heart wasn't counted as collateral damage.

I'd learned early on that in the game of love there wasn't guaranteed victory for those brave enough to play. Though I supposed there had been a thrill in trying.

My father used to say that the greatest tragedy in life was letting fear hold you back. Wondering *what if* was the worst sort of fate he could imagine.

One time I'd asked about chasing my dreams, "But what if I fall? What if I stumble?"

"Start asking better questions, my dove. What if you soar? What if you race the stars themselves?"

If I closed my eyes, I could almost hear his booming voice. *Failure just means you're trying and there's no shame in that. Don't let anyone tell you who you are. Believe in yourself. It's your life and you've got to live how you see fit. To hells with everything else.*

If my father was tasked with writing an advice column, he would be the best.

"It's almost midnight," Ryleigh said gently, nodding at the clock. "We're going to be late."

SEVEN
Prince Gluttony

IXIE, AN EXTREMELY affectionate guest, licked up the column of my throat, groaning softly.

"You taste *so* good, Your Highness," she mumbled, suckling my neck again, no doubt spurred on by the sinful tableau taking place in my grand foyer as I welcomed guests to the party. Her teeth scraped against my jugular and I hid my wince. If she nibbled any harder, she'd find herself in the vampire court.

Trays of smoking cocktails passed by, the sharp fragrance of juniper and other winter-inspired ingredients wafting through the air.

I snagged an ice-cold glass, pleased by the theatrical extravagance of the drink. Frozen juniper berries were used in place of ice cubes, and some interesting technique made the top of the cocktail smoke, giving off that wonderful wintry note. The aromatics heightened the taste as I sipped the citrusy gin, enjoying the slight fizzle that popped over my tongue.

Sight, taste, and smell had all been perfectly engaged; my drink masters had outdone themselves tonight creating the signature cocktail of the evening.

Though some guests were finding more interesting ways to sample their drinks.

At House Gluttony we took feasting *very* seriously. Despite what a slew of rumors suggested, it started as a way to needle Miss Saint Lucent when she'd once written I wouldn't know sin from virtue, and I ought to relinquish my sinner's crown.

I'd wanted her to eat her words. Literally. So, I'd had a long table brought in, taking up most of the entryway, and forced guests to walk around it to enter the rest of the House of Sin.

I recalled with wondrous clarity the moment Adriana had walked in and drunk her fill of the sight that first evening. I'd made sure she'd secured an invitation to the event.

Shock—and what I'd sworn had been a spark of intrigue and desire—had marred her features before the mask of disdain slipped back into place.

But it had been enough to satisfy me. I knew then I'd won that round, even if she'd never admitted to it. I'd kept the table there as a staple of my House from then on.

There was no food or drink served on it. Guests were permitted to indulge in their fantasies, gorging on attention and their partners for all to see.

One such public display was happening now.

I watched as a threesome took turns disrobing, then slowly made their way onto the table. One male took an ice cube from his drink, then ran it over his lover's breasts, getting her nipples perfectly hard before lathing his tongue along the tight buds. The moment she arched up, he hooked her legs over his shoulders and feasted on her like he'd been starved.

She thrashed across the table, her expression one of pure bliss as she groped her breasts.

A second male stroked himself to the scene, then, after bending toward her ear and earning an emphatic nod of approval, he fed his cock down her throat.

I finished my gin and set it on an empty tray. Miss Saint Lucent hadn't arrived. A fact that wasn't surprising, considering she no longer reported on gossip. Still, my attention seemed to wander to the door more than I cared for.

Another couple joined the table, and it became a mix of limbs and body parts entwined in impressive ways. If Miss Saint Lucent were here, she'd scorn the overindulgent orgy.

A throat cleared, drawing me back to the matter at hand.

Aside from greeting my guests, I was giving an interview.

Speaking with scandal sheets was part of my duty to keep up appearances and divert their attention while my House continued its secret efforts to unearth what had caused the dragon attacks.

At least for now the more the reporters focused on me, the less they might look for the next big story. I cocked my head at the reporter—his light hair was slicked back, allowing his aquiline nose to dominate his otherwise delicate features.

Perhaps that was what made him seem so haughty and full of himself.

"Is it true, Your Highness, that your grand 'feast' table is based on a private feud between you and House Lust?"

Anders. Anderson. Something pompous. He'd been firing off questions for the better part of an hour and despite him being one of my sinners, I was ready to smuggle him past Merciless Reach and feed him to the dragons. He was far less engaging than Miss Saint Lucent.

I gave him a lazy grin, dragging my companion closer, earning a pleased giggle as she pressed her generous curves against me. She started unbuttoning my shirt.

Anders watched, rapt, as her fingers deftly moved to the next button, slowly exposing my bronze skin and the top half of my tattoo. A second lover, Rosaline sank to her knees, running her nails up the front of my legs. It felt good but I remained unaroused.

If I closed my eyes, though, if I allowed my mind to drift to forbidden thoughts and desires, I could remedy that.

My eyes remained good and open.

Anders shook his head, seeming to recall he was working and not indulging in debauchery tonight.

"Well? Does House Gluttony have a secret war with House Lust?"

"Come now, do you think I'd waste my time with a subpar court?"

"Rumors suggest you're both aiming for the title of prince of pleasure. Do you have any comment on that?"

"Lust might rule over carnal pleasure, but surely my House of Sin proves there's much pleasure to be found in other areas."

Anders looked like a dog who was intent on going after a bone.

My brothers and I got along well enough in private, but we all culti-vated a certain image for the realm. We had our own sibling rivalries, but nothing as serious as going to war with one another like some gossips claimed. Anders opened his mouth to ask another inane question, when Val strode over, inclining her head.

I'd never been more thrilled to see my second. "Yes?"

"A note arrived for you, Your Highness."

I gave my would-be lovers a wolfish grin.

"Why don't you two indulge each other for a while?"

My companions were only too happy to oblige.

I disentangled myself from Vixie and Rosaline as they began kissing, all but forgetting me as their embrace deepened.

I turned my back on the dullest reporter of our generation and focused on the note. The cobalt parchment was crisp, the ink silver. It was from my House of Sin.

Wolves are prowling in circles of darkness.

I folded the message back up. It was code. And I suddenly had a very interesting adventure to embark on. I schooled my features into the per-fect mask of a devilish rake, allowing innuendo to drip from my tone.

"If you'll all excuse me, I have an invitation I would be foolish not to indulge."

❄ ❄ ❄

I moved as silently as a shadow as I stalked my brothers, mindful of each cobblestone I stepped on. Snow added to the challenge, but the thrill of being caught during the pursuit fueled me to forge ahead. My prey mean-dered down the block, unaware of my presence.

For all their combined cunning, Lust and Envy were rather easy to track as they made their way through the winding streets of the night district. It made me suspicious; were they truly trying to be stealthy or was it a diversion? Perhaps I was simply paranoid.

That they were sneaking around my circle without my permission, and it was grounds for war, was another matter entirely. I could end this right now, reveal myself, but then I'd miss out on seeing just what they were up to.

It had taken less than thirty minutes to locate them. Now I waited, picking my way through the shadows to see where they were heading, curious to discover which of my demons were selling information to our rivals. Perhaps I'd strike gold and find Adriana's informant too.

I trailed my brothers, keeping a block between us to remain unseen, hunting them as I would any ice dragon or creature of the north.

I scanned their wool cloaks, impressed they'd attempted to disguise themselves at all.

Of course, the gleaming polish of their fine boots ruined their attempt to mask their wealth. Lust's lack of focus I wasn't surprised by; he was always more interested in finding pleasure or toying with it, but I expected better from Envy, master of detail.

They casually strolled down the cobblestone street, projecting an innocuous image of two friends in search of a good time. At the next cross street, they turned right.

I waited several beats before following, just catching them as they walked into one of the many restaurants on the block. Fire pits roared in pots out front, warming guests who'd chosen to dine outside despite the snow that fell almost constantly.

I breathed in the aromas of grilled meats and savory meals that filtered out each time a door was opened. My circle was known for its many eateries—unsurprising when so many liked to indulge in food and drink. I inhaled once more, fighting off my own desire to partake in something greasy and delicious. Not far from here a bistro cut potatoes into thin strips, fried them, and dusted them in salt and hot pepper the moment they came out of the oil.

Turning, I scanned the street. I needed a place to wait without drawing attention. An alleyway with a decent number of shadows was directly across from the restaurant.

I aimed for it, glancing around once before slipping down the narrow, darkened path. At the end there was a rubbish bin with a lid half falling off. I looked up at the roof of the building. It wasn't too far from the ground, but it was high enough that I couldn't simply jump.

I could use my wings but didn't want to risk anyone seeing me, thus alerting my brothers that I was prowling around the area.

I exhaled, my breath coming out in a puff, my heart beating double time as I dragged the rubbish bin under the nearest window, cursing as the metal loudly scraped against stone, then quickly stepped onto it. The thin metal bent under my weight.

I jumped high enough to grip the ledge, my fingers sliding over the ice before getting a firm grip, and slowly pulled myself up.

If stealth wasn't needed, I'd already be up on the roof. Instead, I took my time. One wrong move would send snow and ice careening over the edge.

I scaled the building, finding handholds and footholds, moving as fast as I could until I finally reached the roof and rolled onto it. I dusted my hands off, then took up my position near the edge. I had a perfect view of the restaurant below.

A few demons passed by on the street, unaware their prince lurked above.

Drunks linked arms, singing tavern songs. Demons laughed and shouted as they tossed snowballs at one another, the mood light and untroubled. No one was looking toward the sky in fear, no whispers of ice dragons attacking any Prince of Sin. All seemed to be well.

It would be a good night for my circle.

Except for the two princes who didn't belong here.

I waited, gaze locked on the restaurant Envy and Lust had entered.

A few moments later, my brothers were back with a waitress, being seated on the outdoor patio, purposely choosing a table half blocked by a fire pot.

It would have done its job of hiding their features had I still been at ground level.

Food and drinks were served quickly, and I settled in for what appeared to be the most boring spy mission of my existence. They picked at their plates, shared a few laughs, and called for a second round of drinks. I closed my eyes, fighting the urge to fly down and demand to know what the hells was going on. Patience was a hunter's strongest ally.

If I waited long enough, I was bound to discover something.

Nearly a quarter of an hour later, I was rewarded. A cloaked figure strode up to their table; envelopes were exchanged like they were part of some espionage novel.

Envy looked inside his, nodding curtly, then the cloaked figure disappeared into the shadows.

For another hideous stretch of time, nothing happened.

Finally, once I was on the verge of revealing myself, demanding to know what they had planned next, my brothers finished their drinks, then stood.

To my utter delight, Envy removed something from his envelope.

A small object gleamed in the firelight.

A key.

Runes glowed as my brother ran his fingers over it.

I knew the precise location that key unlocked. A place they really ought to have asked me about before taking it upon themselves to visit.

Grinning to myself, I turned to the next building and jumped across to its roof. I would permit them their adventure, to see exactly what they were after and who would be giving them the information. Once I knew that, I'd leave a message for my brothers to come find me as soon as they finished their little outing to the Seven Sins.

If they believed they'd slip through my circle undetected, then unravel my House secrets, they were mad. They needed a reminder that I was the best hunter of us all, and there wasn't anywhere in my circle they could go where I wouldn't find them.

Especially not to my very own private club of sin.

EIGHT
Adriana

THE BUILDING THAT housed the Seven Sins was anything but another nondescript establishment, blending in with the other pleasure halls and taverns that lined the crammed streets of the night district. The club was easily the crown jewel of the circle. It was decadent, indulgent—arguably the most beautiful building aside from House Gluttony.

Alabaster stone walls gleamed in the moonlight, freshly buffed and shining enticingly; the roof had the palest blue shingles, resembling an enchanted castle from a fairy tale.

It looked like the sort of place where dreams and fantasies were real and mundane life faded away. I couldn't help but be caught up in the magic for a few moments.

Music spilled from open doors where patrons of nearby establishments gathered, the scent of food wafting into the cobbled street, making me regret not sampling from the cold dinner platter of pickled vegetables, cured meat, and cheese Carlo had offered earlier.

Ryleigh led us down a narrow snow-covered alleyway, empty save for us, then stopped before a solid metal door.

I shivered in place, both from the cold night air and from an odd sense that tonight would either be very good, or very bad, for reasons I couldn't yet identify.

"Watch."

Ryleigh held the magic key to the center, and the door immediately shimmered, then disappeared, revealing an empty corridor inside.

Ryleigh pulled me through the opening just as the door materialized behind us again, sealing us off from the alleyway.

And just like that, we were in the Seven Sins.

Well, the empty corridor leading to the main lounge, at least.

Magic sizzled over my skin, the glamour already working to disguise me.

I was grateful for the moment of privacy to steady myself. I stared down at my borrowed shoes, the heeled slippers as clear as ice.

I swallowed the sudden lump in my throat, my nerves buzzing. The first hurdle was crossed; the club had granted me entry. Now I needed to do my best to get information for my article without giving myself away. Glamour would hide my identity, but if I asked too many pointed questions, someone was bound to figure out my job.

"Ready?" Ryleigh whispered.

"Almost."

On the short walk over from the Scene Stealer to the Seven Sins, Ryleigh had quietly told me about the layout—on the main level there were seven lounges that connected to the central lounge, each dedicated to a different sin.

Upstairs, personal rooms were available to rent and could be used for whatever the patrons wished: private gambling, trysts, or anything else that was craved behind closed doors.

Downstairs housed an indoor lagoon, bathrooms, wine cellar, and a place for masks to be replaced or clothes to be changed to keep up the guests' anonymity as they left.

On the very top floor was a roof with a botanical garden, known for its wide variety of night-blooming flowers and trees, though according to Ryleigh, it was hardly ever used. Most enjoyed the seven lounges or the lower levels, leaving the roof empty each night.

I couldn't recall where the exit was and didn't like the idea of being trapped when Ryleigh and I parted ways.

"How do we leave?" I asked, staring at the spot where the door used to be. "Oh!"

I clapped a hand over my mouth. I'd forgotten my voice would be disguised by the magic too. I sounded like sin made flesh; my voice was sultry and seductive, practically a low, inviting purr that made my own nipples harden.

Ryleigh shot an amused glance my way. I took a moment to really *look* at her instead of focusing on my surroundings. Her glamour was stunning. Her brunette hair had shifted to a luminous golden chestnut, her face a bit more heart-shaped than before, her lips lush and full and made for all sorts of sinful things.

I wondered how I appeared, then reminded myself to focus on work, my surroundings. Tonight wasn't about pleasure. For me, at least.

I glanced around.

A solid, beautiful mural-covered wall was now in the door's place, the pale blues and icy white hues of the wide-open sky undoubtedly meant to be soothing.

Two towering ice dragons flew through the air, their scales sparkling like diamonds, their iridescent eyes glimmering.

They were the most majestic, fearsome creatures in the realm, and I couldn't help but stare at their giant forms, twisting through the clouds, so free and unencumbered. I'd only ever seen an ice dragon once at House Gluttony, and that had been from a distance. Whoever the artist was, they'd caught the essence of the elusive dragons beautifully in the mural.

But even the stunning art of the northern sky couldn't quell my rapid pulse.

I wasn't claustrophobic, but I despised being trapped. Right now, I was as far from the ice dragons and their freedom as possible. I might as well be stuck in a deep, dark cave.

"How do we leave?" I asked again, ignoring the dulcet tone of my voice.

"Relax, Ad." Ryleigh took my hand again and strode down the wide corridor. "The exit is at the other end of the club. If you need help, ask someone tending the bar."

She paused in front of an ornately carved set of double doors, turning to look me over.

"You're sure this disguise is okay?" I asked.

I knew I could trust the magic, but what if it failed?

I reached up, my fingers brushing the edge of my mask.

It was solid pale blue lace, and I didn't expect it to hide my features at all, considering only a slightly more condensed patch of lace covered my eyes, but it had. If, by some terrible luck, the glamour failed, the mask would do its job well. Ryleigh had the same one on and I hadn't been able to tell it was her on the walk over here.

"You're perfect." Ryleigh kissed my cheek. "Have fun tonight."

"I'm here strictly to work."

"You can do both."

Before I could say anything else, she pushed the doors open, revealing a candlelit, sensual lounge. It was beautiful, luxurious—utterly enchanting, like a dark fairy tale sprung to life.

Music played from some unseen source, the sound heavy on low tones and notes, the beat thumping in time with my heart. It was much different from the familiar string quartets at parties and balls hosted by nobles. Couples danced to it, swaying their hips, their heads bent close.

Bold hands traveled up along silhouettes, slow and seductively.

In the far corner of the chamber more daring arrangements were set up for couples who wished to feed darker desires in public.

Cages suspended from the ceiling swayed as couples entered them, slamming the doors behind them as they began to engage in wicked games. I watched as one masked lady in a beautiful leather bustier chained her lover's hands behind his back, commanded him to kneel, then swatted him with a riding crop.

Without any other sort of foreplay, she pulled his hard cock out and ran the leather along the shaft. It was impressive that he was already turned on.

Perhaps he really enjoyed being ordered around. I tensed as she slapped the underside of his erection, the tip glistening with his arousal. Pain must be his preferred vice, and she was more than willing to give him what he wanted.

It was certainly one way to seek thrills.

I scanned the rest of the room, searching for the best place to sit and hopefully talk with Ryleigh until I settled into the atmosphere and read the guests for the best target.

Low tables and velvet couches in various shades of dark blue provided intimate seating arrangements around the perimeter of the room. Silver-frost flowers with their silver-tipped petals spilled from lapis vases, the scent a cool, fragrant floral that soothed and enticed.

Every couch was already occupied, which was a shame. I would have preferred to sit there until I decided who to approach first.

On the far right, a bar carved from a solid piece of lapis gleamed from the little orbs of iridescent Fae lights that were strung from the ceiling.

Bottles of spirits lined the wall behind the bar from top to bottom, sending prisms of color shooting across the shiny bar top as they were taken from the shelves, flipped theatrically, and poured into waiting cut-crystal glasses and tumblers.

The lounge teemed with glamoured guests, their masks similar to mine and Ryleigh's, though some were made of metal and gleamed menacingly in the light. The music suddenly grew louder, the new beat a primal, faster melody that dared patrons to move in time to it.

Hinges on the metal cages groaned as they swung furiously from side to side, the lovers now completely lost to their passions, uncaring of their audience.

I swallowed thickly, my pulse racing.

A few masked faces turned our way, my nerves igniting in a rush from the onslaught of attention. I was used to blending in, to remaining on the periphery until I'd taken in a whole room. Here I was very much on display. And my exquisitely short dress was only encouraging everyone to look their fill. Instead of being the one who sought out their target, I was very much prey. My mouth went dry.

"Should we get a drink?" I asked.

I couldn't hear Ryleigh over the music.

I turned, ready to repeat myself, but she was gone. I thought I caught the back of her head disappearing into one of the private rooms off the lounge.

I sighed and faced the bar again, choking back a scream at the masked stranger leaning in, blocking my view. "Want to dance?"

"I—"

He didn't wait for my response; his arm was suddenly around my waist, tugging me close. I didn't feel caged, precisely, but I certainly didn't appreciate his arrogant approach.

He spun me around the dance floor, much too quickly, and I squeezed my eyes shut. His heat, the crowded room itself, the quiet chatter that seemed to turn into a full buzz—everything had my head spinning faster than my wretched dance partner as we moved around and around.

My stomach had already been knotting itself together and I felt my mouth start to slowly fill with saliva. It was all too much too quickly. Glamour or not, if I threw up on the dance floor, I would never see another invitation to this club again.

I pushed back, locking my arms straight out, and he finally stopped spinning us.

"Excuse me," I mumbled, then rushed to the far end of the room, praying he wouldn't follow me. Somehow, even in a den of sin, murder would probably be frowned upon. Even if the victim was a miserable beast who didn't feel the need to seek a consenting dance partner.

Hiding was an undignified term to use, but if one wanted to call slinking into the shadows to gather myself that, then perhaps I *might* be avoiding the dancer. For his sake, mostly. I wasn't entirely sure I wouldn't knee him in the groin if he attempted that again.

After a few moments, my breathing resumed a normal rhythm and my stomach settled. The dancer found a new partner who seemed to enjoy his antics, so I made my way to the bar and ordered a brandy.

While I sipped it, another patron edged his way in beside me. Hope kindled again. Perhaps he might be someone I could glean information about romance from.

When I snuck another glance his way, he flashed a key at me. This one didn't have runes on it, which meant it probably opened one of the private rooms.

Why he was showing it off to me like a prize pig at a country fair was unclear.

When I didn't immediately jump up and give a standing ovation to his offering, he moved it closer. As if proximity would spark a greater impression.

My eyes crossed in the height of seduction as he waved it inches from my nose.

"I've secured a private room for us."

I glanced at the other patrons sitting nearby. "I think you've mistaken me for someone else, sir."

"You're here. I'm here. In a den of vice, I'd say the only one who seems mistaken about the purpose of this club is you."

I drew in a deep breath. Romance wouldn't be his strong suit, then.

"Lust isn't the only sin to enjoy here."

He ran his attention down my body. "No, but it's the most fun. Now then, are you coming or not? I've got to meet my intended at the theater in an hour and this cock won't suck itself in the meantime."

I seriously reconsidered my decision to attend this den of iniquity for my article.

Surely, even with sin and vice on the menu, manners and flirtation were not obscene requests, along with wanting a lover who wasn't already spoken for.

"Forgive me, sir. But if your tongue is this bland during a simple conversation, I can only imagine other areas where it would be equally disappointing."

His mouth dropped open.

I tossed back the rest of my drink, slammed the empty glass on the bar, then headed toward the stairs before my temper got the better of me and I was banished from the club. Which wouldn't be the worst fate at this point.

Much to my horror, this male wasn't as easily deterred.

He shouted from a few paces behind me. "Hey! You, there! Stop."

I didn't turn back. There was no way in any of the hells I'd be interested in him. I bumped into patrons, excusing myself as I tried to put distance and bodies between us.

"I intend to prove you wrong about my tongue!"

Gods help me. That wasn't a challenge I wished to take him up on.

Giving up on making another scene, I finally reached the stairs and raced up, my breath coming in short bursts. I needed to breathe in the outside air, feel the coldness on my flushed skin, and escape the idiotic guests who knew nothing of seduction or romance.

After what felt like a year of rushing up endless stairs, I finally came to the end and pushed the door open at what I prayed was the rooftop.

A blast of icy air hit me, and peace immediately settled into my bones. I gulped down a few lungsful of wintry air, my nerves dissipating with each deep inhalation. My sister was far more affected by crowds, but occasionally I fell into that same trap.

I waited, body tensed as I kept my back pressed to the door, but after a few moments, no one else emerged onto the roof.

I exhaled, thankful I'd successfully dodged two uncomfortable situations.

I pushed the unpleasant experiences away and soaked in every detail of the roof.

I'd left a nightmare only to walk directly into a dream.

The rooftop garden was exquisite, bursting with a sea of vivid wintry colors. My attention swept across the space, my heart fluttering for an entirely new reason.

Flowers in various shades of blue, from cobalt to navy and periwinkle, and even complementing shades of white and silver, glowed under the moonlight.

Near the far end was a tall, gnarled frostberry tree.

I loved the tiny ice-coated pale blue berries that sparkled, so I aimed for it, wanting the comfort of its night blossoms and strong trunk to lean against.

I stopped before it, quietly cursing myself for letting two idiots run me off. It was getting late, and I was still no closer to writing my first Miss Match column. Whether I wanted to or not, I needed to go back downstairs and start asking questions.

"First time?" a deep voice said from the shadows.

I whirled, my heart hammering against my chest as I squinted into the darkness, eventually making out the lone figure across the way.

Based on what Ryleigh had said about the rooftop, I hadn't expected anyone to be up here, and he'd been so still my attention initially skipped right over him.

Now that I saw him, I couldn't understand how I'd missed him.

He leaned against the wall of a water tower, his masked face tipped up to the sky, an empty highball glass dangling from his fingertips, glinting in the moonlight.

"Sorry. I didn't see you there."

"Mm."

I waited for another moment, but he said nothing else. This stranger clearly didn't want company, and I knew all too well what that was like, so I made to leave, when he spoke again.

"You didn't answer my question."

I paused, glancing back. He was a cheeky one. "Why are you alone on the roof?"

"I'm not."

Insufferable male. Of course he wasn't *currently* alone. "If this is how you behave with company, then I understand why you're up here, sulking by yourself."

A soft chuckle rumbled deep in his chest, not at all an unpleasant sound.

I waited for him to show off a key, to demand I engage in sin or force me to dance. He did nothing of the sort. He kept his attention fixed to the sky, happy to indulge in light conversation, no demands or expectations. Just pleasant small talk. He might be perfect...

I hesitated for only a moment before I moved closer, studying him in the darkness.

Surely he must have some flaw. Claw-tipped fingers. Crude breath. Little devil horns sprouting from his ass.

He was tall, well toned but not bulky, broad shouldered, and even without seeing his face, I sensed he had no trouble in the romance department.

I wondered what he really looked and sounded like without the glamour. Perhaps he was two inches tall and was related to hobgoblins and trolls. Though I somehow doubted that. I'd wager my entire paycheck that he was no stranger to receiving an abundance of attention.

It was in the way he held himself—sure and confident, like the world would bend to his will, seeking his attention, even knowing it would be fleeting.

Stubble lightly dusted his cut jawline, making him appealingly rugged instead of unkempt. He was a feast for the senses and knew it, given the curve of that wicked mouth as he no doubt sensed my open perusal of him.

If anyone could simply hold a key up and expect lovers to fall all over the opportunity to follow him into the deepest, darkest corners of hell, he would be the one to get away with it.

Yet he didn't use that to his advantage.

His hair was dark, but whether it was light brown or black I couldn't tell. And it didn't matter. He might be handsome, but he was not nearly as enticing as completing my first Miss Match column and collecting my check.

I took him in again, this time with the intention of engaging his mind enough to distract him from his thoughts. Tonight wasn't a loss for me just yet. Here stood my salvation.

"Have you ever been in love?"

He snorted, finally dropping his focus away from the sky and whatever had been holding his attention. I couldn't see his eyes but felt the heat of his gaze move along my costume.

Something about his aura shifted along with his posture, his attention suddenly feeling dangerous in the most intriguing way. Like standing too close to a seaside cliff as the wind whipped at your limbs, dragging you perilously closer to the edge.

Or maybe it was how a mouse felt when a hawk noticed it and realized it was famished.

I wasn't naive enough to think myself the hawk, especially as a charge built in the space between us. But I *was* daring enough to hold my ground, curious to see what happened next.

Which was completely unlike me. *Work,* I quietly scolded myself. I was here for work only. He didn't seem to notice my silent battle, thank the old gods for small mercies.

"That's quite the loaded question for a pleasure club, Lady Frost."

A clever nickname, considering my costume. I hid my fascination, curious to see how he reacted to my next move.

"Not really. You looked like you were contemplating something vast. Love, loss; those are typically the biggest culprits of intense longing. It was either that or you're constipated."

He tossed his head back and laughed, the tension between us breaking with the rich, pleasant sound. My heart gave a little flip. I'd scowl at it for being foolish if I could.

"Your wooing skills are horrendous."

"That's because I'm not trying to make you fall in love with me. I simply need advice on how to move on from my last heartbreak."

"And you thought coming to this club was the best place to discover that?"

His tone was highly amused. Rightly so. I'd wanted to surprise him, hopefully sparking enough interest to answer my questions.

Ryleigh would certainly be impressed with my attempt. I *could* flirt when pressed to. Or maybe I simply liked flirting with this stranger who had a deep, alluring laugh.

One I had no business being fascinated by. Trolls and hobgoblins, I reminded myself. I was enticed because of the glamour and nothing more.

I lifted a shoulder and dropped it, aiming for casual.

"Why not? I imagine lots of patrons are running away from something. Hence the masks and secrecy."

"Or perhaps they simply crave a night of sin-fueled adventure."

"They could do that in any one of the brothels, taverns, or pubs in this district."

"Not really. Here they can truly let go, indulge in anything they wish without anyone in their daily life knowing. This club is escapism at its finest."

"You're here to escape?"

"Aren't you?"

I leaned against the wall beside him, considering.

Maybe it was that simple and I'd been overanalyzing it. Maybe this club was also popular because it indulged in a bit of adventure and danger too.

The fear of being caught, discovered, was also an aphrodisiac of sorts.

Not all the patrons might be craving distraction, but some probably were. And of those few, perhaps that was how they were coping with heartbreak.

Could engaging in a bit of harmless fun until the heartache passed be the best advice?

My mind spun with the revelation. That might be the perfect opening advice for my Miss Match column. I didn't have to be an expert on romantic partnerships. I simply needed to figure out how to assist with emotions on a broader scale.

Losing someone was something I could relate to. When my father died, aside from missing his presence, the routine of our daily life being disrupted was the next hardest aspect to overcome. I'd had to work extra hard to set tasks for me and my sister to fill the void.

Otherwise, the hard days grew unbearable.

Doing something to break the routine might help someone through loss, not simply romantic loss either.

My masked companion mistook my quiet contemplation for something it wasn't.

"Perhaps you should visit Lust Lounge. I'm sure there are many patrons who would be happy to help you get over your heartbreak, Lady F."

"That might be true, but I highly doubt they could help me with love."

"Ah. I understand now."

"What?" I asked, noting the teasing edge in his tone.

I couldn't recall the last time someone was so playful with me. It was disorienting.

And…*fun*.

As if sensing my unexpected delight at our interaction and knowing it would both drive me crazy and hook me deeper, he plotted his next move in the most torturously slow way.

He leaned in, bringing his mouth tantalizingly close to my ear. His breath tickled the stray tendrils of my hair, the sensation intoxicatingly sensual for such an innocent act.

He paused just long enough for my pulse to speed in anticipation, a hunter well-versed in taking down prey. I knew from an article I'd researched that fight-or-flight responses physically aroused, often causing attraction; he not only appeared to know that, but also deftly utilized the skill.

Heat pooled low in my belly the same moment goose bumps rose along my flesh. I was startled to realize how badly I wanted to kiss him.

"You're cynical, Lady Frost."

I laughed softly.

"Isn't it odd how whenever someone has one iota of common sense, they're called cynical? Lust and love are wildly different."

"Spoken like a true pessimist."

"Perhaps that would be true if two patrons didn't just accost me downstairs. I assure you, it wasn't love that fueled them to pursue me."

He froze. "You were harmed?"

"Not at all." I waved off his concern. But when he didn't seem content to let it go, I added, "It really was nothing. Just two males who didn't have decent manners. That's all. I'd rather not think about them now."

He was quiet for a moment. "I would hate to leave you alone on the roof, but eviscerating anyone breaking the club rules would be a worthy task. How do you feel about blood?"

I couldn't help but laugh at that. "How utterly romantic. It's no wonder you're here and not happily at home with a wife."

The tension finally broke as he smiled.

"If you're fishing for information, I'd expect you to ask directly."

He was near enough now that the heat of his body warmed me. And I rather liked it. I swayed a little closer, seeking more of his warmth.

"But no, I don't have a wife waiting at home for me. Though sharing a bed sounds nice."

Against my better judgment, a smile curved my lips. I enjoyed a good battle of wits, and he was a worthy opponent tonight. It had been years since I'd spoken with someone who gave as good as they were getting.

We were in a pleasure club, making his agenda clear—he probably wanted me in his bed tonight—but the pursuit was a pleasant diversion, one I admired. He was learning what I liked, leaning into it, giving me just enough of a taste to crave more.

It was a delightful mental seduction. One I couldn't ignore if I tried.

He wasn't at all like the brutish male who'd stolen a dance earlier and hadn't cared one whit about my wants. Nor was he like the male who'd demanded I go to a private chamber with him. This stranger seemed to get pleasure from enticing *me*. He wanted me to choose him.

He was a wicked flirt.

"What are you escaping from?" I asked.

"At the moment, I'm not running from anything, Lady F. Unless you want me to leave."

There was no mistaking the desire in his tone for anything else.

My pulse ticked faster. I had what I'd come here for—a solid direction for my column. I could go home, grab my quill and inkpot, and draft my article. Then I could crawl into my cold bed alone, shivering and wondering *what if*. What if I stayed, what if I flirted a bit more, what if I kissed him like he was the last being alive and had some real fun for once?

The responsible thing to do was to leave now.

Or I could stay for a little while longer, indulge in a distraction.

Normally, the decision wasn't hard at all. I'd leave the first moment I had what I needed for an article. My stranger didn't push, didn't attempt to talk me into staying. He simply waited for my choice. And that was the most attractive quality of all.

By now my sister and stepmother were tucked into bed, sleeping soundly, and I *could* spare an extra hour or so here without fear of missing my deadline.

His company was pleasant. The emotions he stirred in me even more so.

The firewood needed to be replenished tomorrow after I got paid, so I knew my room would be even colder than usual tonight.

There were a hundred reasons I could come up with for choosing to stay. The truth was, I didn't need to create any excuse other than wanting to be here, now. Enjoying the moment.

I had so few moments like this in my life: carefree, fun, easy.

Temptation grew.

I glanced sideways at the masked stranger; he was much larger compared to me than I'd originally thought. He seemed like the sort of male who knew how to throw his weight around in the bedroom, taking charge while also being considerate.

A polite alpha. Dominant but sensitive. A male who took control, who owned. But only behind closed doors. *The ultimate dream,* I thought wryly.

"Your smile is devastating," he said, tracing my lower lip with his thumb.

A spark of heat ignited at the simple caress. His touch hadn't been tentative or shy; he'd been watching me, gauging my interest. Then he'd acted.

Again, unlike the man from the dance floor, who'd just taken what he wanted.

This stranger didn't give standard compliments, which I appreciated. It meant when he offered one it had been earned through his careful insight. I wasn't sure how I knew that with certainty, but I did.

I also liked the mystery aspect of it all, the thrill of the hunt, the tension of the cat-and-mouse game enticing me enough to play.

He'd made the first, subtle move. Testing to see if I'd welcome his advances.

He was bold enough to make his intentions clear but wouldn't push further.

Another trait I found attractive. It made me want to throw my responsible nature aside for one night and do wicked, dirty things with him.

"What will you do about it?" I asked, baiting him.

"Are you issuing a challenge, Lady F?"

"If I am?"

"I am not one to lose."

He moved until he stood in front of me now, one arm pressed against the wall at my side, the other gently cupping my face. His legs brushed against mine, sending a thrill of anticipation shooting through me from each point of contact.

We were in a pleasure club. And the time for talking was through.

In direct contrast to my ice queen costume, I wanted passion and fire, a night to indulge in fantasy, forgetting the harshness of reality for a while.

This stranger was perfect. He'd take down his prey, then move on to the next, seeking adventure and thrills in the chase. No messy emotions, no true names. No regrets.

"Neither am I."

Feeling bold enough to go after what I wanted, I gripped his shirt in my fist and dragged him to me, earning a surprised huff before his mouth crashed into mine, the kiss a punishing, delightful claiming that set my blood aflame.

My stranger was *exactly* the sort of male I'd hoped he was.

My lips parted on a contented sigh and his tongue swept in, expertly caressing mine.

He groaned into my mouth, ravishing me as he pressed me harder up against the wall, my short skirt riding higher.

I cupped his face, his stubble-roughened cheeks driving me wild.

It had been far too long since I'd felt desired. And there was no doubt that this stranger wanted me madly. He drew back for a moment, his forehead pressed to mine as he panted.

I couldn't tell for certain because of the glamour, but I'd swear he seemed utterly shocked by his response. I had no time to think about it; in the next breath, his lips were on mine, and I was once again lost to him.

He hoisted one of my legs up around his hip, the refined move meant to please and tease. I couldn't tell who it affected more. The new position had his hard length pressed against my core, sending sparks of sensation through me with each delicious thrust.

I wasn't sure he was consciously moving his hips; it seemed as if he'd surrendered to the demand of our bodies. And I was all too pleased.

This kiss...I'd never felt something so passionate before, so untamed.

I melted into it, giving myself over entirely to the sensation, the seduction.

My lips were swollen, bruised things that craved more delightful punishment from his. And he was all too willing to oblige. He gently bit down on my lower lip, smiling against my mouth as a bolt of heat went through me and I clawed him closer.

He was immensely talented with his mouth; I'd need to write an ode to it one day.

His hand splayed against my thigh, pinning me in place, his command over my body already a wonderful prelude to a night I wouldn't soon forget.

He tore his mouth from mine, kissing up the side of my neck, taking the lobe of my ear between his teeth next.

"Unless you tell me to stop, I'm going to worship your body, my lady."

It was already his to do as he pleased with from the kiss alone.

And he damned well knew it.

"Saints curse me. If you stop, I'll kill you." I breathed as his mouth moved along the column of my throat, both devouring and savoring me at once. Goose bumps rose where his stubble passed over my soft skin, and I yearned to feel more of it in other sensitive areas.

His clever fingers dipped between the chains holding the side of my gown together, his bare skin on mine sending another heady rush through my veins.

"I'm no highborn lady, though."

"Perhaps not in title. But tonight, you're *mine*."

He moved his hips again, this time with knowing purpose, hitting a spot that would certainly send me over the edge if he kept that motion up, proving his statement correct as he swallowed my moan with his next kiss.

Gods, I wanted him. But a sudden realization struck, sending reality crashing down on me like an upturned bucket of ice water. This wouldn't be a hard-and-fast evening like I'd originally thought; this male would take his time, wringing pleasure from me for hours.

And while that seemed like the most wonderful nighttime adventure I could imagine, I couldn't risk missing my deadline. No matter how tempting he was.

I broke away from our kiss, breathing hard, my body already protesting the absence of his as he leaned back just enough to search my face.

Whatever he saw, even with my mask on, was enough for him to know our night was done. My stranger slowly set my leg down, smoothing my skirt and bodice with his large hand before adjusting his trousers.

"I—" I froze at movement behind him.

We hadn't been alone.

"By all means," the new stranger drawled. "Don't stop on my account. Things were getting good."

My companion stiffened, then glanced over his shoulder, cursing. "You were supposed to send a note when you were done. Give us a bloody minute."

The other male laughed softly but retreated down the stairs.

"Are you all right?" he asked, his tone gentling. "If I misunderstood..."

"No, no." I shook my head. "You didn't misread anything. It's just... complicated tonight. Poor timing."

"Indeed." He leaned in, lightly kissing my cheek. "The timing couldn't be worse."

I nodded but said nothing. What else was there to say? Our little tryst was over before it could really begin. And it was for the best. I had to leave now too, and tomorrow wasn't a possibility because entry to the club wasn't guaranteed again.

"I apologize for my companion." He motioned toward the spot where the other male had been. I would swear he was stalling, unwilling to part just yet. "He was raised by wolves."

A small smile played across my lips. I'd never been caught in the act before, but there was a slight, dark thrill about being watched that didn't exactly make me feel scandalized.

The masked stranger took a step back. And part of me regretted breaking our kiss early. It felt like I'd lost something special before I'd realized its value.

"I'm sorry, Lady F. I must go."

He hesitated, then came forward again, pressing something cold into my palm.

I glanced down at a key in the shape of a seven, my pulse fluttering madly.

"Come back tomorrow at midnight," he said. "I'll be waiting for you here. Just to talk, if that's all you desire. And if you'd prefer to just escape and find someone else, that's fine too."

My fingers closed around the key, my attention locked on it.

What he'd just offered...

I went to thank him, but when I looked up, my stranger was already gone.

Dear Miss Match,

How do I get over my latest heartbreak?

Sincerely yours,
Stuck in Love

Dear Stuck,

If the object of your affection broke your heart, break your routine. (Much less messy than breaking their limbs and going through the hassle of court hearings and facing the gallows.)

Jesting aside, Miss Match's advice is to do one thing each day that brings you joy. Whether it's admiring the sunrise or sunset, gazing up at the stars, going for a walk in nature, or taking a moment to be kind to someone else.

Court yourself. The right person will eventually come along and see what a diamond you truly are.

Yours,
Miss Match

NINE
Prince Gluttony

*Y*OU *LIED*." ENVY'S dagger pierced the flesh at my throat. Heedless of the blade, I jerked my chin at Lust, signaling for him to stand at the end of the alley, blocking us from any witnesses.

Lust gritted his teeth but followed my silent order, knowing Envy was putting us at risk. This part of town was rife with spies, making the dark alleyway a perfect place for them to lurk.

Ice soaked through my cloak, soothing my own rage as Envy leaned into his weapon and pressed me harder into the wall. He was beginning to test my patience.

"I should decapitate you now."

"You can try." I bared my teeth as a trickle of golden ichor leaked from the wound, dripping onto my collar.

Violence simmered in the air between us, primed and ready to ignite.

Part of me wanted to give in to the growing urge to fight, fuel my sin by the thrill of it.

Tempting as it was, we were in public. I inhaled deeply, then exhaled, my breath streaming out in a cloud against the frigid air.

We hadn't made it out of the night district, and aside from spies and informants prowling the streets, anyone could stumble down the alley and find two princes brawling. It would be the sort of gossip they'd happily sell to scandal sheets for a heavy coin purse.

If any rumor-hungry columnists found out, they'd start digging into possible reasons for the fight, and everything I'd been doing to hide the attack on our hunting party would be destroyed.

I could dispatch my brothers from my circle easily enough, but sending them back to their territory would only delay obtaining the information I wanted to get from them.

Hence why I'd allowed them to visit the Seven Sins in the first place tonight. Aside from patrons engaging in trysts and debauchery, it was a place where secrets could be won in games of chance. Lust had done just that—won a card game that paid in information.

After his win, I sent Val after the informant who'd given my brothers the intel and would see to him personally later. My coffers were practically limitless—I'd pay twice as much for his silence from here on out. I'd pay him triple to find out who Adriana Saint Lucent dealt with.

Overall, things had gone well this evening.

To avoid gutting Envy with my House dagger in the middle of this alley, I focused on the unexpectedly pleasant night I'd had while waiting for them to finish their game.

It had been years since I'd actually wanted someone in my bed.

Even with Envy's dagger gouging my flesh, and the threat of a spy coming upon our little trio, I couldn't stop my mind from flashing to the heated encounter.

That kiss…It awakened something in me, something long dormant.

I ought to kill my brothers for interrupting what promised to be a thrilling evening. I'd thought I'd been cursed to never take another lover, but tonight proved that theory false.

I'd been close to making Lady Frost mine, right there on the damned roof.

Maybe I should stab my brother, then return to the club, consequences be damned.

If I had another more pleasurable way to feed my sin, then I didn't need to worry about missing the next hunt and not fueling my hunger for adventure.

Lady F had been a welcome surprise for multiple reasons. I *liked* her. Immensely.

Envy's blade pressed harder, drawing my attention back to the here and now. His eyes flashed with barely leashed anger. If he didn't get himself under control, *my* leash would snap.

Lust whistled low, a signal someone was coming.

I knocked Envy's blade away. "Take this to my throne room. Now."

I didn't give him a chance to respond. I magicked myself to my castle, stripped my suit jacket off, and tossed it across my throne as I waited for my brothers to transport there next.

The silver dragons carved into my seat of power seemed to crave blood as much as I did right now, the sapphire gemstones in their eyes catching the light of the fire that raged in the oversized fireplace across the room.

I longed to collapse into the plush cobalt velvet cushion and kick my feet up.

Instead, I faced the carved double doors, hand on the hilt of my dagger, waiting.

If Envy wanted a fight, I'd give him one.

In seconds my brothers appeared in the throne room, stalking forward, their weapons hidden. That they waited until we'd reached my House of Sin before they'd struck spoke to the severity of our issue. If secrecy wasn't needed for the good of the realm, they would have attacked in the streets, the brawl drawing all sorts of unwanted attention.

We Princes of Hell weren't known for our restraint.

Envy stopped before me, his chest nearly brushing mine. I smiled at him; there were no witnesses to worry about now.

I held his stare, the tension growing palpable. I could have my dagger lodged in his chest in seconds. My hand grazed the hilt. Diplomacy wasn't my strong suit and the thrill of the attack made my blood sing with my power.

I pulled my blade just as Lust stepped up behind Envy and tugged our brother back a few paces, trying to defuse the situation.

"Both of you, *stop*."

Lust glared at each of us, waiting until he was sure we'd gotten our-selves under control before turning his own anger on me.

"This is bigger than normal inter-House secrets," he said. "A broken treaty doesn't just impact your gods-damned court. Were you and Wrath going to tell us?"

I locked my jaw. Which was a good enough answer for my brother.

"Bloody hell, Gabriel," he muttered, going for the liquor I kept on a bar cart near my throne. "What were you and Wrath thinking? If word spreads of this to citizens in the other courts—"

"It won't." I cut him off. "I've handled it."

Envy shook his head. "You didn't bury it deep enough, or else our spies wouldn't have had anything to report. How, exactly, did you and Wrath manage to keep his injury quiet?"

"Are we sharing House secrets now?" I asked. "Would you care to explain the true reason behind your game with the Unseelie King? I'm sure *that* had nothing to do with your court and all the gossip circulating on why you'd warded it from the whole damned realm. Find any hexed objects lately, brother? You know, since that technically impacts *all* of us?"

Envy's mouth pressed into a hard line.

"Didn't think so." I grabbed a bottle of demonberry wine. "The attack on Wrath was unfortunate but won't be repeated. As you know, the alpha addressed the dragon who attacked, and no true harm was done to anyone."

"There shouldn't be *any* ice dragon attacks, even on us immortals," Lust said. "The pact forbids it. You are supposed to ensure the agreement stands. It doesn't matter if it was a onetime event."

It was jarring to learn this for the first time, so I allowed my broth-ers a moment for their worry. The last ice dragon massacre had killed hundreds of demons from each circle, along with an equally staggering number of dragons.

Under the direction of their alphas, each one of the seven different dragon packs had flown in and chosen a House of Sin to try to claim as an extension of their territory.

For the first time in their long lives, each dragon alpha had put their own differences aside and plotted together. It had been the single largest dragon attack in our history.

After the failed attempt to take the land south of Merciless Reach, I hardly ever heard from or saw the other six dragon packs. Partly because the pack I suspected was led by Silvanus claimed the land closest to my House of Sin and they were among the most ferocious dragons; they had no qualms about fighting their own to establish dominance. And partly because the dragons had suffered such a great loss they didn't wish to tempt fate.

The massacre was something no one wanted repeated, dragons and demons alike.

"It won't happen again."

"You can't guarantee that," Envy said. "What if another dragon gets infected with the same blight that caused the first attack?"

"Nothing is ever guaranteed." Because of the clause that granted them a meeting of their choice, I had to share *some* information. "My hunters are watching the pack. If there's any hint of a change, I'll know."

Lust paced. "I don't like it. What the hell infected them to begin with? That's never happened before, right?"

I shook my head. "I have a select team of experts looking into the matter now."

"Reporters will be all over this story," Envy said, "working the entire realm up into chaos."

"Gods' blood." Lust's expression darkened. "Tell me that journalist doesn't know."

"Keep up. Miss Saint Lucent is an advice columnist now," I reminded them as I poured a goblet of wine. "Hence my earlier victory."

"Wonderful." Lust walked away, pacing. "She knows."

"She *suspects*," I corrected. "And regardless of her suspicions, she's now writing advice about love, which should occupy her well enough."

My brothers were quiet a minute. Unfortunately, I didn't think it was due to being so wildly impressed that I'd rendered them speechless.

"Let's lay this out there," Envy said. "You've been engaged in a *very* public war with a columnist who loathes you. Somehow, she has information on the dragon attack—the first in more than a century—and as a solution, you forced her into writing an advice column on a subject she despises."

When he put it like that, I might see *some* merit in his worry. But I knew Adriana valued her job too much to risk being fired. A fact I'd concluded after seeing her fight so passionately to keep her column before she knew I'd entered the office.

"And you believe, by some wild stretch of the imagination," he went on, "she'll simply let the dragon story go in favor of listening to you, the male she hates, now more than ever?"

I adopted that arrogant mask we all preferred to wear, shrugging as if bored by their worry. "What else would you have me do? Host a tournament royale between the seven Houses of Sin to divert attention away from the dragons?"

"Yes." Lust stopped pacing and spun around. "Give the people what they want, Gabriel."

Envy chuckled, catching on right away. "Brilliant."

"No," I said, irritated by what I suspected they were getting at. "Don't even suggest it."

"*You* just proposed the idea, dear brother. And you're going to do exactly what the realm wants," Envy said. "You're going to host a competition to find your match."

"It was sarcasm," I deadpanned. "I know these are trying times, but do keep your wits about you."

"No. It's brilliant. You're going to invite Miss Saint whatever to be the official reporter, the only one permitted to write about it," Lust added.

"Make her move in while the competition is going on," Envy said. "You'll keep her close and distracted. She'll have no time to hunt down dragon rumors if you're keeping her occupied."

"Have you both gone mad? The last thing I need is to worry about having anyone live in the castle while I'm trying to keep the dragon incident from the public and research ways to avoid anything like it in the future. Most especially the reporter who wants nothing more than to destroy me for some saints-forsaken reason."

"I'm sure it has nothing to do with what happened at that ball," Envy said.

My brows drew together. "Which ball?"

"The All-Sinners Ball. From what I remember, things went poorly between you two after that."

"You're mistaken," I said. "There has never been any warmth between us, before or after that event."

"I left early, but Lust attended." Envy turned to our other brother, his gaze calculating. "What do you remember?"

"About the All-Sinners Ball?" Lust lifted a shoulder. "Not much. I do remember the spectacle of the viscount finding him with the viscountess, though."

Envy was silent for a moment.

"Miss Saint Lucent—"

"We could argue the point all night." I cut him off. "That was a decade ago and no longer matters. End of discussion."

Envy's gaze narrowed. I could practically see the gears turning in his mind.

He must have been wildly drunk that night to believe Adriana Saint Lucent, the silver-tongued, blue-haired hellion that haunted my nightmares, had felt anything except disdain for me from the very start.

The All-Sinners Ball had been the talk of the realm ten years prior—it was a chance for commoners and nobility to all mingle, regardless of station, in hopes of finding a match. All sinners from every House of Sin of marriageable age were invited, Miss Saint Lucent included.

It was the first time I'd ever met her, and the image remained damnably burned into my memory. She'd been positively stunning in her shimmering silver gown, earning attention from everyone in attendance, including myself.

I thought she was the most beautiful, wickedly smart demon I'd ever had the good fortune to meet. I'd started dreaming up ways to impress her, to make her crave me the way I'd suddenly craved none but her.

Then she'd opened her cursed mouth to let me know exactly what she thought of me, and whatever fantasy I'd had of her was promptly slain.

"Back to the issue at hand. I'd be willing to host a tournament to keep the scandal sheets occupied," I said. "Each House of Sin could challenge—"

"It won't be as impactful as a competition with higher stakes," Envy interrupted. "Each Prince of Sin will choose one participant to compete for your throne."

"Except I'm not interested in finding a consort."

"Perhaps not, but you'll adhere to the rules of the pact and do what's best for the realm," Envy said.

He had me there.

"Strike a bargain with one of the participants if you must," he said, reading my resolve to play whatever role I needed to in order to keep my circle safe. "Give them enough coin to break off the engagement after the stories die down in the press. Find someone who cares more about fame than true love."

"Exactly. The relationship doesn't have to last," Lust added, "but a competition for your heart will create the kind of realm-wide distraction we need to figure out if the ice dragon attack truly was one of its kind or if there's a bigger threat at stake."

He didn't elaborate, but I suspected he was worried the witches—our greatest enemies—might be responsible. Which would mean war was brewing.

Without scouring my library for other causes of the attack, I couldn't rule out the possibility of the witches casting a spell or hexing the dragons.

Unaware of my silent worry, Envy nodded. "Involving Miss Saint Lucent will ensure she reports on what we want her to."

"I don't like this," I said, pacing away, already knowing it was the right move. I couldn't guarantee that the dragon threat was over. And

I needed to ensure that if something else happened, the realm would be fixated elsewhere. "Too much can go wrong."

"Things already went wrong," Envy said. "It's time to set them right before things get worse for us all." He strode forward, clapping a hand across my chest. "Do what you must. But keep the reporter close until the competition ends."

Any good leader knew the first rule of battle was to keep your enemy closest.

I supposed it was time to treat this as the most important skirmish between me and Miss Saint Lucent to date. Personal feelings aside, I'd even court her if I had to.

Anything to keep her where I could watch her closely.

"Miss Saint Lucent is here, Your Highness."

I'd cleared my throne room of any members of my court still sprawled across various pillows and tables from the riotous party I'd thrown last night, not wanting an audience for what promised to be a battle of wills.

"Might as well send her in, Jarvis. Let's get this over with."

My butler inclined his head, then disappeared to fetch my esteemed guest.

I glanced at the freshly stocked bottles of demonberry wine lined up on a table near my throne. Once I was through with this charming task, I was going to reward myself with an entire case of wine and even more lovers.

If I was to be accused of the role anyway, I might as well enjoy some raking and ravishing, now that my appetites seemed to be returning in that area. Unless my newfound desires were solely for one mysterious lady...

The doors swung open, revealing the female of the hour.

And she was in a *wonderful* mood.

She lifted her chin as she strode to the dais, her gaze sharp as daggers as she pinned it to me, holding my stare like she could murder me with it if she concentrated hard enough.

Gods' blood. The woman had an impressive glare.

I should have assigned her to the royal guard instead of the advice column. Miss Saint Lucent would certainly make a formidable opponent on the battlefield.

Or perhaps she'd scare the ice dragons into submission.

If all else failed, I might enlist her in the royal hunting guild.

She came to a stop before the throne, dropping an abysmal curtsy, then returned those icy blue eyes to mine. They glinted dangerously, her cunning mind likely thinking up a thousand silent hexes.

A prickle of…something not entirely unpleasant rolled down my spine. Her defiance made the monster in me sit up and take notice. I inhaled deeply, then exhaled.

Once I was in control again, I gave her a bland smile.

"Miss Saint Lucent," I said, mindful of my tone. Best not to poke the viper. Yet. "Always interesting to see you."

"If only that were true."

I raised a brow; it was true or else I wouldn't have been able to say it. Those were semantics for another day. Now I wanted to get this over with and jump off a mountain to clear my thoughts of my mystery lover.

"I've asked you here today—"

She snorted.

I waited, silent and watchful. She didn't utter another word or sound. Not out of respect, but to spite me, if the look on her face was any indication.

I cocked my head to one side, eyes narrowed.

"Is there a problem, Miss Saint Lucent?"

"Demanding my attendance 'at once' is hardly *asking*, Your Highness."

"Must you always be so disagreeable?"

"No, I suppose I ought to feed your ego like everyone else."

This female would be the end of my sanity.

I leaned back in my throne, steepling my fingers, gaze sweeping over her, calculating. And perhaps it was to provoke her too. I didn't have to use my supernatural ability to read emotions to know she positively hated when I looked her over.

Which sent a thrill through me akin to the thrill I felt when hunting dragons. No one ever mentally sparred with me like the hellcat standing before me. I found myself intrigued by whatever delightful nightmare she'd unleash from her mouth next.

"You clearly have something to say. So, go on," I said. "Aside from breathing, what grave offense have I brought to you now?"

"I was in the middle of work when your summons came. Now I may lose my position since I'm not currently writing the advice column *you* so graciously put me in charge of. Only for you to call me disagreeable when I'm not simpering before you. This whim of yours—whatever it may be—will likely cause my family to be homeless. So please do forgive me if I am a little *disagreeable* over the abuse of your power, Your Highness."

I looked her over carefully, this time without the intent to irk. She had no idea of my whims, and she ought to be thankful for that. She might have a silver tongue, but I had a dark hunger. One that she could never handle, no matter how bold she appeared.

"You no longer need that job."

She arched one brow impressively. "Oh? Has a secret benefactor come forward with an inheritance? Have they appointed you with the honor of sharing that information with me?"

Such a smart mouth.

My attention fell to her cursed lips, lingering a moment too long. Lust's taunt from the night before came back, unbidden. Along with the memory of my masked beauty from the Seven Sins. A prickle of awareness hit me.

I wrenched my gaze back up.

Her hand drifted inside her cloak. It looked like she was checking to see if she had something. Hopefully it wasn't a dagger she planned on throwing at my face.

She caught my curious look and dropped her hand, scowling again.

"I'm offering you a position as my official royal reporter. You and your family will move into House Gluttony at once."

Silence stretched between us. Normally, I could sit here all day, waiting for her to break it first, if only to drive her mad. But today wasn't a regular day; there was much to do and little time to accomplish it all before nightfall. I fought the urge to glance at the clock.

When she still didn't respond after another moment, I pressed on.

"My staff will pack your belongings and transport your family via carriage. You won't have to worry about anything. To make up for any inconvenience, I'll pay your landlord to hold your residence for the next several months as a bonus."

Color rose in her cheeks, the blush pleasant against her pale skin.

My traitorous cock took notice, unperturbed by her hatred.

An image of her tied to my bedposts, flushed from more interesting activities as she writhed against my silken sheets, crossed my mind.

I needed an ice bath and a mental examination. Immediately.

Clearly my subconscious had a deviant streak worthy of ballads if it took my favorite fantasy and imprinted her face on my secret lover. Though maybe it was further proof that my appetites were back with a vengeance.

As if she'd plucked that lusty nightmare from my mind, she leveled me with a glacial look, reminding me she would never submit.

"Well?" I drawled. "Have I rendered you speechless with my generosity?"

"Hardly. I'm simply stunned you believe I'd accept your offer. I am wholly uninterested in leaving the *Wicked Daily* and I certainly don't wish to live here."

I ran a hand through my hair. It was already done. Surely she could see the merit and advantage of what I was offering. Ultimately, we'd both win something.

"I've been careful to not have any rumors spread," I said, "so you'll get the honor of breaking the story first, but I'm hosting a realm-wide competition to find a potential wife."

Her expression shuttered.

Not quite the reaction I'd expected. I tamped any curiosity down.

"Since you're the only columnist allowed to write about each event, you'll be courted by every major publication once it's all said and done.

You've been granted exclusive access to each potential match. Interviews with them, me. Anything you need to craft exciting stories. I want this to be the talk of the Seven Circles for the duration of the competition."

"You speak as if this deal has been finalized."

Her tone mixed with her expression indicated she'd already figured out what I'd done.

If she expected me to feel guilty, she was sorely mistaken.

Outwardly I was the most affable of the Princes of Sin, but we all had our demons to contend with.

It didn't matter if she felt like I'd trapped her—for the good of the realm, I'd do worse. And it wasn't as if she wasn't going to benefit handsomely in the end.

"Your rent has already been paid." I leaned forward, narrowing my gaze. "Your salary will be one million coins. Per article. Are you sure you want to turn down this opportunity, Miss Saint Lucent?"

She looked me over, her eyes glittering with annoyance. It was truly remarkable how unimpressed she was with me, considering my reputation. I understood that look, though—I'd seen it in the ice dragons. Miss Saint Lucent didn't enjoy being trapped or reined in.

And I'd done both.

I fought a smile.

For better or worse, my rival was now bound to me for the next several weeks.

"Yes. I believe I am turning it down."

She dropped a slight curtsy, and it was only her abysmal attempt at propriety that allowed me a moment to school my shocked expression into indifference before she rose.

I hadn't expected her to be grateful, but I didn't think she'd turn the offer down.

To say the salary had been excessive was an understatement. Some of the wealthiest nobles didn't earn that much coin in their long histories. I'd estimated a minimum of seven articles, but it would likely be much more before the contest ended.

I couldn't tell if the odd emotion I felt was admiration or annoyance. Or some perverse mixture of both. Adriana Saint Lucent despised me enough to turn down what would have been the deal of a lifetime. She wasn't foolish, which meant there had to be a personal reason.

And that was the most dangerous kind.

We held each other's stare for an intense moment. That level of hatred was an issue I needed to investigate. I knew she disliked me, but it seemed a bit excessive, even for a sinner with an affinity for gluttony.

Envy and Val were both right to worry. I needed to keep a better watch on Adriana. That much intense emotion was highly motivating. And the last thing I needed was a reporter who'd stop at nothing to uncover my darkest secrets to use against me.

This went deeper than a petty rivalry. And I intended to find out when it had started.

She finally withdrew her gaze from mine and started to walk away, pausing only to say quietly, "I'll have the landlord return your payment."

"Keep it."

She looked ready to argue but thought better of it as she swiftly fled.

I watched her go, granting her a reprieve for now, already strategizing my next move. She'd temporarily won this round, but I was no honorable hero who'd graciously accept defeat. I'd use any means necessary to claim ultimate victory.

I lived for the hunt, and she'd just made herself the most appealing target to take down.

When I sparred with Adriana Saint Lucent again, she'd be tied to me one way or another. Even if that meant I had to chain her to my bloody side.

A dark thrill rolled through me as I stood from my throne, intent on stalking my prey. It might not be an ice dragon hunt, but the thrill of taking her down was possibly greater.

TEN
Adriana

"Heavy-handed, arrogant, or not, it *was* an incredible opportunity, Adriana. I can't believe you turned it down."

Ryleigh wasn't wrong, but I was too riled up to agree now.

Her disapproving tone also wasn't helping to ease my own worry. Out of everyone in my life, I thought she'd unequivocally side with me. That she didn't made me question everything.

Immediately after I left House Gluttony, I went to the *Wicked Daily* to see if my suspicion had been correct, finding my desk had indeed already been cleaned out.

Axton had seen fit to take my job from me and give me a new one without any thought or care to what *I* might desire. It had taken several hours to clear things up with my editor and secure my position again, mostly because we had to wait for Axton to confirm my story. And the prince didn't deign to respond to my correspondence until he'd *felt* like it.

Arrogant. Royal. Hoarfrost demon. I hoped his bollocks were attacked by fleas.

He was nothing like the stranger at the Seven Sins. The stupid, wonderful masked male I couldn't stop thinking about while my real world came crashing down around me.

Even in Axton's throne room, I'd been distracted, imagining the way my stranger had pressed me against the wall, igniting my passion as much as Axton ignited my annoyance. I'd reached for the secret key I'd kept hidden on me half a dozen times throughout the day.

I stopped pacing, forcing my mind to focus. I couldn't help but wonder if I'd let my feelings for Axton ruin a perfectly good opportunity. Though "perfectly good" was grossly understating the salary.

My stepmother was out with my sister at the modiste we couldn't afford, and Ryleigh arrived at my home directly after work, listening dutifully as I verbally skewered the prince for more than an hour. Now, though, she was losing patience. We didn't feel other sins—like envy—strongly, so I knew she wasn't jealous about the offer. Still, I would feel better if I could just explain it in a way that made sense.

"There's no way I could work for him, especially how he went about it," I finally said.

"He's a prince. What do you expect?"

"Common decency? Basic manners?"

"He's an arrogant prick, but he's generous with his coin, Ad. That salary would have bought just about anyone."

There was that odd note in her tone again. Perhaps I was being overly sensitive. I brushed it away. We were best friends, and she'd always taken my side when it came to the prince.

"If I allow him to walk all over me, I'll have only myself to blame for feeling less than. It's a matter of principle. Sometimes that's more valuable than coin."

Though it was hard to stand by my principles when my family would be the ones suffering. I'd tormented myself for hours, wondering if I'd made a mistake. One *million* coins per article was more than I could fathom. Maybe I was the worst sort of fool. A principled one.

I sighed before dropping onto my worn mattress and hugged my pillow to my chest. What really chafed was the fact that it *was* an incredible opportunity. A dream chance at eventually writing the stories I wanted to and being well compensated for it.

And all I'd had to do was sell my soul to the damned dark prince and write his epic love story first.

I might not have the obscene salary, but a new idea was taking shape. I'd need to meet with one of my informants, set everything up just right if I hoped to pull it off...but I might still find a way to work around my current reporting restrictions. That it would also pay the prince back for making me wait around all day for him to help me secure my job again was a bonus.

I felt for the magic key again, annoyed that I was so distracted by what it symbolized.

For some reason, I'd kept it a secret from my best friend. Ryleigh was already on edge, and I hated to add one more thing to argue over.

Guilt gnawed at me when Ryleigh sat next to me, rubbing small circles on my back.

Maybe she was just upset for me, knowing how much that coin would help, and not upset *with* me. I should tell her about the invitation to the Seven Sins. But my mouth remained stubbornly shut. I didn't want her to think the stranger had any part in my refusing Axton. I knew it wasn't true, but she'd get that starry-eyed look and endlessly push me to indulge in romance.

"It will all work out, Ad."

"I know. At least I won't have to suffer through courtly games and cutthroat royals all vying for more power. While writing stories that make the whole Seven Circles fall even more madly in love with the one male I hate. For good reason."

Ryleigh was silent for a few moments. She knew too well why I despised Axton. Why there would never be anything but animosity between us. She'd been there that night it all went horribly wrong, but she'd been with her own lover and missed the worst of the show.

It wasn't just the heartbreak and embarrassment; it was the realization that I didn't belong in his world and never would. Just as my stepmother always claimed.

Some nobles had been horrendously cruel to me at the ball that night, but I'd done my best to hold my head high, trying desperately to not allow any tears to fall until I was home.

I'd failed in that attempt. But not because of what they'd called me.

Sometimes not saying a word was the most hurtful action.

Love conquers all. Or so the philosophers and poets claimed. Love was the magic that crossed realms, breached worlds, and threaded them together.

True love also had the power to slay the strongest dragons, the greatest evil. It was what the fairy tales told us time and again. But I discovered those were just stories, enchanting because they were pure fantasy, written by dreamers.

In my experience, if you made the grave mistake of falling for a prince when you were a pauper, reality quickly knocked you back to your senses, bruised and battered with your reputation much worse for the wear. My prince hadn't swept in to save me that night, so I saved myself from further heartbreak and never looked back.

"Would you prefer to take his offer?" Ryleigh asked. "He must have really wanted you for the position. I have little doubt he'd hire you if you asked."

I'd hate myself more than I hated him if I allowed him to purchase my future.

"No. Having to watch him fall in love and writing about it would be worse than continually being shat on by a flock of birds, millions of coins or not."

Ryleigh flashed a devious smile.

"Indeed. I can't imagine anything worse than valiantly walking through a storm of bird shit while having millions of coins rain down on you too."

We chatted for a little while longer before eventually parting ways. Ryleigh had an event to attend for work, and I had...I had a key that had been tempting me all day.

I *should* go to the night district to meet with one of my informants.

I still wanted to run down every possible lead on the ice dragon rumors. But damnably, I craved flirtation a tiny bit more. It had to be some strange anomaly. If I met my stranger one more time, my curiosity would be sated, and I could continue with my normal routine.

My sense of intrigue was a result of our being interrupted the evening before.

It certainly had nothing to do with the stranger himself. Or my desire to get drunk on his intoxicating kisses once more. He was a craving. Something sweet to indulge. And once I'd satisfied that taste of debauchery, I'd never think of him again.

Tomorrow I'd resume my dutiful life as the responsible reporter. I'd find a way to get revenge on the prince and earn some coin in the process.

Tonight, I'd drown out thoughts of Axton's competition and attempt to buy me with someone I wanted to spend time with.

Someone who'd stolen my mind well before I'd stolen that first kiss.

Meeting him would be my own secret, one I was unwilling to share with anyone, even Ryleigh.

For now.

I stepped onto the rooftop garden of the Seven Sins; the night flowers were already in full bloom, the petals shimmering from a fine dusting of ice that caught the light of the crescent moon. I inhaled deeply, the fragrant, sweet scent of frostberries standing out among the many floral notes. My attention swept across the empty space. The stranger with the smart mouth wasn't waiting for me in the shadows. I was early, but only by a few minutes.

I tried not to focus on my doubts. I'd learned the more you sank into them, the more they tugged you under.

Though hope was such a fickle thing to grasp and hold on to as well, like snowflakes swirling through the air; you might be lucky enough to catch one, but too quickly it disappeared.

I wasn't sure what I hoped for tonight, but for the first time in ages, I was eager and nervous and excited all rolled into one. Thoughts of work and being responsible and worrying about the future or my slightly strained visit with Ryleigh all melted into the background.

Tonight, I felt like that nineteen-year-old who'd taken a chance and dreamed.

I drifted closer to the roof's edge, where a stone railing lined the perimeter. I hadn't gotten close enough to really look at it last night and loved the detail that went into it.

The posts were carved to look like dragons standing upright on their hindquarters, their wings extended to keep patrons from accidentally falling over the edge.

It was dark and whimsical with a hint of danger. It reminded me of the prince's throne. Dragon art graced many homes and businesses since Axton had a fondness for the creatures and hosted hunts regularly.

Most denizens of the Underworld were influenced by what the seven Princes of Sin enjoyed, so our circle's affinity for the legendary creatures wasn't unusual.

I ran a finger along the dragon's wing, marveling at the sheer majesty of the design.

The stone was cold, frost coated, not unlike the ice dragons they'd been modeled after. Real dragons were forbidden from flying over our circle without the prince's permission, but their territory was close enough that occasionally you might spy one in the far distance, a smudge on the horizon.

I looked beyond the rooftop, at the world glittering before me.

Up here, the night district was breathtaking. Stone buildings looked quaint nestled together with the snow drifting down in lazy flurries. In fact, it appeared as if the sky had been brought to earth, the lights in the taverns and pubs twinkling like golden stars.

My focus moved upward until House Gluttony came into view, the large limestone castle rising high in the distance like a great beast, watching over us all from the snowcapped mountaintop it perched upon. I wanted to hate it but couldn't.

I imagined the prince was hosting another lavish party right now, indulging in all sorts of debauched acts. Axton's reputation for being a rake was well-known and well-earned.

Against my near-constant attempt to forget, I vividly recalled the exact moment he'd stepped into that role, and how quickly he'd forgotten anyone else in his quest to feed his ever-hungry sin. Of course his reputation had been a little scandalous from time to time before then—he was a Prince of Sin, after all. But what he'd become after—someone who'd break hearts without care or remorse—was something else entirely. He was likely already abed with multiple partners, drinking until the sun rose and news of his competition to find a wife spread.

Soon the streets would be filled with visitors from other circles, all coming to witness the damned prince find his perfect match. It had been ten years since our...disaster. I knew he'd eventually take a wife but didn't expect for it to sting quite so much.

I heaved a sigh, my breath puffing out in front of me, the chill in the air slightly tempered by magic that kept the rooftop from freezing.

Several minutes passed, the boisterous laughter slowly rising from the street, reminding me that I was alone once more, watching from the shadows.

The masked stranger hadn't kept his promise.

Disappointment weighed heavy in my chest. I hadn't sorted out what, exactly, I'd wanted to happen tonight. If I wanted another stolen kiss or more.

I'd enjoyed verbally sparring with the stranger, and the idea of finding someone else this evening held little appeal, though I *could* go back downstairs and find a willing partner. But it hadn't just been physical—though that part was spectacular. I really liked his company.

My gaze found its way to the damned castle again before I wrenched it away.

I took one last look at the lively district, then turned toward the stairs, halting at once.

There, standing under the night-blooming frostberry tree, was my stranger.

"What in the name of the old gods are you doing?" I pressed a hand to my chest.

"Admiring the view."

He strode toward me, his gait sure and confident. There was something attractive about his unhurried steps, his focus hot as I imagined it traveling over my mask, then continuing downward, hungrily feasting on my costume, then moving on to my curves.

His perusal was downright indecent in the most breathtaking way. He admired every inch of me before dragging his attention upward again.

He looked ready to devour me.

I couldn't stop myself from flushing at his appreciation, though I was pleased by his response. It was nice to know someone desired you madly every once in a while.

I'd visited Carlo and had worn the same ensemble as last night. The glamour only worked on the physical form—clothing and jewelry were untouched. I'd wanted my stranger to recognize me in case the glamour gave me a different face.

"I didn't think you'd come."

"A proper gentleman ensures a lady *always* comes first."

My lips curved. Clever, ridiculous male. "That line is old and tired."

"Thankfully I am not."

He stepped up to the railing beside me, leaning over it casually. With his mask, I couldn't tell where his gaze had landed but assumed it was on the patrons dancing in the street below, belting a popular tune that was horridly off-key, but endearing.

"You seemed to be deep in thought," he said. "What were you looking at so intently?"

I settled back on the railing, glancing out across the city. "House Gluttony."

"Ah." He sounded less than impressed. "Dreaming of taming the prince's wicked heart by visiting his bed like every other maiden in the realm?"

"Hardly."

His attention shifted to me, a smile touching the corners of his lips. "Interesting."

"What is?"

"Most fantasize about making the debauched prince fall in love."

"Well, I believe he's already in love."

"Oh?" His grin grew wider. "Who's the lucky winner of that prize?"

"You haven't figured that out?" I tsked. "He's very clearly in love with himself." I added a touch of humor to my tone to avoid ruining our banter. Gabriel Axton wasn't going to tarnish my night. "What about you? What do people say of your reputation?"

"That I am a ruthless lover, far more exciting in bed than any prince. Even one ruled by sin."

"Oh, gods." I smiled. "You're either visiting from House Envy or House Pride, aren't you?"

"I can't very well tell you my secrets," he teased back. "Unless of course you share some of yours with me first. Like, perhaps, your name?"

My heart raced as I looked him over. He was fishing even though he knew it was against the rules. If he was curious about my real identity, that would be disastrous.

"This club is supposed to offer anonymity," I reminded him. "You're far too curious for either of our own good. I'd hate to be banished from here."

His grin remained in place.

"Fair enough. You'd rather not discuss last night, then, either, I presume?"

"I already told you. I had to leave or else I would have been tempted to stay."

He was quiet for a few moments, his attention shifting back to the patrons who'd continued to spill into the alleyway below. Snow had been shoveled to the far side, piled high, granting them access to the exit doors of their lounges and pubs.

"You wanted a distraction from your heartbreak," he said. "A night of fun."

I didn't bother correcting his assumption; I didn't have any heartbreak. Well, recently, at least. In order to keep my identity hidden, I couldn't tell him I was a writer in need of research. It wouldn't take long for him to piece together who I was based on my questions; Miss Match was the only romance advice columnist in the realm.

"Most come here in search of fun. I'm no different."

"Most come here, my lady, to give in to other sins."

Fair point.

"Which sin did you come here to indulge?"

He strummed his fingers over the railing, seeming to consider his answer carefully.

My curiosity grew with each second that passed.

"I'd rather show you, Lady F. *If* you're up for an adventure."

His tone held a dare. And as much as I hated to admit it, even to myself, my sin of choice was gluttony, if only for the fact that chasing thrills was one of my greatest secret desires.

I'd come to this club knowing there was a very real possibility of living out my fantasy with him tonight. This adventure, this night of passion, would sustain me for the wretched weeks to come as I watched the "unattainable bachelor" finally become attached.

But only if I allowed myself to indulge in what my mysterious stranger was offering.

My pulse raced as the evening finally took a deliciously tempting turn.

I didn't know his name. I couldn't begin to guess his eye color. But I knew with certainty he would make tonight an evening I wouldn't soon forget, if his last kiss was anything to go by.

"What sort of adventure were you thinking of tonight?" I asked.

He turned to face me, his expression impossible to read with the damned mask.

"How brave do you consider yourself?"

I nibbled on my lower lip, the motion snaring his attention as if I'd laid a clever trap. "I consider myself fairly bold. Which I suppose is brave in its own way. Why?"

Anticipation thickened the space between us as he drank his fill of me again.

"Bend over the railing."

My breath caught. This was the Seven Circles, a realm that thrived on sin, so I was no simpering miss. Therefore, I hadn't expected him to court me, for saints' sakes, but his low, guttural demand shocked me for a moment.

Then a wonderful heat spread through me. The idea of giving up control, of granting someone else leave to make decisions, was...enticing.

No, not someone, *him*. This stranger who tempted and distracted me far too much.

I clearly needed to seek help. I made a mental note to stop by the apothecary this week; surely the witch running it had a brew to mend my broken sanity.

"Pardon?" I asked, stalling.

His smile was sin incarnate.

"Afraid, Lady F?"

"Hardly."

"Good." He took my hand, drawing it up to brush a kiss across my knuckles. "Tonight, I'd like to be in total control. Do you take issue with that?"

Under any other circumstance, I'd take great issue with it. But his thumb slowly stroked along my pulse point, his touch as far from sin as it could be, yet I already desired more.

I shook my head. "No, I don't take issue with that."

He leaned close, brushing his lips across mine. A bolt of heat traveled through me at the brief contact, my eyes fluttering shut. It was so light, teasing. I immediately wanted more.

He moved that tempting mouth to my ear, his voice a low whisper filled with sinful intent.

"Bend over the railing."

I took a steadying breath, then did as he requested, the stone cold enough to bite into my palms as I braced myself. I gripped harder, forgetting the sting as my attention fell to the ground.

I hadn't realized how high up we were. The idea of him catching me before I could fall sent another thrill racing through me. It was an enormous amount of trust to put in a stranger.

Which was maybe the second indication I needed to seek a royal healer.

But the fear...the fear had adrenaline racing through me, and each of my senses heightened in a way I'd never experienced before.

My body practically buzzed and throbbed, and he hadn't even fully kissed me or touched more than my wrist yet.

"Ready?" he asked, his voice low and deep as he swept a lock of hair back and tucked it behind my ear.

He was such a dichotomy—sweet and considerate, yet wickedly devious. I couldn't predict his next move and loved the challenge.

I swallowed thickly, then nodded, excitement rushing through me. All of a sudden, panic took over.

"Wait."

He didn't move at all. "If you're not comfortable, say the word."

I glanced back over the edge. It was thrilling, and I did trust him...as much as I could trust someone I didn't know at all. Logic overrode my need for adventure.

"Why don't we save this particular thrill for another time?" he asked. His nose grazed the side of my jaw, sending another rush through me as he leaned in. "I have other ideas if you're game?"

"Such as?"

He offered me his hand, then walked us to the garden. "Face the frost-berry tree and brace yourself against the trunk."

The same rush raced through me as I flattened my hands against the rough bark. "Like this?"

"Perfect. Comfortable?"

"Yes."

"Good."

He kicked my feet apart, his hands circling my wrists, securing them to the tree.

"I can hear your heart racing," he murmured against my ear.

"How peculiar. It's almost like I'm in a club of sin while a masked stranger orders me around a rooftop garden."

"Such a wicked tongue."

"Most aren't excited by that realization."

He stepped closer, his front pressed firmly against my back.

I inhaled deeply; he smelled of cedar and something spicy—perhaps cardamom.

I wanted to arch into his touch but couldn't. He'd pinned me expertly in place. But not before I felt his arousal. Gods. I'd felt it last night, but it was impressive, to say the least.

"You must be courted by fools, then."

His hands left my wrists, only to slowly slide up my silhouette, his touch reverent as he skimmed my arms and neck, taking his time to caress each layer of silk, the slight rustle of fabric an aphrodisiac of its own. He continued his upward exploration until he reached my unbound hair and paused, his fingers sliding through my loose waves.

The wig hid my natural color in case the glamour failed, but I worried he'd stopped because he sensed it wasn't real. A moment later, he gathered my hair to one side, carefully winding it around his fist, then tugged my head back until my attention was wholly on him.

I said a silent thank-you to Carlo for ensuring the wig remained in place during any rough play. Which, as my stranger held me firmly in place against the tree, my hair in his fist, his hungry gaze devouring me, I realized was exactly his desire.

He had me right where he wanted me, railing, tree, or wall, it didn't matter. He liked control, or rather, domination.

He leaned down, his lips so close to mine I felt them move with his next words.

"One day I'll fuck that pretty mouth."

His lips brushed against mine again, whisper soft and sweet. Such a dramatic juxtaposition to his filthy words. My body responded to that low growl, his wicked promise. A slick heat gathered between my thighs. I wanted him to do all sorts of things to my mouth.

"Come all over that perfect tongue."

His free hand rested against my throat, his touch light but possessive.

My body was contorted in a way that gave him complete control, but instead of panicking, I parted my lips on a sigh, and he finally kissed me the way I desired, his tongue sweeping in to claim mine.

He happily took command, setting the pace until I was lost to the drugging sensation of his lips moving against mine. The kiss was neither rough nor sweet, but an exploratory adventure he seemed to savor. He was learning what I liked, driving me to the edge of insanity.

My palms dragged over the rough bark of the tree the way I wanted to touch him.

My writer's mind started envisioning all the wonderful ways his tongue would feel, swirling over different body parts with that same languorous motion. He'd peel my bodice down, exposing each inch of skin to sample like his personal feast, driving me wild but making me wait for the payoff until I thought I'd die. He'd slowly taste his way across the globe of my aching breast, drawing closer to the taut bud that craved his attention.

I imagined he'd suck and tease, pulling it into his mouth in a rhythmic way before laving it with his tongue again, and I clenched at the thought. I hadn't realized I'd been rubbing against him until he tugged my hair a little harder, the hint of pain making me throb with need and bringing me back from that blissful stupor.

This male certainly knew how to kiss someone senseless.

Heat pooled between my thighs, his tongue stroking mine mixed with the imagery he'd created causing the most erotic fantasy.

My heart pounded in time to the increasing throbbing of my body, my mind still very much aware that I was pressed against a tree while he had me by the throat.

I expected him to move those wicked hands lower, to curl his fingers around the hem of my skirt, to tug the material upward, to relieve the ache building inside me.

Instead of devouring me, he took his time, content to drive me wild with his kiss alone.

In what could have been an hour or a moment, he finally drew back, releasing his grip on my hair, his other hand lightly stroking my throat as if it were precious.

We hadn't done more than kiss, but it felt like the most thrilling, sensual experience of my life. I wanted *more*. My sin of choice awakened fully, my craving almost all-encompassing.

He pressed his lips to mine, gently, then dropped his hand.

"I'd like the pleasure of your company again, Lady F. Same time tomorrow evening?"

I must have lost much more of my senses in that kiss than I thought. With his body gone from mine, I could easily spin around to face him. "What?"

"Tomorrow. You. Me. This rooftop garden. A bottle of demonberry wine."

If I didn't have this cursed mask on, he'd be able to read the incredulity I knew was flashing in my gaze. "Sir, this is a pleasure club. I'm here for one night of distraction."

His mouth curved in amusement.

"By my count, this is already night two."

I waved my hand, agitated. "Semantics. You know what I mean."

"Why settle for just one or two nights when we can prolong it? Draw out the pleasure. I'm not some inexperienced lad who can't restrain myself around an alluring lover."

"How noble and so very self-centered of you."

The whole male species ought to be magicked away to an island to live out their days of idiocy in peace.

He drew back. "Wanting to see you again is selfish?"

"Deciding you'd like more than one night without consulting me is brutish. And not in the same sexy way as pinning me in place and ordering me around in the bedroom."

"I apologize." A smile twitched at the corners of his mouth. "Allow me to make my blunder up to you tomorrow evening, Lady F."

He held up a silver key, the runes glowing softly.

"We'll draft up the rules of play together," he said, still offering the key. "Deal?"

Accepting another key to this club was a dangerous proposition.

The more time we spent together, the greater the risk of one of us discovering the other's true identity, glamoured or not.

A cynical part of me wondered if that was his plan before I dismissed it.

I was being paranoid.

Normally it wouldn't matter if anyone found out who I was, but I didn't want my private life to become fodder for the scandal sheets.

Ironic, considering how I'd earned my living. But there was much at stake, and I needed to succeed.

I silently considered my options.

If I didn't agree to meet tomorrow, our paths might never cross again.

And somehow not spending the night with my stranger would feel like a tragedy, especially with how he made my body feel with his kiss alone.

I wanted to be braver tomorrow and brace myself against the railing. I wanted him to do wicked, wonderful things while my heart raced and my body soared.

The trouble with indulging one time was it often led to indulging a second time, then a third, still craving more. The next thing you knew, you were addicted.

This stranger awakened a hunger in me, and I knew I couldn't rest until it was sated.

I took the magic key from him, securing it in my bodice.

One more night.

Then we'd part ways for good.

ELEVEN
Prince Gluttony

THE FASCINATING, QUICK-WITTED female exited the Seven Sins, and I forced myself to remain on the roof and not follow her home. Uncovering a guest's identity was against club rules, but I found a thrill in breaking even the strictest decrees. Especially since I'd declared them to begin with.

The glamour made it impossible to tell from her voice or physical appearance, but I *needed* to know who she was—the only one in years who'd reminded me my sin hungered for more than adventure. A small suspicion crept in, but I kept dismissing it.

Still, the desire to track down the truth, to unravel her secrets, was almost as alluring as the royal hunts I organized each month. If not more so.

She captivated me in a way that spelled disaster.

In a time when *all* I should be focused on was my court's safety, winning my war with Adriana, and the bridal competition about to be launched, Lady Frost crept beneath my skin, infected my thoughts. I blamed it on the fact that I hadn't taken someone to my bed in years.

There had only been one other time I'd been initially consumed by a potential lover. Her crystal blue eyes had been bottomless pools I'd wanted to dive into. They'd turned to ice when she'd noticed my attention, and I realized then and there I'd never survive the plunge.

That realization hadn't stopped me from dreaming, though.

I ran a hand through my hair, cursing. If my hunch proved true... *complicated* was certainly one word for it, though it might end up solving one of my problems. Even if it created a slew of other issues. I *had* to be wrong. Adriana Saint Lucent couldn't be the mysterious Lady F.

Fate wouldn't be so cruel as to offer me a taste of all I'd craved only to reveal it was poisoned and I'd been a fool once again.

If I unfurled my wings and took to the air right now, I could solve one mystery tonight, then fly the sixty or so miles over to Merciless Reach for an update on the dragons.

Indecision warred within. I suspected I was looking for threads to tug that didn't exist.

For some horrendous reason, I *liked* imagining it was my enemy moaning softly against my mouth, finally submitting to my domination the way I craved. Which was probably why the club's glamour had chosen to give her the hair color of my rival tonight.

I'd been fixated on Adriana all day, wanting to devise a plan to keep her close. It made sense that the club's magic would pick up on that, giving her pale blue locks to torment me.

One thing patrons were unaware of about the magic that concealed them was that it often played into their hidden desires. They couldn't see what they looked like to anyone else, but to their partner for the night, they took on cravings too scandalous for them to verbalize.

That my lover had pale blue hair was an indication of madness. Or my sin at play.

Not many in my circle knew my true nature. It was one more secret I kept hidden, choosing who to share it with after careful consideration.

My favorite pleasure was inflicting a delicious sort of punishment during consensual bedroom games. I had an unquenchable desire to dominate, to have my lover submit to every depraved whim while begging for more. Chains, riding crops, spanking a lover when the mood struck—some might confuse it for an affinity to House Wrath, which would be scandalous for a prince who ruled a different sin. But my desire wasn't anger based, it was indulgence in its truest, darkest form.

Imagining my enemy—the one female in the entire realm who refused to submit to my charms—coming apart in my arms, bending to my will... it turned me on more than it should.

Indulging in fantasy fed my power, and I certainly needed to be at full strength if another attack occurred. Which explained my abhorrent fixation.

I stared as the mysterious Lady F strode with confidence down the cobbled street, tugging her fur-trimmed cloak up to protect herself from the gently falling snow.

I dragged my attention away from her retreating form just as she turned onto the nearest cross street, leashing my inner urge to follow. Her identity shouldn't matter right now.

My focus needed to remain on the ice dragons and my plot to bind Adriana from discovering the truth.

With an impressive amount of restraint for a prince ruled by excess, I turned from the railing and headed for the door, intending to grab a drink before I left.

Val burst onto the roof, a wild look in her eyes. She wasn't in glamour, and the terror radiating off her would bring a lesser demon to their knees.

A sinking, cold feeling swept through me. Either Adriana had broken the story about the first incident, or the dragons had attacked again. Neither scenario was good.

I was in motion, standing before my second in two long strides.

"Here." She thrust a letter at me. "This just arrived from Merciless Reach."

"By courier or—"

"They used magic."

That meant whatever happened had occurred only minutes before, not hours like if they'd sent a missive by horse.

I ripped open the envelope.

Battle in progress, Jackson taken. Bring help.

"Send word to Houses Wrath, Lust, and Envy at once." My wings erupted from my back, beating the air as I lifted from the rooftop. "Tell them to *transvenio* to Merciless Reach *now*."

I didn't wait for Val's response.

I shot through the stormy sky, ignoring the ice pelting my face, hoping against all odds I wouldn't soon be witnessing another ice dragon massacre in the making.

Chaos greeted me the moment I touched down outside the giant raised portcullis of Merciless Reach. I strode through the courtyard gate and past the fortress's double doors, which were flung open, my attention scanning the hellscape before me.

It looked like what it was—the aftermath of war.

Bodies were strewn along the stone floor in various states of injury, lining both sides of the huge entrance hall. I took them in quickly; all seemed to be breathing. No deaths that I could see so far, though death would have been a mercy for some.

Hunters writhed on the floor, some burned by the icy dragon fire, others dripping blood. The air was scented with piss and other feculent odors from the surprise battle.

Agonized cries drowned out almost every other sound. Dragon fire acted like poison, slowly sinking in, continuing to burn an ice-cold swath until its victim had frozen from the inside out. Cures were possible only if they were administered early on.

Helga, the on-site healer, was in the thick of things, barking orders to her assistant while tying off wounds and smearing herbal pastes.

"Get the dragon bane! Heat the wound!"

She spared me one look before diving back into her work, healing those she could.

"Dear gods, make it stop!"

A young huntress screamed as Helga pressed a cold compress to her face, trying in vain to save the woman's eye from the dragon fire scorching its way under her skin.

Little black veins of poison fire traveled higher, slowing marginally as Helga made an incision and pressed the dragon bane to the wound.

Another hunter clutched his side, gasping. It looked like he'd been clawed, his leathers hanging in tatters off his thick frame.

I stripped off my suit jacket and tore it into strips. "Hold on."

Taking extreme caution to not injure him further, I rolled him gently, then tied a length of my jacket around his middle, staunching the blood flow the best I could.

I moved down the line, doing whatever was in my power to assist.

Demons reached for me, clawing at my hands, my trousers, begging for relief.

Felix burst into the chamber, dropping another injured hunter on a cot someone had just brought in. He saw me and hurried over, issuing a quick report.

"A sudden attack on our camp began nearly an hour ago. Five dragons ambushed our training party, two miles west. One moment we were sparring in hand-to-hand combat, the next we were in full battle. I would've sent word sooner, but it took time to get the injured to safety."

His gaze swept through the makeshift triage.

"No deaths in the field. Several injured as you see."

Felix was in his fifties—still very young by demon aging standards—but the fine lines around his mouth had deepened drastically, as if he'd aged tenfold tonight.

"Jackson?" I prompted.

He shook himself from his thoughts.

"Was taken thirty minutes ago. Due north of the wall. Looked like the dragons were heading toward the barrens."

The barrens were located just beyond the mountain range—a frozen tundra that mortals would liken to the arctic region in their world. It was flat, covered in ice, and almost uninhabitable except for a few creatures like dragons, hell wolves, frost bears, and tundra deer.

"He was still alive?"

Felix wiped his brow, ignoring the blood dripping from his own head wound. "He was still fighting."

"Lock the building down. Keep everyone inside the fortress until further notice. Understood?"

The outpost was well fortified, made of stone slabs too thick for the dragons' fire to penetrate and warded by magic as an added precaution. There was only one area of weakness—the windows, but they were strategically placed to avoid any true harm.

The command I issued also served a less noble factor I needed to consider. Depending on what we discovered, I might need to wipe the hunters' memories. A decision I loathed to make, but I couldn't risk another breach with so much at stake.

"For the good of the realm" was a motto I was growing to despise.

Felix seemed to read what I hadn't said, his expression turning stark but understanding.

Duty. Loyalty. Honor. It was the vow each hunter took when being admitted to the guild. And that very notion had the hunter hitting his chest twice to prove he stood with me.

"Yes, Your Highness."

Magic burned the atmosphere, prickling my skin. *Thank fuck.* I swung my cloak over my shoulders and headed for the door. Seconds later, shouts rang out in the courtyard.

My brothers appeared in smoke and fire, one after the other from their circles, using the transportation magic similar to when Fae shifted from one location to the next.

Each wore a similar expression: vengeance.

They stalked forward to meet me, their dark cloaks billowing behind them like shadows of death. I strode out to meet them, leading them to the area where Felix said the dragons had fled.

"This way."

We didn't move like mortals through the pass. We used the strength and speed that made us *Other*. The qualities that made us feared realms wide.

Within seconds the four of us had traversed several miles, finally picking up a trail at the base of the mountain. The disturbance in the snow indicated the dragons had separated into two groups. Or best-case scenario, Jackson had gotten away and raced off on his own.

"Lust, Envy. Go around the western side. Wrath and I will continue directly up."

Our group veered into different directions and carried on the search.

I flipped the hood of my cloak up, the thick wool doing little to stop the wind from lashing out as snow fell hard and fast around us, obscuring a clear view of the star-pricked sky.

It was the perfect night for an aerial attack. Especially for creatures whose frosty scales blended in with the wintry elements.

I closed my eyes and inhaled, the crisp scent of pine mingled with faint traces of musk. And something worse.

"Hear that?" Wrath asked, voice pitched low.

I nodded.

My grip on my House dagger tightened, the sound of our enemy growing closer. Leather snapping down from a punishing altitude along with a high-pitched shriek broke the otherwise peaceful silence of the night. At least one ice dragon was circling high above. Maybe two.

They weren't far ahead of us, and the hope that we weren't too late drove me forward through the punishing terrain, my brother right on my heels as we tracked the creature.

I couldn't stop wondering which dragon had been infected now. Silvanus? Symon?

There was no good answer. Whoever it was, the alpha would put them down if we didn't get to them first. The thought made my stomach clench, even knowing it had to be done for the good of the realm. Questions I had no answers to swirled through my head as we marched onward. How had this dragon been infected? Had he or she been in contact with Hectaurus?

I shut all thoughts and worries down, save for the hunt.

The treacherous woods beyond Merciless Reach were usually a quiet, eerie place at night. But this wasn't a typical evening.

Now my brothers and I forged ahead with our recovery mission.

There were no other signs of Jackson struggling.

Which didn't bode well for him or for our realm. I cursed myself for not taking Felix aside earlier in the day, ordering him to train the new initiate hunter at House Gluttony before he set off for Merciless Reach again.

He was young, so much yet to learn, so much growing left to do.

It had been a long time since I'd prayed, but I asked the old gods for mercy.

Wrath studied the woods to our right, his muscular body primed to attack. Out of all our brothers, he was the one who thrived on discord the most; it fed his sin and thus his power. Whatever injury he'd had left from his attack was gone now thanks to the battle-inducing magic.

A small gift amid the nightmare.

We trudged our way up the steep incline, the snow mixing with sleet at this elevation adding a complication we didn't need.

Snow crunched underfoot, alerting anyone or anything nearby to seek shelter. Aside from the occasional beat of dragon wings, it had been a while since I'd last heard any other creature fleeing our path.

Between us Princes of Sin and the restless dragons, nothing good would come from lingering here tonight. Even the fiercest solitary Fae that called this place home knew to run.

I scanned the forest, the shadows beckoning like bony fingers for us to move deeper within the woods. A few lone moonbeams broke through branches laden with snow and ice, illuminating the evergreen canopy above us with a silvery pallor.

Everything about this night felt haunted. I wondered if it was the spirit of the hunter I'd failed, coming back to curse us all. I banished the thought. I had to believe Jackson was alive.

On the western edge of the mountain, I sensed Lust and Envy already moving in, their violence thrumming like a battle drum within my own chest, a call to arms.

My attention landed on a dark splatter several feet away on the ground, my stomach tightening at what I suspected I'd find. Or rather who.

I motioned to Wrath, then picked my way carefully to the spot, already dreading being correct. I scented the blood before I was certain we were standing near remains.

I knelt at the base of the gnarled tree, dusting the thin layer of snow from the leathers. My House Crest was splattered in gore, and five large claw marks scarred the leather chest plate.

It had been all but shredded.

I moved aside, allowing my brother a clear view. A steaming pile of entrails and the tattered battle leathers were all that was left. It was a miracle we'd found that much.

I swore. Given the warmth still clinging to the leather, we'd likely missed them by moments. Seconds, perhaps.

Which meant the dragon had purposely left this for us, planning its attack for the biggest emotional impact, knowing we'd figure out it had waited to finish its prey until we were close.

Wrath's sin slipped its leash, the ground rumbling beneath our feet, shaking the snow from the heavy branches. He'd come to the same conclusion, and if he didn't control his legendary anger, he'd start an avalanche.

From the opposite end of the forest, Lust and Envy cursed under their breath. With my senses heightened to my full power, I heard them clearly as they shifted course and quickly made their way up and over the mountain to us.

My own rage rattled its cage, but I shoved that emotion deep down, forcing a controlled calm to descend.

"Hunting guild."

There were only about eighty official guild members, made up of the best males and females in my circle. Each year five or six hopeful initiates tested, but only the best were granted entry. Some years we didn't add any new members to the guild. With more training, it was very possible Jackson would have eventually sworn his oath.

I pulled what remained of the fighting leathers from the snow, flipping them over to read the name etched into the inside of the chest plate, confirming what I knew.

"It's Jackson."

Wrath's expression didn't shift, but the burning rage in his gaze flared.

This time, the ice dragon didn't simply attack; it had killed. And it had done so in the most provocative way, its mission to start a war between us clear. This wasn't like the first attack—there was no bloodlust or chaos. The dragons struck the guild and picked off the weakest link, driving him north and toying with him until we'd closed in.

That proved they were aware of what they were doing.

The alpha's claims that it had been solely due to madness seemed like one more clever ploy. I hadn't detected a lie, but sensing that sort of deception with a dragon wasn't the same as knowing when another demon, Fae, vampire, witch, or mortal lied.

Even we Princes of Hell had our limits.

I expelled a long breath, concentrating on breathing in slowly, then exhaling. The more I controlled my reactions, the clearer my mind remained. And I needed to keep my emotions under control—otherwise I'd focus on just how crushing this was. Beyond the horrible loss of my initiate hunter, the potential loss of power and weakening of my court could be astronomical.

After this murder, there was no chance for a hunt next month. Which meant I had to make it through several more weeks without my greatest supply of power.

My attention snagged on the giant prints left in the snow. "Three dragons."

Wrath's hands curled into fists, his focus shooting skyward as a dark shadow passed over us, a taunt and perhaps a dare.

We'd been watching the sky when a sudden shout broke the stillness.

"On your left!" Envy yelled.

I spun as the first dragon seemed to be born out of nothingness, stepping from the shadows of the forest, towering at least ten feet above me, its crimson eyes glazed over with a vacancy I'd never seen in an ice dragon before.

I froze.

Ice dragons' irises were iridescent.

There were no variations in color. Ever.

"See that?" I asked.

"Any idea what it means?" Wrath asked.

I shook my head. "Maybe a spell or hex."

Our conversation halted as the dragon took another threatening step in our direction.

It took a moment to spot the scar carving a swath along his chest. Silvanus.

My breath lodged in my throat. Whatever looked out from Sil's eyes wasn't familiar. Hatred and madness burned bright. His gaze narrowed on me, nostrils flaring.

No hint of recognition flickered in his eyes. Only a ravenous fury, aimed directly at me.

I mourned my old friend, the little hatchling who growled even when nudging his head against me, quietly asking to be petted.

Shiny ruby-red blood coated his snout, fresh from his kill. That deadly mouth opened wide, his shriek piercing the night. Silvanus was calling in his packmates. Whether they were infected or not wouldn't matter—they'd all descend into the madness of the kill.

Adrenaline rushed through my veins.

"Sil?" I yanked my dagger from its sheath, slowly pivoting as the dragon circled us. "You in there somewhere?"

Silvanus's eyes remained vacant as he shook his head, his scales sending prisms of light bouncing through the forest.

Wrath and I exchanged looks.

The dragon's unfocused gaze was also at odds with the cunning he'd shown moments before with his kill. We didn't have time to consider the implications of that or his eye color.

Three more dark shapes appeared from the night sky, growling and snarling and spewing white flames of ice, their eyes shining with an unholy light as they descended upon us.

Whatever hope I had left of this ending with the smallest amount of bloodshed vanished.

The dragons hovered for a few moments, their beating wings sending out arctic gusts that would have killed a mortal.

Thankfully it did nothing but fuel me to attack.

My House was at stake.

My demon murdered.

No matter that I'd raised these dragons, that I'd considered them my friends; I would do what needed to be done for the good of the fucking realm.

Even if that meant I needed to destroy them all.

I bared my teeth, a feral snarl tearing from my chest as I sprung at the first beast. Because that's exactly what Silvanus was now—a feral creature who wished to eradicate me and my brothers from this realm.

My House dagger glowed like a fallen star as it arced through the night, aimed straight for the dragon's heart. He lunged at the last moment, deflecting my blade.

I spun and slashed, my death dance well choreographed and brutal.

Out of the corner of my eye I saw my brothers locked in their own battle dance, their unforgiving expressions illuminated by flashes of light that glinted off their weapons.

They'd put together what I had; they knew our only way out was to kill. And we were born to obliterate everything that dared to stand in our way.

Blood and fire, tooth and claw, demon blades and untapped rage left one dragon severely injured, three more escaping into the sky before we could set off after them.

Wrath's wings erupted in a fit of rage. But I needed him here.

"Halt!" I looked at my brothers, at their blood-drenched clothes, their glowing blades. Then I jerked my head at the dragon lying at my feet, Silvanus. "Help me get him up."

Wrath magicked his wings away, then stooped down to the dragon, a look of worry marring his stoic face. "Will he make it?"

Silvanus's chest heaved from exertion and injury. He tried to get up, then collapsed.

He wasn't dead, but he would be if I didn't get him to a healer soon.

"We'll take him to House Gluttony, get him healthy, run some tests. I'll keep him locked away until we figure out what's going on."

Envy wiped his dagger across his trousers, then sheathed it. "How, exactly, are we going to sneak an injured thirteen-thousand-pound ice dragon through your circle?"

"Clean him up, put a party hat on him, and tell anyone who asks that he downed a field of demonberries?" Lust offered.

Wrath shot him an annoyed look.

I bent down to where Sil struggled for breath, my own chest aching at the sight, and ran a gentle hand along his flank. "I'll send word to the witch."

Lust shook his head. "I don't like it."

I understood why. The way the dragons behaved tonight made it hard not to wonder if witches were involved. Their behavior was so erratic, so unnatural, it reeked of witchcraft.

"Have any other ideas?" I asked.

Envy glanced at Wrath, his brows arched high.

The general of war sighed. "I'll ask my wife."

I nodded in assent. Emilia's mortal family had been witches, so she knew spells and could work them better than any other magic wielder I'd met. Without delay, Wrath magicked himself back to his circle. Envy crouched beside me while Lust stood with his arms crossed a few paces away, his attention locked on the injured dragon.

"If it's caused by magic," Envy said quietly, "we need to let Pride know."

I raked a hand through my hair, cursing. "We'll call a summit."

Smoke swirled through the snow, crackling like fire. Once it cleared, Wrath and Emilia stood hand in hand, dressed in their signature black and gold.

Emilia's hair was woven with flowers, the dark curls falling loosely down her back. Under her cloak she wore a long, billowing gown that wasn't at all designed for the frigid temperatures of the north. She must have been in the middle of tending to some House affair and had left at once. I wanted to gather my sister-in-law in my arms, twirl her around, and share a laugh. But I couldn't. Not with Sil barely clinging to life and an initiate hunter who'd been slain.

Emilia's expression fell when she saw the blood-soaked leathers.

Then she noticed the dragon.

She dropped her husband's hand and rushed to its side, going to her knees before the giant beast, uncaring of the snow that seeped through her skirts.

My brother fisted his hand, probably to keep from dragging her back, even though Emilia was by no means mortal, and she'd likely go to war with him if he tried.

Her rose-gold eyes met mine. "You raised him, Gabe?"

I swallowed thickly, nodding.

"I'm so sorry."

She turned her attention back to the dragon. Her eyes flared with her power as she scanned him from head to tail.

"I don't see any spells but need more time to really work." Emilia glanced back up at me. "I can transport him to the dungeon, but you need to go there first. Use this." She handed me what looked like a small gold coin. "It will act as a way for me to locate you once I begin the spell."

I closed my fist around the coin, shot Silvanus one last look, then magicked myself to the dungeon to wait.

TWELVE
Adriana

"Nyx?" I waved the unmarked envelope at my informant, dragging her attention back to me. "You'll get this to the printer today, right? It's imperative it goes public this afternoon."

We were tucked into the shadows of a cryptlike pub aptly named Eternal Rest at the far edge of town. It was dark and dank and housed more spiders than paying patrons.

Cobwebs collected in thick, sticky clusters in the corners, an ode to every horror story ever penned. The tables were made from scavenged parts of broken caskets. One could only hope that they hadn't been occupied before being hacked into furniture, though given the rumors about the owner's taste for blood and fall from vampire grace, anything was possible.

It seemed most came here to die some sort of death. Be it reputation or the utter demise of one's sanity. Or perhaps murder by drink.

I wasn't positive, but judging by the bitter taste of the tea I was politely sipping, I couldn't rule out the possibility of being poisoned. I half expected my throat to swell shut, my eyes to bulge, and to keel straight over at any moment. I hadn't thought to write out my last will and testament before the meeting and only mildly regretted it now.

Maybe I should have opted for hard liquor like my fidgeting companion.

Nyx guzzled shot after shot of ice-flower whiskey like it wasn't just after six in the morning and that sort of thing wasn't frowned upon even in a realm built on sin.

Though, given the clientele at Eternal Rest with their preference for blood shots, most hadn't seen their beds in the last decade, so perhaps time was indeed relative.

She ran a hand over her shaved head, a shiver rolling through her as her hood fell back.

I'd never seen her so...shifty. Which was saying a lot, as that was her standard mode of operation.

Nyx finally settled her attention on me, her milky irises almost glowing in the dark.

"You wanted to know about the club, too, right? The Seven Sins?" she asked.

I nodded, forcing myself to not reach for the magic key I kept on me.

"Rumors. Nothing concrete."

I raised my brows. "Who are people saying owns it?"

"Maybe all the princes. Except for ours."

That made no sense whatsoever; it was the first time I'd heard that rumor.

"Why would Gluttony permit other Princes of Sin to fuel their power here?"

She lifted a shoulder and dropped it. "I'll get your paper printed, miss. And see what else turns up about the club, though whoever owns it has been sought in the shadow network for years. Whoever they are, they covered their tracks well."

Nyx jolted in her seat when the door slammed open. I'd been working with her for years and she'd never been this on edge.

I narrowed my eyes. "Is everything all right?"

"Might be the time to visit family on the Shifting Isles."

Her gravelly voice made the fine hair along my arms rise.

Or maybe it was her cryptic warning. Nyx hadn't looked inside the envelope; she didn't know what mischief I was up to. Therefore, her warning meant something else scared her. And anything that scared Nyx would likely make anyone else wet their pants.

"I don't have family there."

"Neither do I. But I'd find a reason to get out of here. That's for damn sure."

Across the pub, two demons who'd been engaged in a vicious card game stood abruptly, their chairs clattering to the floor. They began brawling, bashing mugs and glasses and any other items they could at each other.

Shards of glass flew through the air, stopping short of our table by mere inches.

I kept my attention split between the fight and my informant. "Are you planning on running?"

Nyx tossed back the rest of her whiskey, tapped her empty glass against the table, then eyed me. I swore under my breath and called for another round.

Once she had her next shot, she settled back, her gaze darting everywhere.

"Gluttons for thrills and adventure or not, I think a good many will be on the run soon. After what happened to that hunter last night."

A chill worked its way down my spine that had nothing to do with the blast of frigid air that swept through the pub as the two brawlers were tossed out.

"Stop talking in riddles or there won't be any more whiskey. What happened?"

"That new initiate hunter? Jackson Rose. He's dead. Word in the shadows claims he was done in by a dragon. They say he was eaten whole."

"That can't be true. His family isn't high-ranking, but he's noble. There's been no official statement from the castle or mention of death."

"Another oddity, but that doesn't make what I said less true."

A high-pitched ringing began in my ears. There had to be some mistake. I'd seen Jackson a little over a week before. He was young and brash, and quite possibly the worst dancer in the realm, but certainly not *deceased*.

"How do you know he's dead and demons aren't just gossiping?"

"Passed by his family's house this morning. They hung his leathers outside the door." Nyx nestled into her cloak, seeming ready to bolt at the next opportunity. "If you don't believe me, go see for yourself."

I fought the urge to tug my own cloak around me. Jackson *couldn't* be dead. He'd been a drunken fool, certainly, but to have him wiped from the realm so young...

I glanced at the half-empty room. The bartender swept the broken glass into a pile, the sound of the broom scratching across the broad floorboards. It reminded me of sharp nails.

The Eternal Rest was rather...quiet. Even with the brawl. Normally, whenever I met Nyx here, one could count on at least three brawls happening simultaneously.

If Jackson was killed by an ice dragon, if those rumors were circulating through the network of shadow spies...then hunting down information would be next to impossible.

Was that what happened to the first informant who'd told me of the ice dragons—had he run instead of selling his intel to the highest bidder? It was terrifying enough to know a Prince of Sin might have been harmed, but when no other information came forward, it was easy to dismiss as fiction. Now, with a rumored death, things were growing much more worrisome.

If a prince could be attacked and a hunter killed, what chance did any of us stand to survive?

I turned back to Nyx, a new question forming on my lips.

But she was gone.

I huddled in the doorway of the building directly across from Jackson's family's town house, plush hood pulled low to protect me from the howling storm.

Nyx was correct: Jackson had passed on to the Great Beyond.

I stared at his leathers, hung with great care on the entrance, a symbol for all who came to visit or who simply passed by to pay their respects.

Any loss of life was heartbreaking, but there was an overarching sense of foreboding that hung in the air. Perhaps that was just me. Aside from one or two spies who fled, no one seemed worried about the dragons.

Because they didn't know.

I'd check the paper later today to see the official statement; surely there had to be one considering Jackson's role as an initiate hunter of the prince's prized hunting guild.

Something about the armor unsettled me.

I couldn't quite figure out what, though. The leathers seemed...unused.

Given how fresh Jackson had been to the guild, that wasn't too surprising. As an initiate, he'd only been in the field for a short while.

Gusts of wind covered them lightly with snow, obscuring them from further scrutiny.

It was probably nothing. And yet...that nagging little voice named Intuition couldn't silence the sense that *something* wasn't quite as it seemed.

Perhaps the tea had been poisoned and paranoia was a side effect.

Or maybe they weren't his leathers. If Nyx was correct, if the second ice dragon attack was true, then it stood to reason Jackson's leathers would have been marred or destroyed.

If that was the case, it was highly suspicious for them to attempt to hide that. An ice dragon attack that ended in the death of a citizen was news everyone in the realm should know.

The death of hunters north of Merciless Reach wasn't terribly common, but it wasn't unheard of either. The elements normally were to blame—the harsh cold was nature's finest assassin and it killed indiscriminately.

The more I mulled over the condition of the leathers, the more uneasy I became. There was no good reason to change his armor. Hiding an attack would take plotting, planning.

But was Prince Gluttony, the male who went out of his way to show the circle he was a debauched rake, truly cunning enough to devise a plan to keep us all in the dark?

Several minutes later, a grief-stricken woman who I could only assume was Jackson's mother opened the door, her eyes swollen and bloodshot, as she carefully dusted snow off his leathers. She seemed to be operating on sheer force of will alone. Though I suspected it was love.

Unconditional love made warriors of us all. It gave you strength to carry on, to show up for the one you lost. It set your own emotions aside. I'd known what that was like with my father.

As difficult as it had been, I'd stayed by his side, offering him sips of water to wet his dried lips until he could no longer swallow. Then, instead of running away, hiding from the inevitable, I held his hand, reminding him of all the good times we'd shared, watching as his chest stuttered, then started, taking my breath with it each time.

It had been like that for four weeks. The constant state of alarm, the worry, the knowing that one time his chest wouldn't rise again.

Dreading it.

Then on that final night, it finally stopped. I'd stared for hours, unbelieving, though it hadn't come as a shock. His body had grown so cold. So stiff. Still, I couldn't let go.

Unconditional love had kept me there, right by his side, as he crossed. No matter that I wanted to run away, to scream at fate, to crawl into a ball and sleep the pain away, never emerging again. Part of me wanted to die that day too. But life can be like the day; it goes on no matter how hard we try to force it otherwise.

So, as Jackson's mother lovingly tended to his leathers, I understood it was because she was still caring for her baby, even after he'd gone.

A million questions burned through me, but I refrained from crossing the street. It would be reprehensible to question a mother who'd just lost her son.

I stared for a few more minutes before making my way to printers' row a couple of streets over, mind churning. If Jackson had been killed by an ice dragon...a shudder wracked through me. I could think of no other logical explanation for his sudden demise. Impossible as it seemed, I'd bet anything that we were standing on the brink of disaster.

If the ice dragons were no longer adhering to the pact that kept the

Seven Circles safe, it was only a matter of time before they set their sights southward.

And our circle was the first territory they'd pass.

A new sense of urgency had my pulse pounding as I walked faster down the street.

I'd have to work twice as hard and twice as fast to turn in my Miss Match column on time while focusing on my original investigation. But no matter how difficult it would be, I'd find a way to accomplish everything.

I had to hunt down all the information I could on ice dragons, as swiftly as I could. It wasn't about breaking the story of the century anymore. It was about the safety of my family. My friends. The entire realm.

Finding out every bit of information I could on what was actually happening needed to become a priority, no matter how much the meddling prince had tried to thwart me.

If we understood why the ice dragons were attacking, *if* they were attacking, then we could find a way to stop them.

A shadow passed overhead, drawing my attention up.

This time it was a storm cloud, but I couldn't help but feel a note of alarm as I watched it move along the horizon.

I wondered if perhaps it was a warning that a different sort of storm was moving in.

One that had the potential to destroy us all.

THIRTEEN
Prince Gluttony

*T*HICK LAYERS OF straw crunched under my boots as I entered Sil's dungeon. I'd had several bales brought in to cover the stone floor where Silvanus lay on his side, chained and unconscious.

Despite...everything...I wanted him to be as comfortable as possible.

"Anything?" I asked.

Emilia glanced up from where she crouched beside him, shaking her head. "I still don't sense any direct spells on him."

I leaned against the wall, considering other options.

"Would the dragons need to be cursed individually?"

"Not necessarily. But usually there's some trace of witchcraft that's detectable." Emilia stood, dusting off her hands. "Spells and hexes have magical threads. If witchcraft was used, it wasn't done to the dragons themselves."

"Can you tell if it was placed on me or my court?"

"I wish I could, but I can't sense anything like that. Someone could have cursed your ability to protect your court, which is an indirect spell, not actually placed on you. If that makes sense?"

It meant someone could have cursed or hexed me in a way that covered their tracks. Again, not disproving the witch theory. But not proving it either.

Frustration welled deep within me. I had no more answers now than I did yesterday.

Emilia looked at the dragon one more time, then made her way to me, pulling me in for a hug. "You know you have the full support of House Wrath. We'll figure this out."

I offered her a tight smile but said nothing as she left.

I couldn't help but wonder if this was part of my circle's private curse, if there was some game I needed to win or debt I needed to pay to make things right.

Two of my personal staff, Ricard and Wright, demons who'd sworn an oath of secrecy as part of their elite position—and who I trusted implicitly with this most delicate situation—wheeled a barrel of ice water in, wrenching me from my thoughts, their gazes fixed on the slumbering dragon.

I sensed their fear as they hurried to unload the supplies I'd requested, the tension in their movements belying the outward indifference of their expressions.

Wright folded a few lengths of clean linen and set them beside the giant tub, quickly stepping back toward the cell's opening. He hadn't taken his attention from the dragon.

"Will that be all, Your Highness?" Ricard asked, rubbing warmth into his hands.

"For now. See to it that no one enters the dungeons without my express permission."

"Yes, Your Highness."

Both demons bowed, then hurried out of the cold chamber, their teeth chattering all the way down the corridor. Demons were long-lived, not immortal like us Princes of Sin, and I'd forgotten how unpleasant it was for most to be so near an ice dragon.

Once I no longer heard their hurried steps, I set about my work.

I hung my overcoat on a hook by the door and rolled my shirtsleeves up, grabbing the linen and dipping it into the water. It was cold enough to make my bones ache. Which meant it was the perfect temperature for a dragon who breathed ice.

I lifted Sil's enormous chin, gently wiping his snout in soft motions, removing the dried blood from his scales.

I ignored the growing pang in my chest. Jackson didn't deserve his fate, but it was hard to hold any true hostility toward the creature before me. Whatever was going on with Sil wasn't his fault. Something was impacting him, making him literally see red and attack.

I dipped the linen back in the barrel and wrung it out, watching as the water turned pinkish. I wanted to hear him sass me about doing a terrible job, while almost doing a dragon's version of a purr.

Mortals had puppies and kittens, and I had Sil to love and raise before releasing him to the pack.

The giant dragon lay on his side, his flank rising and falling in that same labored way it had directly after the fight. Once I finished cleaning him off, I ran a hand along his icy scales. The dragon didn't stir. He'd been in the same unconscious state since Emilia magicked him here.

"What happened to you, Sil?"

The dragon remained asleep.

No one knew what to make of it. And we were out of time for discussions. I'd sent word to each House of Sin, calling a summit for later today. With the pact broken, each prince needed to be brought in and debriefed. It was no longer simply a House Gluttony issue.

Wrath, Lust, and Envy had taken leave to rest and clean up here while Emilia had tried to detect any spells for me. The plan was to meet Greed, Sloth, and Pride at Merciless Reach after we'd privately discussed the competition and set the parameters for each suitor.

With everything that had happened over the last several hours, I'd almost forgotten about the whole ordeal of pretending to find my match.

I stroked the flat expanse between the dragon's closed eyes, watching as his lids fluttered a few times but remained shut.

"On my crown, I'll figure out how to save us all, Sil. Just hang in there for me."

"Your Highness?" Val's soft voice drew my attention from Silvanus. "If you still want to speak with Felix before the others arrive for the summit, you need to leave now."

I wrung out the linen and set it on the side of the barrel, then stood, wiping off my hands.

It was time to play the part of the prince again.

Val's expression was one of deep sorrow as she watched Sil struggle for breath. "Has he come to at all?"

"No. But he will."

I adjusted my sleeves, slipped my overcoat on, and Val handed me my crown. It was time to meet my brothers and decide the fate of the dragons and our realm.

"We'll give Lust two minutes, then start without him," I told Wrath and Envy. Neither of my brothers was happy with the delay. I left them to quietly argue and searched the skies that normally teemed with dragons from Silvanus's pack.

All was eerily still. Calm. The quiet before the proverbial storm. I couldn't stop from worrying that the dragons had pulled back to plan a better battle strategy.

I stared at the giant wall that spanned from Merciless Reach all the way across the northern border, separating the wild, brutal land here from the southern territory below.

A moment later, the door behind me creaked open, drawing my attention to the matter at hand.

"You're late."

My tone was as cold as the welcome I received from Lust.

Instead of slinking into the chamber quietly, he shut the door hard enough to rattle the saucers and cups of tea and coffee set up along the breakfast sideboard in my private meeting hall at Merciless Reach. Given the sensitive nature of what we would be discussing today, using the outpost and its warded walls made the most sense. Not to mention, it was isolated enough that no one would know all seven Princes of Sin had gathered.

I had Felix bring the hunters and initiates out to practice sparring in the far eastern camp, so only Helga and her assistant remained on-site. Helga was in her healer's chamber, mixing tinctures and remedies to keep in stock, and wouldn't leave unless ordered to. Even then she'd put up a fuss unless someone was bleeding to death.

Wrath, Envy, Lust, and I wanted to sort out the details of the competition and get the announcement underway before Pride, Greed, and Sloth arrived for the summit. I had a feeling they wouldn't want to discuss a fake hunt to find a wife after they heard about the dragons. An official royal reporter was waiting at the printer, ready to spread the news today.

Lust flashed a small menacing smile my way, immediately setting me on edge.

"Apologies. I slept in."

My magic alerted me to the lie. No doubt our other brothers sensed it too. Lust had been out entertaining lovers again. And I wanted to put my fist through his face for being so cavalier.

Though, given his dark mood, his night—morning, really—hadn't gone as he'd planned.

None of us had slept much and our frustration over last night's events had our tempers running high. After we'd secured Silvanus in the dungeon, we'd taken Jackson's remains to his family, staying to see him off to the afterlife.

We'd altered their memories, a decision that weighed heavy and didn't settle well for me. Or my brothers. We might be wicked, damned things, but we had our own morals. Gray and skewed as they were, there were some acts even we—the morally compromised—questioned.

My brothers were anxious to get the summit over with and get back to their circles, to the seats of their power, to protect their courts, but had agreed it was best to delay their departure for a few hours.

I wanted this competition ironed out and announced. Now more than ever, it was imperative to keep our realm focused elsewhere.

Lust proceeded to fix himself a cup of coffee and added a frostberry pastry to his plate before finally gracing us with his presence.

He sat on my right, completely ignoring me in favor of slowly licking the frosting from his pastry.

"Mm. Reminds me of that sweet little hellion from last night," he said. "Gods, do I love that club. I need to look into opening one in my circle."

"The Seven Sins?"

"Not sure why it's called that when so many patrons are clearly only interested in my sin," Lust quipped.

I directed our attention back to the matter at hand.

"Sloth, Greed, and Pride will be here within an hour. I want the plan for the competition finalized before then. We'll have each House of Sin appoint their own suitor," I said. "That will give seven suitors an opportunity to—"

"Seven isn't even a decent orgy," Lust interrupted. "We'll appoint two per House."

"I'm not hosting an orgy. I'm supposed to appear to be looking for a potential wife."

"I actually agree with Lust," Envy said. "If you choose two per circle, including one suitor from a well-established noble family and one suitor from the general public might be the way to go."

Wrath sat back in his seat, arms folded across his broad chest. "It's a decent idea; it'll get everyone's attention."

"Exactly. Appointing a member of the general public guarantees it's the talk of the Seven Circles, because it involves everyone," Envy continued.

"Good, it's settled, then. Two suitors per circle. On to the parameters of the competition," Wrath said. "Each week one suitor will be sent home. Weekly elimination rounds would—"

"No," I interrupted. "With fourteen participants that would mean drawing this out for three and a half *months*."

"Come, now, Gabriel. It will hardly be an inconvenience to entertain lovers, unless you're scared of being compared to House Lust."

Lust's gaze was filled with challenge.

I narrowed my eyes. I was certain now that whatever had happened last night hadn't gone in his favor; he was out of sorts and itching to fight.

"I have no issue entertaining suitors for months on end," I said. "I do have a circle to run and a court to look after. I can't spend all my time playing in bed."

"You could eliminate more in the early stages, if it proves too taxing for you."

"I assure you my stamina won't be an issue."

"Of course not," Lust said. "You let everyone else do the heavy lifting."

Envy made a strangled sound, choking off his laughter. Probably because Wrath kicked him under the table. Wrath exhaled, then glanced up at the ceiling.

Lust was pushing me too far.

"What is your issue this morning?" I demanded. "If you'd like to host the competition, by all means. Take up that mantle. You're clearly succumbing to either envy or wrath, and I don't have time to entertain *you*."

"Careful," Lust said, a low note of warning ringing in his voice. "That's not an accusation you want to make lightly, Gabriellis, especially when you've been lusting after someone you hate for years."

Our gazes clashed and held, like two titans battling it out.

Silence fell like a thick blanket of snow.

"If you're referring to Miss Saint Lucent, have the intestinal fortitude to say it."

Neither of our other two brothers dared to move. It took a lot to push me out of my mask of carefree rake, and Envy and Wrath sensed that trouble was near.

Lust was needling me, which meant either he thought I needed to spar, or he did.

I took in the shadows under his eyes, his hand fisted around his coffee.

Whatever his issue, Lust wasn't really upset with me.

I wondered then if the prince of pleasure had met someone who hadn't been impressed, who'd ignored his advances.

That would certainly be a first. And would explain his desire to brawl. Lust hadn't replenished his power through carnal pleasure, and he likely needed to find some other source.

Instead of feeding his need to fight, I brought the focus back to the competition.

"Every House of Sin will host a drawing for one suitor. We'll include commoners and nobility to keep it exciting, while also keeping the number to seven suitors." I would not be swayed on this. "That way it will accomplish all that you've laid out."

Envy shrugged. "It works."

"Glad you think so," I said, not hiding my sarcasm. "I'm announcing the competition today: details on how to enter, who can enter, and when the drawing will take place. It will dovetail with the private investigation we're doing at each of our Houses of Sin."

Wrath eyed me speculatively. Whatever he was about to say, he held his tongue. A knock at the door alerted me that our time to discuss this portion of the event was done.

Pride, Greed, and Sloth were here.

"Enter."

Val stepped into the room first, her expression tight. "Princes Greed and Sloth."

Our two brothers entered without preamble, eyeing us all as they took their seats.

They couldn't look more different if they tried. Where Greed was all bronzed hair and eyes, Sloth was icy eyes and nearly white hair. Both could stick a dagger in your gut and not bat a lash, though, much like each Prince of Sin.

Greed's coin-colored gaze swept around the room, skimming the half-eaten food and drinks, pausing briefly on Wrath before he aimed it at me.

"Gabriellis. I assume you've got a reasonable explanation for inviting us after the meeting already began."

Sloth's ice-blue stare seemed to pierce me as it slowly drifted over the room. Unlike Greed, he said nothing incendiary; he simply raised a pale brow, waiting.

I ignored them both, shifting my focus to Val. "Where's Pride?"

"He sent his regrets, Your Highness."

Silence descended. I counted until the urge to invade my brother's gilded castle passed.

"We called a summit, not high tea. He is aware of that, correct?"

Val winced from the drastic drop in temperature but nodded. "He said he has House matters that take precedence."

"What, exactly, does that prick think is more important than ice dragons attacking?" Lust quipped.

I blew out a frustrated breath and dismissed Val with a nod. "His missing wife."

"You mean the wife who *chose* to leave his ass?" Lust folded his arms across his chest. "He needs to take a hint."

"And we need to focus on matters of war, not romance," I snapped. "Now, Greed, Sloth, as I mentioned in the missive, we sustained an attack that resulted in death late last night."

I gave my brothers a rundown of what had happened, not sparing any detail. From Wrath's attack to Jackson's death and the ambush on my hunters. With each new bit of information, Greed's mood darkened, and Sloth's indifference shifted to something harder, more cunning.

Sloth was the most well-read of us. Instead of debauchery, he *lived* for unraveling issues, whether spells and hexes or medical in nature. I could see his mind spinning with possibilities—it wouldn't surprise me if he already knew which section of his library to investigate first. The mood in the chamber was rife with displeasure, but I continued.

Lastly, I informed them of the plan to host a bridal competition, with the hope that it would be enough to distract reporters and keep attention far from the ice dragon situation until we all resolved it quietly.

I finished the report with letting them know Emilia hadn't detected any spells on Silvanus, and Greed sat forward, his gaze narrowed.

"But she's not *certain* witches aren't involved," he pressed. I shook my head. "Isn't Sursea still being held prisoner at House Pride?"

"As far as I know, yes. Does anyone have different information?" I asked, looking at Envy in particular. He shook his head.

"Then it's time to go to House Pride and speak to the witch." Greed glanced at each of us. "If witches are responsible, you know it's somehow tied back to her."

It was a fact none of us could deny. Sursea was the root of all our animosity with witches.

Sursea was known as the First Witch throughout the realm, since she was the first witch born of goddess blood to spawn magic users. Unlike the children she spawned, who were long-lived, she was immortal and as dark and twisted as they came. She'd hexed several objects that wreaked havoc to this day in the hopes of destroying us, her greatest enemies.

The witches weren't humans who practiced witchcraft—they had power in their blood, aided by herbs and spells. She hated Pride, hated us all, and when our dear brother decided to marry Sursea's daughter against our warnings, all hell had broken loose. Quite literally. It set off a chain of events that ended in each of our Houses being cursed.

"I'll make arrangements to travel to House Pride as soon as I'm able to." I heaved a sigh. "Anyone oppose the idea of using the bridal competition to divert attention?"

Greed pressed his mouth into a hard line. Envy and Lust remained quiet.

Wrath met my eye.

"The competition will create a nice cover story for why we're all in and out of your circle too. Once it begins, you and I can take turns leading expeditions to track the aggressive pack," Wrath said, sitting forward. "Every other night. We'll see if we find anyone else above the outpost who's had any issues with the dragons. I doubt the attacks on me and then Jackson were isolated. There's got to be some solitary Fae who's seen something. Even if it was a witch roaming around."

I nodded in agreement. "Lust and Envy, double your research teams if you must. Sloth, track down any potential cause. Hexes, dark magic, bad takeaway food—nothing is off the table. Your library is the most extensive; I'm sure you'll find something we can use."

The knot in my shoulders eased a fraction. I felt like I had regained some control of this situation. But I wouldn't rest until the threat was eradicated.

"What, exactly, is the timeline for the competition?" Sloth asked. "Meaning how long do we have to search until the realm erupts into chaos?"

"Today I announce it. In two days, we'll announce the suitors. By the end of the week, I'll welcome them to my House of Sin. Hopefully the news cycle will—"

Someone rapped at the door. I counted until the urge to slay the demon foolish enough to interrupt us passed. "Enter."

Val's expression was a cross between fury and murder. Wrath took notice, no doubt siphoning some of her emotions to fuel his sin.

"Apologies for interrupting, but you need to see this, Your Highness."

I took the newspaper sheet from her, scanning it quickly, before cursing every last devil-fearing saint I could think of as I crumpled it in my fist.

"Has there been another attack?" Envy asked, rising, his emerald wings shooting forth.

Not in the way he thought, but it certainly felt that way.

I exhaled slowly, then shook my head.

"Miss Match just broke the news of the competition."

Is Love the Most Dangerous Adventure of All?

Dear Sinners,

You'll notice today's Miss Match column is a bit different, but no less romantic in nature. Perhaps it's the former scandal sheet writer in me, but I cannot keep such a *delicious* secret to myself...

It has come to my attention that His Highness, Prince Gluttony, the unattainable bachelor himself, will soon announce a competition to find his match.

With a reputation for ravishing and raking, it will undoubtedly be entertaining to see who will overindulge in masochism by choosing to be tied to him in unholy matrimony for eternity.

Time will tell how this storybook romance will unfold. Though it is important to note, most fairy tales are, in fact, cautionary stories.

My advice? Unless you'd like a lifetime of disappointment, I'd avoid entering this love arena.

Until next time. Stay scandalous, sweet sinners.
Miss Match

FOURTEEN
Adriana

"Did you hear?"

The high-pitched screech that followed the statement drew my attention up from the limited selection of lantern oils. A small group of women jumped up and down, a newspaper held between them.

A sardonic smile curved my lips. I wasn't certain, but the vampires living all the way down on Malice Isle probably heard their excited cries.

I went back to perusing the jars of oil, trying to find something I could afford this week. The entire circle had erupted into chaos after my special article went out this morning.

Each time I imagined how furious the prince was, I couldn't help but grin. It was certainly time someone gave him a taste of his own high-handed behavior. I had no idea that "Stay scandalous!" would become the new phrase du jour and knew he'd positively *loathe* it.

Another squeal erupted, this one remarkably louder than the first.

I glanced around the market stall, half expecting small woodland creatures to have responded to the shrill noise, tails fuzzed and tiny claws at the ready, prepared to valiantly free their endangered brethren at any cost.

When no impending squirrel stampede occurred, I returned my focus to the group of three young women waving the paper around, my ears tuned for gossip as they chatted excitedly. Old habits perished a slow death, it seemed. There probably wouldn't be a time when I wasn't ready to report on some delectable scandal.

"The prince confirmed the Miss Match rumor! He's looking for a bride. Anyone can enter the competition!" the first one squealed. "You simply add your name to the drawing."

"Imagine being Prince Gluttony's wife?" said the second, a dreamy tone in her voice.

"Let me see—" The third one swiped the paper away. "Where do you enter?"

Prince Gluttony clearly had tried to take back control of the situation, and it seemed his confirmation announcement was doing just that. Unsurprisingly, no one was heeding my advice.

I all but rolled my eyes. Not at them. They had every right to dream of their happily-ever-after. I was already over the damned prince's stupid competition, and it hadn't yet begun.

I could only hope to fall into a fugue state until it ended. Perhaps I'd visit a temple and make a sacrifice to the old gods on the way home.

Or maybe I'd stop by the witch's apothecary to take a tonic. Though, humor aside, I had much more serious matters to focus on. I'd scoured my network of informants on the way back to the *Wicked Daily* this morning, and none were in their usual haunts.

I'd need to set out again later to see if I could locate any of them after dark. Until they came out of hiding, there wasn't much more information I could glean on the ice dragon situation. Or if there were any more rumors circulating around Jackson's death. No official report had been printed; all anyone was talking about was the stupid competition.

My stomach twisted. I still couldn't wrap my mind around the fact that he was dead.

Hopefully my informants would have more to report on than the prince's news.

More than the details of the competition, I wondered who'd taken the position as his royal reporter. If we were in House Envy, I might be *slightly* jealous, knowing what I did of the hefty salary he'd offered.

"Will that be all?" Donovan, the vendor, asked, nodding to the small container of oil.

"It's ten coins more than last week," I pointed out. "And half the size."

He lifted a shoulder. "Still cheaper than the rest."

I sighed and handed over the coins.

There was no point in trying to haggle with Donovan. I'd done business with him for years and his prices were firm. I'd need to find a creative way to balance our budget this week. Hopefully I could find a better deal on vegetables. Meat was certainly out of the question thanks to Sophie's demand for a new gown combined with the raised price of oil and my visit with Nyx.

Donovan jerked his chin at the growing crowd behind us. All the screaming had drawn curious shoppers, all jostling closer to hear the prince's news.

Excitement ignited as if the market had been doused in the emotion, then lit, the news spreading like wildfire among the hardworking citizens of the realm.

My column was being whispered about right alongside the royal news—something my editor would be pleased by, despite my going rogue this morning.

Miss Match was now an authority on breaking all news relating to romance. I sincerely doubted Prince Gluttony had intended for that to happen.

I smiled to myself. Celebrating small victories was highly underrated.

"He'll choose a wife from common families as well as nobles!" someone cried.

My triumphant smile faded as I glanced at the paraffin on the table.

I wondered if stuffing my ears with wax was more dangerous than being subjected to hearing more about the *wonderful* prince.

Donovan wrapped my purchase in brown paper and handed me the package.

I tucked the glass jar into my satchel, mindful of any accidental elbows swinging my way as the small pathway between stalls grew even tighter. If any of my supplies broke, my family would be in dire straits this week.

"You entering that competition, Ad? Might win yourself a prince."

Donovan waggled his brows in a move meant to be suggestive but unfortunately made him look spasmodic. I offered him a polite smile. I had a masked stranger who was already causing me enough romantic distractions without adding sadism to my list.

"I would rather gouge my eyes out with a dull spoon."

"Really? Only a dull spoon?" a familiar irksome voice drawled much too close.

I stiffened as the male of the hour circled me, his features hidden under a dark cloak.

Axton looked like the sort of male mothers warned their daughters about. The bad, tempting ones who were terribly exciting for all the wrong reasons.

"After your little stunt this morning, I was hoping for something a bit more creative from the exquisite mind of Miss Match. Or perhaps I expected you to *stay scandalous*."

He angled his face toward mine, his hood shifting enough to grant me my first good look at him. Oh, the prince was indeed furious. He loomed over me, eyes flashing.

Axton was formidable when he chose to be—dark, dangerous, his gaze penetrating deep enough to pierce your soul. His expression was colder than steel and just as hard. Here stood the demon often hidden behind the roguish prince.

For a second, I forgot how to breathe.

That bladelike gaze suddenly swept over me, darkening further before he flicked it back up, pinning me with it once again. Whatever he'd been searching for, he hadn't found.

But *I'd* finally found my senses.

I looked Axton up and down, knowing he loathed when I did it, my expression perfectly unimpressed with his temper. "Why are you dressed like a grandmother in the dead of winter?"

His lips twitched, not quite forming a smile. Which put me on alert again. I had a feeling he'd hunted me down and this marketplace meeting was no coincidence.

I considered darting into the crowd, running as far and fast as I could. If he put this much effort into finding me, whatever message he'd come to deliver wouldn't be good.

He seemed to read the thought before I'd finished it. The prince took another step in my direction, his body much, *much* too close to mine now. He didn't have to utter a single word or threat. I knew if I ran, he'd chase me. There was one truth even I couldn't deny: Gabriel Axton was legendary for being ruthless when it came to the hunt. I did not want to end up his prey.

A little shiver went through me at his proximity.

One he noticed, given the knowing smirk.

"I like to hear what residents of my circle really think of me. Even the minor few who'd prefer to be maimed rather than wed me."

Much as I would have loved to offer a cutting remark, the continued squeals and giggles surrounding us proved I was alone in my loathing. Even married women and grandmothers were getting swept up in the fantasy of catching Gabriel Axton's attention.

I pressed my lips into a firm line, unable to retort as his fan club grew riotous. The twinkle of amusement in his eyes said he knew I was out-numbered too.

"Well. I can see you're very busy. Enjoy your afternoon of spying and ego stroking."

"Not so fast, Miss Match." There was no longer any amusement in his tone. "You and I need to have a little discussion."

"I'll be happy to schedule something in. Have your staff contact the *Wicked Daily*."

He gave me an incredulous look.

I turned on my heel, ready to make a dramatic exit, and promptly collided with a giant of a man. Glass shattered in my satchel, the scent of oil stinging my nose and eyes as I bounced backward, my fall broken only by the several other bodies pressed close.

I glanced down at the liquid staining the canvas bag and leaching onto my best day dress, wondering at the sudden dizziness taking over. I'd never been one prone to fainting spells, but the smell mixed with the crowd suddenly made my knees weak.

In the next breath I was hauled off my feet, carried to the safety of an empty alley.

I squeezed my eyes shut, praying that my hero wasn't my nemesis.

"You smell atrocious."

I cursed the old gods. Prayers were for saints, not sinners, apparently. I drew in a few deep breaths, then glowered at the shadow of my savior as he towered over me.

"This is all your fault."

"The part where I told you to storm into the pathway *was* rather rude of me."

I ignored the sarcasm dripping from his tone. I had worse problems to contend with.

I bent down and peeled my satchel open, wincing at the broken glass that grazed my fingertips. I let out a shaky breath, my worst fears coming true. Oil coated *everything*.

I stared for a few moments, trying to collect myself as my world came crumbling down around me in a sudden, violent heap.

My parchment and new quill were ruined, along with the bit of ribbon I'd purchased for Eden. I couldn't afford to replace the items and get enough food for the week.

I'd already gone through my allotment of paper from the *Wicked Daily,* and no matter that my Miss Match article was popular, Mr. Gray wouldn't hand out another sheet. Without the parchment, I wouldn't be able to draft my next column.

Which meant we'd go hungry for another week. And if I couldn't scrape together more coins soon, I'd miss a second column.

Tears pricked my eyes.

Axton swore and knelt beside me, pulling the bag from my grasp. "Are you hurt?"

Only emotionally. I gave a slight shake of my head, unable to speak without giving away the full extent of my despair. My eyes remained locked on the cursed satchel.

"Adriana."

Axton's voice was soft as he peered inside the bag. Wonderful. I was now being pitied by the worst possible male in the realm.

I straightened, willing myself to not show any weakness.

"I really must go."

"Adriana, I—"

I spun on my heel and fled, only realizing as I pushed my way through the crowd that I'd forgotten to curtsy. And I'd left the remnants of my satchel behind.

But as the tears finally came hard and fast, I couldn't find the will to drag myself back and face the prince. He'd already seen me cry once, and it was something I'd vowed he'd never witness again.

"Ad! *Look!*"

Eden's cherubic face was alight with excitement when I walked through the door a few hours later, defeated and spent. I'd tried to barter with the shopkeeper who sold parchment to no avail. I'd even begged to work for them, if only for one piece of parchment.

"Can you believe it?" Eden said, tugging on my arm.

I shook myself out of my despair and looked up, halting at the sight.

There were at least half a dozen people swarming around our small front room. Bolts of fabric hung over the settee, the colors lavish and beautiful.

My attention swept from the silks and cottons to the stacks of parchment being delivered. I went on alert at once.

"What's going on?"

"This good here, miss?" A young male pointed to the weathered table, his arms filled with paper.

When I couldn't find the words, my sister swept in. "That's perfect, thank you."

I blinked at the abundance of goods, unsure if I was hallucinating. "What is all this?"

My sister rushed to my side, hugging me close. "The prince! He sent a note. Whatever did you do to him?"

I must have gone into the fugue state after all. Or perhaps inhaling the oil did something nefarious to my brain. It was hard to escape the noxious scent, as it had soaked through the bodice of my dress. Surely that was the only reasonable explanation for this show of excess.

"Pardon? Did you say the prince? As in Axton?"

"Of course I mean Prince Gabriel. Here!" Eden handed me the cobalt-and-silver note.

It was indeed stamped with the House Gluttony crest.

My heart pounded as I broke the dragon seal and flipped it open, suspicious of what his motive for this stunt was. He clearly had some angle he was working. I'd been reporting on him long enough to know that Axton never did anything out of the goodness of his wicked heart.

He'd taken the time to track me down in the marketplace; he'd had a reason. One he wouldn't simply drop just because I'd run off.

Dearest, insufferable Miss Saint Lucent,

Consider the gown a gift to those who'd otherwise suffer your stench with the spilled oil. It's most certainly not an apology for ruining your parchment. Or your day.

His most charming royal highness, unrepentant rake and rogue,
who I assure you has no issue with staying scandalous,
Gabriel Axton, Prince Gluttony

"Oh!" Eden sighed dreamily from over my shoulder. "He is as generous as he is charming, wouldn't you agree?"

I flashed my sister a dubious look as I folded the paper back up.

"Yes," I said dryly, "whenever a gentleman calls you insufferable, then comments on saving others from your clothing's stench, it most certainly points to generosity and charm."

Eden's smile wouldn't be dimmed as she looped her arm through mine, steering me toward the obscene abundance of fabrics. "Say what you like, dear sister, but he is an absolute dream. He's even purchasing new gowns for me and Mamma!"

My suspicion grew.

The prince was definitely up to something. He'd been furious when he'd cornered me earlier. There was no way he was rewarding me after I'd broken the news of his competition first.

Whatever his plan, I'd bet money I didn't have that it furthered his cause somehow.

I kept my thoughts to myself.

"He is?"

"Indeed." Eden motioned to the bedroom she and my stepmother shared. Her voice was filled with hero worship. Wonderful. Another Axton fan was living in our home now. "Well. He doesn't necessarily know they're for us personally. He instructed the modiste to measure everyone in the household for new attire. Mamma is getting fitted now."

My sister's smile appeared frozen in place at that part. Which meant my stepmother was using her usual charm on the dressmaker.

Before I could excuse myself to rescue the woman, another knock came at the door.

Eden clapped her hands, then darted over to answer the door to whoever was calling on us now. I'd never seen her so animated before, and despite my growing alarm at the prince's obvious plot, I refused to ruin her fun.

A parade of servants wearing House Gluttony's livery deposited satchels of groceries on the kitchen table. Fresh fruit and vegetables and bread that smelled divine. Along with cured meats and hard cheese. It was more food than we'd had at one time in a decade.

The surprises weren't nearly close to being over. The next knock brought another set of servants, this group carrying jugs of oil and new lanterns.

I dropped onto the small settee, completely at a loss for words.

Axton might believe he was simply needling me over the market incident, but no matter his motives, this one act would save my family from any more hardship for the next several weeks.

The good feelings for Axton were of course short-lived when the modiste swept into the small main room and began clucking at my attire, demanding I stand at once, then not so subtly encouraged me to burn my entire wardrobe. Perhaps *she* was my punishment.

Hours later, and several bolts of fabric lighter, the modiste and her assistants finally left our home. I collapsed onto the settee next to Eden, completely spent from the afternoon's marathon fitting. Axton certainly had ulterior motives, but it would have been foolish to refuse the goods for my family, especially after I'd turned down that obscene salary.

In a week's time I'd have a new cloak, shoes, short boots, unmentionables, and five new dresses. Axton had proven once again that he indulged others to fuel his sin. I knew it was only a matter of time before he let me in on this nefarious move. For now, though, I'd let my sister prattle on with stars in her eyes, waxing poetic on the generosity of the handsome prince.

My stepmother swept out of the bedroom, a cunning gleam in her gaze as she waved today's paper around like a victory flag.

I didn't need to see the headline to know it was regarding the realm's biggest news.

"Your sister is going to become a princess," she declared, cold eyes on me. "I entered Eden's name earlier this afternoon."

Sophie raised one impertinent brow, daring me to object.

It didn't matter that I had no designs on marrying the prince; it was the cruel way my stepmother glared like I needed to be reminded that I'd failed so spectacularly at winning his heart. As if I'd ever forget that fateful night ten years ago when I'd been made into the laughingstock of the circle by the very prince lavishing our household with gifts.

Sophie had been positively livid when I'd come home from the All-Sinners Ball. She'd called me a stain upon our family and refused to find me a suitable match after that. In all honesty, she hadn't tried very hard before then either.

My stepmother held the paper up, jabbing her finger at it. "This is the match of the century. And our family *will* win his throne."

How foolish of me to think it was supposed to be more about winning his heart.

Eden looked at me, her expression a mixture of worry and...hope as she bit her lower lip.

After today's extravagant showing, she had a crush on the prince.

Any protestations I might have voiced died in my throat.

I would certainly not be entering my name for the silly competition, but if Eden had a chance at true happiness, far from Sophie's toxic reach, I'd choke down my own feelings for Prince Gluttony.

Foul tasting, wretched, and all.

FIFTEEN
Prince Gluttony

$\mathcal{A}$FTER A SUCCESSFUL venture to the market to enact my plot to find Adriana *and* potentially unearth my secret lover's identity, I returned to House Gluttony feeling fractionally better as I headed for the royal library. Despite my brother's House of Sin being a giant library, I was unwilling to leave all the research to Sloth.

Not because of pride or any other sin, but because of the simple fact that I had one of the best collections of books dedicated to the history of ice dragons.

There *had* to be something useful in one of them. I refused to think otherwise.

I strode with purpose, filtering through theories uninterrupted. This time of day, as an afternoon storm rolled in and my court was slowly recovering from the previous night's parties, my House was quiet, the hallways blissfully empty.

It wouldn't remain this way for long.

With the news of the competition out and the participants' drawings scheduled, there would be a new layer of complications I'd need to contend with. But that worry could wait.

I traveled down the winding corridor of the east wing, the ice-blue silk panels of wallpaper depicting ice dragons in flight and battle. With each scene I passed, the beautiful artwork felt more like a taunt than an ode to the creatures I so admired.

My hunter had been slain, which meant my circle had been attacked.

There was no greater motivation to use every moment I could to uncover something that might help.

I paused outside the library's ornately carved doors, haunted by the creatures I'd spent decades adoring. Two dragons faced each other, mirror images of ruthless beauty that seemed poised to attack. They were crafted of birchwood, and the artisan had used my tattoo as inspiration. The dragons alerted anyone who entered that they were guarding the vast knowledge of my kingdom.

I pushed the doors open, taking a moment to breathe in the scent of leather and ink as I made my way to the back section, where hundreds of years of dragon history were shelved.

I pulled book after book from the floor-to-ceiling cases, stacking them high on a table, and rolled up my sleeves. I *would* be successful today; failure was not an option I'd accept.

The first book was more observation of dragons—from hatchlings to adolescents to adults. What they ate, how they behaved, mating dances and rituals, battle tactics, nesting; everything was keenly observed and reported on. The second history was from hunters at Merciless Reach, detailing skirmishes and any insights gleaned from battling the great beasts.

I called for a cold supper, barely stopping to eat as I scanned book after book.

"Gods' blood," I swore, rubbing my temples. "There's got to be something."

I went over our summit, turning over the conversation with my brothers. Greed's suspicion about witches wasn't far off from my own fears. I would need to pay Pride a visit soon.

There had to be a way to get Sursea to talk; surely I could find out what she wanted most and offer it up. Within reason. I picked up the next book. At first there wasn't anything, then, just as I was about to quit for the night, a note scribbled in the margin caught my attention.

I read the passage over, hoping it truly was as promising as I thought.

No scientific proof to date, but one scholar posed an interesting question. Might a tonic created from royal vampire venom thrall dragons into speaking mind to mind without the need for a witch's spell? Regardless of outcome, it might be worth pursuing.

I could have kissed the scholar who'd scribbled the idea. Emilia hadn't detected any spells and yet Silvanus still hadn't woken up. I wasn't sure what else could cause a dragon to slumber in such a way that nothing roused it. Royal vampire venom might be exactly what I needed.

For the first time in what felt like ages, a spark of hope ignited in my chest.

I rang the servants' bell located in the library and within moments Jarvis arrived.

"Your Highness called?"

"Send a missive to the new vampire prince requesting an audience within the hour."

Jarvis cleared his throat delicately. "And if he declines?"

"Insist. Blade's court is in a precarious position; he doesn't need another enemy. But he could gain a favor if he chooses correctly."

Jarvis bowed at the waist. "I'll send the request straightaway, Your Highness."

Blade was no fool. He'd granted me entry to Malice Isle shortly after my request was sent, even going so far as permitting me to use my magic to transport directly into his castle.

It was obvious he was angling to turn this meeting in his favor, and I was prepared to offer the support of House Gluttony should he need it. *If* he played nicely tonight.

After dethroning the previous vampire prince by a brutal show of violence—at which my spies reported Envy had been present and played a large role in his mysterious game—Blade's court had become increasingly divided. Warring vampires and their bloodlust were issues no one wanted to deal with; they could be too unpredictable, too driven by instinct.

One faction had immediately sworn fealty to him, despite the fact that his eyes were dark crimson and not the typical blue of royals. The second faction wanted to place a blooded heir on the throne. During this time of upheaval, the new prince needed all the allies he could get.

Word in the shadows claimed Blade would soon be in the market for a political union and he might seek to wed outside the vampire realm.

I stood in the darkly Gothic antechamber of his throne room, toeing at the bloodstone-checkered tile, awaiting the announcement of my arrival.

Zarus, the previous prince, had an affinity for all things blood colored, proving taste was truly subjective. I had to admit the stone *was* unique, but if I had a penchant for guzzling blood, I wouldn't drench my castle in the color. Best to leave some things understated.

The collection of iron sconces twisted into finger bones added an extra layer of the darker season charm, something mortals called Halloween or fall.

Flames on the candles danced, casting odd shadows around the chamber.

Val was eerily still beside me, dressed in the battle leathers all hunters wore. Her knives were on full display, the belt strapped to her hips slung low and stocked well.

"A bit on the nose, isn't it?" I asked my second, trying to soothe the strain. She flicked her attention to my boots, watching as I kicked at the bloodstone.

"Did you expect anything less for a leech?"

"Impressive collection of knives, demon."

Val spun on her heel at the sound of the low, gravel-like voice, a knife already in each fist. She would have had her blade pressed to the new prince's throat if his hadn't already found its way to hers. Blade had earned his name well.

I grinned. Not many beings ever snuck up on me or Val. Even fewer lived to tell the tale. The vampire prince had a reputation as wild as mine, and his truly was earned.

"Blade."

"Axton."

I jerked my chin at his weapon. "Greeting guests with your namesake is poor form."

His answering grin would have had a mortal pissing themselves. It made me like him more.

"Your second calling me a leech in my own court is in equally bad taste."

A hint of fang gleamed under the candlelight.

I leaned in, squinting. "Tell me, how often do you sharpen your fangs to get that menacing sheen? Once a week, twice?"

His booming laughter rattled the sconces. He slipped his dagger back into his holster.

"Come." Blade strode down the corridor, away from his throne room, glancing over his shoulder with that shit-eating grin. "We'll have a drink."

Val shivered in place.

This was going to be an interesting night.

Blade swung open the door to what appeared to be a vampire kitchen. No staff bustled around, which was either a very good thing or rather unfortunate. Giant hooks hung from the ceiling, leaving no doubt what they were used for.

"Well, then." I stepped across the threshold and glanced around. "This is wildly unsettling."

"Don't worry"—Blade smiled—"you're not here to be drained and served to my court."

"How comforting," Val mumbled, eyeing the giant slab of ice conveniently placed under the hooks that seemed to be keeping urns of blood cold enough to become slush.

The kitchen was dank, smelled metallic, and boasted overflowing amounts of fruit and jugs of wine—all plum colored and highly suspect.

Blade grabbed three glasses from a cabinet and set them in front of us, pulling a flask from inside his suit and pouring out what I prayed was straight whiskey. Or maybe arsenic.

He clanked his against Val's first, eyes gleaming with mirth as she recoiled.

"Well?" He tossed back his drink and slammed the glass down. "What are we bargaining for tonight, Prince?"

There was no sense in working my way up to it. I knew from interacting with the vampire over the years that Blade was direct and appreciated the same approach.

"I need your venom. A vial or two, if you please."

His brows shot up at that. He scrutinized me closely now. "Is this some weird fetish your court is trying out? You know, I *have* heard interesting rumors even all the way down here."

"I'd be relieved if it was. But no. I have other reasons."

His dark crimson gaze held mine for a few moments. He knew I couldn't lie, so what I said had to be the truth, odd as the request had been. Maybe he was wondering if I was mad.

Blade folded his arms across his chest, leaning a hip against the wooden table that served as an island from hells. Gods only knew what was prepared on that ghastly thing.

I had to consciously keep my lip from curling at the thought.

"You can't make a vampire without an actual vampire."

Val snorted. "I assure you, you have nothing to worry about on that account."

His attention slid to Val. There was something in his look that reminded me of a lion who was considering if a fight would be worth the effort to expend his energy.

The spark that flickered to life indicated it just might be.

"I am willing to offer something favorable in return," I said, using the tone of the jovial rake I was known to be. "Rumors suggest *you* need friends, desperately."

At that he snorted. "*Desperate* is not a term I'm familiar with, now or ever. I need a mate. And I need an heir. Know anyone who'd be a good match?" He didn't take his amused gaze from Val, enjoying antagonizing her far too much. "Word around the realm suggests *you're* about to be a bit of an expert with finding a bride."

"Alas, it's regrettably true. But I'm sure plenty will want the second-most infamous rake in the Seven Circles once I've retired the crown. Your prospects will brighten faster than those pearly white fangs."

He cocked his head, losing a bit of the humor as he looked me over again.

It seemed our negotiation was about to begin.

"I want a favor of my choosing at any point in the future. Friends are fickle. Relationships change. I want a sworn oath, right here and now, or you can go home without any venom."

Val stiffened. She hadn't been expecting his request, but I had. It was the only way for a prince in crisis to guarantee an ally remained his without fear or second-guessing. We were in the Underworld and none of us came here by way of shining morals.

Unlike us Princes of Sin, vampires couldn't detect lies.

Still, I hesitated to agree. What Blade wanted was no small request.

Demons were like Fae in one regard—if we swore an oath or vow, we needed to adhere to its terms or the magic binding us would wreak havoc, often causing a tiny inconvenience like death.

Immortals tended to get a little touchy about that sort of thing and rarely entered into any binding agreement. Myself very much included.

Being prepared for his request didn't stop my visceral reaction to it.

Silence stretched as I considered my options.

While I'd waited for Blade to accept my request for this meeting, I'd tried to come up with an alternate bargain that would be equally appealing.

I hadn't found anything then, and that remained damnably true now.

One edge of his mouth curved up as my fingers tapped a beat against my dagger's hilt. He knew he had the upper hand.

I thought of Jackson and how his fate might become that of many more.

My grip tightened on my dagger as I unsheathed it. "Fortunately, this will hurt. You."

Blade's eyes gleamed with triumph. He hadn't been as confident as he'd let on.

He held his palm out to me, not even wincing as I dragged the blade across his skin, tearing into it as if it were no more substantial than butter.

Once I did the same to my own palm, I waited.

"I bind the Prince of Gluttony into a favor of my choosing, at a date of my choosing, in which he will not hesitate to act upon the request at once."

I repeated the words, watching with a bit of satisfaction as the stoic vampire finally showed a hint of pain. His throat bobbed slightly; the sensation, I'd been told, was like hellfire crawling up each of your veins as it bound a Prince of Hell to someone.

For my part, my pulse beat more rapidly, my breath coming faster as my magic infused the agreement. Blood oaths were a little different than the vow I'd just sworn. A blood oath didn't cause pain. But they were also typically shorter than a vow.

Once Blade straightened, he grabbed a vial from the same cabinet he'd taken the glasses from. He held it to his fang, and I watched in horrified fascination as royal-blue glowing venom filled the container. When it reached the top, he pulled his fang away, licking his lower lip as Val made a gagging noise and took the vial from him.

"Are we through here?" Val asked, handing the vial to me.

I nodded. The venom was not exactly ice-cold when I grabbed it, but it wasn't warm by any means. Vampires were certainly as far from warm-blooded as they came.

Val shot the prince an inscrutable look. "Thank the gods. I'll be in the corridor."

"Always a pleasure, little sinner," Blade mocked silkily. He turned his attention to me. "If you're hoping to thrall someone, administer it at dawn or twilight. It'll have the most potent effect then."

As soon as I returned from Blade's court, I briefly considered visiting the Seven Sins to see if by some miracle Lady F had waited several hours for my arrival. Despite the chaos of my life lately, I craved her company in a way that grew more ravenous with each passing day.

Of course, I still had my dark suspicion regarding her identity.

And that drove me wilder than anything else.

I'd have an answer to that question soon enough, though.

While I was in Malice Isle, my spies had been watching Adriana's house tonight, ready to report on any movements. No one had informed me that she'd left. If I went to the Seven Sins and my mystery lover was there, I could've ruled out my rival once and for all.

Instead of feeding that desire to track her now, I flew to Merciless Reach, tonic clutched in hand, and went straight to the command center chamber.

"Any updates?"

Felix looked up from the maps spread across the table. "No new dragon sightings, no attacks. Hunters have been staying near the outpost per your orders, Your Highness."

"Wrath patrolled tonight?"

"Yes. You just missed him. I accompanied him, then came here to see if any area stood out for our next search."

I ran a hand through my hair. "You checked their nests?"

Felix shook his head, his expression as tight as I imagined mine was. "Didn't want to risk sending a hunting party that close on the off chance they have any hatchlings. And Prince Wrath was concerned with the bar-rens. He wanted to make sure no other alphas had sent scouts to see what this pack was up to."

"And?"

"No sign of any other packs."

Thank the wicked gods for that. The vial of vampire venom weighed heavily against my chest. I didn't want to offer any false hope, so I kept it tucked away.

"I'll check the nests on my next patrol."

With a pat on Felix's shoulder, I transported myself back to House Gluttony. Unease followed as I made my way to my private chambers, trying to anticipate the dragons' next move.

It was an effort in futility and not the best use of my energy.

Blade said the ideal time to administer the venom would be dusk or dawn, and dawn was still a few hours away. No matter how much I wanted to forge ahead and give Silvanus the venom, I needed rest. It was going to be a hellish few weeks and I couldn't risk looking tired and run-down when the whole realm would be watching my every move.

I stripped off my clothes and crawled into bed.

I tossed and turned, my mind flooded with images of crimson eyes, steaming entrails, and the expression on Jackson's mother's face when I'd delivered the news that her only son had been killed in an accident. It was the closest to the truth I could give her without lying. If I didn't uncover the truth behind the dragon's madness, many other families would be grieving.

The dreams continued to torment me, but this time they took a wicked approach.

Lady Frost's cobalt-and-silver hair fanned across my pillows, her glamoured face half hidden by a mask as I trailed openmouthed kisses along her silky skin. She was the most exquisitely devastating thing I'd ever seen. Even in my dreams she was a feast for the senses.

I admired her nude form, lovingly caressing her, exploring every inch of her as I worked my way down her body, my new favorite uncharted territory.

I pressed a chaste kiss to her inner thigh, then moved my way back up, loving her cursed protest that I left her wanting. I'd devour her soon enough. But first...

I took her mouth in a searing kiss, pressing her against the mattress, my desire for her burning away all thoughts and worries. I wanted to flip her over and slap her pert little ass, watching her squirm from the sensation as my hand dipped lower, spreading her arousal as I spanked her to climax.

My cock ached with the need to claim her, but I craved her taste on my tongue more.

Half asleep, half aware, I stroked myself to the dream, my grip tightening as I moved up and down my shaft.

In my vision, I kissed my way down her lithe form again, this time intent on feeding her every desire. Like a sinner hell-bent on redemption, I worshipped every part of her before I fitted myself between her legs, hoisting each one over a shoulder to spread her wide; a prince finally sitting down to his feast.

I looked up the length of her body, wanting to watch her as I brought my mouth to that secret place between her thighs and—

I lurched backward as her dark hair faded to a pale ice blue.

My pulse pounded furiously when the glamour and mask fell away next, revealing the truth I'd been avoiding seeing.

Her mouth curved into a familiar taunting smile as she dragged her attention down my body in the most gloriously slow sweep, finally settling it on my twitching cock. The tip of her pink tongue swept across her lower lip before she sank her teeth into it.

A raw hunger crossed her features, reminding me it was only a dream.

My hips involuntarily thrust forward, forcing me to pump into my hand, a bead of precum leaking from the tip. She didn't remove her gaze from me, as if fascinated by my desire.

I watched, frozen in either horror or deep fascination, as she trailed her fingers along the curve of her breast, past her ribs, teasing her lower belly, before dipping lower...

Gods' fucking blood.

I pumped my fist over my cock, watching as she pleasured herself, her fingers circling her glistening clit before sinking deeper.

A soft moan slipped past her parted lips, making me impossibly harder. I'd never fallen victim to my brother's sin of choice before, but in that moment, I envied her fingers.

She withdrew them as if she'd known exactly what had snared my attention, then swirled them across her arousal, stroking herself torturously slowly.

I couldn't look away if my cursed soul depended on it.

I wanted to throw her back and sink into her, setting a punishing rhythm, pounding hard and fast until she clenched around me and we both shouted our release.

Hatred, it turned out, *was* a powerful aphrodisiac. I'd never been more aroused by the thought of making a lover fall apart.

My sweet nemesis lifted one hand to her breast, kneading it as she continued to play with herself for my pleasure and hers. My world narrowed down to just us.

There was no mystery lover. No Seven Sins. No looming dragon threat. Just the female I wanted to bring to her knees...

Our hands worked in tandem, keeping pace as if competing to see who would finish first.

Rivals even in this most intimate moment.

She kept those cool eyes fixed on me in the most erotic show of defiance I'd ever seen as she rode her fingers to climax, spreading her thighs to make sure I drank my fill of her.

My orgasm followed immediately, erupting all over her stomach.

And my sheets.

I jolted up in bed, skin damp with sweat, cock at half-mast.

Devil's blood. I hadn't come so hard in a long time. I fell back onto my mattress, chest rising and falling rapidly as I caught my breath.

Even awake, I couldn't rid myself of the twisted fantasy that had played out. Maybe witches were involved—I certainly felt like I'd been cursed.

I pushed myself into a sitting position, cleaned myself up with my already soiled sheet, and rolled out of bed. I padded over to the wash-basin and splashed icy water on my face, then straightened up, glancing at my reflection in the mirror, unsure what to make of that...

Punishment.

That's what that was, and my sin loved it. The sadistic bastard.

Unable and unwilling to go back to bed, I quickly dressed and headed for the dungeon.

Dawn would break soon, which meant it was time to feed Silvanus the vampire venom.

Once a Rake, Forever a Scoundrel

By Miss Ryleigh Hughes, the Wicked Daily

Dear Sinners,

On the same day as his grand announcement of the competition to find a wife, Prince Gluttony's servants were spotted entering the residence of a certain journalist he's been feuding with. Rumors are running wild regarding what, if anything, the gesture means.

Most whispers suggest it was simply one more taunt in their public war. And I'd have to agree. It's no secret that there is no love lost between these two.

Aside from practical gifts—like parchment and quills—Ms. Escoffier, modiste to the elite, was seen removing several bolts of her prized fabrics from her shoppe. Was it another calculated move to infuriate the reporter who's given him hell over the years, or a way to charm the circle?

Anything is possible when it comes to this rake of the highest order, though this journalist doesn't believe his rival will be amused by the public spectacle.

Whatever his motive, this bold move sent a flood of new suitors racing to enter their names for his competition this morning. Lines of hopeful brides twisted through the streets leading to the palace. The wait was so long, servants brought steaming mugs of hot chocolate to those waiting in the frigid temperatures.

Perhaps building a frenzy was his true goal all along. If so, bravo, dear Prince. You've certainly charmed your way into more hearts, even if you've made a greater enemy in the process...

As the colorful Miss Match said, until next time, sweet sinners. Stay scandalous!

SIXTEEN
Adriana

AFTER A MORNING spent unsuccessfully trying to track down any of my informants in an effort to work off my annoyance over Ryleigh's article, I walked into the *Wicked Daily* and glanced at my overflowing desk. My stormy mood grew darker.

Stacks of envelopes spilled onto the floor, no doubt filled with questions for Miss Match. If any of them ended with *stay scandalous!* I vowed to move to the forest and live out my days as a hermit. Then I'd no longer need to think about the prince or the ice dragons; I'd be too preoccupied with entertaining all my imaginary friends.

Something was happening in the circle. Something terrifying enough to send even the most hardened informants into hiding.

Short of sneaking into the castle and infiltrating the prince's staff, my next opportunity to gather information would be at either the Scene Stealer later this week or Axton's stupid competition. I penciled in the play on my calendar.

Intermission was a wonderful time to gather information—almost everyone who attended was there to gossip. Hunters and nobles close to the prince always made an appearance, their need to boast unmatched by even the most scheming of matchmaking mammas.

I'd linger around the perimeter, blending in with the shadows as they freely spilled their secrets in poor attempts to impress one another.

Although, there was one more avenue I could explore sooner: the Seven Sins club. It certainly had everything to do with unearthing any new leads on the rumored dragon attacks, and nothing at all to do with the stranger who haunted my dreams.

A troubling suspicion was taking shape, one I needed to resolve soon.

My stranger had a seemingly endless supply of runed keys at his disposal. He had to either own the club or be involved with its management somehow.

And if I uncovered the secret owner, I had a feeling I'd know exactly who my stranger was. The owner might be a successful merchant, or a devious noble.

If gossip was to be believed, the club might also be owned by those who had access to each Prince of Sin's castle. Could my stranger somehow be part of Axton's court?

The idea had crossed my mind earlier, but I'd dismissed it. What if he was a trusted advisor to the crown? Or a thief or an assassin? The most troubling thought of all was one too blasphemous to even consider.

I took the key from my cloak's hidden pocket and turned it over. I had no idea if it would even admit me to the club if I tried to use it.

"Good morning!" Ryleigh burst into the office, shaking snow from her cloak. "How is the lovely Miss Match this fine morning?"

I shoved the key back into my pocket and gave my friend a withering look she ignored. "Let me guess. An anonymous tip was sent in, and you were the lucky one who got the article?"

She flashed me her most winning smile as she set her desk up. Parchment, quill, inkpot, all lined up neatly. It was her way to settle her nerves and think over her approach to conflict.

"It was either me or Julian."

I'd figured as much, though it still stung considerably to know my friend had spread that rumor. And she didn't seem all that apologetic about it. We'd never fought before, and we'd never kept secrets before either. I couldn't help but wonder if my guilty conscience was creating this little rift between us. I exhaled, letting the matter go.

At least she'd spun some of the story in my favor—Julian would have been much worse.

"Sophie is furious. She made me swear to smooth things over with the prince for Eden's sake."

I pulled my fresh parchment out of my new satchel, cringing only slightly at the supplies Axton had purchased, supplies the entire circle now knew about. I reminded myself that Ryleigh was my friend and she'd done me a favor. If I repeated it in my head enough, I'd believe it.

Though I'd also repeatedly chanted that the tavern singer with mesmerizing eyes would profess his undying love at his last concert, and that hadn't come to pass.

"Why is she so concerned about Eden? She and the prince have never even met."

"Sophie doesn't want Eden's reputation tarnished before the winners are chosen."

Ryleigh rolled her eyes. "There are several *thousand* entries, according to my source. I highly doubt your sister will be chosen." She jotted a few notes down, then leaned across the aisle. "Who do you think sent the tip in?"

"Who do you think?" I whispered, even though we were the only two in the office. "It reeks of Axton. He's plotting something."

Ryleigh snorted. "If it was an attempt to charm more suitors, I'm afraid it worked. Did you see the line leading up to the castle this morning?"

I wished I hadn't. The streets were packed with people jostling one another, desperate to submit their names before the drawing later today. It had been a nightmare trying to squeeze my way down the avenues to the shadow network part of town.

Nyx hadn't been nursing a whiskey at Eternal Rest, and neither had any of my other regular informants. More proof that something was stirring in the shadows. It couldn't simply be the dragon rumor or Jackson's death that scared them off, one by one. But what?

I glanced at the clock on the far wall; the minute hand was suddenly moving much too quickly. Today was the big day—the hopeful bride from House Gluttony would be chosen.

Suitors from the other Houses of Sin had already been picked by their princes and announced in the paper last night, but in dramatic fashion, Gluttony had waited until last to choose the suitor from our circle.

I wouldn't be surprised if everyone in the circle gathered outside the grand entrance to House Gluttony at high noon today.

According to the official royal report published this morning—as read to me by my *very* enthusiastic sister who'd been up before the sun to snatch the paper—a giant urn was filled to the brim with eligible ladies' names and was being guarded around the clock from any nefarious plots to remove the competition.

Rumor claimed that Axton would choose one name and announce it right there on the spot, his intention undoubtedly to create an even bigger spectacle of his hunt to find a bride.

One thing I could say about Gabriel Axton—he knew how to work the papers.

I read over one of the new questions, then quickly tossed it aside.

Do you believe Prince Gluttony is a good kisser? If one counted all the asses he kissed on a regular basis to gain favor, then I supposed he was.

Alas, that fell into the *personal opinion* column, so I couldn't share the advice.

I opened the next letter. Someone wanted to know if hate sex was as wondrous as others often claimed and would I mind terribly sharing what I knew of Prince Gluttony's wicked tongue.

I balled the letter up and considered using it as kindling.

Finally, there was a question worth considering.

Dear Miss Match,

I've had bad judgment in the past, but I've just met someone new. How do I trust myself?

I couldn't help but think of my stranger from the Seven Sins. I'd been experiencing this feeling lately myself. At night, long after everyone had turned in for bed, when the streets were eerily silent and I'd finished writing, I couldn't stop myself from wondering if my stranger was the best sort of indulgence—or another great mistake.

There really was only one way to find out.

In between hunting down reliable information about the dragons and writing my column, I needed to unravel the truth behind my stranger's identity. All while keeping it from my closest friend. This was precisely why I avoided romantic entanglements—my life had become far too chaotic over the last week or two.

Ryleigh jotted a few notes down on her own parchment, unaware of my inner struggle. "You think Prince Gluttony will choose a commoner or noble?"

I set the letter aside in the *yes* pile. It would be the perfect follow-up article. "Don't know, don't care."

"Are you sure? What if the gifts didn't have a plot or scheme attached to them?"

I didn't like the skepticism lingering in her tone.

I turned my full attention to my friend. We were skirting around a subject I refused to acknowledge.

I'd already been down this path with Axton, and it was a road I didn't wish to travel again. It had taken years of needling him in the papers before people slowly forgot our history.

For his part, Prince Gluttony had never once mentioned our former… association.

I wasn't sure if that bothered me more or not.

The spark of annoyance I felt now wasn't because of the prince for once; it was because of the blasted situation. I understood how invasive it was to have my personal life shared widely across the realm, and this time it was worse. It was that fact alone that made me lash out.

"If this is about Axton's show of gross overindulgence, you ought to know better. He didn't do it to be kind. He did it for his own gain. Probably to try to charm me so I don't continue to write about him, or it was some half-assed attempt to distract me."

"Ad—"

"There is *nothing* that male could ever do to change my opinion of him. He is still the same selfish, spoiled rake he's always been. I cannot wait for him to find a wife to torment. Hopefully she'll be as disloyal and petty as he is, and they'll live a long, wretched life of misery together with incredibly dull and boring sex."

I regretted the harshness of my words the second they left my lips.

Ryleigh swallowed hard, her attention fixed to some point behind me.

I inwardly groaned. I must be cursed by some wicked fan of Axton's. Magic *had* to be involved with his uncanny ability to sneak up on me.

"Again?" I knew before I turned that the prince would be there. I gathered my courage and swiveled in my seat. And there he was.

Quiet rage simmered in his hazel gaze. He'd heard my lovely speech in full, then.

I opted to lighten the mood. "Someone ought to place a damned bell on you."

Axton gave me a look filled with such icy malice, chills raced down my spine.

He stared for a long, silent moment, then directed his impressive glare at Ryleigh.

"You wrote that asinine column about us, correct?" Ryleigh's eyes widened as she nodded. Axton scoffed, his attention once again landing on me. "Such loyal, *unselfish* friends you have, Miss Saint Lucent. Using you for their own gain."

I flinched. His barb landed because it had *felt* like that.

"She didn't—"

"She did, actually." Axton folded his arms across his chest, head cocked to one side, daring me to contradict him. I couldn't. "Would you like to try another excuse or are we through? I've got a wife to find and torment, after all."

"Our editor received the tip from an anonymous source. Perhaps you should take your complaint to your own infamous court. Or yourself."

The look he cut my way could wither the hardiest northern flower.

"Do me a favor, Miss Saint Lucent. Don't attend the name drawing today. I don't want you anywhere near the event."

Without uttering another word, he strode for the door.

The devil must have been working his brand of dark magic overtime. I was up and out of my seat like a shot, darting after the prince, Sophie's warnings to think of my sister's future spurring me into action.

He'd only made it to the first step outside when I caught up to him.

"Your Highness, stop."

I hadn't intended for my voice to be so loud, but the sound practically echoed in the sudden stillness of the bustling morning streets.

Axton stiffened.

It took a moment for my brain to catch up with my error. I'd commanded the prince in public. And, given the spectacle of his competition this morning, it hadn't gone unnoticed.

Several passersby stopped to gawk, jaws hanging wide, their attention volleying between the prince and myself, waiting to see how he'd react to such an impertinent breach of rank.

At least I'd quelled one rumor: there was no secret affection between us.

Axton slowly pivoted to face me, his expression coldly aristocratic.

If looks could kill, I'd be greeting my maker this instant.

He closed the distance between us, taking my arm as he retreated into the *Wicked Daily,* dragging me along with him like some primitive cave creature claiming his mate.

To avoid creating any further gossip, I went silently, though my mind was alight with all manner of wicked retribution.

"You are an absolute nightmare to my sanity." His voice was a low growl as he kicked the door shut behind us. "Forget picking suitors. I ought to take you over my knee and punish you in front of the whole damned circle later. Really give them something to talk about."

It was absolutely crass and abhorrent, but my pulse started to flutter wildly at the thought. How dreadfully inconvenient to start thinking of my masked stranger now.

Axton's attention snapped to mine, his nostrils flaring.

Gods' blood. I'd never wished for the old gods to strike me down in a raging bolt of lightning before. But there I was, peeking up at the ceiling, hopeful as ever.

Unsurprisingly, no errant bolt from a merciful deity put me out of my misery.

As a Prince of Sin, Axton could sense desire. And he'd certainly noticed, given the sudden intensity of his expression. He dragged his attention over me, his eyes blazing with some emotion I couldn't quite identify. For a moment, it felt like he'd burned away every layer of my defenses and saw every secret desire I'd ever had.

In the next instant, his expression shuttered.

"Are you fevered?" he demanded.

"No."

"Chilled?"

"No. Why?"

"You clearly must be ill if you're—" He abruptly shut his mouth, adopting that roguish grin he wore so well. "I don't wish to catch whatever malady you're suffering from."

The devilish look he flashed my way said that wasn't all he was concerned about, and we both knew it. Ryleigh was doing her best to ignore us, but you'd need to be comatose to not feel the strange tension building in the office.

Axton's attention shifted from me to the desk, and I could almost swear I saw the gears turning as if he was contemplating bending me over it now, tempted to spank me right there on the reporting room floor, uncaring if we had an audience.

His sin made passing up indulging a great effort.

And curse it all, my body wasn't at all put off by the idea.

I needed to take a plunge into the coldest northern lagoon to purge myself of whatever hex I had to be under. There was no way in the seven hells I'd permit myself to be turned on by *him.*

I smiled sweetly. "Fear not. I still despise the unholy ground you walk upon. I simply wished to apologize."

His gaze narrowed. Whether from my apology or my attempt to hide my reaction, I couldn't tell. After a lingering moment, his expression shifted to that of an unaffected rake.

"Such an honorable young lady," he purred, knowing full well I couldn't stand when he used that low, seductive tone on me.

And just like that we were back to barely tolerating each other.

"Yes, well. Honor is a concept you ought to adhere to once you take a wife. Difficult though that may be for a scoundrel such as yourself."

"The only female in the entire realm who'd be miserable as my wife is you. Isn't it fortuitous that you and I will never happen?"

I flinched. If he'd stabbed me with his House dagger it might have hurt less.

Once upon a time, I'd thought he would be perfect for me. Because *he'd* made me believe in his brand of fairy tale, right before I discovered he was the villain the stories warned us about.

I should have known better than to delude myself into thinking a Prince of Sin could ever be reformed into Prince Charming.

"It appears we finally agree on one thing. I would never marry you, Your Highness."

"Good. I don't recall asking and never will."

And that has always been the issue, I thought crossly.

I sat back at my desk, promptly giving him my back.

It was wildly inappropriate, but I didn't care.

He'd just coldly reminded me why I'd curse him until the end of days.

SEVENTEEN
Prince Gluttony

I SWEPT INTO THE dungeon, settling my gaze on Silvanus's slumped form as the team of healers and Val made room for me, their hushed whispers ceasing upon my arrival.

The mood was as ominous as the dragon's current condition. Aside from me, everyone was in heavy winter cloaks, their hoods pulled low like assassins to withstand the brutal temperature.

I took the vial of royal vampire venom from my suit jacket and crouched down to get a better look at Sil. He'd barely been breathing when I visited him at dawn. Instead of risking hurting him with the unknown effects of the venom, I'd called in the healers to stabilize him.

The ice dragon looked only marginally better now.

His normally luminescent flank remained duller than normal, more unpolished silver than sparkling iridescence. A twinge of worry slipped between my ribs like a blade. It had been several hours since the healers first began tending to him. I'd expected a bit more positive progress.

"Has he woken up at all?" I asked.

"Not yet." Val stepped away from the healer she'd been speaking with, eyeing the venom in my fist like it was cursed. "You trust the leech?"

"I don't have to trust him to use the venom." I motioned to the door. "Everyone aside from Val, exit the chamber. I don't want to take any chances if he jolts awake."

What I didn't have to say was if he jolted away and wanted a snack.

The healers left the chamber in a swish of cloaks, looking relieved to be sent away.

"Do you think it's wise to test the venom when he's so...still?" Val's question was the same one I kept asking myself.

I paced. The name drawing was in an hour. Blade had said the best time was dusk or dawn, but not the only time. If I gave Sil the venom now, I'd have a limited amount of time to interrogate him if it did work. And if it didn't work, then I'd have to leave him and pretend all was wonderful in front of my entire circle.

A feat I could normally accomplish, but this time I feared the strain would begin to show.

Val drew me to the side of the dungeon, her voice dropping low even with no one else near. "There's something else you need to know. Dragons were spotted flying over Merciless Reach. They fired trackers at them, but none pierced their hides."

"Gods' blood. Will nothing go right?"

I rubbed my temples. I didn't like the fact that the dragons had flown near the outpost.

Especially today. The sixty or so miles by land weren't far by sky to my House of Sin.

The crowd already gathered outside my castle was immense; it would be the perfect target for bloodthirsty dragons. The crowd wouldn't be able to escape quickly, making them even more appealing.

If they struck today...it would be unimaginable. There was no way I could cancel the drawing without causing a bigger scandal; I had to move forward with our plan.

I glanced down at Silvanus. Tonight, no matter his condition, I'd attempt the venom. For now, I needed to focus on making it through the next several hours.

I faced Val.

"I want extra hunters stationed between here and Merciless Reach. Keep them hidden to avoid any rumors or creating unrest," I said. "Send word to House Wrath. I'll need him to reinforce the perimeter today. But

I don't want any of his court spotted here. I'll fly up as soon as I can after the drawing."

Val nodded. "How did your meeting go with the reporter?"

"She'll be there."

"You're sure?" Val's tone was filled with skepticism.

I thought back to our encounter this morning. "It's the one thing I'd bet on today."

Adriana had been full of surprises, but one truth remained—she'd ended our little meeting feeling a renewed sense of hatred.

Which meant she wouldn't miss the name drawing for all the money in the realm. At least I wouldn't have to divide any of my forces to have someone watch her. From here on out, the closer she remained, the easier it would be for me to monitor her movements.

"Has the modiste sent an update yet?"

"The items will be delivered by morning, Your Highness."

I exhaled. Finally, something was going according to plan.

"When Adriana arrives," I said, walking toward the cell door, adding a bit of swagger to my stride in preparation for the grand event, "I want eyes on her at all times."

EIGHTEEN
Adriana

EDEN CLUTCHED HER cloak tightly in her fist, her knuckles bone white. Her normally golden skin looked pale as she glanced around at the other hopeful suitors filing into the area marked for entrants. I couldn't tell if it was the crowd or her nerves, or both.

She'd never enjoyed being trapped in large gatherings. Even at the mere thought of a crowded ballroom she'd break into hives.

I stood with her near the entrance of the circular drive, sinking deeper into my cloak as the next blast of arctic wind howled down from the mountains.

It was cold enough to make me think ice dragons were circling high above, their wings producing an extra chill meant to subdue their prey before they attacked.

I glanced up, shivering at the thought. For once, I hoped the rumors were false.

"You don't have to do this if you don't want to," I murmured low enough for my stepmother to not hear.

"It's not that at all. I *want* to be picked." Eden's gaze cut to me and lingered. I made sure to keep my expression carefully blank. "There's just so many people."

"As long as you're certain."

"I am. Very much so." Eden swept her attention around, dropping her voice to avoid anyone overhearing. "It wouldn't be the worst fate to marry a prince, Ad. Especially someone as charming and generous as Prince Gluttony."

I scoffed, earning a look of admonishment from my little sister.

"I don't know why you dislike him so much," she said. "I hope you give him a chance."

"I didn't enter my name into the drawing." Thank the old gods for that. "But if you get chosen, I'll mind my tongue."

She gave my hand a little squeeze, then made her way into the waiting area.

Sophie and I lingered with the rest of the families just outside the castle's entry, waiting for the prince to emerge and choose someone's fate.

I quietly mulled over my exchange with my sister. I hadn't realized that she might be nervous about *not* being chosen. And it was rather foolish of me. Axton was a handsome prince.

Powerful in more than one way. *Of course* I knew she'd been smitten.

Ever since he'd bestowed our household with gifts, Eden had been speaking of him almost nonstop. Her dreamy tone suggested she felt as if the sun rose and fell based on his whims. Every morning this week she'd rushed out to get the royal report and read it to me, determined to make me see why he'd be the perfect match.

A knot of unease twisted deep inside me.

My sister was too young to know what had transpired between me and Axton at the All-Sinners Ball, and I'd certainly never divulged anything of our history to her.

If Eden *was* chosen, then I'd be forever linked to the prince. And I'd be happy for her since she seemed to want it desperately. Wouldn't I?

A flash of sitting around the table with Axton while he showered my sister with affection crossed my mind. Would it be sincere or a way to forever needle me?

It was such a wildly unpleasant thought, I jolted when fire erupted from several low containers set at even intervals around the driveway and the castle's exterior, warming the air.

It was dramatic but practical. A flare for gaining attention that

Gluttony excelled at, much as I'd claimed otherwise in my articles. I closed my eyes, wishing I had stayed at the *Wicked Daily* and missed this event. Knowing the prince, his next move was about to happen.

A cannon shot fired, right on schedule, followed by heart-shaped blue and silver petals raining down over the crowd. It was romantic and made more than one lady fan themselves.

Several columnists jotted notes, Ryleigh, drooling Julian, and pompous Anders included.

It was odd not being one of them, huddled together on the stairs of the castle, waiting for the prince to make his grand entrance, quills held at the ready.

Truth be told, I'd rather be hidden among the crowd for this particular event.

Finally, Prince Gluttony emerged from the castle, striding down the steps until he reached the low stage that had been set up. His grin was wolfish, the gleam in his eyes positively wicked. His crown sat askew on his head, further playing into his role of proud rake.

He looked like he'd just rolled from bed, and the crowd couldn't get enough. They screamed and stomped their feet, shouting his name in a chant that made my teeth clench.

"Gentle demons of the realm, welcome!" His voice boomed above the clamor, silencing the excited cheers. "It's with great honor that I stand before you, humbled by the overwhelming enthusiasm for my search to find a consort."

Another loud cheer went up, forcing the prince to pause his speech.

"Without further delay, let's see who our suitor is, shall we?"

My mouth was suddenly dry as I rolled onto my tiptoes, trying to spot Eden's blond head in the crowd of hopefuls. There were thousands of entries. Her chance of being picked at random was slim. Yet my heart was pounding hard, and my palms were damp within my gloves.

I couldn't tell if I'd be happy or horrified if she was chosen.

"For the House Gluttony suitor…" Axton thrust his arm into the urn containing the names, making a grand show of fishing around. "Nobles, hardworking sinners, which will be granted a chance at their own fairy-tale ending?"

I kept my eye roll internal. How very arrogant to declare himself a storybook prince.

The crowd was wild now; the idea of a commoner finding their happily-ever-after with the handsome, devilish prince was the stuff dreams were made of.

My stomach twisted into knots.

He wasn't going to choose Eden.

I knew it.

With near certainty.

Yet my ragged pulse suggested otherwise.

I suddenly became aware of several sets of eyes turning my way, the columnists all stealing glances in my direction. I commanded myself to breathe. To look as bored as possible, to appear completely unaffected by all the pomp and circumstance taking place on the stage.

An impossible feat when I realized *why* everyone's attention had shifted to begin with.

Axton had spotted me in the crowd, his expression thunderous. For one horrifying moment, I thought he'd come storming over and put me over his knee like he'd threatened.

Honestly, given the narrowing of his gaze, he looked like he was contemplating doing just that. An unwelcome heat spread through me. Perhaps I *was* coming down with a fever.

Instead of slinking away, I offered him a slight incline of my head, refusing to be cowed by his displeasure.

Despite his high-handed banishment earlier, I never would have left my sister to face this crowd alone.

My stepmother shot a look of disapproval my way, her mouth pursed so hard it looked like she'd sucked on a salt-encrusted lemon.

The prince finally wrenched his attention back to the matter at hand, and I loosed the breath I'd been holding. A few more moments and we could all go home.

I kept my attention locked on the stage, watching as he repeated the same dramatic gesture, finally fishing a single piece of paper out of the mass of hopefuls, then raising it up. His expression was impossible to decipher.

He started speaking, but a strange ringing in my ears drowned out his words.

My stepmother pinched my elbow, hard, and everything came rushing back.

"Congratulations, Miss Regina Trombley!"

I sagged with relief. Eden flashed a look over her shoulder, her expression laced with disappointment. She started to make her way toward us, shoulders hunched in defeat.

Sophie practically fumed beside me, but it was of little consequence. I hated that my sister looked so miserable. Eden reached us and took my hand, squeezing it gently. She'd had enough of the crowd. And her dreams had been dashed. Despite my own tumultuous feelings for the prince, I hated that she was deflated.

"Is Miss Trombley here?" Axton asked, his voice carrying across the chatter.

Someone nearby pushed their way to the front, but I couldn't quite see who it was with so many people packed so tightly together. "Your Highness?"

The crowd began tittering as it parted, granting me a good look at the newcomer.

The person who'd stopped before the stage was no simpering young miss; she was a spinster by choice.

A cold dread swept through me.

"Yes?" Axton asked, all charm.

"Miss Trombley is no longer in the running. She ran off with her beau to the Shifting Isles just last night."

If he was disappointed, it didn't show. Axton didn't miss a beat. "Well, who am I to stand in the way of true love? Congratulations are still in order to Miss Trombley and her chosen one."

Sophie shoved Eden back toward the area where suitors were supposed to wait. I flashed her a scathing look. Couldn't she see that her daughter was miserable in such confined quarters?

I was so aggravated I missed the drawing.

"And the suitor is…Miss Eden Everhart!"

The world came crashing to a halt. My sister's last name was the same as mine: Saint Lucent, not Sophie's maiden name.

I shot my stepmother a horrified look. "What game are you playing at?"

Sophie simply smiled back. "It's no secret that the prince despises you. If you'd been able to charm him, we wouldn't be here now. So why should your sister suffer for your failings? I told you she deserves to be a princess, and now she is one step closer."

I looked at my stepmother, really took her in. Her confident smile. Her calm demeanor. Eden's name being chosen wasn't at all a surprise to her. A dark suspicion took shape.

I leaned in, dropping my voice so no one would overhear. "What did you do?"

"What any other parent would do for their child." Her tone was injected with venom.

"A spell?"

Sophie's attention darted around, indicating I was correct.

She'd used magic to secure Eden's win.

"Smile, darling. The realm will be watching us all. If you ruin this for our family, I vow to make you regret it for the rest of your days."

NINETEEN
Prince Gluttony

"Your Highness! Over here, Anderson Anders, from the *Sinners' Rumor*, we spoke a few days back. Do you have time for a few questions following the grand announcement?"

I flashed my most dashing smile, careful to not bare my teeth as the reporter stepped into my path, trying to block my retreat. Pompous Anders truly grated on my nerves. It took every ounce of diplomacy I could muster to not check him with my bulkier mass.

"No questions today, Anders. Please direct all inquiries to the official royal reporter."

I waved to the remaining crowd who lingered in my circular drive, then headed to the stables to saddle up my hell horse. The stable hands nodded as I entered Magnus's stall and prepared him for the journey. The enormous stallion loved riding out to Merciless Reach, feeling the icy wind claw at us as he pushed himself to speeds that should break every law of nature.

Hell horses weren't like mortal horses—they were faster, more powerful. He'd race the sixty miles in just under an hour and still not be spent for the day.

It was often a punishing and invigorating ride. Exactly what I needed after the spectacle of this afternoon. I mounted him and within seconds we were tearing across the grounds of the castle, heading straight for Merciless Reach.

I closed my eyes, allowing the joy of the ride to take over. Memories of more innocent times rushed into my mind. Emilia hadn't taken her horse Tanzie riding with us in quite some time; it seemed we'd all gone from one crisis to the next over the last several years.

I hoped to rectify that soon.

Magnus clattered over the gravel road leading up the mountain and out of town, his mane whipping about as he unleashed his full power and drew me back into the here and now.

What felt like mere moments later and not an hour, we were drawing up to the wall dividing the uninhabited land to the north from the Seven Circles below.

A shadow passed above, and Magnus stamped his hooves. We were being hunted.

I kicked my heels into his sides, and we shot off again, racing to the stables inside the fortress. Another shadow followed us, the fierce cry of dragons piercing the otherwise quiet of the day. Magnus bolted through the gates, racing the dragons and getting us under shelter as the first blast of dragon fire came from above.

Hunters who'd been standing near the stables scattered, darting in zig-zags to the safety of the warded walls of Merciless Reach. I didn't follow them.

I tossed the reins to a stable hand, dismounted, and took to the skies, immediately locating the two dragons. Their eyes glowed crimson, the color frightening against the backdrop of snow and ice. Once they spot-ted me, they spewed more unholy flames, narrowly missing me as they gave chase.

Before I'd gone a mile Wrath joined me, called in no doubt by Felix at the first sign of attack, and the two of us raced toward the far north, using every advantage we could to lure the dragons away from the out-post and what lay beyond.

The ice dragons' shrill cries echoed behind us, confirming we'd snared their attention and they'd given chase. My pulse thrashed through my veins, my adrenaline pumping hard.

That had been too damned close. My hunters knew what they signed up for when they joined the guild, but no one deserved to live under fear of constant attack.

I flew as fast as I could toward the mountains, noting the moment Wrath peeled away and sped toward the nearest dragon. His wings, once emitting a bright white fire, were now jet-black and menacing as he gave chase.

For once we looked like exactly what we were: avenging angels, fallen from grace to battle the worst creatures in the realms. Together we provided a tantalizing target for the dragons; they couldn't resist the lure of taking down other apex predators. Any hunters that might have snared their attention at first glance were soon forgotten.

Wrath angled back toward me, his expression thunderous. We'd come dangerously close to disaster. Merciless Reach was warded, but if the dragons slipped by us, the houses and towns beyond were not. I'd need to investigate devising some way to magically protect my demons. One that wasn't a constant low-level drain on my power.

A familiar mountain range rose like an angry god before us, its jagged slopes reaching up to curse the sky.

My brother glanced my way, waiting. I gave him the signal we'd used countless times. As the mountain pass came into view, he veered to the left while I aimed to the right.

We'd split the dragons and wait for them to give up and fly back to wherever they'd been hiding and follow them there. The bellowing cry behind us indicated they'd hesitated—giving us the advantage, which was exactly what we'd wanted. That one moment allowed us to pull ahead, diving below the tree line, camouflaging ourselves.

I plummeted to the ground, tucking my wings in tight, forcing my chest to still. The dragons flew past in a blur of iridescent scales and white wings, aiming for the highest mountains to the north. I took to the sky again, intent on stalking them, and cursed.

They were gone.

I flew in the direction they'd taken, scouring the terrain below. It was an exercise in frustration. Caves and evergreens blocked my view. I spent another hour combing the area, listening for any slight bleat or snarl, any flutter of wings.

Nothing. It was as if the dragons simply ceased to exist.

I circled the mountain one last time, then headed back to Merciless Reach.

Wrath was already there, his expression as dark as I imagined mine was. I jerked my chin, indicating he should walk with me. I didn't want any of the hunters to overhear us.

"Did you manage to get a tracker on any of them?" I asked.

Wrath shook his head. "They anticipated the move and blocked it."

I pushed my hands through my hair, swearing. "They've got to be cursed. I can't think of one other thing that would cause them to oscillate so much. Sometimes they seem to know exactly what they're doing, other times they don't."

Wrath stared off into the distance, his gaze settling on the bruised mountaintops smudging the horizon. Snow started coming down in heavy clumps. Soon it would be a whiteout. The perfect conditions for the ice dragons to blend in.

"The witches have been quiet since the last raid," he said, breaking into my thoughts.

"I know. I haven't heard any news about them from my spies in months."

Wrath and Emilia had run into trouble with them a few months back at House Greed, where the witches had staged an attack, the first in a long time. And while the demons had won the skirmish, the witches were never silent for long.

"The dragons could be a distraction," I said. "Maybe they want us focused here while they infiltrate House Pride."

Wrath folded his arms across his chest. "Did he ever inquire about the summit?"

"No. You think he's planning something of his own?"

Wrath shrugged. "He hasn't been growing slumber root to relax in the garden after work."

An idea formed at that.

Slumber root was a flower that was powerful enough to knock a demon prince out cold, so it should act the same on a dragon. Perhaps it was time to get some plants for my healers to work with. Rumors had been circulating for some time that Pride had grown an entire field of slumber root, making us all wonder what he was really up to.

Out of all of us, he might be the one who wore the most masks in public. No one ever truly knew what motivated Pride, aside from searching for his missing consort. Even his reasons for that were constantly up for debate. Did he truly miss her? Was it all a hit to his cursed pride? Or was there another reason he was so desperate to track her down?

If he'd been anticipating a war with witches for some time, it explained why he wasn't concerned about the dragons. He'd have expected some form of retribution or subtle attack. If that proved true, it would have been nice of him to let us all know.

I watched the mountains fade from view as the storm blew in harder.

It felt like our entire realm was under attack. Malice Isle had just deposed the old vampire prince, forcing Blade to hunt for a bride to settle the unrest.

The Unseelie court to the west was scrambling under its own new leadership.

And if the witches *were* plotting something by way of the ice dragons here in the north, we'd be facing possible war from almost each direction.

I exhaled. "Let's hope we're wrong about the dragons' being cursed."

Wrath met my gaze, his expression as guarded as mine. "We need to talk to Pride. Do you want to send a request from your House or should I?"

A slow, wicked smile curved my mouth.

"Neither. I say we show up there now. You game?"

My brother's grin matched mine. Entering a different circle unannounced could be an act of war. A fact that made Wrath's sin tremble with anticipation. Literally. The ground rumbled hard enough to cause a sheet of snow to career off the wall.

I gave him a flat look.

"Keep it together, heathen."

With a dark twinkle in his eye, he winked. In a blast of smoke and shadow, he transported himself to House Pride.

"Thanks for the warning," I muttered, preparing to summon my magic next. "Gods-damned prick."

I'd just pulled in my power when Wrath came blasting back.

He smashed into the fortress wall, putting a slight dent in the stone. He was furious as he stood, brushing himself off. I didn't think it had anything to do with the disheveled state of his clothing, though Wrath *was* particular about it.

I swore.

"He warded his circle?" I guessed.

Wrath nodded. "And he better have a damned good reason for it."

My brother stormed off, likely preparing to magic himself back to House Wrath. I had little doubt he'd be sending a missive to our secretive brother, and it wouldn't be a thinly veiled threat. When Wrath's sin ignited, we could only hunker down and prepare for war.

It was the last thing I needed to worry about. It was troubling enough that Pride had closed down his circle—and peculiar timing. I wanted to know exactly what he was doing, and if it was in any way impacting my circle, Wrath wouldn't be the only one he'd need to shield himself from. The might of House Gluttony would come for him.

I made my way back to the fortress and climbed the stairs to the command room. "Val?"

My second glanced up from where she was studying a map. "Yes, Your Highness?"

"Get Pride here immediately. Tell him House Gluttony will declare war if he doesn't come now and bring slumber root."

"That will definitely get his attention."

"That *is* the idea."

Far better for me to piss him off than have Wrath storm House Pride. There were only so many fires I could maintain at once.

Val bowed and left to send the missive.

I strode out onto the parapet, needing to breathe in the cold air to settle myself. Pride wouldn't take long, especially if he wanted to keep his secrets to his court. Less than thirty minutes later, Felix cleared his throat and stepped onto the roof. "Prince Pride is here."

He'd no sooner made the announcement than my brother's form filled the threshold.

My attention swept over him in assessment.

Outwardly he looked the same as always.

Not a hair out of place or piece of lint on his suit. His cravat was perfectly knotted at his throat and even the scar that ran through his lip seemed to add to his regal edge. There was a tenseness around his mouth that belied his casual demeanor.

Pride's silver eyes gleamed like daggers as he watched my hunter hurry back inside. The storm wasn't the only cause of the frigid temperature drop.

When we were alone, he flung a bag of slumber root at me.

"A war, Gabe? Over a gods-damned weed?"

I was in no mood to deal with his cavalier attitude tonight.

I shoved him against the wall, satisfied by the clack of his teeth from the sudden impact.

"If it's only a weed, why, then, are House Pride's grounds covered with them? I've heard rumors your circle is starting to look less than pristine. That's so very strange for a sin like yours, where appearances are everything."

He narrowed his gaze but didn't respond to the strike at his power.

"You seem to have missed the part about ice dragons attacking, Luc. Remember the summit you couldn't bother to attend? Try taking your head out of your ass and care about something outside of your immediate desires."

A muscle in his jaw flickered but he still remained stubbornly silent. I knew exactly why he wasn't saying a word—he couldn't lie and wasn't about to tell me the truth.

I grabbed the slumber root. "Felix?"

Felix returned to the parapet. "Yes, Your Highness?"

"Have Helga turn the slumber root into a liquid we can shoot into the dragons. Or a paste to cover needles—whatever she can come up with the fastest. We need a way to quickly administer it if they attack."

"Straightaway, Your Highness."

Felix took the little satchel and did as I'd commanded, leaving me and my brother alone once again.

Pride raised his brows. "Is the threat really that serious?"

"A hunter was killed. What do you think?"

He lifted a shoulder, adopting an attitude of nonchalance. "An unfortunate event to be sure. Do you think they'll attack your House of Sin soon?"

"If we're sharing House secrets, why don't you go first? You can start with the field of slumber root or whatever plot you're hatching for your consort."

My brother's hand balled into a fist before he quickly released it.

We would get nowhere if we kept needling each other. It was time to set any animosity aside and see what my brother might know about witches and their possible involvement.

"I'm looking for anything that might cause the dragons to go mad," I said. I didn't miss the way he flinched. The bastard was definitely keeping secrets. "You wouldn't happen to know a spell or curse like that?"

"Why would I?"

"Your mother-in-law is currently in your dungeon, is she not?" I asked. "Perhaps she's mentioned something along those lines or boasted about using a spell on a Prince of Sin."

"Sursea hasn't spoken a word in nearly a month." He looked out at the courtyard below. Hunters hurriedly took shelter, their focus darting to the sky. "You don't need a witch to break a curse."

"I'm aware. But I do need to know what spell was used or who the target is."

"Then I'll leave you to it."

"Not so fast." I was before him in the next breath, my dagger pressed to his jugular. "I want to speak with Sursea. Now."

Pride schooled his features into a mask of forced politeness. "Very well. I grant permission for a five-minute visit. Meet me in my courtyard now."

I dropped my blade. "After you, then."

With a mockery of a bow, Pride magicked himself to his circle.

I summoned my own magic and in a crackling blaze of fire and smoke materialized beside my brother right outside his castle.

We weren't exactly alone.

Pride's helmet-wearing guards stood in a circle around us, blocking my view of the grounds. His smile was anything but friendly when I raised my brows at our greeting squad of doom.

"Make haste, dear brother. By my count, you've got four minutes remaining."

"You haven't even taken me to Sursea yet."

His grin was downright wicked. "I only granted you a five-minute visit. You didn't specify that they had to be with my mother-in-law exclusively. You have three minutes and forty seconds left at House Pride. I suggest you spend it wisely."

Fae-like bastard. "Take me to Sursea now."

Pride and I strode up the gleaming stairs to his castle. The moment we entered his gold-leafed foyer, he immediately turned to the chamber on the right. Guards stood outside the door, bowing as Pride motioned for them to grant us entry.

I was about to stab my brother with my dagger when he pushed the door open, revealing a sight I hadn't expected to see.

"Sursea."

I walked into the finely appointed chamber. It was a far cry from the dungeon setting I'd been led to believe she resided in. It looked like a suite straight out of the mortals' Versailles.

Silk-covered walls, gilded molding, frescoes and paintings and sitting areas fit for a king.

Sursea perched on the edge of silk settee, staring down her nose at me. She raised a dark brow but didn't respond. Pride stepped in and closed the door, pulling a pocket watch from his waistcoat and giving me a mocking smile.

"Time's ticking, brother."

I faced the witch. "I need answers."

Her expression was as placid and unmoving as a still lake. If it wasn't for the cunning glint in her eyes, I'd think she was in some sort of magically induced stupor state.

"Are you mute?" I asked, moving closer. "Under a spell?"

Pride exhaled. "She's protesting her captivity."

I narrowed my eyes on her. "So you can speak; you're choosing not to?"

She lifted her hand, suddenly finding her nails worthy of all her attention. A slight twist of her mouth indicated she was having fun. She always did love toying with us Princes of Sin.

No matter. I only needed to read her nonverbal responses.

"Did you curse the ice dragons?"

She glanced up sharply, then went back to studying her nails.

"Time's up." Pride snapped his pocket watch closed. "Get out."

"Thank you for your generous hospitality." I smiled, then turned to Sursea and offered a condescending bow. "And thank you for solving that one mystery for me."

I turned and left the room, relieved to finally close out one theory. The witches weren't behind the attacks. Or, if they were, it hadn't been orchestrated by their leader. Sursea had been surprised and her reaction hadn't been feigned.

Short though it was, it had been a very successful visit, but now it was time to get to the dungeon and test out the venom. The witches were off the playing board for now, but there was still an ice dragon issue that needed to be resolved.

Hopefully I could get Sil to speak more easily than Sursea.

TWENTY
Adriana

SEVERAL HOURS LATER, my sister and stepmother finally returned home.

"Eden and I will be moving into House Gluttony for the duration of the competition," my stepmother announced, giving me a pointed look. Maybe I hadn't hidden my nerves as much as I'd thought. "I expect you'll mind your behavior. Understand?"

I bit my tongue so hard I nearly drew blood. My war with Axton wasn't entirely my fault.

Eden gave her mother a surprised look. "Ad can't stay here alone, Mamma. People will talk."

"Who shall know?" she asked.

"Any columnist who looks into the families of the suitors, for one," Eden said. I blinked back my surprise. Eden normally never contradicted her mother. "It will be better for her to remain by my side. If she stays home and the truth of our connection is revealed, people will say there's a rift and it will cause a bigger scandal than if we get ahead of it."

My brows rose. It was a valid argument, one my stepmother was having trouble disagreeing with. I didn't want to take Sophie's side, but living with the prince while the competition was underway would be...torture.

"You're very kind, Edie, but your mother is correct. I should stay here. My presence will only cause a scene in the castle. Everyone knows how much we dislike each other. And it wouldn't be fair if he took that out on you. Axton needs to focus on the suitors, not feuding with me."

She gave me a pleading look. "Please. I can't imagine not sharing each moment with you. This is the most thrilling event of the century! Please say you'll come. I promise you'll change your mind about him once you see how lovely he can be."

"Edie," my stepmother chided, "stop being dramatic. You only need to worry about the prince right now. Not gossiping with your sister."

My sister's eyes started to glisten with unshed tears, her lower lip trembling. "But what if you're both wrong? What if he thinks we've tricked him and I lose the competition?"

Sophie shot me an annoyed look, as if I'd created that issue.

I felt backed into a corner. I wanted to avoid the competition at all costs, but the investigator in me saw an opening. One I'd be foolish to turn down.

Moving into the castle provided me with a very good excuse to poke around and see what rumors I might unearth without my network. My informants were off the playing board until I could locate them again, which limited my sleuthing.

If I was caught digging into Axton's secrets…my sister would suffer the consequences. But if I didn't discover the truth, the whole realm could suffer instead.

"I'll go with you," I said softly. Hoping if anything went poorly, she'd forgive me. "When are we expected there?"

Sophie looked ready to murder us both. Instead, she lifted her hand, testing to see if her hair was still as perfectly plaited as before. "A carriage will be here first thing tomorrow."

I excused myself to my room under the guise of packing, relieving myself of any more hostile looks from my stepmother or doe-eyed recountings from my sister about Axton's generosity.

It took all of thirty minutes to put my clothing in an old trunk; all the while the key in my pocket practically hummed its insistence.

Despite the chaos of the world, there was one place I was determined to visit before anything else went terribly wrong.

❄ ❄ ❄

If there ever was a much-needed time for an escape, tonight counted as one. After visiting Carlo to don my disguise, and paying him a handful of coins I could ill afford to keep our arrangement from Ryleigh, I stood outside the Seven Sins, heart racing in anticipation.

Snowflakes freckled the hood of my cloak as I stared at the unassuming door.

I had no idea if the key would even work tonight, but desperate times called for desperate measures. I swore my eagerness was strictly due to gathering information for my column and about the dragons. But I knew if any of the Princes of Sin were near, they'd know it was a lie. I wanted to see my masked stranger. I craved his company no matter how hard I tried not to.

With a prayer that someone would be looking out for me, I held it to the door, waiting as a few tense seconds ticked by. Just when I started to draw my hand back, the door disappeared, granting me entry. I expelled a quiet breath and hurried inside, aiming directly for the bar.

"What's your poison?" the masked bartender asked, shaking a violet-colored cocktail, then pouring it into an elaborate glass.

He slid it down the bar, the drink stopping precisely in front of the woman who'd ordered it. It was impressive. Noting the elongated ears poking out from his golden-blond hair, I guessed he'd used a bit of Fae magic. Light court, given the color of his locks.

"What do you suggest?" My voice carried over the excited din of the club.

I glanced around, searching for somewhere to sit. The club was as packed as always, couples already paired on the dance floor and lounging on the sofas.

Since I wasn't certain my masked stranger would even be here and it wasn't yet midnight, I decided to soothe any nerves by taking a cocktail up to the rooftop.

The bartender paused in the preparation of his next drink, looking me over. I wore the dark blue wig again and the "ice queen" costume, as Carlo had dubbed it, but there really was no telling what the glamour allowed the Fae to see.

He didn't hesitate to answer, "Winter ale."

"I've never heard of it."

"We've never stocked it before—and probably won't again. We were owed a favor."

Intrigued, I ordered the ale and took the tankard, sipping the frothy upper layer. It was delicious. Like mulled spices soaked in a light ale, then mixed with warmed brandy. It shouldn't work together, but it was a wondrous match. It felt like I was sipping on a chilled dessert.

Fortified for an evening of either very bad or very good decisions, *if* my stranger arrived, I made my way up to the rooftop garden, taking my time as I passed by rows of night-blooming flowers, their fragrances a feast for the senses.

If my stranger was here, I wondered if I should apologize for not keeping our date, or if I should see how he reacted first.

I still had a burning curiosity about his identity, one I had no business indulging.

I paused once I noticed the figure leaning over the railing. From the back he looked to be the same height and build as my stranger. Still, I wouldn't be certain until he spoke.

I moved on silent steps, my pulse speeding for some reason.

Perhaps it was simply excitement rushing through my veins, anticipation of what was to come, what we'd been leading up to all week. Or maybe I liked him and was nervous our time together was almost over. Which was a foreign concept to me.

"Nervous, Lady F?" he asked when I got close, his focus still fixed on the city.

I moved to his side, letting out a quiet breath of relief. I didn't realize how much I'd been worried that he might not show up tonight.

I'd only known him for a few days, but his companionship was a welcome relief. Especially after the events of the day. Potential dragon attacks. My sister being the suitor. My network going as silent as the dead. My run-in with the prince at the office. Moving into his castle tomorrow...Today might be worse than the All-Sinners Ball.

Instead of letting on that my thoughts had been consumed by the past, I focused on my companion. Tonight, I vowed to be present, to think of the here and now. It was our last time together and nothing would ruin it.

"Not at all. I was admiring the view."

A small smile curved his lips, his head tilting slightly in my direction. "I thought that line was old and tired."

"Luckily, I am not."

Once again, I used his own words from the last time we'd spoken, earning a delighted chuckle from him. I allowed myself a moment to relax and soak in the lighthearted banter.

My stranger turned to me, and for one drawn-out moment, I forgot how to breathe.

He dragged his attention over me, and I swore I felt his hunger turn ravenous through the layers of magic and the mask keeping his true face from me.

For the first time, I wished to see him. To read each flicker in his gaze, to decipher exactly what he was thinking and feeling. To ink it permanently into my memory.

Which was not something I should desire tonight or ever.

He was looking at me so intensely, I wondered if he'd somehow figured out how to see through the magic disguising me.

"You're dangerously beautiful."

"Dangerous in what way?"

"In the way that I can't stop thinking about you."

A pleasant flush came over me. "I can't decide if that's very good or very bad."

He laughed, the sound so rich and dark it was addicting. "Neither can I."

I took a sip of my drink, hoping to cool the warmth spreading through me. I should be trying to figure out who he was, subtly asking if he knew anything about the dragons or the silence of the shadow network. If anyone knew anything about secrets, I imagined he might.

Yet I wanted to hold this moment in my hand, keeping it to myself for a while longer.

"Let's say it was a good thing," I said. "What's got you the most curious?"

He scanned me again and I couldn't help but feel like he was memorizing every detail.

"I wonder why you're here with me."

"Where else should I be?"

"Curled up in bed with someone who adores you, who'd never be foolish enough to let you go. Who'd spend his days discovering details that bring you pleasure."

I felt my cheeks warm pleasantly. "You're quite the flirt."

His mouth twisted into an impish grin.

"I also spend an unfortunate amount of time wondering what you look like, the color of your hair, the shade of your eyes. I want to know who you are, what occupies your days."

He paused, as if waiting to see if I would offer any information up. Clever, clever male.

I gave him a coy smile of my own.

"You'll need to try much harder to wrangle secrets from me."

"Very well, Lady F." His playful grin turned downright sinful. "I must confess, I spend the most time thinking about what it'll feel like to slide that pretty costume off and worship every inch of you. I dream about the silkiness of your skin, the quiver of your thighs. You've got me in a vise-like grip and I'm eager to return the favor."

My heart decided it was a wonderful time to start racing.

I returned his open perusal. His dark-blue suit was cut to his frame as if it had been molded to him—showing off his toned muscles and all the work he'd put into looking like a god. His clothing indicated he had money to spare, though I wasn't sure if he was nobility. Since glamour didn't change clothing, I knew he had to have some wealth.

I wondered what he did for work, assuming it had to be something where his body was a weapon itself. Perhaps a royal guard or member of the hunting guild. Or the owner of a secret club of vice…

I'd felt the power of his body when he'd pressed me against the railing and couldn't stop myself from envisioning exactly how he'd look as I'd peeled each of his layers off.

"If you keep looking at me like that, we'll never make it to a private chamber, Lady F."

I ran my gaze over him again, partly in challenge and partly because I couldn't stop myself. "Maybe I want you to take me right here. Over the railing."

I don't know what possessed me to suggest that.

Maybe I wanted to take him up on his offer from the other night. Or perhaps I was still thinking about what the prince had said earlier, about taking me over his knee.

As much as I hated to admit it, I craved that show of untamed desire.

He paused for a moment before his mouth hitched up on one side.

"You are full of surprises."

He glanced at the street below, where several patrons were spilling out of nearby establishments, their voices loud as they downed more spirits and celebrated, as he seemed to consider my request.

Shouts of Axton's name carried upward, quickly followed by my sister's name. It was startling to hear strangers cheer for her.

Not that I wasn't happy they threw their support behind her. It just brought the very news I'd been running from back to the forefront of my mind. Any levity I'd felt from our flirtation slowly dissipated. No matter where I went, the damned prince was lurking.

"I wasn't sure if you'd come here tonight," my stranger admitted. "With all the celebrations."

I hesitated before responding. He hadn't mentioned anything about me standing him up last night, which made me wonder if that meant he hadn't shown either.

If he wasn't here, then what had kept him from our date? My intuition told me to tread carefully, that some unknown trap might be laid.

Another whoop for the prince went up through the crowd below, saving me from having to answer him directly.

"I think it's actually quite sad," I admitted. "Choosing a potential partner from a name in a bowl."

He snorted. "When you put it that way, it's rather unromantic, isn't it?"

"Lonely, I imagine."

I was startled by the realization. Normally, I couldn't give two cares about the prince and his lack of meaningful relationships. But now that my sister was involved, it bothered me.

"Bloody hell. We're a sad pair of sinners tonight."

I smiled at that. "It's unfortunate, but true."

Our conversation had started off promising, then the crowd ruined it with the reminder that tonight was only a distraction. Tomorrow I'd be moving into House Gluttony with my sister and stepmother and the rest of the suitors.

"Well, then. It looks like there's only one way to salvage our evening," he said, his voice laced with teasing. "If you'll pardon me, Lady F. I shall return in a moment."

He bowed over my hand like a valiant knight, then left me on the rooftop, curious about what his plan was.

A few moments later, he returned, a fur throw clutched beneath one arm and a silver tray laden with desserts balanced on the other. Perhaps he really did own the club. The thought sent a thrill through me, the secrets he'd have access to, the gossip. He might be a very good contact to have indeed. Good for business and pleasure.

I couldn't help but laugh as he made a grand show of laying out the fur, then serving me one of the pale blue petit fours after I'd settled down for our impromptu picnic.

He set the tray filled with the rest of the desserts on the ground near us, then tapped his petit four against mine.

"Cheers to indulging in your sweet company tonight, my lady."

The strangest thing was, he sounded genuinely pleased. As if sitting together on a fur blanket while the world cheered below was everything he'd hoped and more from our evening.

"I would have thought you'd be disappointed," I said. "This *is* a pleasure club."

"Ah. Well, this is all part of my master plan to make you fall wildly in love and share all your secrets with me." His grin made butterflies take flight in my stomach. "It's working, isn't it?"

I smiled down at my next petit four, thankful for the lack of light. "With confidence like that, my new guess is you're definitely from House Pride."

We chatted for a while longer, sharing light, fun conversation without touching on topics that were too difficult.

Finally, once the last little cake was devoured, he brushed his hands off and stood.

"Will I have the pleasure of your company tomorrow?" he asked, helping me to my feet.

I sank my teeth into my lower lip. Tomorrow I'd be living in House Gluttony and sneaking away might be difficult, but I'd find a way. I fought the urge to ask about his access to the keys to this club, not wanting him to change his mind about the invitation.

There would be more opportunities to subtly ask about his life tomorrow.

He'd certainly been digging into mine all night, and I wanted to know if there was a larger reason behind his curiosity.

I thought back to the question for Miss Match, about trusting yourself after previous mistakes. Maybe my stranger was simply inquisitive because he liked me, but I needed to be sure of his motives before I handed over my trust.

Finding out who he was outside this club would go a long way to soothing any remaining fears of admitting to what I actually wanted. There was one secret I couldn't keep hiding from—what started as a fun night of passion was slowly turning into something more. I shouldn't want to keep indulging when there was so much else I needed to focus on. Yet the idea of setting him aside…it made my insides twist. Surely I could find a way to balance it all.

"Only if you promise to bring more dessert."

The slow, wicked smile curving his lips indicated far more interesting things would be on the menu tomorrow.

I suddenly couldn't wait to see what delicious treat he had in store for us next.

My handsome stranger might have ulterior motives for hunting down my identity, but he wasn't the only one willing to break some rules to accomplish his goals.

One way or another, I'd unravel one mystery that haunted me.

He drew my hand up to his lips, brushing a kiss across my knuckles.

"Until tomorrow, my lady."

Maybe it was a trick of the moonlight or the glamour at play, but I could have sworn his eyes suddenly twinkled like he'd won some secret match. I also couldn't help but think his innocent tone had sounded a little like a promise.

Whatever his silent vow was, I couldn't begin to guess.

But I'd be on guard until I knew.

I withdrew my hand and offered him a little wave, pretending I wasn't at all suspicious.

"Sweet dreams."

TWENTY-ONE
Prince Gluttony

For the second time, I watched the mysterious Lady Frost slip into the shadows and forced myself to remain where I was. One thing I'd learned by mastering the art of the hunt was that patience won in the end.

A peculiar mixture of frustration and admiration filled me as she moved down the street, unaware that my attention still lingered on her. In this I at least had the upper hand.

Our mental game was well matched; for every move I made, she kept pace. She was wildly smart, a trait I'd applaud if it wasn't directly impacting my investigation and need to discover who she was. If I didn't need to meet with Val in a few minutes to discuss the competition and the suitors' arrival, I'd take to the skies now.

All my existence I'd been the dragon stalking my prey.

Now I'd encountered another dragon unafraid to circle me. It was alluring stimulation and would certainly make for interesting bedroom sport. That it also fueled my sin was a bonus. I needed all the power sources I could get now that the dragon hunts were off indefinitely.

Sweet dreams. For a second, I'd held my breath, convinced she'd known exactly what I'd done in my dreams the night before. How I'd come to the image of her laid out on my sheets.

I banished the memory before it got me into more trouble and replayed our earlier exchange, thinking of how I'd approach it differently.

My interrogation had been subtle, and she'd not only recognized it right away; she'd called me on it. I'd wanted to pin her arms above her head and punish her pretty lips with a kiss.

I'd need to plot my next move more carefully.

And I needed to get my own hidden desires under control so they didn't interfere. The club's glamour had given her the same pale blue hair she'd had the last time I'd met her.

A taunt or hint that I was on the right track, I wasn't yet sure, but I was closing in.

I felt the thrill building, a steady thrumming in my pulse, urging me to take her down. It was difficult to turn that innate drive off, to not act when I was so close to victory.

When the hunt took over, I became attuned to even the most minor details, cataloguing everything, turning them over with a critical eye.

Lady F's fantasy had given me a solid clue. I didn't for one second think it was a coincidence that she'd wanted me to bend her over the railing. And I didn't think it was entirely due to the fact I'd asked her to brace herself on it the last time we'd met.

One thing I was certain about—if my hunch proved true, I now knew how to keep her close and ensure our interests aligned until the dragons were handled.

When she found out the truth, she'd be livid, of course, but by then it would be too late. There was one other name Adriana sometimes used to describe me, Ruthless Rake.

For once she'd gotten something right; the first part was true. I'd become the most despicable, ruthless bastard in the realm if it meant keeping my demons safe.

As my quarry strode away, I reminded myself it was temporary. The modiste had sent word that she'd have the items delivered first thing in the morning.

By midnight tomorrow, I'd have my answer.

And shortly after that, I'd hopefully have ensnared my rival once and for all.

Dear Miss Match,

I've had bad judgment in the past, but I've just met someone new.
How do I trust myself?
Yours in scandal but hopeful for love,

Distrustful

Dear Distrustful,

I'll admit this is a rather difficult predicament. Learning to trust yourself as you give love a second try is a little like taking a chance on a patisserie that gave you food poisoning.

Do you attempt to sample from that dessert bar again? Or will you fear sweets giving you the runs for the rest of your days and avoid them at all costs?

It may be a silly comparison, but it's done to prove a point. You cannot avoid love because of one experience that left you fevered and queasy. One bad pastry doesn't mean all desserts are rotten.

Just look at Prince Gluttony — if anyone is legendary for making bad romantic decisions that leave his lovers wishing they'd been struck by food poisoning instead, it's our Prince Un-Charming. Yet he's fearlessly charging into uncharted territory with his competition to find a mate — reforming his rakish ways. Or so he claims. If he's not worried about ending up hugging his royal commode, then you shouldn't be either.

Stay scandalous, sweet sinners.

Yours,
Miss Match

TWENTY-TWO
Adriana

OUR RENTED CARRIAGE clattered over the cobbled streets, the coach jostling so hard my teeth clicked together and my backside bounced several inches off the bench seat.

My stepmother sat as primly as a queen, pretending the carriage was as fine as anything, even as her heeled shoe stuck out noticeably from her gown, planted firmly to keep her from catapulting across the coach.

After she'd laid into me for the better part of an hour for comparing the prince to intestinal issues in my latest column, she'd been doing her best to ignore me.

My sister had been more amused, biting her lip to stifle her laughter. At least someone appreciated my hard work. If one looked past the references to troubled orifices and royal commodes, it was sound romantic advice.

Eden fussed with her new gloves, tugging the lace gently at the wrists. "What do you think the competition will be like?"

Her attention shifted to me, her expression torn between hopefulness and worry.

I lifted a shoulder. "I really haven't heard any rumors. I imagine it will be extravagant and excessive, given the prince's sin."

It was the nicest thing I could say and hopefully it would be enough to quiet her unease.

Eden nodded, seeming only partly mollified. "I wonder what the other suitors are like."

Sophie waved her hand dismissively. "Don't expend your energy on them. Focus on how to please the prince."

My attention shifted to the window. The tall fence surrounding the edge of House Gluttony came into view; soon we'd arrive at our destination.

A large shadow passed over our carriage, drawing my attention upward. "Did you see that?"

Sophie and Eden shook their heads.

"What did you see?" Eden asked. "A dragon?"

She sounded far too excited by the prospect of that. As if they weren't meant to be feared.

"Why on earth would you think it was a dragon?" I asked instead, wondering if gossip had spread beyond the shadow network and I'd somehow missed it.

Eden gave me a look that indicated I was rather dull. "Because the prince adores them? It would be quite a thrill to see one flying over his castle as we arrive."

My sister had me there. It would be keeping in line with Gluttony's flare for the dramatic.

I pressed myself against the window, trying to peer up. There was a slight overhang above the window, blocking my view of the sky.

"It was probably just a cloud," Sophie said, rolling her eyes. "You always were too fanciful. Stop finding mysteries that don't exist."

I hadn't been the one to suggest it was an ice dragon. Instead of arguing, I spent the remainder of the ride watching for another sign that something was amiss in the sky, but the shadow never returned. And we'd ground to a sudden halt.

We had arrived at House Gluttony.

"Remember," Sophie said sternly, glancing between me and Eden, "there's a throne at stake. Behave accordingly. *Both* of you."

A footman dressed in House Gluttony's blue-and-silver livery helped us down, then set about retrieving our trunks. The modiste had worked overtime and finished all our new clothes; it was incredible what the prince could achieve when he tossed enough coins someone's way.

Eden and I fell into line behind Sophie as she made her way up the castle's wide stone stairs, head thrown back in a show of high-born arrogance I'd never wish to emulate.

"Good afternoon, Miss Everhart. Mrs. Everhart and Miss—" The butler's eyes widened a fraction. I'd attended events here for years, so we were well acquainted. "Miss Saint Lucent. What a surprise."

If Jarvis wished to ask about my connection to one of the suitors, he was too well trained to do so. His smile never faltered as he ushered us into the foyer.

"Your private chambers are located in the south wing. If you'll follow me this way, I'll take you there now."

My attention swept across the foyer, noting immediately that a table Axton typically stationed there—where guests feasted on one another and engaged in all manner of sinful tableaus—was now gone, replaced by a giant crystal vase filled with flowers.

I'd been distracted by the prim setting and cursed when I noticed my sister and stepmother were already ascending the gilded stairs at the far edge of the chamber.

Not wanting to cause a scene already, I grabbed my skirts and hurried along, hoping to catch up to them without anyone realizing I'd been gone.

What I didn't expect was the door to my right to open so suddenly, or for the prince to come striding out so fast. We collided in the most catastrophic manner.

I bounced off his hard chest, falling backward, and the damned prince tumbled with me, hoisting me up at the last moment so my fall was broken by his body.

I lay there for a second, trying to recall if I'd pissed off any of the old gods in my articles to receive this level of punishment. Alas, it was simply poor luck and terrible timing.

I shoved myself to a sitting position, my palms unintentionally sliding along the defined ridges of his abdomen, and I couldn't help but notice the muscles flexing under my touch.

I wondered if it was possible for the earth to open and swallow me whole. Anything would be better than facing Axton in such an undignified manner. I'd practically petted him.

I went to stand, but his hands shot up and gripped my hips, forcing me to remain where I was.

I glared down at him.

"I beg your pardon, Your Highness. You're causing a scene."

Challenge entered his expression. "I can think of more efficient ways to cause a scandal."

Before I could ask what sort of illicit substance he'd been sniffing, he subtly ground his hips upward, his grip on me unyielding. If he'd been trying to stun me into silence, it worked.

I realized at once what the issue was. He wasn't keeping me there to make a scene; he held me there to avoid one. My mouth snapped shut.

We were in a precarious position for more than one reason, but the only one that concerned me was how my sister would feel if she knew the prince she spoke so highly of was hard as granite beneath me. I knew he couldn't change his rakish ways overnight.

Instead of drawing attention to his *situation*, I held his stare, giving him a silent vow that I'd keep this between us, a temporary truce in our war. But it would cost him.

A tense moment passed before he spoke.

"Why in the seven hells are you here, Miss Saint Lucent?"

I gave him a prim look. "If you'll unhand me, I'll happily tell you."

A dark gleam entered his gaze. "I find you're much more agreeable like this."

By this point, we'd drawn the attention of my stepmother, my sister, the butler, and at least one other courtier who'd been coming down the stairs.

They all stood frozen, as if a spell had been cast and they couldn't move. I understood why. I was straddling the prince in the middle of his foyer, his hands bunched in my skirts.

From their vantage point it probably appeared as if we were in the throes of passion.

But up close, the tightness of his jaw indicated he was furious. He was likely holding on to give his hands something to do aside from strangle me.

As far as entrances went, this was a disaster for my sister. At least the stiffness in his trousers had diminished. Gods only knew what *that* had been about. He certainly didn't harbor any affection for me. Perhaps he'd been locked in an office, stroking himself to his one act of cleverness like I'd imagined weeks before. The thought *almost* made me smile.

"My sister is Eden Everhart. One of your suitors. Now let me up, you heathen."

He released me as if he'd been burned.

I'd just managed to get to my feet, smoothing down my skirts, when his large hand wrapped around my arm.

He flashed a boyish grin at our audience, earning blushes from almost everyone.

"If you'll excuse us for one moment. Jarvis, please see Miss Everhart and her mother to their suite. Miss Saint Lucent will be there shortly."

The prince didn't give anyone an opportunity to respond.

I shot Eden an apologetic look and caught her hiding a grin behind a gloved hand before I was whisked in the opposite direction. In mere seconds Axton had us in his private study, the door slamming shut to drive home that this wasn't to be a pleasant chat.

I kept my jaw locked, unwilling to say a word. It would only make this much worse.

He jerked his chin toward a high-backed chair. "Sit."

"Shall I heel next?"

I clapped a hand over my mouth. But it was too late. I'd unleashed the demon. Axton advanced on me, his expression impossible to read as he raked his gaze over me.

"*Don't* tempt me. I would do unspeakable things for you to obey my every command."

As a Prince of Sin, he had the ability to influence someone's behavior if he wanted to. I'd never known him to use that power, but the intensity flashing in his face made me reconsider how serious he was.

I backed up quickly, dropping into the aforementioned seat.

He followed me down, planting his arms on either side of the chair. He was close enough now for me to see the ring of green in his golden-brown eyes.

I wet my lips, my mouth suddenly bone-dry.

His pupils dilated as he tracked the action, a hunter forever stalking his prey. He leaned in, and for a horrifying moment, I thought he was going to kiss me.

I swallowed thickly, forcing my breathing to remain steady, commanding my pulse not to race.

Axton was too skilled to not read the traitorous signals. His attention swept over me, cataloguing every action, his face inching closer as if he craved a taste of my lips, even knowing the price of that particular indulgence. He moved until his breath mingled with mine.

"What part of *stay clear of me* is difficult to understand, Miss Saint Lucent?"

Whatever madness had fallen over me vanished.

I set my jaw, remembering that he was the bane of my existence. Whatever had happened in that foyer was the result of the tumble temporarily knocking our common sense away.

"I would love nothing more than to do just that." I glared right back at him. "Since you chose my sister, I find my options limited."

"Who put her cursed name into the drawing?"

He'd stoked my ire with that.

I poked him hard in the chest, hiding my wince. I might as well have struck an iron statue. He grinned down at me.

"Do not speak of my family in such a manner."

"I'm trying to sort out if this is some devious plan hatched on your part to infiltrate the castle and spy. I assure you I have nothing but the utmost sympathy for your family."

The devious plan to infiltrate his castle and spy had happened *after* she was chosen. That was exactly the sort of incriminating information he'd love for me to share.

I glanced down, noting his favorite bits were in the perfect location should my knee suddenly jerk upward. Muscles *did* spasm on occasion. I had just cause, surely, to get away with it if mine happened to jolt into him.

He leaned closer, his gaze full of challenge.

"Do it and I promise you'll be over my knee, Miss Saint Lucent. Though that didn't feel like such a deterrent to you yesterday, did it?"

I balled my hands into fists, ignoring that taunt and the ember of heat that sparked low in my belly. "Do not punish my sister for wanting me here to support her."

At the reminder of his hunt to find a wife, he finally straightened, but he didn't step back.

"If you cause any trouble for me, I'll disqualify your sister from the competition. Have I made myself perfectly clear?"

I nodded. "I don't plan on being here much during the day, nor at night if I can help it. I have work to do."

"Good." He stepped back. "The less I see you, the better."

TWENTY-THREE
Prince Gluttony

"WHAT'S WITH *THAT* look?" Val asked, eyes narrowed as she entered the war room tower.

I raised my brows, all innocence. "What look?"

"It's the face you make when you're close to winning a hunt. Or scheming."

I shrugged. "When am I not partaking in either of those wicked delights?"

"Hmm" was all she said before flipping through the new files my scholars had brought. I'd already gone over them—nothing new to help us uncover the underlying cause of the dragons' condition. I glanced at the clock. It was almost dusk. Tonight, if the dragon had come to, I'd give Sil the vampire venom and hope to every wicked sinner in the realm it worked.

Val's mouth pursed as she tossed the files aside.

We'd known each other too long for her to take my response at face value. Before I'd asked her to step into her current role, she'd been one of my best hunters.

She'd grown up in a small village just south of Merciless Reach and its wall and had spent almost all her time as a child in the woods stalking dragons. Val lived for adventure almost as much as I did, but she was much more cunning in her approach.

I hadn't filled my second in yet on my plot to tie Adriana to me. And even though she'd counseled me several times throughout the years to either bind the reporter, banish her, or stop sparring with Adriana Saint Lucent in public, I hesitated to share my plan.

I replayed the glorious run-in with the hellion this morning.

I'd learned several valuable things from our *accident*. My spies reported that Adriana had left her home in a rented carriage, and it was heading toward my House of Sin.

Intrigued, I'd waited in the parlor, watching from the shadows as the conveyance rolled to a stop. All eyes had been on Adriana, tracking her every move, so they hadn't been paying attention to who she'd been traveling with.

Her arrival was an unexpected delight, especially when I saw who'd gotten out of the carriage with her. Sometimes Fate was a cunning bastard. I owed him a drink.

I manufactured a meeting, knowing it would grant me a prime opportunity to take her measure, physically comparing her to my secret paramour from the Seven Sins.

Glamour could create a fine illusion, but some basic truths remained, such as height and size. When she'd run her hands up my body, all quiet temptation and hooded eyes, I'd been distracted from my mission, struck with the memory of my dreams.

Twice now, the female who hated me above all others had been aroused. Her animosity wasn't for show, either. I sensed the emotion on more than one occasion. But that arousal—that was also present. She desired me physically and despised that fact.

If we hadn't had an audience, I would have slowly stroked my hands along her sides, just to see if she'd roll her hips forward, seeking friction against me.

Or if she'd lean close and wrap those pretty hands around my neck instead.

There was one instance where I might permit *that* delicious debauchery, and it involved her—I slammed the image away before it devolved.

The point, I'd gathered, was I could use that attraction to my advantage.

There might be hope of distracting her with my charms yet. Somehow, I doubted it, which was why I'd gotten another idea. I was eager to sort out all the pieces of the competition, give Sil the venom, and get to the Seven Sins. Tonight, I'd be victorious in at least one endeavor.

"You need to be careful," Val said, wrenching me from my silent plotting.

"Regarding?"

"Whatever you're planning with the reporter. I heard about your little collision."

"Accidents do happen, even to us princes."

She shook her head. "You have seven suitors living here now. They're not going to want to share your attention with anyone else, let alone the reporter you hate."

"Any other words of wisdom on how I ought to behave?"

"You don't need the realm turning on you now. If I've noticed how much attention you've been paying her, how distracted you've been, others will too."

The room chilled with my annoyance. I didn't come here to be counseled on my public image or deterred from my plan.

"Your job, dear second, is to ensure the competition goes smoothly. And my job is to play my part during the day and solve our little issue by night. What I plan in between is no one's business. Need I remind you what they say is essential in war strategy?"

She crossed her arms, annoyance radiating from her stance.

"Keep your enemies close, Val. Don't, for one second, think I don't know exactly who Adriana is to me." I narrowed my eyes, my jaw straining from biting back the force of my own aggravation. "That hasn't changed in a decade. Right now I need to keep her where I can see her. And I don't particularly care how it looks. If you notice anyone growing suspicious, I expect you'll see any rumors squashed. Understood?"

"Yes, Your Highness."

"Good."

I scanned the latest report she'd brought from Merciless Reach, my good mood darkening. "Is it true the dragons might be turning on their mates?"

She heaved a sigh. "Hunters reported blood in nests, indicating brawls between mated pairs. Nothing concrete to go on yet, but we're closely monitoring the situation."

I raked a hand through my hair.

Every time I thought the situation couldn't turn bleaker, it did.

Val went to leave, then paused in the doorframe. "Your Highness?"

I glanced over. "What is it?"

"When you omit the truth, your eyes narrow right before your jaw tightens. You might want to address that so no one else picks up on it."

"It's impossible for me to lie. You know that."

She gave me a rueful smile. "Are you certain?"

Before I could demand that she clarify, she turned and exited the chamber, leaving me to wonder about our odd exchange.

I decided the stress of our situation was to blame and headed down to the dungeons.

Silvanus stirred as I entered his cell, the first sign of alertness he'd shown in days.

Hope burned in my chest as I made my way over to where he lay in the straw. He'd nestled down into it, another sign he'd been active or aware enough to move his body.

"Sil?"

His flank lifted on his next breath, working slightly faster at the sound of my voice.

Praise every wicked god there was.

I knelt beside him, withdrawing the vampire venom from my jacket.

I only had an hour or two before I needed to make an appearance at the welcome dinner. Now was the best time to finally see if the dragon could be thralled into speaking.

I didn't waste one moment. I carefully peeled back his lips and shoved the tiny vial into his mouth, holding it shut with both hands as the mighty dragon finally came alert.

Silvanus thrashed against me, nearly knocking me off-balance as he staggered to his knees, then pushed up to his feet. I held on, my feet dangling five feet off the ground, until I saw the column of his throat finally work. He'd swallowed the vial whole.

I leapt backward, giving myself enough room to look directly into his eyes.

They were as red and vacant as the last time I'd seen him awake. I had no time to mourn.

"Silvanus. Tell me if you've had any meetings with witches over the last three moons."

His pupils constricted, his mouth yawning wide. A stream of icy fire spewed around the cell, coating the stone in thick slabs of ice. I dove at the ground, rolling out of the way.

Suddenly, I heard his thoughts.

Chills raced down my spine as I grabbed my dagger.

Kill, kill, kill, kill, kill.

Enemy.

Kill.

"Silvanus. Do you know who you are?"

The ice dragon's shrill war cry was the only response I got.

Kill, kill, kill, kill, kill.

"Silvanus. *Stop.*"

That time, I'd used the power of a Prince of Hell to force compliance.

The dragon's frantic chant ceased.

I leaned closer, ready to hear whatever he said next, my pulse pounding wildly.

With a roar that shook the room, the ice dragon lurched forward and collapsed. I rushed to his side; my own breath lodged in my chest.

I waited another beat. Silvanus didn't stir.

He was out cold again.

I watched as his flank finally lifted with his shallow breaths. He was alive, thank the gods, but I'd used all the venom.

"Silvanus?" I slowly dragged a hand down his icy side. There was no tensing of muscle, no sign of movement to indicate he'd heard me.

I straightened from where I crouched and began pacing. The dragon remained in that unconscious state.

"Fuck!"

I kicked the ice-covered wall, ignoring the pain that lanced up my leg.

I was no closer to knowing what plagued the dragons now than I had been before. I wasn't sure if Sil's worsening condition was due to his injury or if being away from his pack was somehow to blame. He'd never fully recovered after our fight and I wondered if he ever would.

I shoved my hands through my hair, spared one last look at the dragon I'd raised and loved fiercely, then made my way to the cursed welcome dinner, praying to any god that would have me to make it through the night without raising suspicion.

TWENTY-FOUR
Adriana

Sᴏᴘʜɪᴇ ᴡᴀꜱ ꜱᴇᴇᴛʜɪɴɢ by the time I was escorted to our chambers.

"You see?" she cried the second the butler closed the door. "She's a walking scandal! Let's hope the prince overlooks your connection. This couldn't have gone worse."

If anyone knew how aroused he'd been for someone who wasn't in the running to become his wife while his actual suitors arrived at the castle, it might be considered worse.

Alas, I kept that secret to myself. Not to spare him, but to avoid ruining my sister's dreams, even if they included a lifetime with my sworn enemy.

"You're lucky the press hasn't arrived yet." Sophie's tirade continued as she paced. "Imagine how embarrassing that would have been for Eden. Being known as the suitor whose sister plowed down the prince. What were you thinking?"

I perched on the edge of the closest settee, exhausted from the battle of wills.

"I didn't plan to collide with the prince," I said. "It was an accident."

Eden sat beside me. "I know. Was he terribly upset?"

I thought back to the look of shock and horror that had played over his features. That could have simply been due to his physical response to our collision.

"Not too upset. More surprised, I think."

Sophie poured herself a drink from the sideboard in our luxe sitting room. When I first walked in, I'd barely registered any details of our private chambers, and they were exactly what I'd expect from a prince who thought more was more in every sense of the word.

Settees and chaises and tables, silk-covered walls, plush woven rugs. More decorative pillows than I'd ever known existed in one realm, stacked to almost spilling across each seat.

Bookshelves filled with books and baubles, a gilded sideboard stocked with every spirit known to man and beyond. Plus we each had our own bedroom located off the sitting room and our very own bathing chambers, a fact I'd been told by Jarvis on the endless walk up.

I wanted to escape immediately.

"From here on out," Sophie said, "you will avoid the prince at all costs. No attending events, no encounters in hallways. We don't want his hatred for you to impact Eden's chances at winning his hand. It will be a miracle if he doesn't send her home simply because of your unfortunate association. Do I make myself clear?"

"As crystal," I said, glancing at the clock.

Blessedly, right as Sophie opened her mouth, a knock came at our door.

A footman delivered a letter addressed to Eden with the House Gluttony royal seal and exited. My sister read it over, jumping in place as she shared the *wonderful news.*

"Each suitor and their family have been invited to join His Highness tonight; he's hosting a welcome dinner!"

"I'm afraid I'll have to miss it," I said, lifting a hand to my head. "I'm coming down with a migraine."

Sophie gave me a pleased look, but before I could even make it to my private bedroom, a dress box arrived with my name on it. A note accompanied the package.

My teeth ground together so hard I feared I'd break them. It seemed I'd be attending tonight's grand event after all. His Highness *insisted.*

Sophie snatched the note out of my hand, then crumpled it. I swore her eye twitched.

At Eden's curious look, she explained. "Your sister will be joining us. By order of the prince."

My sister squealed, completely overjoyed by the turn of events; Sophie looked murderous. And I wished I'd taken up Nyx's warning and visited nonexistent cousins on the Shifting Isles.

Thankfully my sister didn't seem upset at all by my less-than-graceful entrance, and if she had been, the prince had restored her good mood with his *generous* invitation.

"Well? Go get ready," Sophie snapped. "It seems we'll need to make the best of things."

Through my cracked door I listened as Eden chatted about the new gowns, the lady-in-waiting who'd been assigned to her, and the abundance of jewels at her disposal.

I'd never known my sister to care for the finer things, but she'd also never been granted the opportunity. I'd done my best to take care of us all, but it had barely been enough to keep food on the table. I was happy she had something to feel joyful about.

Even if the source of that joy was Axton.

A flash of our collision had me grinding my teeth again.

Attending a welcome dinner was the last thing I wished to do, but the sooner I got dressed, the sooner I could slip away and meet my stranger at the Seven Sins.

I closed my door securely and glanced at the opulent bedroom.

Silk-covered walls, plush carpets, and gilt-covered furniture took up a large portion of the floor space. There was also a floor-length mirror propped against one wall, and a rolling rack someone had already filled with my clothes.

Piled in a neat stack on a settee were several boxes from the modiste. Earlier I'd only opened one package—the traveling dress I wore now at my stepmother's insistence. Curious about my new wardrobe, I opened the rest of the packages, admiring the skilled work.

The fabrics she'd chosen would all complement my complexion and coloring in ways I'd never experienced before. The designs weren't ostentatious at all, the simplicity hinting at her skill in crafting clothing that would make the wearer the true gem.

I held one dress up in the mirror, admiring how my eyes sparkled from it.

The cloak was perhaps the most stunning piece—the material reminded me of a dragon's hide. It was pure white but had pale blue and silver slivers that curved into scales.

The material was one I'd never encountered before—not quite cashmere but in that family. It was soft but thick and made me want to wrap myself in it at once.

I'd be warm even in the most frigid temperatures, and its softness encouraged one to stroke it. I put it aside and opened the box that had just arrived, dreading what was inside.

As I pulled the sparkling gown from its package, its frothy ice blue skirts cascaded to the floor, the iridescent gemstones sewn across the bottom catching the light.

For a moment, I stopped breathing.

I'd been wrong before. *This* was the most incredible thing I'd ever seen.

It wasn't lost on me that the color was close to my natural hair color and the iridescent gemstones were reminiscent of my "ice queen" costume.

Suspicion worked its way under my skin. Had the prince somehow found out I'd been attending the club of vice and was warning me to keep his secret, or he'd share mine? Or was this simply an ode to the shimmering winterscape we called home?

Maybe I was reading into things too much. It was just a dress.

A sharp knock at the door yanked my attention to the clock. I needed to hurry if I was going to be on time. I opened my door, expecting to see Sophie's furious face, but the person standing outside my bedroom took me by complete surprise.

"What are you doing here?" I asked, hugging my friend.

Ryleigh gave me a bemused look. "Surprising you. And working. The prince invited a select group of columnists to meet the suitors."

An idea slowly filtered in at that. I hid my smile.

Tonight wouldn't be so bad after all. Miss Match would be attending, and I'd make sure to share every salacious detail in my next column.

A familiar male swept in behind Ryleigh, his gaze turning sharp as he took me in.

"I also brought in the cavalry." Ryleigh nodded to her former flame. "I heard you were invited tonight and figured you'd need some help. Make him regret his old mistakes."

I gave my friend a soft smile. I hadn't realized how much I dreaded attending this dinner, having to sit by quietly and watch Axton break someone else's heart. Possibly my sister's.

"Well," Carlo said, sniffing the air. "I see we have much to do and little time to do it. Sit."

He pointed to a small velvet-cushioned stool in front of him.

I did as he requested and within seconds Carlo had unleashed the full might of his talent. Brushes passed over my face a few times, for eyes, cheeks, and lips.

I simply sat back and let him work his magic.

After what felt like only a few moments later, he clucked his tongue. "There. I've performed a miracle. And we've finally gotten to utilize your natural beauty."

He snapped his fingers and an assistant I hadn't noticed gathered up his assortment of makeup and brushes and they swept from the room as quickly as they'd entered.

I couldn't tell if I was impressed or terrified.

"Carlo is certainly a force of nature," I said, gently touching my hair. "How do I look?"

I went to look in the mirror, but my friend shook her head.

"Not yet. Look after you're dressed." Ryleigh gave me an appreciative once-over, then held the gown up. "I can't imagine what something like this costs."

"Probably best to not be too curious about it."

Ryleigh raised her brows but didn't comment. An awkward moment passed between us. Probably the first in our whole friendship. I wasn't sure where the tension was stemming from but knew Ryleigh had to feel it too.

It was possible even though I'd paid for his silence that Carlo told her I'd been visiting him before attending the Seven Sins. Maybe she was wondering why I hadn't shared that with her and was hurt I hadn't extended an invitation for her to join me.

Guilt gnawed at me again, yet I still couldn't bring myself to talk about my stranger, especially not now.

"Is the prince providing everyone's wardrobe for tonight?" she asked, her tone indecipherable.

"I believe just for Eden and us by default. He wants his suitor to reflect his sin. You know how much Axton enjoys showing off. I'm sure this pales in comparison to Eden's gown."

Ryleigh stared at the dress for another moment, fingering the jewels. "If you say so."

The sleeves were made of dozens of strands of diamonds, artfully hanging at different intervals, reminding me of jeweled wings. The bodice was understated by comparison—the same frothy material as the skirts gathered just off the shoulders and formed a matching V in the front and back, not too scandalously low, but tasteful and tempting.

It had to be worth tens of thousands of coins. More than my annual salary at the *Wicked Daily* by far. I hoped I didn't accidentally spill something on it at dinner.

I was already on edge without worrying about the expensive gown getting damaged. I couldn't help but think of the money being better spent in the community.

Standing there, bedecked in jewels, I feared I'd seem as frivolous as the nobles who'd taunted me all those years before. I had no idea how I would hold my tongue around Axton for the next several hours without ruining my sister's chance at happiness.

A maid entered the chamber next and helped me step into the gown, and after a few moments of primping and adjusting the straps, I looked myself over in the mirror. My lips were a little fuller, my lashes a bit longer. All my features were subtly enhanced by Carlo's talent.

Ryleigh let out a low whistle. "Gorgeous. He's going to regret not making you his, Ad."

"That was ten years ago and I'm sure he's as relieved as I am it didn't work."

But I *was* feeling better about having to attend tonight's opening event.

Axton might be getting ready to indulge his sin and court seven women, but I wouldn't look like some wilting wallflower he'd left on the shelf. I hardly recognized myself.

My hair fell in long, loose waves that tumbled down my back, brushing against my exposed shoulder blades each time I moved. A small headband encrusted with diamonds pulled the top part of my hair back, showing off my slender neck.

I looked like a Fae princess.

My palms suddenly dampened. "It's a bit much for dinner, isn't it?"

"Not at all. I totally get why Axton chose this for you."

"He chose it for Eden's image," I reminded her. "He's hoping to make her look like a cosseted princess and her family worthy of a royal title if she wins."

"Say what you want, but that gown was designed for you, Adriana. Everything about it is you—the color, the way it looks like your Seven Sins costume."

A bolt of ice flew through my veins, ruining the moment.

"Coincidence, I'm sure."

Ryleigh's gaze ran up and down the dress.

"Actually, not the Seven Sins costume. He made you look like a blade. Beautiful, but lethal. People will certainly be talking."

Before I could feign a fever and stay hidden up here until it was time to sneak away to the Seven Sins, Ryleigh spun me toward the door.

A bead of trepidation rolled down my spine as I looked myself over once more.

If Axton wanted to make me into a weapon, he must be anticipating a battle. But the question remained: was the war between us or was some new skirmish about to begin?

"Ready to face the gossips?" Ryleigh asked with a wry smile.

We were normally the gossips.

I took a deep breath and nodded. "We'll find out."

Dinner wasn't supposed to be anything extravagant. Just a simple meal for the seven suitors and their families before the upcoming week's festivities.

Axton wouldn't know subtle if it gently tapped him on the shoulder and whispered in his ear. Or, preferably, punched him in the loins.

As we waited outside the royal dining hall in awkward clusters comprised of families, suitors, and a handful of reporters, performers served appetizers that were more circus act than fine dining. Which, I supposed, was aptly done considering the ridiculous bridal competition we were being subjected to.

I subtly glanced around the room, pleased I recognized each suitor. Years of reporting on gossip had finally paid off.

Erudite Monroe from House Sloth nestled into a corner, her nose pressed into a book.

Ava Rice and Omen Seagrave, of House Greed and House Envy, respectively, were on opposite ends of the room, staring daggers at each other. Which wasn't surprising since rumors suggested their fathers were at war after a bad gambling debt was called in.

Allure Whitlock of House Lust held court with almost every reporter, save for Ryleigh. And the House Wrath suitor, Cobra Pierce, was born into a legendary line of fighters. No proof ever came to light, but there were whispers about her previous lover dying mysteriously on a hunting trip hosted by her father. I made a mental note to not get on her bad side.

Ryleigh stood across the room, chatting with the House Pride suitor, Miss Vanity Raven. She exuded her sin of choice in all ways—from her haughty expression to her shimmering pale locks, Vanity didn't suffer from lack of confidence in any capacity.

If I were to size up the competition, I had to admit, she'd probably be one to watch.

The prince himself had failed to make his grand appearance, and I supposed it would be entertaining to see how he'd make an entrance without a lover tucked under each arm.

Conversations hushed as the predinner show took an interesting turn.

One performer held skewers of marinated meat in the air like swords; a second spit flames, torching them all to a perfect medium rare. Another spun plates on a long stick, then tossed them, one plate at a time, to the young women gathered around.

Sophie's eyes gleamed with triumph as Eden snatched her plate from the air with grace.

I prayed my plate would knock me out cold for the remainder of the dinner.

Alas, I caught my dish like a proud seal at one of Axton's old themed parties and fought the strange urge to curtsy at the polite smattering of applause.

Once everyone had been served their skewers, the delighted suitors all cheered as the performers bowed.

I took a bite of meat, hating that it might be the best thing I'd ever eaten. It was cut so thin it practically melted in my mouth, and the flames added a wonderful charred flavor that complemented the sticky sweet and spicy marinade.

Before I could take another bite, another performer came around, holding a balloon above my plate. He pointed to a bracelet that looked like a pin cushion because it was one.

"Take a needle and pop the balloon over your dish, miss."

Brow knitted, I did as he suggested.

The balloon burst and hot red pepper slices and chopped cilantro rained down across the skewer, adding a bright pop of color to the dish. It was a feast for the eyes and the mouth.

The performer beamed and went to the next group, another balloon in hand.

I silently cursed Axton. This over-the-top show wasn't simply to dazzle; it elevated the taste of the food. If he was hoping to impress his potential brides, he'd damnably succeeded.

Each reporter frantically scribbled notes with their quills, no doubt ready to sing his praises across the gossip columns tomorrow morning.

I swiped a glass of demonberry wine from a passing tray, waving off an offer to probably have it torched or infused with the tears of my enemies.

"Suitors. Families," Jarvis intoned. "Dinner will be served shortly. If you wouldn't mind, please head this way. We'll call you in soon. Reporters, this is where we bid you good evening."

Ryleigh gave me a finger wave and left with the other reporters from around the realm. I watched her depart and wished she could have snuck me out under her skirt.

Alas, I held my head high as we moved like good little cattle toward the dining hall doors, corralling ourselves for the short wait to be seated. Within moments, the first group was called. Erudite Monroe finally closed her book and went into the dining room without a backward glance. Eden shot me an apologetic look as she and Sophie were escorted in next.

Cobra and Allure were called in, followed by the two sparring families from Houses Greed and Envy, leaving just me and the House Pride suitor.

Vanity stared at me from where she already waited outside the royal dining hall, her gown made entirely of diamonds. Her expression was otherwise blank, but I didn't miss the cold sweep of her attention as it passed over me. I waited, breath held, for the cutting remark to follow. My gown was ridiculous for someone who wasn't in the competition.

She flicked her attention away just as quickly, dismissing me.

I slowly exhaled. I couldn't do a thing about anyone's private thoughts, but at least she hadn't mocked me for a dress I hadn't even chosen. I'd heard Vanity was nice enough, but my own history made me fear the worst when it came to anyone so privileged.

Perhaps I was overly sensitive, but once upon a time I had been viciously scorned for the crime of wanting to fall in love. I'd been reminded that I was no one—no title, no wealth, no powerful connections. Just a commoner who was so clearly attempting to rise above my station.

And here I was, in a gown that cost more than several years of my salary, feeling that same insecurity from a decade ago creep in.

"Miss Raven, Miss Saint Lucent." A footman greeted us. "If you'll follow me."

I held my head high as I followed him to my chair.

Blasted Axton was already seated at the head of a large horseshoe-shaped table. I quickly averted my gaze once I caught Sophie's disapproving scowl from the seats to his right.

The dining chamber had been turned into an enchanting forest, complete with real frostberry trees in giant urns, their branches lit with glittering Fae orbs, and wintery flower garlands running down the center of the giant table.

I froze mid-step. It wasn't a forest. It was an interpretation of the Seven Sins rooftop garden. I gave myself a mental shake and hurried along to my seat. I was imagining things.

Blessedly, the prince didn't seem to notice my steps falter.

In fact, he hadn't seemed to notice my arrival at all. He laughed heartily at something my sister said and I tamped down any unease. Other guests didn't suffer from Axton's oblivion. They watched me like I was about to burst into song and dance and entertain them all.

I sat beside my stepmother and took a sip of my wine, ignoring the lingering stares the best I could. Finally, after I nearly finished my wine, Axton disengaged from his riveting conversation and stood.

"Thank you for the honor of your company this evening." I felt his attention finally land on me and refused to glance up. "My decision will not be an easy one, but I promise to give each of you an equally fair chance at seeing if we are a match. Now please enjoy your meal. I'll speak with everyone privately soon. Including ten minutes to chat with family members."

Absolutely wonderful. The night just got even more thrilling. I prayed for me and Sophie to be called soon so I could leave this nightmare shortly after.

"How long will we, the suitors, have with Your Highness? Enough time to promenade through the garden?" Allure asked with a definite purr in her tone. Sophie's face darkened as she shot the prince a subtle look to see how he'd respond. House Lust was clearly her biggest threat.

Axton's expression remained rather neutral. "Tonight is only about conversation, Miss Whitlock. I'll try to keep it around ten minutes for everyone."

I almost snorted but somehow managed to keep myself under control.

My nerves got the better of me, so I called for another drink. I sipped my demonberry wine, watching the silver demonberries twinkle like little stars in the liquid.

Time seemed to pass in excruciatingly slow increments, the passage being counted by each course that was brought out. Before the final course was served, Axton excused himself and requested that Eden join him outside. Sophie all but beamed as they left arm in arm.

I wished to sink below the table and disappear.

As the hour dragged on, I requested another glass of wine, followed by another, wishing winter ale was also on the cocktail menu.

I couldn't recall the last time I'd indulged in more than one or two glasses of wine and blamed the idle hours and sheer boredom for throwing caution to the wind and downing a fourth. It had been two hours since dinner began, so it wasn't as if I was a drunken fool.

But I did have a *much* better time while I waited. And a lot of the lingering fear about having to speak to the rake slowly melted away.

Finally, after what felt like an eternity, Val motioned for me to follow her outside. "You're next."

Sophie stiffened beside me—she hadn't been summoned. And, for once, I wished for her company.

"What about my stepmother?"

Val's smile was brittle. "He wishes to speak with you alone."

"Why?"

"I suppose you'll find that out once you talk to him."

I glanced from Sophie's tight smile to the clock. It was growing late. "Do you know how long this will take?"

Val ignored me in favor of hurrying me through the dining hall and outside.

The prince wasn't on the veranda as I'd thought. I followed Val down the stone stairs and into SilverFrost Garden, the prince's private pleasure gardens, my head buzzing pleasantly.

Perhaps I should have left that last glass of wine untouched.

I silently chanted to remember to behave for Eden's sake. That I wanted to mitigate damage with the prince, not throttle him. That the sooner I spoke to him, the sooner I could sneak off to the club and lose myself in my stranger's embrace.

"He's straight ahead." Val paused at the end of the path, nodding for me to continue by myself.

On a beautifully carved bench at the end of the path, half hidden by swaying willow trees, the prince lounged. My attention swept over him, noting the dishevelment.

His collar was unbuttoned, his hair mussed. I couldn't tell if he was tired or if the suitors had ravaged him. Given his reputation, I'd wager the latter was true.

Annoyance rose in a wave. He couldn't seem to help himself, and I'd had enough. My little sister's heart was on the line, and I wouldn't allow him to shatter it like he'd done to mine.

"Axton."

"Adriana."

I joined him on the bench, doing my best to sit as far away as I could. Which wasn't far, given it was meant to seat two people. It also didn't help that his legs were spread comfortably as he leaned back like the royal pain in the ass he was.

I felt his attention on me but didn't take the bait. By my estimation, I only had to suffer through nine more minutes with the rogue.

"You're upset."

"You're much more astute than I give you credit for, Axton."

His leg brushed against mine as he shifted closer.

"Care to enlighten me why?"

The wine must have loosened my tongue more than it already was.

I faced him, wanting to see his reaction. "You said tonight was only about conversation. And judging by the state of your hair, I'd say that isn't true."

He was silent for a minute as he held my stare.

"Are you jealous?"

"Don't flatter yourself. I'm just tired of being correct when it comes to you. My sister deserves someone who will guard her heart, not destroy it carelessly. Not only can't you keep your word, but this gown is also ridiculous."

I wasn't sure why I blurted that last part out. But I'd been sitting in the damned dining hall for hours while he'd been entertaining his suitors, and I wanted no part in this.

I had much more important things to do with my time than wait around for him to ravish everyone. It was closing in on midnight, and if he prevented me from visiting Carlo to don my disguise before meeting my stranger, I would commit regicide.

"Hmm." Axton leaned closer. "I thought the gown was rather lovely on you."

If he thought flirting was going to soothe me, he was sorely mistaken.

"Have you ever even considered what this much wealth could do for your citizens?"

His brow quirked up. "Tell me what you'd do differently."

"With the money you spent on it, you could have fed an entire neighborhood. Done some true good in our circle. I would have donated it, spreading the abundance around. Instead, you feed your desires. Constantly. You can't even make it two hours without being a rake. I don't know if it's your appetites you need to sate or the need to indulge others."

"And?"

"And I'm wondering how on earth your reputation is so wonderful. The gown was clearly a clever plot to have your suitors mock me. I don't belong in this dress, and you know it."

He was quiet for a moment.

"You have very strong opinions of me. Yet you've never actually asked what my motivations are."

I laced my hands in my lap. "It's obvious."

"It is, is it?" He made a derisive noise, shaking his head. "Allow me to give you another perspective. Outwardly, yes, it seems obscenely extravagant, but this gown? It provided work for many members of my circle. Members who have previously refused any donations."

I sat straighter, eyes narrowed. He looked entirely sincere. "I'm listening."

He ticked them off, one by one.

"The jeweler, the dressmaker, the cobbler, and even the several bolts of fabric the dressmaker had purchased. Each of those establishments was given business, enough to hire more employees who'd needed work too. To you, what you're wearing is wasteful, and I understand why you'd think that."

He gently plucked at the strands of diamonds, letting them fall through his fingers. He was careful to avoid touching my skin.

"You see indulgence. What I see are the families who have earned income, doing what *they* love. The dressmaker hired two assistants who needed work; not only do they have employment now, but she can take on more clients. The jeweler's family also made more off that one sale, for this one gown, than they do all year. If that means I've helped ease their burden, even by a fraction, then I can live with your opinion of me being less than flattering."

The slight buzz from the wine burned away. I searched his face, looking for any hint of deception. He kept his attention on me, his expression earnest. I was at a complete loss.

"Your Highness, I…" I wasn't sure what to say.

He held my stare.

"Members of my circle have repeatedly asked for help with their businesses. The parties I throw, the gowns, the food; *everything* serves a singular purpose: to aid my circle. They may refuse my donations, but they welcome my business. So I give it to them as often as I can."

"To feed your power."

"To care for my court. A weak prince is a danger to his people."

Axton stood, offering me his hand. Our time together had ended.

I stared at it for a long moment before finally accepting his help up. What he'd said...it sounded like he'd meant it. And that was a problem.

It shifted my thoughts, throwing me dangerously off-kilter.

I'd never considered the shoppe owners and businesses, how they felt about the prince.

The extra staff he'd hired, the chefs. Even the performers tonight; everyone had likely been paid handsomely.

Father used to warn me that our intentions shaped how we viewed the world. If I looked for the negative, I'd always find it. And if I saw the positive, I'd find it in spades.

My feelings had clouded my view. I saw overindulgence because I *wanted* to.

But, in truth, Axton provided income to countless people, something he seemed passionate about and not duty bound to do.

I was starting to understand why the realm liked him so much. Grudgingly, I had to admit he would make a fine match for my sister. If only the thought didn't cause my stomach to ache.

Hopefully that was simply the wine festering.

He gave my hand a gentle squeeze, then let go as he stepped back.

"When you take the gown off tonight, I hope you at least acknowledge the good it's done. You are free to donate it and do what you like with the coin."

He started to walk away, then stopped.

His hands curled into fists, and after another long pause, he finally turned back to me.

"Just to be clear, I didn't so much as kiss any of the suitors tonight. I was too busy thinking of how distractingly beautiful you are in that gods-forsaken dress to indulge anyone else's desires."

The confession looked like it cost him dearly.

While I struggled to come up with a response through the maelstrom of emotions cycling through me, he offered a slight bow, then left.

TWENTY-FIVE
Prince Gluttony

A TWIG SNAPPED ON the garden path a few paces behind me. I whirled, dagger drawn, and squinted into the shadows. I expelled a breath.

"Mrs. Everhart."

I'd been distracted by my conversation with Miss Saint Lucent and hadn't been paying attention to the slight prickle of awareness that indicated I was being watched.

"Your Highness."

Eden's mother tucked a long quill into her coiffed hair, adopting a look of innocence that was as believable as a viper claiming it wasn't venomous as she stepped out from behind the silverfrost bush and onto the path.

"I was just admiring the gardens. I've never seen so many silverfrost flowers in bloom. They're as lovely as I've read about in the scandal sheets."

She hadn't lied, but there was an air of falseness that rang in her statement. I glanced down at her hands. Ink smudged her fingertips.

How very curious. From my first impressions of her, I wouldn't have taken her for someone who'd ever design to dirty her hands. Unless it somehow served a greater purpose for her—like securing a royal match for her daughter using any means necessary.

My instincts went on high alert.

It seemed there truly was a snake in our midst.

"You appear to have taken a turn and lost your way." I held out my arm in a show of princely charm and manners. Though nothing disguised the edge in my tone. "Shall I escort you back to the dining hall?"

Her gaze lingered on where I'd left Adriana.

Something about her hesitation slowly raised my hackles.

With a pinched look that made her appear slightly constipated, Mrs. Everhart took my proffered arm. She couldn't be more different from Eden or Adriana if she tried.

"How exceptionally kind of Your Highness to offer to escort me. I needed some air and wandered a bit too far, it seems."

A dark suspicion rose as I glanced back at the ink on her hands. Adriana had accused me and my court of feeding information to her editor, but for once that wasn't true.

There were two other witnesses in her home who had details of the items I'd given her.

Eden. And Sophie Everhart.

All at once, I understood. Sophie had been spying on her stepdaughter, hoping to sell more information to the gossip sheets. How utterly ruthless. I imagined inside gossip fetched a handsome amount of coin.

Silence stretched between us, one I purposefully refused to fill. I found the guilty often prattled on, hoping to distract from their wicked behavior. Soon enough, Sophie broke.

"Did you have trouble with my eldest, Your Highness?" she asked. "Adriana is not blood related, thank the gods for that. She's entirely too high-strung and opinionated to be an Everhart."

I kept my pace slow, my muscles loose. Inside, annoyance ignited in a blaze, and I didn't bother to stomp it out.

"Disowning someone based on the notion of blood and speaking about it so freely to a stranger is a sin I find far more appalling than a woman who speaks her mind."

Sophie's mouth snapped shut so loudly, I heard the clack of her teeth.

I hid my smile, not quite finished.

"In fact, I find it rather odious and boring when former nobles think of themselves too highly. It reeks of pride, and as you're aware, that isn't my sin."

We made our way to the terrace stairs, and I paused at the bottom, finally dropping my arm. Sophie's jaw was so strained from biting her tongue, it gave me a delightful burst of elation.

The only one permitted to needle Adriana was *me*.

"Thank you, Your Highness. Good—"

"One last bit of advice, Mrs. Everhart." This time I didn't mask my expression. I allowed every bit of the demon to shine through as I held her stare. "It would be unwise for you to sell any more information about me or your daughter to the press again. I would hate to disqualify Eden because you've been running interference. Do I make myself perfectly clear?"

She swallowed hard, then gave me a deep curtsy.

"Yes, Your Highness."

"Wonderful. Good night."

I watched her slink up the grand staircase, then disappear into the dining hall. Hopefully it would be the last time I'd need to deal with the woman.

One issue settled, I turned on my heel, heading back down the path and out of the garden.

Anticipation thickened the space around me.

It was nearing midnight and the charge that had been steadily building all day was coming to a head. I could have taken the easy route and sent my spies after Adriana, but that wouldn't be quite as exciting and it wouldn't feed my sin.

Instead, I'd called them off, wanting to indulge in the thrill as the hunt came to an end.

In less than an hour I would solve one mystery and the suspense was growing delightfully unbearable; it was the sweetest sort of torture and I allowed myself to fully indulge. I couldn't tell if I was more excited by the prospect of being right about Lady F's identity, or if I was simply looking forward to seeing the woman who'd made me *feel* so deeply again.

I wound my way through the garden, getting as far as the evergreen wall that signaled the edge of it, then glanced around. All was quiet, except for the pounding of my pulse. And that wouldn't be calming down anytime soon.

When the clock struck the witching hour, I would finally know if Lady F and my rival were one and the same. Tonight, one way or another, my hunt would end.

It was time to discover if the gods were indeed merciful to sinners like me.

An ember of hope sparked deep in my chest, growing stronger with each moment that passed. I didn't think I would be able to put out the fire even if I wanted to.

I glanced around the empty garden again, then pulled out a pocket watch. I scowled down at the time piece. The second hands must be cursed by witches to move excruciatingly slow.

I shut the damned thing and tossed it into the nearest frostberry bush. I would be early but couldn't bring myself to wait around anymore.

I unfurled my wings and shot into the night, aiming directly for the Seven Sins and what felt like standing on the precipice of realm-shattering change.

TWENTY-SIX
Adriana

THE MOMENT I stepped onto the roof, I saw him.

If I listened closely, I swore I heard a choir of angels singing on high, though that thought might strike me down since I had a most unholy plan for this evening.

After dashing over to Carlo's to change into my Lady Frost costume, I'd stopped at the bar to acquire another winter ale, grateful for the excuse to sip it and allow myself a moment to drink my secret lover in.

A pleasant chill worked along my body as I admired my stranger. He was straight out of a fantasy, tall, dark, mysterious...And tonight, he would be mine.

No more hesitations. No more distractions.

I wanted him to stamp any unpleasant thought from my mind; I wanted him to take my mouth in a searing kiss, then turn my body inside out. I wanted to forget Axton's earnest conversation earlier, his confusing motivations for overindulging. The fact that he'd called me lovely and seemed to hate that it was true. He was my enemy.

Perhaps not in the sword-and-dagger sense, but in the *he'd villainously broken my heart and now I'd made it my life's mission to destroy him back in the press* sort of way.

My feelings for Axton this past decade had been simple—iced over, frosty—now they were beginning to thaw and I wasn't sure what to do with that unwanted puddle of emotion.

Between the prince and my stranger, my life had spiraled into chaos.

I needed to wrangle it back, focus on work, on the ice dragons, on anything but romance. At least in my personal life.

Tonight, I'd indulge my physical desire then walk away from my stranger and this club for good. Tomorrow, I would remind myself of all the ways I hated the prince, and I'd fill my days with writing my column and forgetting my stranger and that this secret romance ever existed.

"I see the crowd of admirers are back," I said. "I'm willing to ignore them if you are."

"I got the impression that you might enjoy an audience, Lady F."

He slowly pivoted to face me, and I swore his breathing all but stopped as he took me in, his attention lingering on my frame for a beat too long.

He recovered swiftly, his mouth twisting up on one side. "Or is it the thrill of potentially being caught that you crave?"

Well, then. We were both clearly eager to jump straight into things.

I took my lower lip between my teeth. I'd never been with a lover in a public setting before, but the desire to do so burned through me. In my own bedchamber, when I touched myself, I'd picture being caught and the mere fantasy drove me over the edge.

"Tell me." He was certainly intrigued. Maybe it was a fantasy we shared.

It wasn't necessarily the idea of being watched that turned me on.

"It's the fear of being caught," I admitted.

He motioned for me to elaborate.

I took a sip of my spiced lager, trying to settle my nerves and consider my thoughts.

"I'm not sure what else to say. The idea of someone witnessing such a private act and being so lost to the moment I couldn't care less if they watched *is* the fantasy. I like the thrill of it all, the danger."

"You want others to feast on the show." His voice was low and seductive. "To indulge and overindulge your desires is part of this circle."

I'd never spoken my fantasies out loud before and I wasn't sure if it was the comfort I felt with the stranger because he made me feel free, or if it was simply the fact that we didn't know each other that made the confession easy.

Still, I felt entirely too vulnerable, sharing so much without learning anything in return.

I took another large sip of my drink.

"It's just a fantasy. I'm not certain I'd ever actually do it. I think it's the danger, the anticipation of possibly being caught, more than someone watching that's enticing. What are your secret desires?"

"To make your fantasies come true."

I shook my head, unable to stop the grin from spreading across my features. He was a shameless flirt. And a liar. At least that put one lingering fear to rest—there was no way he was the prince. They were incapable of lying.

"We are newly acquainted. What were your secret desires before we met?"

His attention returned to the twinkling city as he considered. I wondered if anyone had ever asked him that before, or if he simply didn't wish to share anything personal.

Snow started falling heavily, though the flakes didn't touch us where we stood. The roof of the Seven Sins was warded by magic that prevented the elements from disturbing its guests.

"You want brutal honesty?" he asked.

"Yes. I'd like to know what you're interested in."

He was silent for another moment as if debating his response.

"I want to strip you down, bend you backward over the railing, and eat your pussy until you come all over my face."

I'd been in the midst of taking another sip of my winter ale and nearly choked.

He flashed a knowing look my way.

"What I desire is to have you shouting so loud that every last guest races to this roof, watching as I hook your legs over my shoulders and feast. I want them to know they'll never make you come like I will. That your body is mine to pleasure and mine alone."

He grinned over at me. I must have flushed from head to toe.

"I want your fingers in my hair as you ride my face, lost in ecstasy.

Once you've begged for mercy, and once I'm certain you can't take another moment of pleasure, I want you on your knees, choking on my cock as I ruthlessly fuck it."

I could barely catch my breath after that striking description.

Even with a drink in hand, my mouth had gone dry.

Gods' blood, the male had *quite* the sinful imagination. And wasn't afraid to share it.

He waited for my response, head cocked to one side. From what I could make out of his expression, he was amused, thinking he'd stunned me or perhaps scared me away.

"That was..."

"Graphic? Explicit? Shocking?"

"Well thought out, actually."

He laughed, the sound deliciously dark and tempting, just like his desires had been. "Most don't have that reaction, Lady F."

"You must be courted by fools," I said, once again using his own words from our previous encounters. "Any male who takes the time to think about his fantasies in such vivid detail and expresses them with confidence is intriguing."

"How so?"

"If you're putting that much thought into servicing your partner, it means you're not a selfish lover. You care about giving pleasure as much as receiving it, if not more so."

"You could tell all that by my desire to bend you over the railing?"

"Of course. Your fantasy starts off with pleasing someone else. Only after they've been sated—enough times to beg for mercy—then you crave your own release."

"And that appeals to you?"

"Your mind does, yes."

"If you're thinking of my mind when I'm describing my fantasy, I'm not doing a good job seducing you."

"I disagree. Your imagination is colorful, indicating you wouldn't be a boring lover. And your mouth is downright filthy. Which, under the right circumstances, can be extremely arousing."

I had his entire attention. "What else intrigued you? The physical intimacy?"

"No, not just that. Adding an element of danger—like bending your lover over a railing—while you pleasure them heightens the emotions and physical experience of the act for them. It's all incredibly well thought out."

"I've put a shameful amount of thought into it for far longer than I'd ever admit."

It sounded like an honest confession, but we hadn't known each other for long so he must have meant his fantasy in general.

He leaned against the railing, arms crossed as he looked me over. He'd been attempting to shock me, and it seemed like I'd succeeded in doing that to him instead.

He sighed.

"We're going to have a problem, Lady F."

"Regarding?"

"You want a night of distraction," he said. "And that's perfectly acceptable."

"Except..."

"I already know I am not going to be satisfied with one night."

I sensed there was more he wanted to say, so I chose my own response carefully. "Tonight is the only night I have available for a while. I can't keep coming to the club."

"Neither can I. So you agree we have a dilemma."

A trap was being set, but try as I might, I couldn't quite figure out his plan.

I pressed my lips together, considering more angles.

He couldn't *possibly* be suggesting what I thought.

"I suppose we only have a dilemma if you're unhappy with our time being limited to this one night."

"Perhaps it's my sin to seek overindulgence, but I do take issue with limitations. You seem to have a very practical mind, Lady F. How do you suggest we solve our little problem?"

"We could simply agree it's for the best if we parted ways now."

Even as the words left my mouth, I hated the thought of him agreeing. Whenever someone said "it's probably for the best" it usually meant someone was about to get hurt. When I'd gotten dressed for the Seven Sins tonight, I hadn't planned on wearing emotional armor.

"Or," he said slowly, "we might choose to leave the masks and secrets behind. We can make our own private arrangement away from the club."

I swallowed hard, then glanced out at the city. The snow continued to fall, the storm almost obliterating House Gluttony from view.

I wasn't sure how we'd gotten here.

We were supposed to be two strangers who gave in to our desires for one night of debauchery and fun, no strings attached, no emotions.

No potential heartbreak. Just a simple flirtation.

And yet, tonight hadn't I wanted to unmask him before walking away for good? I'd gotten addicted to our encounters when they should have only been a small taste of fun.

After my one attempt at love, I didn't court anyone. And not simply because I didn't have time to. Though I supposed I'd have more time now that I lived in the castle and didn't have to worry about working *and* tending to our home. At least for the next several weeks.

Which should be more than enough time to indulge in a little romance.

I didn't outright deny his request, so he pressed on.

"In fact, if we don't need to rely on the club or earning magic keys, we could do whatever we liked, whenever we felt the desire or need."

I narrowed my eyes. "You haven't had any issues with finding keys before."

"Luck. And favors."

I was sure there was more to it than that, but he was purposefully dodging the question. I changed tack.

"What exactly are you proposing?" I asked.

At this he finally hesitated. His fingers tapped a quick beat along the railing. "A mutually beneficial bargain. One we both honor until we're sated."

"The terms?"

"We court secretly unless we'd like to go public. If it ever comes to light, we agree to never reveal the truth of where or how we met, then part ways without any expectations of this lasting beyond a few weeks. We indulge in our fantasies, see each other as often or as little as we like during that time. But we agree to keep our relationship private."

I thought about Axton entertaining his suitors for the next several weeks. It would be nice to have someone to distract me at night after I'd hunted down any clues in the castle.

If we both agreed that it was a temporary bargain, that should mitigate any unwanted feelings. Though, truth be told, we weren't doing so well with not becoming interested in each other now. That could just be because we hadn't had our fill of each other yet. Surely once we'd indulged as he'd said, we'd feel differently. I hadn't met anyone I'd wish to seriously court.

This was a passing fancy, one that was intriguing because of the secrecy, the mutual attraction and mystery, the thrill of the unknown.

Right now, we were deep into the stages of pretend. We could make up stories and backstories for each other without the weight of reality ruining our fantasy.

In my mind, he was a fierce royal hunter, a ruthless fighter, an owner of an infamous nightclub, and an indulgent lover. When in truth his everyday life might be as mundane as mine.

"Let's agree to six weeks," I said.

No reports had been published about the length of the competition, but that should hopefully cover most of it so I wouldn't be alone. If I only saw my stranger at night, I wouldn't tire of him. Hopefully.

I prayed his appeal wasn't simply because he was a tantalizing mystery to solve.

"Once our time ends, we part ways," I added. "No renegotiating. No broken hearts."

"Wonderful." His smile was practically warm enough to melt the snow. "We'll swear a blood oath to make it official. Our needs will be mutually met that way."

I hesitated at that, looking him over carefully as I considered the suggestion.

"A blood oath is a bit much for a simple dating arrangement."

It was a magical bond that couldn't be broken, but it would ensure he adhered to the time limit, which suited me well enough to consider agreeing. It also meant we'd work together to achieve our mutual needs, keeping our interests aligned while the bond was in place.

"Maybe." He sounded rather casual about the whole thing. Like he was proposing a walk in the park and not a magical tether to a complete stranger. "But it also grants a certain level of trust between the parties. With a blood oath in play, neither of us could betray the other. Do you trust me, Lady F?"

I would have liked to, but that cynical part of my brain warned me there was some hidden angle I hadn't yet figured out. I studied him closely, but whatever telling details I might have read in his face were disguised by the glamour. No matter how hard I tried to unearth his secrets, I hit an impenetrable wall. The risk, the danger...it had me on the edge, peering over.

If I wanted to know who he really was, there was only one way to find out.

I had a growing suspicion that my first impression of him being a hawk closing in on his prey was the truth. I looked him over again, wondering if I actually wanted to play the part of the mouse, or if I should walk away before it was too late.

TWENTY-SEVEN
Prince Gluttony

$\mathcal{M}$Y PULSE THRASHED aggressively as victory came within reach.

I kept my posture casual, unwilling to spook my quarry into bolting.

Anything could go wrong in these last moments. I needed to proceed with extreme caution like I would when battling the best apex predators.

Adriana was clever, her look guarded as she weighed her options, signaling that she suspected a trap and was testing to see where it lay.

Adriana.

It had taken every ounce of my willpower to keep any surprise from showing when I realized I had been correct: my rival was my paramour.

I couldn't say I was disappointed by the discovery.

The moment she stepped onto the roof wearing the cloak I'd had made specifically for her, an odd sense of warmth spread through me. It hadn't dissipated yet. If anything, it grew stronger. I shouldn't feel relief, but I'd be lying if I claimed otherwise.

Adriana had gotten under my skin for years; it seemed only right that she'd finally burrowed deep inside and made me feel desire so strongly again. Hate and love were so closely bound—we were fools to think we could ignore whatever *this* was forever.

It was clear that she didn't trust me. And she shouldn't. I was up to very wicked things.

"It will also break the club's glamour for us," I added, sensing she was just as curious about my identity. "No more hiding behind magic or masks. If we enter into the bond, we won't have any secrets from each other."

Her brows rose fractionally. "No secrets? I'm not sure how I feel about that."

"Secrets only in the sense of who we are. I won't suddenly be privy to your darkest desires. Unless you'd like to share them…"

Her smile was back in force, lighting up her whole face.

She *liked* when I flirted shamelessly. How ironic since that was the one quality that she took me to task for in the papers.

My rival was full of delicious surprises.

I could only hope she liked them just as much as I did; she was certainly about to have quite a shocking discovery.

"All right," she said at last. "Let's swear a blood oath."

"You're certain?" I asked, watching for any hint or sign that she was opposed to the arrangement and not admitting to it. She nodded, but I couldn't read if there was a lie based on physical motion. "I'd prefer if you consented aloud."

"A true gentleman," she teased. "I consent to the blood oath."

Thank the wicked gods for that.

I pulled a pin from inside my suit, and Adriana raised her brows, clearly wondering at my preparation for the evening. I pricked my finger before handing her the pin to do the same.

She punctured the tip of her finger then held it to mine.

"By blood and by choice, I bind thee to me, for six weeks hence. My wants are your wants, my desires, your desires. I will not act against your best interests, and you won't act against mine. In this, we are united. Bound by honor, or death do us part."

She repeated the words, and when she finished, I felt the magic sizzle between us as the binding snapped into place, tethering us.

Adriana swore and staggered back a step, one hand pressed against her chest as if she'd physically felt the blow.

I reached out to steady her, fingers brushing against her bare skin.

A spark ignited between us in a blaze, setting off a chain of emotions that had me gasping for breath.

And then, all the tension, all the temptation, detonated as if it had been held back for years instead of days and had finally been set free.

I took one look at her, at the ravenous hunger in her gaze as she dragged it over me and came completely undone.

TWENTY-EIGHT
Adriana

ALMOST INSTANTLY, A strange rhapsodic sensation flowed through my veins as the magic settled in, drawing me closer to the masked man before me.

I suddenly wanted to tear his clothes off.

All the teasing, all the tension, it needed a release. *Now.*

I'd never been bound to someone before and couldn't tell if it was his desire or my own or a combination of the two coursing through me in such strong torrents.

But something had shifted the instant our bond snapped into place.

One line replayed in my head:

My wants are your wants, my desires, your desires.

Our desires were definitely aligning, as if we needed any magical assistance there. In fact, I doubted the oath had anything to do with what we were feeling.

This attraction wasn't created *by* magic; it simply *felt* like it.

He seemed to feel the same pull, leaning in, his lips brushing mine lightly before he tugged me up against him, deepening our kiss like a man possessed.

My hands raked through his hair, soft as down as he hoisted me up against the railing, pressing his hips into mine, his arousal already hard and thick between us.

My focus narrowed to each point of contact.

Maybe it was the magic bond settling in, or the chemistry we'd felt from that first night finally unleashing, but I'd never experienced such euphoria from simple touches before.

It felt like the world melted away and left only us, tethered in this one moment. Small but infinite and wholly consumed by each other.

Every touch, every innocent brush of his skin against mine felt like a dream and I wanted to stay lost in it forever.

His kiss was magic on its own, his lips soft but firm as they met mine, over and over.

Each nip of his teeth and slide of his tongue made my body react tenfold, the slickness between my thighs growing. It felt like we were both lost to sensations, completely giving in to our baser wants and desires, allowing our bodies to simply react to each touch and caress.

There was no rooftop, no rowdy partygoers drinking on the streets below us.

Axton and the years of heartbreak were finally a distant memory.

It was me and my stranger and the explosion of desire we couldn't stop.

I ran my hands along the front of his shirt, needing to feel him without any layers between us. He broke our kiss, his hands sliding over my arms in gentle, loving strokes, watching as I undid the first button on his shirt, then the next.

By the time I'd gotten to the last button and slowly peeled his shirt back, I was ready for him to take me right there. He was a carving made flesh. The most exquisite thing I'd ever seen. I'd fallen for his mind first, so his powerful body was simply an added delight to marvel over.

This stranger was entirely too good to be true. And yet here he stood, very real and just as wildly attracted to me.

"Beautiful," I whispered, tracing each hard ridge of his abdomen, my attention transfixed by him.

His entire chest was quite literally a work of art—a tattoo of two silver dragons entwined, facing each other, took up nearly every inch of his skin.

The way the dragons were positioned made it look like two halves creating a heart. Near the bottom of their serpentine bodies a banner bound them, a Latin phrase inked onto it.

Nitimur in vetitum. We strive for the forbidden.

Something like recognition slithered along the edges of my memory, but that was impossible since I'd never seen it before. Any peculiar feeling was forgotten the moment he shrugged the shirt completely off, allowing me a moment to admire him.

I traced each dip and curve of the tattoo, especially enjoying the hiss of breath he released when I continued raking my nails down, pausing at his belt line before dipping below it, stopping just shy of the fierce bulge straining against his trousers.

A male had no right to look so good or be so tempting.

But it wasn't simply his body that aroused me; it had been his mind, his wicked tongue.

He'd captured my attention well before he'd stripped his shirt off, revealing the dark god of sin he truly was.

Once I'd explored every inch of his inked skin, he returned the favor. The glamour hadn't yet faded, so I wasn't sure who he was, but I didn't care. I wanted him. Now.

"I could touch you like this all night, Lady F."

"I'd be happy to oblige." My eyes fluttered shut as I sank into the sensation.

His touch was erotic, a whisper of fingertips gliding along my neck, across my shoulders, dipping between my breasts.

Each caress was a promise, a declaration. A vow of all the pleasurable things to come.

"Taking my time, exploring. Adventuring across the map of your body."

He drew little circles over my ribs, then continued down, stroking and teasing the sensitive area below my belly button, my body moving into his caress, trying to guide him lower.

His cursed hands slid upward instead, a soft laugh escaping those wonderful lips.

He twined his fingers through mine as he tugged me close, kissing me softly again. Like a fairy-tale prince courting a princess. The kiss was sweet, his hands clasping mine sweeter.

Such a vast dichotomy between this and the filthy fantasy he'd shared before. And he well knew it.

I hated to admit it, but I loved the teasing. The way he made me antici-pate and crave each touch, wanting him to both end my torment and pro-long it until I couldn't take another moment of it and we both succumbed to this intoxicating need.

He unclasped our hands and traced each line of my corset, slowly tug-ging at the strings, undoing them only enough for him to replace his fingers with his mouth.

"You have no idea how long I've wanted to do this."

From the earnest sound of his voice, he made it seem like years, not days.

He kissed down the column of my throat, then along my décolletage, slowly, maddeningly peeling my bodice down to draw the top of my breasts into his warm mouth.

Patience might be a virtue, but we were in a club of sin.

He moved upward again, nuzzling my neck. "Is there something you want, Lady F?"

"You. And you damned well know it."

I felt his smile on my skin. The heathen knew exactly what he was doing.

My hips bucked toward him, needing to feel him pressed between my thighs, the desire to be filled growing unbearable as he played.

He gave in to my silent demand, fitting his body against mine as he began a slow, rhythmic grinding of his hips against mine, hitting a spot that made me see stars.

"Like that?"

"Yes." My legs widened of their own accord, my short skirt riding past my thighs, inviting him closer, needing him to claim me. His hands fell to my bare skin, his attention caught on where our bodies connected. If he didn't touch me soon, I'd lose my sanity.

Finally, blessedly, he knelt before me, his hands clamped onto my legs, both to hold me steady, prevent me from falling back over the railing, and to slowly push my thighs apart.

"Brace yourself against the railing. We're going to give the people on the street a show."

A small whimper escaped my lips as I gripped the railing, leaning back to gaze up at the snow falling like mad around us. I was completely at his mercy; one wrong move and I'd go tumbling back, falling to the ground several stories below.

If that didn't speak to trust, I wasn't sure what would.

Over the sound of my own blood rushing, I heard people chatting in the alleyway below and could only imagine what they'd witness if any-one happened to glance up. My skirt was short enough that they could already see up it.

My pulse sped faster, both in fear and in excitement as his attention turned to my inner thighs, his openmouthed kisses trailing higher.

Gods above. He was going to make his fantasy a reality and I was all too willing to play along.

He slowly peeled my undergarments down my legs, helping me step out of them before tossing them aside. Cool air brushed across my sensitive flesh, the sensation freeing as I bared myself to my stranger and anyone else who glanced up or stepped onto the roof.

He gripped the bottom of my skirt, guiding it higher, exposing me more.

"You're beautiful." He dragged a teasing finger across my body, his touch wrenching a moan from me. "Already deliciously wet for me, Lady F."

I swore, my breath catching, as he chuckled and repeated the motion.

He circled my clit, then pushed the tip of his finger inside me before withdrawing it.

"Or are you drenched for them? Knowing they can see everything I'm doing to you."

My attention dropped to him, my chest heaving.

He looked like a masked angel who'd fallen with one purpose in mind. "Touch me."

Without uttering another word, he bent forward, his mouth replacing his fingers in a shock of sensation that made me arch into it as if I'd been struck by lightning.

The first stroke of his tongue dragged a moan from me, my body tight-ening around him. It was like he was savoring that first taste of whipped cream. The next slide of his tongue dipped inside me, and I forgot anyone else was in earshot as I cried out, begging for more.

If his kiss had been magic, what he was doing with his tongue now was a gift from the old gods.

"Fucking delicious."

He feasted like I was his own personal dessert and he'd been deprived of indulging in it for too long. He didn't seem to care if we were caught either; he spread me wider, making love to me with his tongue, completely focused on making me feel incredible.

Right then I believed his reverent tone from before, that he'd spent decades plotting this move, not a week. That he'd dreamed of all the ways he'd make me call out for him.

I threaded my fingers through his hair, holding him against me as he expertly lapped at my body. I was so close to falling over the edge, so ready to drag him there with me.

The glamour seemed to fade now, leaving only his mask in place. I hadn't noticed before, probably because of the magic, but in his current position, I saw dragon wings tattooed across the whole of his back, cresting at the top of his shoulders.

He rocked back on his heels, pushing two fingers inside me, thrusting while his tongue stroked in tandem. Saints curse me. The male knew what he was doing. He growled his approval, the vibration mixed with his tongue and fingers making me jolt forward.

I wanted to see his face as I came.

"Take your mask off," I demanded, tugging his hair back. "Now."

"Only if you take yours off too." His voice was too low for me to try to recognize it. As if he knew what I was up to, he pumped his fingers once more, his smile growing positively wicked as I bucked into him and nodded. He'd fully distracted me. "On the count of three?"

He withdrew his fingers, then pushed them back in, hooking them slightly, hitting a spot that sent a bolt of heat through me.

"One."

I panted as he repeated the motion.

"Two."

I was on the precipice, ready to shatter apart. And he damn well knew it. We'd been playing this game for days and I would kill anyone if they interrupted.

I reached up, gripping my own mask, ready to shed it.

With his free hand he did the same.

He withdrew his fingers, then thrust in again, my body throbbing with need as he filled me, his tongue flicking against my sensitive flesh.

"Three."

We wrenched our masks off at the same moment he pumped into me, then did a wickedly delightful move with his thumb, pressing it hard against my swollen clit, and the orgasm I'd been so close to having came rushing through me at last.

I dropped my mask, the lace tumbling next to where he knelt in a delicate heap. He didn't notice. He was focused entirely on ruining me for any other lover, intentionally or not.

He hadn't lifted his face, so all I could see were his muscles flexing as he concentrated intently on each reaction my body gave him.

He leaned in as if he couldn't stop himself from tasting me as I came. His tongue flicked over me while his fingers worked me, and I had never felt such ecstasy in all my life.

I gripped his shoulders, my head thrown back as I rode him through wave after wave of pleasure. By now every patron below must have heard us, but I didn't care.

Gods he was incredible.

He continued to feast until the last shudder worked its way through me and I collapsed back, breathing hard. He pressed a small kiss to the inside of my thigh, his touch turning gentle, tender. Like he wanted to drag this out and replay it in his dreams.

Once I caught my breath, I finally glanced down, eager to see him without a disguise, wanting to know if the truth of him compared to my imagination in any way.

But he wasn't quite through with me yet.

Once you've begged for mercy… He was making good on that statement.

His clever fingers began working me into a second orgasm. I rocked against him as he started mimicking the way he'd soon slam himself to the hilt inside me.

I was already close again, already buzzing from what he'd just done to me, and the intensity was almost too much to take as he thrust in and out.

When his other hand closed around his erection, stroking up and down over his trousers as if he couldn't wait to be inside me, it undid any control I had left. I wanted him even more.

I cried out in rapture, and he finally looked up, a powerful, raw hunger in his expression as he watched me shatter once more from his touch.

It was primal. Possessive. And…

Our gazes locked and held, my breathy moan turning into a shout of disbelief at the exact moment I realized who he was.

But it was far too late.

The next wave of pleasure crashed through me and all I could do was ride it out, unable to stop this glorious release from happening, even if it came from *him*.

His fingers were still buried deep inside me, still eliciting pleasure as I clenched around him, my body uncaring about his true identity as it succumbed to the most intense wave of pleasure I'd ever felt. He pumped into me while he stroked himself, his eyes hooded with lust.

I held his gaze, unwilling to look away as I rocked into each of his thrusts and came.

My defiance only seemed to turn him on more, which made me come harder.

Finally, the last of my orgasm passed and I stopped riding his fingers. His grip on his erection loosened, his fist slowing its pumping before stopping.

I couldn't stop myself from looking. He was still hard and hadn't found release. Part of me wanted to unbutton his trousers and see what happened next.

My chest heaved with exertion as reality slowly settled in, breaking the moment.

Gabriel blasted Axton was my masked stranger.

And the damned prince had just given me the best two orgasms of my life.

There was no justice in the world.

Only after he seemed certain I'd come down entirely from my release, he reluctantly sat back on his heels; his hands clasped loosely in front of him as if to keep from reaching out again.

I couldn't fathom why he'd ensured I was sated, even knowing who I was. Perhaps it was his sin that compelled him to make sure I was thoroughly satisfied.

Or maybe he simply enjoyed knowing he had such control over my body.

My attention fixed to his mouth, needing to break contact with his steady gaze until I collected myself. His damned lips glistened with my desire, sending a new wave of heat through me.

Noticing what held my attention, he slowly ran his tongue over his lower lip, pupils dilating. I internally screamed at my pulse to calm itself down. I would *not* be attracted to Axton.

We watched each other silently, like two opponents circling each other, unsure of our next moves.

His hazel eyes narrowed on my wig before returning to my face. I couldn't begin to decipher what he was thinking; my own thoughts and emotions were too tangled and twisted.

"Adriana."

"Axton."

"This is quite an interesting night."

His tone was light, but I knew he had to be reeling as much as I was.

We stared at each other for another silent beat. The prince dropped to his knees, a dark gleam entering his gaze as he slowly raked it down my body, undoubtedly noticing the slight trembling in my muscles from the aftershocks of pleasure that hadn't quite abated yet.

Belatedly, I realized my skirt was still bunched up around my hips. Not that modesty mattered now. The prince had done far more than simply *look* at my nude form.

And there was no way for me to play down the effect he'd had on me. He knew as well as I did that he'd owned my body. My mind, however, was finally catching up to the situation.

He was nestled between my legs, his face mere inches from the place that still throbbed for him. Part of me wanted to put the masks back on and finish what we'd started.

It certainly wouldn't be the first time we indulged.

Axton dragged his attention back up, settling it on me.

Hatred wasn't shining in his eyes. It was something far worse.

And infinitely more complicated.

I needed to get away from him and that accursed look before we did anything else we'd regret tonight. Our minds were clearly addled from needing to overindulge in lust.

He would never commit to—

Dear gods. His bridal competition. My sister. I'd forgotten the blasted rake was hosting a very public competition to find a wife. All while carrying on in secret with me.

He kept his gaze steady on me, watching as I sorted through feelings and facts. He didn't appear to be struggling with the truth; his breathing was calm, his posture relaxed. And all at once I understood. I had been so wrong. So *very* wrong. He wasn't shocked by my identity.

He knew. From the moment I walked onto the roof wearing the cloak he'd had made. The gods-damned demon had set this up days before. *That* was why he'd sent the modiste. It wasn't because of our run-in at the market. It was to prove my identity for whatever he'd plotted next. And whatever *that* plot entailed, I'd entered an unbreakable blood oath with him.

The realization sent me reeling.

I drew back from him, the movement too sudden for where I'd been perched against the railing. My entire sense of gravity upturned.

"Adriana." He reached for me. "Don't!"

With a scream, I toppled backward, falling hard and fast toward the ground.

And certain bare-bottomed death.

TWENTY-NINE
Prince Gluttony

I DIDN'T THINK. I acted.

I dove over the edge of the roof after Adriana, plummeting as hard and fast as I could, willing my body to break any laws of nature daring to stand in my way.

The old gods were smiling down on a sinner like me for once. My arms banded around her, catching her up against my body seconds before she crashed to the ground.

Once I had her, my wings erupted from their magical tether, tearing from my back in a thunderous clap that rent the air, silencing the merriment of the patrons drinking outside.

The sudden intensity of my wingbeats displaced snow from the ground in a punishing sheet that whipped up and out, covering the unlucky few standing nearby.

Anyone looking on would know I'd been at the Seven Sins tonight—there was no mistaking my cobalt-and-silver dragon wings. The scandal sheets would be all abuzz in the morning, given that the suitors had moved into the castle tonight.

That was an issue for another time.

"Are you all right?" I asked, shouting over the wind that violently whipped us.

Adriana swung her legs around my hips, locking her ankles behind my back, pressing herself against me as we shot upward, leaving the night district a mere speck of glowing lights twinkling far below before being swallowed by the storm.

Most inconveniently, my cock was still hard as granite.

A fact she had to be aware of since it was notched against her body.

I gritted my teeth, trying to clear my thoughts. Her skirt was still wrenched around her hips, leaving only my trousers as a barrier between us.

I was trying to be a gods-damned gentleman, but each time she moved, she sent a bolt of awareness through me that had the damned thing twitching at her entrance.

As if she needed anything else to mock me for.

I focused on the icy sleet pricking my wings like a thousand needles, the pain not nearly distracting enough as she shifted again.

If I didn't know any better, I'd swear she was torturing me for the thrill of it.

Adriana's arms tightened around my neck, her skin cold enough to make me shudder. I flew as hard and fast as I could, trying and failing to beat the worsening storm.

She buried her face in the nook of my shoulder as ice and snow pelted us, grounding me in the here and now. Her entire body was rigid apart from her heartbeat, which thrummed wildly against my own chest.

"It's okay, you're safe." I pressed my lips to her ear, trying not to startle her more by shouting against the screaming winds. I didn't need to use my supernatural senses to know she'd been terrified of dying. Rightly so. Another moment and I would have been too late.

My own pulse raced as I shoved that thought deep down, focusing on the present.

I tucked her against me the best I could, offering her what little warmth I could from the freezing temperatures as I tried to settle my own swirling emotions.

Adriana fucking Saint Lucent's sweet taste was still on my lips, distracting me.

I refused to think about how amazing she'd felt, writhing on my fingers, my tongue. When the bond snapped into place, her arousal had slammed into me, amplifying my own.

In that moment, I'd never known such hunger. And now that she knew who I was, I'd likely never know that sensation again.

It was my own fault. She'd wanted one night of distraction. But I'd become obsessed with unraveling the truth of who she was, knowing that if she was my rival, it would not only be the perfect way to keep her close to me so she couldn't break the dragon story, but also the best way to fuel my power while I couldn't indulge in the adventure of hunting the dragons.

I hadn't counted on the fact that the lines would become blurred between duty and passion. Or that I would *like* her.

I closed my eyes briefly, the full weight of my decisions settling in.

My head started to pound.

Suddenly, Adriana jerked back, squinting against the storm. "Where are we going?"

"The castle. You need to get—"

"No!" She almost slipped from my grasp as the snow came down harder. "Please. Take me home. We cannot be seen like this together."

I blinked frost from my lashes, glancing over my shoulder. The storm was growing worse and there was no chance I'd make it back to her neighborhood without her succumbing to the elements. With a muttered curse, I abruptly shifted course.

I flew past the castle, giving us time to privately sort out the mess I'd created and get her warmed up before she got ill or worse. She was also correct: it wasn't as if I could bring her back there now, especially with the castle filled with potential brides.

Her sister. At first it had seemed like a wonderful turn of events; now I wasn't as sure.

I continued flying as quickly as I could, aiming for a cavern on the far edge of House Gluttony, my wings snapping against the storm.

The cave was tucked deep within the evergreen forest that surrounded the castle proper, far from the prying eyes of my courtiers.

It was a mere crack in the mountainside, barely wide enough to fly through unless I pulled my wings as close to my body as I could without losing momentum. It was the perfect location for a demon who craved daring adventures; getting here was impossible without wings.

And on the off chance anyone did make it, I'd warded the cavern from the world, keeping it a secret from everyone. Until now.

Adriana would be the only other soul who entered my personal domain.

It had been my private getaway for a century, a place I could relax and simply exist without the weight of being a prince pressing down on me.

Here I slept on the hard-packed ground, lit my own fires, and lived as simply as one could. I had the necessities—dried meat, beans, jugs of water and brandy. Flint and firewood. A blanket, a few tin cups, and an iron skillet. A spare shirt or two.

Something my court might find surprising since my sin was overindulgence. But the cavern provided me with the thing I craved most.

We careened through the opening, flying at full speed until we reached the place where it widened into a small chamber. Adriana hadn't spoken again and hadn't removed her face from my neck, as if she could force the night to not exist.

I set her down on the thick pelts I'd used as rugs, grabbed the lone blanket from a hook on the wall, and draped it around her shoulders.

For the first time, I wished I had a straw mattress or bedroll to offer.

She gripped the blanket under her chin, teeth chattering.

I quickly lit a fire in the small pit, then crouched before her, my gaze sweeping over her in quick assessment. Her lips were tinged blue, her porcelain skin paler than usual.

Her dress offered little in the way of protecting her from the harsh elements we'd flown through and was completely soaked.

She'd need to take it off.

And the wig.

It was another clever move on her part—wearing something to disguise herself even when the glamour lifted. Adriana had taken great pains to ensure she remained anonymous when entering or leaving the club. It would have been sufficient enough for anyone. Aside from me.

Fate was a twisted prick, but I owed him another debt.

Had she never rushed onto that rooftop, and had I not hunted my brothers that same night and waited for them there—she never would have ended up in my sights. I didn't like the unpleasant emotion that came on the heels of that thought, of Adriana meeting someone else.

A shudder wracked through her.

My fingers twitched with the urge to rub warmth into her. I kept them clasped in front of me, aware that her tantalizing scent still lingered on my skin.

A full moment of silence stretched between us, nearly as painful as the ice attacking my wings. Unsure how to proceed now that she was here and I'd managed to secure a magical bond, I decided to break the tension with humor.

"I've had lovers fall quickly, but that was a bit on the nose."

Firelight gilded the curve of her cheek, the line of her jaw. Taut from clenching her teeth. Apparently, she wasn't ready for my paltry attempts to lighten the mood.

"It won't take long for the fire to warm the cavern. Would you like hot brandy?"

Those ice-blue eyes shone with betrayal when they finally met mine.

"You knew it was me." She hadn't asked; her voice was pitched dangerously low.

I expected her to put all the puzzle pieces together quickly, but just how swiftly she'd done it was impressive.

I drew in a deep breath. It wasn't exactly the first question on my mind, but I'd let my concern go. She was well enough to spear me with that accusatory glare I'd come to expect from her, which was confirmation enough that she wasn't physically harmed.

"Did you really not know it was me?" I countered, unwilling to admit to the truth.

"You were so...pleasant. Mysterious. Unlike the miserable rake you are."

Detecting lies was certainly useful in situations like this.

The fact that she *didn't* answer my question strongly indicated she had suspected it was me at one point and refused to admit it. Otherwise, she would have denied it outright.

"I *am* pleasant." I gave her a wolfish grin. "And you certainly didn't seem to mind my rakish behavior in the club. In fact, I believe you rather enjoyed my filthy mouth."

She offered me a stony look but didn't snap back at me. I leaned closer.

"After you recognized me, you rode my fingers so hard my entire hand became drenched. Maybe hatred arouses you more than the thought of being watched."

She still didn't take the bait.

Worry gnawed most unexpectedly deep within me. Adriana Saint Lucent wasn't one to hold her tongue, especially when it came to me.

I looked her over critically again.

"You should take the dress off and let it dry."

She shivered in place, her knuckles turning bone white as she held the blanket tighter.

"It's fine."

I sensed her lie before her body practically convulsed from the next shudder. "You're going to get hypothermia."

She didn't respond.

"You do realize we'll need to strip naked and curl around each other for warmth should you actually *get* hypothermia?"

Her teeth rattled together. "The fire will be fine."

Another lie. I pushed to my feet, towering over her. Any attempt at maintaining a pleasant tone vanished. The demon prince came out to play.

"Take the damned dress off, Adriana. Unless you secretly *want* to be cuddled up with me naked. Then by all means, keep the thing on. I'll gladly nurse you back to health. You can even put the mask back on if you'd like."

With a glower that was most impressive, she looked up at me. "I can't, you demanding brute."

She turned and dropped the blanket down, exposing the back of the dress and the intricate knots holding the corset portion together. I'd managed to tug the front down a little earlier, but she couldn't shimmy out of it.

Gods' blood. We'd be here all night undoing the damned thing.

"Stand up."

She gritted her teeth but got to her feet, turning to grant me access to the dress as she reluctantly let the blanket fall to the ground.

The shudders started again, more violently now that the blanket was gone.

With a movement so swift, it was only possible with my immortal strength and speed, I unsheathed my House dagger and sliced through the gown, tearing it down the back in a clean line. I tugged both halves apart, tossing them to the ground in the next instant.

There. At least now she'd get warm quicker.

Adriana stood ramrod straight, her naked body cast in shadows as the flames flickered wildly around the cave. She wore clear heeled slippers that reflected the fire, the shoes giving her legs definition. I tore my gaze away from the generous curve of her bottom and plucked up the blanket, wrapping it around her shoulders once more before taking a step back.

"Do you need help removing the wig?"

Her shoulders lifted with her next breath. "Yes."

I hesitated for a beat.

"If you can't do it," she said, her tone uncharacteristically soft, "the fire will be fine."

"I'm a prince; of course I can remove a simple wig."

I hadn't the slightest idea what I was doing, but I was damn well going to claim victory over the accursed thing. I set my attention on her hair and quickly located several hidden pins.

I gently moved her around, using the firelight to find any glint of metal, painstakingly plucking each one out and dropping them to the ground on her tattered dress.

Once I was certain they were all located, I gently tugged the wig back, revealing her pale blue hair. It tumbled down her back in a graceful sheet. The scent of lavender and honey greeted me, likely the soap she used.

I fought the urge to run my fingers through her hair. There would be no need to do such a thing, especially when I saw her hair had stayed dry underneath the wig. I sensed Adriana was only allowing me to address any basic needs, and anything frivolous would be met with scorn.

I tossed the wig onto the small pile of her things, then grabbed two tin cups from the tiny sideboard I'd made from raw timber, pouring a few knuckles of brandy into each before setting them over the fire.

While they warmed for a few moments, I pulled the strips of wool from the old boot I kept them in, using them to wind around the cups, to keep from burning our hands.

Adriana kicked her shoes off and settled back onto the furs, watching silently as I fixed her cup, then gingerly took it, sipping the warm liquid.

Her eyes fluttered shut, some color rising in her cheeks.

"Thank you."

I paused, the muscles in my body tensed. Surely the world was about to collapse.

"That's it. I'm taking you to the royal healer. Now."

She glanced up, a furrow forming in her brow. "Why?"

"You thanked me. You're obviously out of your senses."

She offered me an obscene hand gesture, confirming she was truly on the mend.

I quietly exhaled and grabbed my own mug, downing the warm brandy by half.

I sat across from her, watching as she slowly began to shiver less, my mind pulled in several directions at once. It was the first night I wouldn't patrol the border, visit Sil's dungeon, or meet Val in the war room to go over any reports, and the idea of leaving the realm unprotected from the ice dragons made me more restless than usual.

But there was no way I could explain my absence to my lovely friend, who'd eventually use the information against me once the blood oath was no longer in effect.

Adriana was a columnist first, one who wished to see me fall and had been trying to accomplish that for years, a fact I'd never forget, no matter which lines blurred.

And she was in no condition to be left alone anyway.

She looked me over, her expression impossible to read. It wasn't exactly the reaction previous lovers had had after I'd delighted them with my tongue. The fact I'd abstained over the last several years notwithstanding. Though I suppose I understood her feelings for me wouldn't magically soften because I'd made her come. Twice.

"I thought as a Prince of Sin you possessed some supernatural ability to recognize people through scent."

I arched a brow. "Are you comparing me to a dog?"

A wry smile curved her lips. "Careful. You're setting yourself up, Your Highness."

"We're a little beyond titles, Adriana. Call me Gabriel or Axton."

Her attention fell to my lips, lingering. My body hardly needed any encouragement to respond to her interest. I shifted, focusing on the hard-packed earth.

"Will the bond interfere with the competition?" she asked. "I know there's a physical...aspect to it."

"That aspect is only there because of *mutual* attraction," I said. "The magic doesn't create it. Only enhances what both parties already feel. If only one of us felt certain...urges...the other wouldn't be affected. It is based on consensual emotions, always. The bond took, which meant we both desired it. I couldn't have forced the connection, even if I wanted to."

She was quiet a moment, mulling that over.

The truth was the bond was going to make things very interesting over these next several weeks. If either of us traveled too far from the other, physical ramifications would occur.

"That should be easy enough to avoid," she said at last. "Now that I know who you really are, there's little chance of any attraction resurfacing."

I gave her a mocking grin. She could mentally hate me all she liked; it didn't stop her from physically desiring me. Even now. Which was all the magic I cared about.

"Well," she said, "once the heightened emotions from tonight pass, that is."

I snorted, earning an annoyed glare from her. The fire had properly heated the cavern now, so I tended to my damp shirt, amusement at her denial making me chuckle.

"What's so funny?"

"You aren't lying to yourself exactly, but you also aren't admitting one fact I'm very aware of, darling. And therefore not acknowledging what the magic already senses. Tonight's lingering attraction isn't simply because of our tryst. Or the intensity of the *multiple* orgasms I gave you."

"You're arrogant and wrong, once again."

I raised a brow.

"Am I? I seem to recall that you were aroused enough when I offered to spank you, knowing full well it was me. And not only that, but during our little collision? Don't think I wasn't aware of how your body reacted to mine."

A pleasant flush blossomed across her petal-soft skin.

"If you must know, I was imagining it was my stranger, not you."

Her tone was so prim and proper. If I didn't know what her secret desires were, I'd never guess she'd fantasized about being caught.

"I hate to break it to you." I leaned in, dropping my voice to a low purr. "But I *am* your stranger. And you liked me just fine when I was on my knees, tasting every inch of you."

She took a sip of brandy, then another. As if the liquor would stop the memory from resurfacing. I sensed her arousal now, knowing she was recalling each flick and slide of my tongue, and she didn't despise it. As much as she wished she did.

At least that made me feel better about my own arousal. She couldn't hold that against me when she'd been fighting it too.

"Yes, well. The fantasy has been thoroughly destroyed now."

"Mm. We'll see."

"No, we won't. Now that I know who you are, physically aroused or not, I won't be acting on any lingering...emotions."

The magic of our oath would make that an interesting vow to keep.

Perhaps Lust had been correct—hate sex was best. I might not have been positive it was her until tonight, but our passion had been the thing of legends. Hate and love were strong emotions, the divide between them easily closed. I could have stayed on my knees, pleasuring her for an eternity, and never tired of the sounds she made or the way she tasted.

Until she realized who I was and the spell broke.

Perhaps that made me a despicable bastard, but I'd never claimed to be anything but a villain. Morals were for heroes and the pious. I was a sinner through and through.

"There's something else we should discuss," I said after taking another deep pull of my brandy. "The little fact that your sister is one of my suitors."

Her gaze narrowed.

"If it will create a rift between you, you may take her place."

Her attention was frozen to me, a look of horror slowly spreading across her face. Another punch to my ego.

Or maybe she was just surprised.

I decided to pull the bandage off completely, laying it all out there.

"We suit well enough physically. And we're bound by oath now. It makes sense to see how this plays out." I downed the last of my brandy, relishing the burn. "Will you join the competition and become my suitor?"

THIRTY
Adriana

"YOU CANNOT BE serious, Axton. My answer is no. Absolutely *not*."

The prince gave me a bemused look while he refreshed our cups of brandy, appearing far too relaxed considering the circumstances as he settled back on the furs.

Though I supposed he wasn't as shocked as I was. He'd strongly suspected it was me.

And while I *might* have harbored some passing, deranged fantasy that Axton was my stranger—obviously to live out some masochistic desire for emotional punishment I needed to work through—I had been surprised it was true.

"It's a little late for buyer's remorse, darling. The oath can't be broken."

"But it doesn't mean I have to be a suitor. And I certainly won't ruin my sister's chance at happiness."

"Need I remind you that your will is bound to mine for the next several weeks?"

"I do not recall agreeing to become one of your suitors."

"You didn't have to. And I quote, 'My wants are your wants, my desires, your desires.'" His smile was far too pleased for the situation. "Devil's in the details, as they say."

"Never bargain with a demon prince," I muttered, the familiar motto no longer seeming like a silly fable mothers told their children to keep them out of trouble.

Cursed Prince of Sin.

I exhaled, trying to calm my racing thoughts. *Surely* there had to be some way out of this. I simply needed to make him see reason.

"I will not take my sister's place."

His brows rose. "You'd rather keep what happened tonight a secret from her?"

No, I absolutely wished I could go back in time and remake all my choices that led up to this point. "It wouldn't be the first time," I muttered.

He gave me a puzzled look. "Do you often court the same people?"

Now it was my turn to look confused. "I was talking about you."

He opened his mouth, then closed it. My temper flared as understanding dawned.

"How positively infuriating. You've gone through so many lovers that you don't even recall the time we shared, do you?"

He studied me like maybe I'd gone into some hypothermic state after all.

"You and I have never been…intimately acquainted before tonight." His gaze narrowed. "Unless you know something I don't."

"You have no recollection of the All-Sinners Ball?" I stared at him, wondering if it was possible to suddenly incinerate him on the spot. When he remained damnably unscathed, I gave up trying to torch him with my mind and the conversation as a whole. "Forget it."

"Adriana—"

"Please. This night has already been eventful enough. I'd rather not discuss it."

He seemed unwilling to let it go, but from either the steel in my tone or the hard expression on my face, he finally turned away and glanced at the discarded wig. "Where did you get that?"

"The Scene Stealer."

He seemed vaguely impressed but said nothing else.

I downed the rest of my brandy, holding my cup out for him to splash more into it. There wasn't enough brandy in this cave to get me through the night.

I forced myself to think of anything besides the prince and what we'd just done as he refilled my cup. My column and my plan for it blessedly came to mind.

"I'd like to write a special Miss Match article introducing the suitors. Do you object to me interviewing them?"

Axton studied me for a long moment. "If you're plotting some revenge, then I object."

I smiled faintly at that. "Not this time."

Silence stretched between us, giving my more pressing thoughts an opportunity to creep back in. Cursed thoughts. They were like ghosts in need of banishment. Since we were stuck here for the foreseeable future, I might as well ask what I really wanted to know.

"Why did you keep seeing me when you were hosting a competition to find a wife? Were you always aware it was me?"

"No. And can't it simply be about adventure? I do love indulging in a good challenge."

He didn't *really* answer my first question, indicating he was skirting the truth. My fingers tapped against my cup. If it was a battle of wills he desired, I'd give it to him.

"If you didn't know it was me that first night, there had to be something you…"

I smiled. He might be cleverer than I'd originally given him credit for, but after nearly a decade of watching him for any way to ruin him, I was well-versed in reading him.

"You needed a distraction," I said, paying close attention to his reaction. "That's why you kept seeing me."

"When don't I enjoy a good diversion?"

"Don't you have enough lovers to occupy you on any given night?"

"I'd been taken with you all week. You're quite enchanting when you're Lady F."

And yet, the rake of rakes hadn't *actually* attempted to take me to his bed until tonight. I couldn't quite figure out if that was solely because he'd wanted me to swear the oath to him or if he simply craved me the same way I craved him in spite of his suspicion.

"I've never known you to go so long without feeding your sin."

"My appetites are far ranging and diverse. There are many ways, aside from bedroom activities, to sate my hunger."

"Then why do you spend so much time crafting an image of hopping from one bed to the next?"

He gave me a lazy grin. "Just because I was alone in bed this week doesn't mean I was any less satisfied. I thought of you. Often. Even without the mask."

He was trying to divert my attention by offering a shocking bit of honesty, but it wasn't working. Once my reporter's mind was engaged, there was no quelling the need to uncover the truth. I loved a good mystery, especially one that could lead to my rival's downfall.

What else had he been doing when he left me at the Seven Sins, alone and worked up?

He might play it off now, but he'd been equally aroused. I didn't doubt that he'd tended to himself later on, but what had been more important than his need to overindulge?

Especially when the entire realm was watching him so closely now.

He was up to something—something more than his hunt to find a wife.

I thought back to our first encounter at the Seven Sins, when that second male had interrupted. Had that been one of his brothers or a high-ranking member of his court?

They must have needed him for something important. Enough to leave their typical debauchery behind. Had that been the night Jackson died? Or was there something else going on? I couldn't quite pinpoint the timeline of events. But I would.

We studied each other in the flickering firelight, quietly sipping our drinks.

His attention dropped to my lips, remaining there entirely too long for either of our good. I wasn't sure if he was hoping to distract me from prying into his secrets.

Or maybe he was remembering how our night began.

It took every ounce of willpower I possessed to not return the favor.

Kissing Axton when I had no idea it was him was one thing, but giving in to my desire fully aware of his identity was another.

I hadn't yet determined if my sister truly liked him or if she was simply swept up in the extravagance of courting a prince, but on the off chance she did fancy him, what happened earlier…could never happen again. Not that I wanted it to.

I tugged the blanket closer, realizing I still wore nothing beneath it.

My skin burned with the memory of Axton's caresses, his languorous kisses, aching for a touch I'd never allow from him again. I wanted him to sink into me, ending my torment.

His gaze flicked up, flaring. His eyes were not simply hazel, but an incredible mixture of gold, green, and brown all vying for dominance. They'd been blazing with heat when he'd touched me earlier, the memory making me crave him once more.

He knew. As a Prince of Sin, he could detect arousal.

I couldn't stop my cursed attention from falling to his lap, noting with satisfaction that I wasn't the only one affected by our earlier mistake.

It would be easy to lean into our bond, blaming the magic for anything else that happened between us. We could claim to be overcome from our earlier foreplay.

I could invite him to share my blanket, or crawl onto his lap.

I doubted he'd refuse either offer. We were two adults with needs. We could satisfy them, then move on. Never speaking of it again. He certainly knew how to do that.

He shifted uncomfortably, eyeing the bottle of brandy again. For a brief moment, I almost wished we were back at the Seven Sins, still blissfully unaware of the truth.

If we were still masked, there would be no question of what we'd be doing now.

His gaze locked onto mine. He looked like he was envisioning all the ways he'd make me call out his name—before he wiped his expression clean.

Whether it was for his sake or mine, I couldn't tell. I took another large sip of my drink, listening to the fire crackle, trying desperately to stop thinking about the prince's wicked mouth.

"Are we spending the night here?" I finally asked, breaking the silence.

For a cave, it was rather cozy and welcoming. Despite the fact that I usually didn't like being caged in, I didn't mind it, even if the circumstances that brought us here weren't ideal. It was a night adventure, being trapped with a wicked prince in a cave while a storm raged on. It made for a good story, even if the company could have been better.

I was surprised Axton had chosen something so rustic when his castle overflowed with riches.

Somehow, it suited him more.

He glanced toward the mouth of the cave. "We'll wait until the storm passes."

I drew in a deep breath. That could take hours, but I didn't protest. I wasn't quite ready to face my sister or stepmother. Hopefully by the time I returned, they'd be fast asleep.

"You cannot speak a word of this," I said. "I trust you know this will never happen again. And I think it's best if we avoid each other from here on out."

" 'My wants are your wants, my desires, your desires,' " he quoted. "If that's what you want, then I have no choice but to agree."

His attention slid over me again, this time in quiet assessment.

He stood and rummaged in a small trunk on the far wall I hadn't noticed, returning with an oversized shirt and a thick pair of socks.

"They'll be big but will keep you warm."

My brows rose. Axton was...*doting* wasn't quite the right term, but he was certainly fussing. It was a side of him I didn't know existed. Because he'd kept it hidden.

Or maybe he'd just kept this side of himself hidden from *me*.

The prince was full of secrets, it seemed.

Axton was an enigma, a tantalizing mystery begging to be solved.

Which was dangerous. Or perhaps disastrous for him. There was nothing I enjoyed more than unraveling secrets. And uncovering his truth would be especially sweet.

I pulled the socks on, pleased they almost reached my knees. They were soft and warm and felt like clouds. I felt Axton's attention on me as I stood.

I dropped the blanket, hiding my smile as he cursed and quickly averted his gaze, suddenly finding the bottle of brandy immensely intriguing.

His shirt was so long it hit mid-thigh. I took my time pulling it on and buttoned it much slower than necessary. Torturing the prince might become my new favorite pastime. He'd tricked me into a bond with him. I might as well enjoy watching him squirm as payback.

I settled down onto the fur again and sighed. It felt decadent to be warm and dry.

He ran his attention over me, then flicked it to the fire.

Without warning, he pulled his trousers off, his muscles flexing with the movement, making the tattoos on his shoulders seem to take flight. I had no memory of the ink from our previous time together and wondered when he'd gotten them done. Or maybe I simply had forgotten them over the years, more focused on how horridly our night had gone.

He straightened, standing up with all his proud glory on display.

My mouth was suddenly dry. It was going to be difficult, pretending our passionate encounter on the roof never happened. But that was an issue for tomorrow. Tonight, I stole another look at him, avoiding his lower half and impressive erection.

I scanned his chiseled torso, hating that he still looked like a dark, tempting god of sin.

His real wings had been a sight to behold. He didn't show them off often, and rumors suggested he'd been unable to access them during the realm-wide curse that House Wrath had broken a few months back. I wondered how it felt when he'd magicked them away.

I realized I was still staring and yanked my attention away from his tattoos, trying to ignore the flutter in my pulse as I scooted back, giving him room to do…whatever he was doing.

"Don't worry," he drawled. "I won't bite until you ask me to."

I gave him a flat look. "You mean *unless* I ask you to."

He held his trousers close to the fire, his mouth curving in that frustratingly smug grin as he turned the garment over, drying the other side. He'd already been drying his shirt—something I hadn't even registered before he tested to see if it was dry.

"I said exactly what I meant."

"We just established that tonight was a mistake."

"Maybe." He casually lifted a shoulder and dropped it. "Some lessons are harder to learn than others, especially after you've had a taste of temptation."

The sinful way he said *taste* ignited a flurry of images I couldn't escape.

Which was exactly what he'd intended, the bastard.

His soft laugh carried through the cave as he stood, watching me with dark amusement as he stepped into his trousers and grabbed the shirt.

Much to my misery, he didn't put the damn thing on.

"Need I remind you, yet again, rake, that you are searching for true love."

He balled the shirt up and crouched before me, hazel eyes sparking with mirth. "Is that what I'm doing?"

"You've certainly made it seem that way."

His expression was one of pure amusement. "Here. Use this to sleep on. I'll let you know when the storm passes."

I took his offering and lay back, attention fixed to the mysterious male I thought I knew.

Axton picked up my discarded blanket and draped it over me—all but tucking me in—then moved to the far edge of the fire's light, his face now hidden in shadow.

As I watched the fire play over his bronze skin, I wondered who the real male was. I'd been researching and watching him for years, writing all sorts of scandal sheets about him, but was startled to discover in these quiet moments he was nothing like I imagined.

I wasn't sure if he was better or worse. Definitely more complex.

Sinner certainly, never a saint. Villain, antihero, nothing quite suited him.

He was wicked and kind and aloof. Mysterious and dangerous, yet concerned for others, even someone like me who he disliked. He was brutish and dominant and crass and still retained a sense of softness when the need struck. He was also devious when it suited. Ruthless Rake. I'd forgotten all about that moniker.

Secret keeper. Debauched prince. Tender lover. Arrogant male.

Now more than ever, I wanted to unravel the mystery of Gabriel Axton once and for all.

I told myself it was strictly to help my sister for the competition and to see if Axton's secret had anything to do with the ice dragon rumors, but deep down I suspected my reasons were not nearly as altruistic as that.

I exhaled again. Six weeks. All I had to do was steer clear of him for six weeks. Even with a magical bond it shouldn't be that hard.

I hoped.

THIRTY-ONE
Prince Gluttony

"THERE'S SOMETHING DIFFERENT about you." Lust looked me over, sweat dotting his brow as he dropped to the mat and kicked out, attempting to swipe my legs out from under me.

I danced back, narrowly avoiding contact with his blow.

Everyone assumed Lust was more of a lover than a fighter but never made that mistake again after training with him. He was as wicked as the rest of us when the mood struck.

We'd been sparring in my training room for the last two hours while the new royal reporter worked on the suitors' profiles.

Much to my surprise, after speaking with them during the welcome dinner, a few would truly make fine matches. *If* I was actually in the market for a wife.

The dinner hadn't been the chore that I'd imagined it would be, especially after what had happened with Silvanus. In fact, it had gone so well, I'd planned another dinner for this evening.

I would flirt shamelessly and dance, then sneak off to meet Felix at Merciless Reach for a night of hunting. That it would also help me avoid a certain blue-haired reporter was an added bonus. Try as I might to stop them, my thoughts kept turning to her. More often than I liked.

"You mean my godlike definition?" I lifted my brows. "I've been spending extra time training to impress my suitors. I'm flattered you noticed."

"Definitely not it."

Lust sprang to his feet, circling me, eyes narrowed. Dark hair stuck to his forehead. He needed a haircut and shave. Which meant he'd spent the last few days feeding his sin.

A fact made painfully obvious, literally, given the nail marks down his back.

We healed almost instantly, which meant he'd either gotten extremely rough or he'd used some sort of magic. Lust was the prince of pleasure, his appetites wilder than even mine.

He feigned an uppercut, then swung with his opposite fist, catching me in the abdomen.

I took the hit, then swung back, clocking him in the jaw.

He spit golden blood on the ground, eyes glinting.

"Distracted, brother?"

I landed another quick jab. "My spies report that Envy's scheming. Care to enlighten me why?"

"Does anyone ever truly know why he does what he does?" Lust bounced on the balls of his feet, throwing a punch that would have done serious damage if I hadn't avoided it at the last second. "Wrath said you didn't patrol the border last night."

"Something came up."

"Tell me it was a lead on the dragons and not your cock. You know you're not actually supposed to court anyone, right?"

I struck out, catching him in the shoulder as he turned away from the blow.

"You spend an unhealthy amount of time thinking about my love life. Find someone to court or read a book. Though, judging by your back, you found someone."

"You were with that ice goddess from the Seven Sins, weren't you?" He closed his eyes. "Gods. That dress. I might damn the whole realm for her too. Think she'll be there again tonight? I'll happily keep her company for you while you play doting husband."

I struck him in the center of his abdomen, unable to land the second jab as he reared back, laughing.

I stalked a small circle around him.

"Stop thinking about her."

"She didn't seem to mind me thinking about her when I caught you together."

I tackled him to the ground, and he knocked me off, his grin growing wider as we circled each other again. I bounced on the balls of my feet, shaking off my annoyance.

The damned blood oath was making me feel...territorial.

I kept my jaws locked together, refusing to take my brother's bait.

Which only encouraged him to keep up his taunts.

"Probably because you were dry-humping her leg like a fiend, Gabriellis. Imagine if I unleashed my power on her? She wouldn't be looking for thrills elsewhere. I can promise you that. She'd be on her knees, choking on—"

I landed my next blow, *hard,* and Lust staggered back.

Amusement flared in his eyes.

"So sensitive."

"Would you focus?"

I feinted to the right, then doubled back, missing him by an inch.

He whistled softly when his attention snapped to the doorway.

I refused to look over my shoulder, not trusting his attempt to distract me. *Surely* Adriana wasn't already up to her wicked reporting ways and meddling. Especially after her insistence that we avoid each other and pretend last night never happened.

As if that was an easy task.

I fired another quick punch at Lust, determined to push the rooftop from my damned mind just as she'd asked.

My brother and I traded blows for the next several minutes without speaking. Lust remained uncharacteristically serious as we took turns knocking each other down.

The sparring session was meant to blow off steam but had turned into a brawl.

We fought like the dirty bastards we were. Kicking out, swinging, using our wings to shove the other back, slicing at each other with our daggers.

I released all the pent-up frustration I'd been holding in a flurry of punches and kicks. Channeling all my dark emotions into one goal: beating Lust.

I turned into the demon, shedding all pretense of princely civility as I unleashed myself.

I thought of the latest report I'd gotten from my hunters, how the dragons had gone after a lesser demon last night, maiming him severely enough to cause problems with the other solitary demons.

I should have been tracking the dragons last night. I should have left Adriana once she was sleeping and secure. Instead, I stood guard until morning. Watching her sleep soundly. As if the realm wasn't in danger and I had all the time in the world to spare.

She wasn't a suitor.

She'd never be my wife.

Her gods-damned *sister* was in the running to be my bride. So why then did I stay? The blood oath? I wished to the old gods that was it.

"Gabriel. Stop."

Lust's voice was laced with magical command, breaking me from the fighting trance I'd been lost in. I blinked slowly, taking in the blood, the ravaged training room.

We'd fought like feral animals, the tapestries torn from the walls, the weapons upturned and scattered across the floor. A shield lay crumpled and bent near my feet.

I didn't remember using it.

I looked down at my fists; my split knuckles were slowly stitching themselves together. I glanced back at my brother, noting the swelling going down around his eyes.

"You were starting to frighten her." Lust jerked his chin behind me, his voice barely above a whisper. "And you don't need to start any new rumors."

An odd prickle rolled down my spine.

I turned, already knowing who I'd find, my pulse speeding in anticipation.

Except it wasn't her.

I schooled my expression to hide my conflicted feelings.

"Eden."

She leaned against the refreshment table by the door, a book pressed to her chest like a shield. I wondered how long she'd been there, watching us.

I scanned her quickly, understanding why Lust had fought so valiantly. Eden Everhart exuded grace and poise. She was exactly the sort of challenge my brother couldn't resist.

That she was currently part of a competition to win my hand wouldn't be a deterrent, sham of an event or not. Lust was no stranger to scandal himself.

I crossed the room to her side, pouring a glass of water from a pitcher, trying to adopt that devil-may-care image I'd crafted. I settled back, sipping the drink.

"To what do I owe the honor of your company, Miss Everhart?"

She quietly studied me. "Are you angry, Your Highness?"

"No. Why?"

"You were fighting like you either wanted to end a war or start one."

"Oh, he definitely wanted to start one. Our boy here is in *quite* the mood."

Lust snagged a glass and poured himself a drink, situating himself between us.

I downed my glass by half, hoping to the old gods he'd keep his cursed mouth shut.

Eden glanced between us. "What happened? If it's not too presumptuous of me to ask."

I couldn't help but wonder if she got her inquisitive nature from her sister and thought carefully about how to respond. My brother, however, was a meddling prick and didn't waste any time, saying too damned much.

"I offered to entertain a mystery lover he'd been seeing before the competition began. He got all sensitive and bothered." Lust gave her a lopsided grin. "Seems he's not the sharing type these days."

She ran her attention over me again, one brow raised. Eden looked entirely too much like her sister with that expression.

"You truly are staying scandalous, Your Highness." Her mouth twitched. "It's something I'm sure Miss Match would be very interested in."

Lust nearly spit his water out. "Wait. I was only kidding. You're not really going to have your sister write an article about that, right?"

"Was there something you needed, Miss Everhart?"

"I was wondering if I might tour the kitchens."

My brother leaned in, not wanting to miss a word of our conversation. He really needed to get a hobby that didn't involve gossiping to our brothers.

"I'll meet you down there in thirty minutes."

She gave me a shy smile. "Actually, would you mind terribly if Vanity and I went alone? We're working on a surprise."

I wasn't sure if I should feel relief or concern that two of my suitors would prefer to not spend time with me. Before I could decide, a flash of ice blue caught my attention.

"I don't—"

I stopped mid-sentence, my gaze following Miss Saint Lucent as she hurried past the open door. Unbidden, a memory from last night came roaring back.

Me, nestled between her thighs, worshipping her while she fell apart on the rooftop, her cries of pleasure echoing down on the world below.

Lust elbowed me in the ribs, dragging me back to the here and now.

I shook my head as if to clear it. Eden was here. Asking about the kitchens. I smiled apologetically, hoping I hadn't insulted her too much.

"I don't mind at all, Miss Everhart. In fact, I look forward to seeing what you and Vanity cook up."

Eden's eyes twinkled with mirth as she offered a low curtsy, then left.

I rubbed my temples. I needed to get out of the castle for a few hours. Adriana was already haunting my thoughts, and the urge to track her down the corridor to see what nefarious plot she was up to now was growing rather irksome.

My brother practically buzzed with the need to share whatever was on his mind.

I waited for him to dazzle me with his powers of romantic observation.

Lust remained silent. Stubborn prick.

"Go on." I faced him, arms crossed. "Say whatever clever insult you're practicing."

Lust looked me over, shaking his head. "You're an idiot."

"Regarding?"

"Bloody hell, Gabriellis. How *aren't* you sleeping with that female?"

"Miss Everhart is a suitor."

"I'm talking about her sister. Don't act like you didn't see her hurry by." He set his glass down and sighed. "I can't tell if she'd be the best or worst thing to ever happen to me."

My teeth audibly ground together.

Lust shot an innocent look my way. "Problem, Gabriel?"

I ignored him.

The gods-damned oath had sounded like an excellent idea, but now it felt like a curse.

The territorial rage that seized me at the thought of my brother taking Adriana to his bed was nearly all-consuming. For the next five weeks and six days, I wanted to work my frustration out with my fists. Since that couldn't happen, I needed to hold it together.

I managed to give Lust one of my rakish grins instead of knocking him out. Again.

"I'll see you in two days for the opening event."

Let the Games Begin!
Special Edition: Meet the Matches

Dear Sinners,

Welcome to what the prince has claimed to be *the* event of the century. For the first time in the history of the Seven Circles, one of the seven ruling princes has decided to make a spectacle of love. Today your very own Miss Match has been granted the opportunity to introduce Prince Gluttony's suitors. With each House of Sin represented, things should get *very* interesting here.

House Gluttony: Eden Everhart, of common birth but striking beauty; Eden is the darling of the circle and *the* suitor to watch.

House Lust: Allure Whitlock, daughter of the Duke of Whitlock; Allure is rumored to enchant a great many with her smoldering stare.

House Sloth: Erudite Monroe, daughter to the marquess; this suitor spends her time deep in the research wing of House Sloth, a voracious reader and lover of supernatural history.

House Greed: Ava Rice, of common birth; Ava's parents own several gaming hells in their circle and are rumored to be wildly successful at collecting their due.

House Envy: Omen Seagrave; Omen's father lost their family title in a bad bet at none other than Ava Rice's family gambling den. Their private interactions might be more entertaining than the prince's attempt to truly fall in love.

House Wrath: Cobra Pierce, of common birth but born into a legacy of combat fighters; Cobra is cunning on and off the battlefield.

House Pride: Vanity Raven, of noble birth; Vanity is anything but a raven-haired beauty. With the shimmering golden looks that grace most in her circle, she is one of the most physically stunning suitors. If the prince is thinking with his favorite appendage, she'll certainly take an early lead.

Until next time, stay scandalous!
Miss Match

THIRTY-TWO
Adriana

COBRA, THE HOUSE Wrath suitor, was in the guests' training rooms located on the second floor, tossing daggers at a straw dummy.

Her long ebony hair was braided into an intricate crown around her head, her black leather trousers hanging low on her hips. The gold corset she wore had sheer sleeves that ended in what looked to be metal wrist cuffs. She exuded her House of Sin in every way.

Her gray eyes turned to where I lingered by the threshold. A dagger flew through the air, hilt over blade, then struck the dummy with a loud thwack.

Cobra expelled an annoyed breath.

The dummy's head rolled to the floor.

She shot another look my way, then retrieved her throwing daggers. "You're Eden's sister. And Miss Match, right? Of 'stay scandalous' fame? I didn't get a chance to speak with you at the welcome dinner."

With everything that had happened over the last couple of days, I'd nearly forgotten the catchphrase was still wildly popular. I hoped my smile was pleasant and not encroaching on a grimace.

"Yes." I moved into the room. "If you've got a few moments, I have some questions for the next advice column. I'm working on a special piece to introduce the suitors and hopefully give some romantic advice based on your previous dating experiences."

Cobra lifted a shoulder and yanked her daggers out one by one. "What do you want to know? If you're hinting at the rumors about my father's hunting trip, I'm afraid that's off-limits."

I valued my life too much to stick my nose into *that* scandal.

"I'm only interested in your history with the prince. Anytime you've previously interacted. First impressions. Your hopes and relationship goals. That sort of thing."

She tossed the dagger in the air, watching me. "I actually met Prince Gluttony at the All-Sinners Ball several years ago. He was quite flirtatious."

My brows rose. I didn't recall seeing her there, but then again, I'd been occupied with my own emotional drama that night. I didn't know why the information surprised me.

"Interesting." I scribbled down the note, taking careful pains to not break my quill. "Did either of you engage in anything more serious than flirting?"

She gave me an amused look. "Nothing that would give me an advantage in this competition, if that's what you're asking."

It wasn't and she'd very impressively dodged my question. "Do you recall any details of that night that might intrigue the public?"

And by *the public* I meant me. I was horridly curious about someone else's perspective on that night that changed so much for me. Axton's reaction last night had been annoying enough for me to consider digging into it again.

"Let's see." She cocked her head to one side. "I remember thinking the prince had no shortage of romantic interest. But I don't remember much about what he was doing. It was a decade ago."

Deciding to stretch the truth a bit, I said casually, "One of the suitors recalls him being enamored with a commoner. So much that he'd been on the verge of proposing."

"Oh, how deliciously scandalous." Cobra drew back, her surprise seeming genuine. "I don't remember *that*, but I also was occupied with someone that night, too. She'd had the most interesting feather we were discussing. I recall it vividly because I thought it looked like Prince Envy's razor-like quills. He had quite the legendary rule about lovers then." At my blank look, she waved her hand. "You had to be there. Is the commoner one of Gluttony's suitors now?"

"I'm afraid I don't have that information," I lied.

I asked a few more questions about the competition, her hopes, what she wanted for her future, her ideal romantic date, any relationship advice she had for others, then excused myself.

My intuition was buzzing, but I couldn't quite sort out why.

After my meeting with Cobra, I decided a walk around the castle would do me a world of good for multiple reasons. I found out from Sophie that the suitors were getting ready for high tea with the prince, so I'd set out earlier tomorrow to interview everyone else. Which meant I had time to poke around the castle while everyone was occupied with the competition.

That I was also doing everything in my power to avoid the prince was beside the point.

I couldn't believe I'd nearly walked in on him, shirtless, in his private sparring room. I'd thought he'd be busy courting his suitors, not brawling with his brother.

One glance at his sweat-covered, tattooed body and my mind promptly went straight to the gutter. I vowed to steer clear of that section of the castle for the rest of my stay.

I meandered down the corridors on the farthest edge of the castle. I'd only ever seen the main level where parties were thrown, and House Gluttony was practically the size of a small city.

I veered down to the lower levels. I wasn't sure yet what I was hoping to uncover, but servants were a wealth of information. Perhaps I'd overhear something scandalous.

The ground floor was a hive of activity—servants filtered in and out of the main corridor, busily tending to the castle's needs. Maids with armfuls of freshly laundered linens rushed to and fro, while others polished silver, stoked the fires, and prepped for the coming festivities.

The first phase of the competition was taking place soon; rumor claimed it was something about kissing. I wouldn't be attending, for obvious reasons. The magic that bound me to the prince made me have some primal urges. It wouldn't be very becoming to go screeching at his potential brides and launch myself at them like a rabid monkey. Sophie would be horrified.

The thought made me laugh as I continued my stroll.

Several cooks toiled in a large kitchen. The smell of simmering stew wafted out into the hall as they chopped vegetables and stirred bubbling pots on the stove.

I narrowly avoided a collision as footmen hurriedly removed dishes from the upper guest chambers and carried them down to be cleaned in the scullery.

Chatter from nearly every chamber filled the air with an energetic hum, occasionally punctuated by laughter or an exclamation from one of the servants as they went about their daily tasks. Despite the absolute chaos of the scene, everyone worked together in perfect unison to ensure the efficient functioning of the castle.

If any of the suitors were obnoxious, I'd never know. I didn't overhear one bad word passing between the staff, even down here, where they could speak freely.

I also didn't hear any whispers of ice dragons or sense anything was amiss.

Everyone smiled pleasantly as I passed, nodding hello. They didn't seem to be pretending, but looks could be deceiving. Maybe the prince had altered their memories.

I dismissed the idea as soon as it came.

I strolled along the corridor, peering into some more chambers, curious about what one did with so much space.

House Gluttony really was like its own small city—there was a butcher, sprawling fresh market, bakery, winery, tailor, and several more kitchens. Waitstaff and cooking staff and guest services and event planning. And those were all located on this one floor.

By the time I reached the end of the corridor, where two staircases diverged, I was ready to retire to my room to change. I hadn't unearthed any clues here, so I'd venture into the shadow network and see if any of my informants had resurfaced yet.

Enough time had passed that Sophie and Eden should be at tea with the other suitors, trying to win the prince's wicked heart. Except...I was intrigued by the unique set of stairs.

Maybe it was the writer in me, but my mind spun with stories as I lingered at the crossroads. It certainly wouldn't hurt to spend a few more moments exploring.

One side of the staircase was bright, cheerful, clearly leading up to the main level, where parties were normally held, but the other spiraled down into the deepest, darkest pit of despair, if the bleak stone and medieval torches were anything to judge it by.

I went to take the upper stairs but paused again, my attention sliding to the darkened stairwell, which *had* to lead to some subterranean lair.

Or likely the dungeons. Which wasn't far off from my first impression of "poorly lit torture chamber."

Sophie would certainly pitch a fit if she knew I was entertaining the thought of touring the dungeons. Surely she had some rule against it that meant doing it would be another smudge on my sister's reputation. And really, it was a boring old dungeon. What fun was there to be had?

Firelight flickered as if some underground breeze stirred from far below, the scent of musk or perhaps mildew traveling up with it.

A damp, dark dungeon, then. Wonderful.

Iron sconces were spread far enough apart that most of the stairwell was left in shadow, adding to the medieval charm.

I wasn't prone to superstition but couldn't stop the involuntary shiver from rolling down my spine. It would be a *terrible* idea to go wandering alone down there. Which sent a rush of excitement through me as I shifted course and took that first step into the abyss.

If Axton was keeping secrets, this would be the most obvious location. Which meant it was the last place I'd find a clue.

Logically, I knew there wasn't anything truly terrible down there; it was all within the castle walls. But it was fun to give my imagination the space to craft all sorts of wicked tales.

That was by far more preferable than repeatedly thinking about what had passed between me and Axton on the rooftop of the Seven Sins last night. The desire. The thrill. The absolute horror.

The cursed way my heart raced at the thought of doing it again. I vowed to throw the biggest party of the century to celebrate my return to sanity once the blood oath was gone.

I shouldn't be thinking of the prince on his knees. I shouldn't relive each throbbing moment, yearning for his next forbidden touch. Madness. I was clearly drowning in it.

My hand trailed over the cool stone wall as I carefully descended, my ears pricked for any unusual sounds. Ghosts, goblins, wicked Fae, or bloodthirsty vampires—anything could be housed here, plotting escape and revenge.

Perhaps this was where the suitors had all met. I could imagine none more bloodthirsty than marriage-minded mammas as their heirs fought for Axton's throne.

Sophie would be livid if I was discovered.

My imagination was working double time, the thrill of potentially getting caught spurring me on faster. No one had mentioned anything about any part of the castle being off-limits, so I wasn't *too* worried about getting in trouble for exploring.

The stairwell spiraled down and down, the air growing heavier with condensation as layers of earth swallowed me whole from above.

It was nonsense, surely, but my ears popped, and my pulse thrashed, and I had to remind myself to breathe as the space between the light and shadows stretched farther and farther apart and danger seemed to press in all around me.

Finally, blessedly, I reached the basement level.

Alas, there was no sign of the suitors or the competition. But I'd ventured down and might as well explore a little more.

It was exactly what I'd expect of a dungeon. The floor was made of oversized gray stone slabs, the walls roughly hewn from the mountain House Gluttony had been built upon. Iron chandeliers hung menacingly low from the ceiling, most candles long since burned to the quick.

It was certainly dark, a little dank, and smelled of must and rotting straw.

Cells lined the right side of the wide corridor, the bars humming with magic. Which was unsurprising—the prince would have warded the cells against any magic wielders and supernatural beings that didn't wish to be trapped.

The left side also had cells, but these had solid doors instead of bars, making any curious mind spin with thoughts of all sorts of potential deviant occupants and their crimes.

They weren't any less potent with magic. I involuntarily shuddered at the amount of power feeding those closed cells, the magic making the fine hair on my arms stand on end.

I quietly continued down the corridor, stopping to peer into each of the cells. All were empty and looked like they hadn't been occupied in quite some time.

Inside them thick layers of dust blanketed the ground, undisturbed as freshly fallen snow.

Spiders spun webs in the corners, catching a plethora of skittering bugs.

It was rather disappointing for my imagination, but the rush of possibility and what-ifs had been worth the endless stairs I'd taken to explore. Out of everything I'd toured today, this had held the most potential. Alas, I had to admit that my intuition might be wrong. Maybe Axton really wasn't hiding any dark plot from the realm.

I turned to head back the way I'd come, when a growl rumbled the floor.

Pebbles broke away from the walls from the force of the noise, and I gripped the nearest bars to steady myself. The sound ceased as if it had been silenced by magic.

"Gods' bones. What was that?"

I stood, breathing in and out slowly, waiting for my limbs to stop trembling.

Mouth dry, I faced the opposite end of the corridor again.

The sound had come from the last door on the left. Part of me wondered if it did involve the competition. If so, it would be best for me to run before I was caught.

But...what if it wasn't anything to do with the game? What if it was the break in the case I'd been searching for?

That little devious wretch on my shoulder always got me into trouble. She whispered for me to get closer, to investigate the monster.

Feeling determined, I padded quietly to the door. I might be an advice columnist now, and I might not want to make any more trouble for my sister, but I couldn't walk away from seeing what that was and how I might write a story about it one day. If it was an ice dragon, if Axton was keeping one locked away here...then maybe Jackson *had* been killed by one.

The closer I got to the cell where the noise emanated from, the colder the air became. I slipped over a thin coating of ice. I glanced down, rubbing my hands over my arms.

The frost seemed to be coming from under the cell door.

I studied it for a moment, my teeth slowly beginning to chatter. I wondered if someone had left a window open and if that was why the creature had roared. It was positively freezing.

I waited for some jailer or guard to come check. No one stirred.

I inched closer to the cell.

A small circular window sat a foot or so above the middle of the door. The perfect place to spy on whatever nefarious creatures Axton was hiding down here.

I told myself I was doing it for Eden's sake. Who knew if this would be part of the next test? If I spied now, I could gain her an edge.

I rolled up onto my toes, hands pressed to the cold metal door, a hiss escaping at the icy bite as I peered inside.

A giant crimson eye blinked at me, its size taking up the entire window, making it larger than my open palm.

I opened my mouth to scream but was cut off as a rough hand clamped over my mouth. In the next instant an arm as hard as steel circled my waist, trapping me.

I kicked at the air but couldn't gain purchase as I was hoisted up and dragged away.

THIRTY-THREE
Prince Gluttony

IGH TEA WASN'T what I expected. The suitors were making the competition into something rather enjoyable. Instead of a dull afternoon of being hounded by marriage-minded mammas and their crown-hungry heirs, I was in the midst of an extremely detailed—and rather enthusiastic—conversation about the proper way to clean a kill.

It had all been highly entertaining up until the point when Val received a missive from one of my spies, then disappeared, leaving me to wonder what calamity had befallen my circle now. I should be the one storming off to see to whatever disaster was unfolding.

Instead, I listened dutifully as the House Wrath suitor continued her story.

"…as you can tell, I rather enjoy gutting any hell beast I can stick a dagger through," Cobra finished. "Though I find myself often splattered in blood and offal, it's rewarding to do a good job."

I offered her a polite smile. Cobra was not only fun to talk to; she was also as striking as the serpent she was named for, with jet-black hair that fell down her back and perfectly bronzed skin. She had full lips that begged to be kissed, and it was a shame that even with that tempting mouth, my mind was elsewhere.

And she noticed.

Her deep gray eyes were fixed to my face, her brows raised in expectation.

I suddenly felt like the worst sort of villain for leading each of these young women on. To me, the competition was a way to distract the realm. To them it meant something more.

They all deserved someone who would give their undivided attention. It wasn't Cobra's fault I'd disengaged from the conversation, but I couldn't explain my distraction.

If it were any other time, I would have considered asking her to accompany me on one of my legendary hunts. Cobra was interesting and would make a fine match.

But this wasn't any other time, and these circumstances were far from normal.

I couldn't stop myself from wondering if Val was off to deal with Adriana somehow, and realized Cobra was still patiently waiting for me to speak.

"Your mother must be exceptionally proud."

"No one can skin a tundra deer like my Cobra."

"Indeed." My smile was plastered to my face. I didn't know how I'd forgotten her mother was sitting with us. Perhaps I'd been distracted by the giant saber she was polishing across her lap. "A skill most valued in House Wrath when planning a future, I'm sure."

Cobra set her cup of half-finished tea aside and offered a polite curtsy I didn't deserve.

"Your Highness?"

I blinked at the new suitor seated before me, glancing nervously to her mother. She was golden-haired and golden-skinned, her eyes big and innocent. And familiar...

They were the same shade of clear blue as her sister's.

"Miss Everhart," I said. "It's nice to see you again. Are you enjoying tea?"

She nodded, then glanced down at her teacup.

I waited for her to press her suit, to charm me as the others had tried. I should have known she'd take after her sister and do the exact opposite of my expectations.

I sat forward, my curiosity piqued. She'd been chatty enough during dinner, though it had mostly been about the food and show. Eden had a particular fondness for the pickled hot peppers and spoke at great length about vinegar, of all things.

"How did you enjoy the kitchens?" I asked.

"It was lovely, thank you." She bit her lower lip, then leaned forward. The move was so similar to Adriana's I momentarily forgot where we were. "My sister is rather impressed with your home, I think. She loves to read, and our room is well stocked. Though it's missing some romantic mystery novels."

I sipped my tea, trying to sort out her game. "I was under the impression your sister loathed anything to do with romance."

A genuine smile touched her lips. "And yet you had her editor put her on a romantic advice column."

I felt my own lips twitching in amusement. "Yes, well, I do love to *stay scandalous*."

"A trait you're well-known for, Your Highness." She gave me a shrewd look. "I suppose that's why you sent all those gifts to our home too. To keep the realm talking."

An image of Adriana's masked face on the rooftop of the Seven Sins crossed my mind, her new, billowing cloak that sealed her fate flowing behind her.

Best to not reveal the truth about those gifts, or the way I'd unwrapped them.

I cleared my throat and considered loosening the cravat at my neck.

Has it suddenly gotten warm in here? I might need to open a window.

Unperturbed by my lack of conversation, she pressed on. "In fact, I told her you were rather charming and generous. Despite her protests, naturally."

I narrowed my eyes. "She was opposed to my gifts?"

"Very much so. Initially. Something about the word *insufferable* made her wary."

"But she did eventually come around?"

"Not entirely, Your Highness. Though I wouldn't worry if I were you.

She hasn't cursed your name in at least a week. Which I daresay is progress. Perhaps you ought to try sending her more gifts."

Eden sipped her tea. And I'd swear the move was to hide that cunning gleam in her eyes. I forced myself to refrain from asking about her sister again.

We both knew sending Adriana any more gifts would be a terrible idea.

"And what of you, Eden? What sort of scandals do you find intriguing?"

She leaned in, dropping her voice to a conspiratorial whisper.

"Falling for someone forbidden." Before I could formulate a response, she straightened up, her disposition brightening. "Regarding my sister, I fear you've fallen into the trap she's laid. She refuses to admit it, but I know Adriana secretly yearns for a happily-ever-after."

Just not with me.

The thought was unwelcome. For a multitude of reasons.

"Are you and your mother both big readers, too?"

"In a sense. Mamma likes romances with lots of scandals in them, but I like cookbooks, Your Highness. I'm sure after my last request, it should come as no surprise that spending time in the kitchen is one of my favorite indulgences, though Mamma doesn't permit it often. Or at all. Which was why Vanity offered to accompany me."

My focus drifted to her mother.

I'd had my staff pull information on every suitor's family, taking special care with Sophie Everhart. If memory served from her file, she had been ruthless when she'd been hunting for a husband. She hadn't cared about titles, only wealth.

Adriana's father was a cunning merchant who'd had enough money to rival the Crown.

I wondered at their obvious change of circumstances. Adriana had been in tears over a broken jar of oil and ruined sheet of parchment.

"If you'd like to visit the kitchens again, you're more than welcome to. We'll be sure to keep your mother busy so she can't refuse."

"I doubt my mother would refuse you anything if she believed it would help my cause."

"That's very forthright of you."

"My sister and I do share the same blood."

"Yes," I said, "I'm beginning to see that very clearly."

Eden took her leave and the next suitor sat: Vanity, the stunning noble from House Pride. She was another intriguing choice, and if I had been truly in the market for a wife, it would be hard not to consider her.

I thought of the Miss Match column that hit the realm shortly before we'd arranged the tea. Adriana claimed I'd flirt with Vanity, and she was only partly wrong; I wasn't thinking at all with my favorite appendage. I was considering the tactical aspect. Along with her beauty.

Vanity's conversation flowed easily, the same as it had last night, her gloved hands reaching out to brush against my trousers each time she laughed.

It would be easy to fall into a flirtation with her. I could see us adventuring through life, laughing and finding common interests. Unfortunately, I'd barely registered anything she'd said, I'd become so distracted by whatever had taken my second from the royal tea.

When Val slipped back into the room, she didn't need to utter a word.

Something else had gone wrong.

Her expression gave nothing away to my guests, though.

I couldn't tell if Adriana was to blame or if the dragons had waged another attack on Merciless Reach. The last hour seemed to drag endlessly.

I sat there, smiling and flirting—pretending I hadn't a care in the realm—until the last suitor had gotten her time with me.

Then I stood, brushed my trousers off, and bade them farewell.

My heart raced as I strode down the corridor, waiting until I heard Val's tread behind me.

"Well?" I demanded. "What happened now?"

THIRTY-FOUR
Adriana

I THRASHED AGAINST my captor, trying in vain to smash my head into his, my muffled cries swallowed by his hand.

"You're testing my patience, Miss Saint Lucent. Calm down."

His voice was familiar, but it was hard to place it with his steel-like arm banded around me. He dragged me back to the stairwell, my pulse pounding the entire way.

"If I drop my hand, you must promise not to scream."

He didn't add "or I'll knock you out using magic or any means necessary" but the threat was clear enough from his tone.

"Understand?"

I nodded, and after another painfully long moment, he finally set me free.

I whirled around, stunned. "Prince Envy."

He looked me over coolly, his green gaze calculating and hard. "What are you doing down here?"

I could ask him the same thing. It wasn't typical for Princes of Sin to be wandering around each other's Houses alone.

I tamped down that urge, knowing I was already on the verge of uncovering something very, very wicked.

Another low growl had the fine hair on my arms standing on end.

For a second, I could have sworn Envy looked rattled.

My focus drifted behind the prince, down the long corridor filled with cells we'd come from. And whatever that creature with the crimson eye had been.

If *he* was unnerved by it, that meant we were all in trouble if it got out. I shuddered at the thought.

"What was in that cell?"

"Does Gluttony know you're down here?"

It didn't escape me that he'd ignored my question and responded with another. It was a typical diversionary tactic employed by each Prince of Sin.

My intuition went on alert. I'd bet anything the creature in that cell was responsible for Jackson's death. I'd been checking the royal report daily and they still hadn't mentioned anything about him. It wasn't standard procedure for a noble's death, especially one who'd been trying to enter the prized hunting guild.

"He never said I *couldn't* be down here."

Envy scanned me again, his dark brows slightly knitted. "Let's get you out of here before anything goes wrong."

I wanted to ask if that meant murder but refrained.

"Is he experimenting on that...creature?"

"You are far too curious."

"I'm a reporter; it comes with the profession."

His smile was all teeth. "Curious creatures typically end up dead. I'd be very careful if I were you."

It was advice from a rival court. My pulse raced harder.

"Why are you helping me?"

"I'm not altruistic, Miss Saint Lucent. I promise my motivation is entirely self-serving. Well, almost entirely. I am rather interested in your peculiar association with my brother. You seem to feel very strongly about him. I'd like to know why."

I searched his face. He wore the cold mask of a Prince of Sin well. But there was something else in his expression—there and gone in a blink—that hinted his questions might not be fully selfish in nature. If I didn't know any better, I'd think he was genuinely interested in helping his brother.

I thought of his recent engagement announcement. I'd missed the party but had heard from Ryleigh it was quite the event. Envy had fallen hard. Rumors claimed he and his fiancée had met while he was engaged in a Fae game—a deadly game with a hexed object at stake.

Ryleigh had investigated the matter, always curious when it came to hexed objects and the one that had eluded her all those years ago. She hadn't uncovered what Envy had been after, though. As far as I knew, no one had. His secrets were nearly impossible to unravel.

Which made me wonder all the more why he was here, potentially helping his brother with a reporter who kept needling him in the papers.

Maybe I was reading too much into our encounter; maybe he was just being kind. Or maybe he was helping his brother cover up something that would rattle the whole realm.

I gave him a polite, if bland, smile. "I'm afraid the past cannot be unwritten; therefore, it's best to leave it alone. Good day, Your Highness."

I stole one last look behind Prince Envy, no closer to knowing what that terrifying red-eyed creature was, then headed back up the stairs.

THIRTY-FIVE
Prince Gluttony

To avoid anyone from my court or staff overhearing us, I had to wait until we reached the war room tower before Val could give me the full update.

Her closed-off expression let me know the news wasn't good.

"How bad is it?"

"Here." She handed me the missive she'd received. "Judge for yourself."

Dragons are attacking their young.

Eggs broken in nests. Others torn apart.

Orders on how to proceed requested.

I raked a hand through my hair, cursing. It was unfathomable that they'd turned on their young. Ice dragons lived for a thousand years, but they only produced young every hundred years or so. My court would be in serious jeopardy if the next generation was lost, since the hunts were still the greatest way for me to stoke my sin and power.

A weak prince was a target for witches, Fae, vampires, shifters. My sinners could also align with another court, damaging me further.

I forced myself to go into that calm center, to think, to plot.

"I won't risk anyone else getting attacked. Tell the hunters to stand down. Envy's here for the competition. He and I will go out tonight once the suitors have retired for bed. We'll round up any hatchlings we can find and bring them here to hand-raise until this mess is sorted out."

More than a hundred years ago, I'd had a cave designed specifically to mimic a dragon's nest built not far from the stables. I'd kept Sil and the others I'd raised there until they could hunt and track on their own. It was as close to a natural habitat as possible. And it would be perfect for now.

"Speaking of your brother…"

I raised my brows. "What now?"

"He caught Miss Saint Lucent in the dungeons."

An overwhelming sense of dread swept through me. "Tell me she didn't see Silvanus's cell."

"Afraid I can't do that, Your Highness."

I blew out a breath. "Have her meet me in my private study in thirty minutes."

"There she is. The hellion of the hour."

Adriana flashed me a scathing look as she entered my private study, immediately halting once she saw we weren't alone. I'd called in reinforcements for our meeting.

Lust and Envy leaned against opposite ends of my desk, two perfect images of indifference, though that couldn't be further from the truth. Envy had been on edge since he'd scared her from the dungeon. Adriana had come very close to uncovering our secret.

My brothers were all scheduled to arrive later tonight for the first part of the competition tomorrow morning, but I'd wanted Lust and Envy here for this meeting to hopefully encourage Adriana to behave for the duration of the competition.

Her little excursion into the dungeon was precisely why keeping her chained to my bed would be ideal. In all honesty, I hadn't entirely ruled that out. The only thing stopping me from doing just that was the suitors. And the unexpected warmth the idea spread through me.

Cursed magic bond.

"I hear you've been exploring instead of working diligently on your column," I said, watching her closely. "Did you encounter anything interesting?"

She pressed her lips into a hard line.

We both knew she'd stumbled across something *very* interesting. It was only a matter of time before she kept digging into the matter I was desperate to hide.

My gaze swept over her. I could magic her memory away to ensure my secrets remained hidden. I *should* magic her memory away, as my brothers had so kindly pointed out. It was the wise move for the realm. And yet I couldn't quite bring myself to tamper with her mind.

Therefore, it was time for threats.

"Allow me to sate your overactive imagination," I drawled. "What you witnessed will be a test that takes place at some point of the competition. As such, I expect you'll keep it to yourself. I'd hate for your sister to be disqualified for interference."

I motioned to my brothers.

"Since they have suitors in the competition and a vested interest in it being run fairly, they will be watching to ensure you don't revert to your gossip-centered, *stay scandalous* ways."

"If you didn't wish for me to wander the castle, perhaps you ought to set rules."

"As if you'd follow them."

"I think we both know I'd follow them for the next...five weeks and five days."

Lust and Envy hadn't known about the blood oath, and while Adriana's comment was seemingly innocent, they were well acquainted with how oaths of that nature worked.

Their heads whipped in my direction, their gazes blazing with incredulity.

I would never hear the end of it now.

I shot Adriana a frustrated look. For her part, she'd gone pale. She hadn't meant to let that secret slip out, which went a long way toward thawing my ire.

I motioned to my brothers. "Leave us."

They both flashed devious grins at Adriana but kept their opinions to themselves, knowing it was my court and I'd proceed how I wanted to with it.

Miss Saint Lucent rose from her chair as well, but I shook my head, and she sank back down. "Not you. We have a private matter to tend to."

"I have nothing more to say to you, Your Highness."

"You seem to have plenty to say. Even when you ought to remain silent. Why stop now?"

I pulled her chair back, then circled around her again, noting she'd straightened up in her seat, her chin notched a degree higher. Defiant. And brave.

I stopped before her, then leaned against the desk, enjoying the flare of annoyance coming from her as she quickly pieced together why I'd tugged her chair back.

I'd granted myself just enough space to sit in front of her, forcing her to look up at me.

"You need to play nicely, Adriana. Not everyone knows about our little bond. I'd prefer to keep it that way from now on."

"Don't call me by my first name. We're not close."

I motioned to the little space separating us. "I'd say we're fairly close. Our previous night of debauchery notwithstanding."

A pretty blush rose on her cheeks. Knowing her, it was from annoyance.

"I was unaware that walking around was offensive."

"Walking is perfectly acceptable, and you know it. Snooping is quite the opposite."

"Unbelievable. I was doing my best to avoid *you* and your ridiculous bridal hunt. The dungeon was the last place I'd expect to find you or a test; it's not the height of romance."

My lips twitched with amusement. She had me there.

"If you're looking for an apology..."

I gave her one of my most charming smiles. I hadn't been, but now that she'd offered...

"On your knees."

Tension crackled in the space between us.

She looked me over, her gaze as frosty as the tundra. This woman would choke before she ever cowered before anyone due to rank or station. Not from pride, but from principle.

An admirable trait. Even if it pained me to admit it.

"No."

"I'm your prince. That was a command."

"You cannot force yourself upon me. Regardless of previous... mistakes."

"Such filthy thoughts." I smiled. "I want you groveling, Miss Saint Lucent. Now get on your knees."

She held my gaze, her hatred glimmering and palpable as she slipped off her chair and slowly sank to her knees before me. I watched as she winced from the kiss of pain.

My private study had a solid limestone floor and no carpet to buffer her body from the hard, cold surface.

I stood there, arms crossed, holding her defiant glare. So different from the passion I'd seen the night before, the searing heat. My Lady Frost was anything but cold when it came to the bedroom. Too bad that version of her was gone.

Though the current female was remarkable.

Many hunters twice her size and brimming with violence from the moment they came screaming into this world would have dropped their attention from mine by now.

Most couldn't maintain direct eye contact with a Prince of Sin for long—their innate sense of preservation kicking in, alerting them an apex predator had homed in on them.

Minutes slowly ticked by, silent and tense. Any one of the suitors or their managing mammas might knock at the door, hoping to gain favor, especially after our intimate high tea. It would cause quite the scene should they discover Adriana on her knees before me.

But I found I quite liked her there.

She wouldn't apologize for spying unless ordered to. And I had no issue handing out orders. If she didn't obey, she'd be punished.

As I took in the slight pressing of her legs together the longer she knelt before me, I had the oddest inkling that she might be amenable to certain tactics.

Well, will wonders never cease?

I didn't think her reaction had anything to do with our bond.

I reached down, lightly tracing her jawline, slowly tilting her chin up.

Just as I suspected.

She didn't bat my hand away, nor did she skewer me with her tongue. Hatred still burned red-hot in her eyes, but there was something new flickering there, too.

Something I recognized at once, even if she didn't.

Most sinners in our circle were gluttons for punishment, and Miss Saint Lucent *liked* a hint of pain. More than she'd ever care to admit, especially to the likes of me. Regardless of how I'd made her feel on that rooftop garden when she didn't know who I was.

I stroked her jaw, enjoying the domination, the control, the sensation of my callused fingertips tracing her petal-soft skin. My sin ignited, the power flowing through me in a delightful spark. Her eyes fluttered shut, the long, inky lashes resting peacefully against her cheeks. I had a very good idea of what she was fantasizing about.

When I told her to get on her knees, she'd accidentally given the truth away. Perhaps it was something she'd kept hidden even from herself, but it was our dirty secret to share now.

I ought to be worried about what she'd seen in the dungeon. I should be flirting with my suitors. Or combing through my scholars' files on dragon illnesses now that I was certain the witches had played no part in my court's perils. But here I stood, captivated.

I could blame being wholly engulfed on my sin, but it rang false.

"It must truly be terrible, Miss Saint Lucent."

Her eyes shot open, her hands instantly curling into fists at her sides.

For a moment, she'd forgotten how much she despised me. I could practically see her private struggle to leash her curiosity, to force her attraction away. I understood.

No matter how much I couldn't trust her, no matter how much trouble she'd caused me throughout the years, I still craved her. It used to be a secret fantasy I barely acknowledged.

"What is?"

"Wanting to wrap those perfect lips around my cock, hating me as you do." I pressed my thumb into her mouth, her lips parting almost eagerly at the intrusion. "I wanted you on your knees to apologize, nothing more."

When she didn't bite down, I pumped it slowly in and out, watching as she tried once more to squeeze her legs together while kneeling. Saints curse me. She was something.

"As I recall, you said you wouldn't be attracted, magic bond or not."

Her tongue swept over the tip of my thumb before she sucked it harder, and I felt the corresponding tug deep in me. My cock hardened.

Indeed, Miss Saint Lucent had a filthy little secret, too. One I couldn't stop myself from indulging in, no matter how foolish it was while the competition raged on in the press.

If anyone walked in now, with my trousers tented and my thumb pumping into her mouth, there would be little I could say that would make it seem innocent.

Part of me didn't care. Our time at the Seven Sins had ended, but that didn't stop this insufferable craving we shared.

She wanted to take me down her throat and I wanted to indulge her desire.

Given my reputation, a little deviance would be expected. But being caught with Adriana after our public war would certainly overshadow the competition in the scandal sheets.

Still, as she continued to take my thumb in her warm mouth, I longed to unfasten my trousers and give her exactly what she and I both wanted, consequences be damned.

I reined in my own attraction, denying us both our interlude.

"Each time you defy me in public, you'll be punished in private."

Her velvet tongue flattened, welcoming my thumb deeper.

"And I think you might enjoy it as much as I will."

I wasn't foolish enough to think she'd submitted fully. She wanted to bring me to my knees too. Get me as aroused as she was. But I was in control now. Just as I'd always be.

I played a little longer, then pulled free, watching her reaction carefully.

There was one more secret I'd like to unravel about this rival of mine. What she'd choose would tell me everything I needed to know about how to keep her close.

"I'm offering you a choice of punishment for today's little excursion. Choose to have me spank you. Or remain on your knees until dawn."

THIRTY-SIX
Adriana

THE PRINCE'S SOFT, sinful words repeated in my mind, stunning me into silence.

If it wasn't for the dull ache of pain radiating up from my knees, grounding me in the here and now, I'd swear I was in the throes of a terrible nightmare.

Surely I couldn't be considering his *punishment*.

Or, worse yet, feeling slightly aroused by the idea of it.

When I told him I wouldn't end up in his arms again, I meant it. The scoundrel had issued it as a challenge, and I had fully intended to win.

And yet, here I was, on my knees, completely, horridly aroused not a day later.

I was still shocked I hadn't bitten his cursed thumb the second he'd slowly pushed it inside my mouth. He'd taken me by surprise, and I'd been caught up in the sensation and the way it had made my imagination run wild. Biting him had been the last thing on my mind.

When I closed my eyes, I'd envisioned his hand tangling in my hair, tugging my head back as I took him deeper, my tongue following the hard ridge of his cock. Before I'd known my stranger was really Axton, I'd fantasized about doing just that.

Horrified by my physical response, I wracked my brain for a solid reason for my depraved fascination. I didn't harbor any secret desire for the prince; on the contrary, I couldn't stand him.

It *had* to be a result of our stupid oath. And of course the fact that we hadn't slept together.

If he'd bent me over the railing and given me several more orgasms, surely this wouldn't be turning me on right now. That was it. A simple, reasonable explanation. My stranger had wound my hair around his fist and that was exactly what I'd just pictured the prince doing.

That my stranger *was* the prince was beside the point.

I exhaled a quiet breath, relief spreading through me. It wasn't Axton's dangerously low purr or wicked intentions; it was the vision of my masked stranger demanding those same dark acts that made me want to comply. It was the idea of being caught in his private study, on my knees, taking him down my throat, that turned me on. Replacing Axton with my stranger granted me leave to fully lean into my arousal, to sink into the fantasy without boundaries.

I'd *liked* it when he'd kicked my feet apart that first night, taking control.

I also liked the fear coursing through me now, the thrill of someone walking in, finding us engaged in a new type of war. I'd be the one on my knees, but that's precisely where I'd take him once I was through with him.

Gods, I wished Axton's identity was never revealed. I'd give anything to be with my stranger now. I closed my eyes, imagining it had been him pumping into my mouth, tasting like salt and sin as I swallowed him down.

It would be so easy to pretend I wasn't in the prince's private study, his castle filled with hopeful brides, as I unbuckled his belt, slid down his pants, and made him regret denying me.

"Adriana."

Axton's tone held a note of authority. And, if I wasn't mistaken, a hint of yearning.

Had he been suffering from this madness since we last parted too?

The constant craving. The memories. The unquenchable desire. Part of me hoped he had. That he was as haunted, as disturbed and distracted too.

"Choose."

Remaining on my knees until dawn was out of the question. I had to get out of this room and this temptation before I did something I'd regret.

My body thrummed with a need so powerful I ached. And it had nothing to do with the pain of kneeling on the stone floor before my wicked prince.

"You're supposed to be finding a bride," I said. "Not indulging in your sin."

"You're delaying the inevitable. Now choose."

My attention swept around the room. It was papered in dark cobalt silk, the chairs made of supple leather, the desk strong and seductive like its owner.

I shook myself from my idiocy. Axton was a plague I needed to eradicate from my system. Immediately.

"Blood oath or not, I'm not going to submit to your depraved whims, Your Highness."

"Your choice is to remain on your knees, then?"

"My choice is to carry on with my day, far from you and your debauchery. I already apologized about exploring the dungeons. What more do you want?"

The look he flashed my way had my pulse speeding and throbbing in all the right places. He looked like he very much wanted me to choose the first option, to sprawl across his knee.

"I'm debauched?" His mouth curved. "I've said nothing of this being a sinful bedroom game, Miss Saint Lucent. When I ordered you to your knees, *you* were thinking of my cock, while I was only after an apology. A charge you didn't deny, by the way. Your thoughts slant toward naughty places all on their own; don't blame me for your inner deviant. I simply aim to please."

I mustered up my most haughty tone. "Let's get this over with. I have an article to draft up and plans later."

His hazel eyes sparkled devilishly. "Say the words, darling."

"My choice is corporal punishment." I gave him a saccharinely sweet smile. "Obviously, I need to satisfy my inner deviant. Shall I bend over the desk, or will the chair do?"

Gods, did I hate the male.

His knowing look called me on the fact that I didn't consider this a punishment at all.

Axton shrugged out of his suit jacket, tossed it across the high-backed chair behind his desk, then slowly rolled his shirtsleeves up, watching me intently as his bronzed skin came into view.

He had plenty of lovers to tell him of his beauty. I was mostly intrigued with the power behind the corded muscles of those forearms, wondering what he did to earn that level of definition. He finished rolling his sleeves, then crossed his arms.

"Anyone might walk in on us," he said.

My breath lodged in my throat.

"Then I suppose you'll need to explain yourself if we're caught."

He was the picture of pure male arrogance as he gazed down on me. I was horrified to realize how wet I'd gotten between my legs. How painfully I ached with need.

I *wanted* his hands on me. And he knew it.

"Much as I hate to pass up this glorious opportunity to put you over my knee," he said, not sounding at all sorry, "I'm afraid I must prepare for tomorrow's event. Make sure you behave until then or else next time I won't be merciful. You may rise."

I bit the inside of my mouth so hard I nearly drew blood. I rose as gracefully as I could, unwilling to give him the satisfaction of seeing my anger at his dismissal.

He gave me one more wolfish grin, then strode toward the door, pausing once he'd reached the threshold.

"I'll have some items sent to your chambers to ensure you remain entertained there and don't cause trouble between now and tomorrow's grand event. You can punish yourself for as long as you desire, though fair warning: the toy you'll probably choose as the best punishment was modeled after me."

"Filthy, despicable bastard," I muttered, brushing down my gown to avoid strangling him.

Dark laughter echoed from the corridor as he left, annoying me more.

Before it faded, I swore I heard him say, "You have no earthly idea, darling."

To avoid running into Axton again before the first public suitors' event in the morning, I called for a maid and asked for the next Miss Match column to be delivered to the *Wicked Daily*.

Mr. Gray had sent a missive earlier this morning, threatening to personally pick up the article if it wasn't on his desk by noon. Apparently, the "Meet the Matches" special was another raging success for our paper.

Ryleigh had been inundated with reporting on all the gossip swirling around but managed to send a note my way, filling me in on early whispers of who the favorite suitor would be. Thus far, most had singled out Eden and Vanity based on my write-up.

A strange feeling twisted my stomach into knots. I *wanted* my sister to be a front-runner but struggled with what I'd do if she really won. Especially as my secret encounters with the rakish prince became more…complicated. I'd need to do a better job of avoiding him.

Which shouldn't be hard if I spent all my spare time researching dragons.

I glanced around the shared sitting room. The little library caught my eye.

Several books looked to have been delivered sometime that morning, mostly mystery romance novels and adventure stories. But others, located near the top, which I reached by standing on a settee stacked with several pillows, looked promising.

The one I picked was an ancient-looking thing almost hidden on the upper shelf; its cracked leather binding had pages half dangling from where they'd been sewn to the spine.

It was about different creatures living in the Underworld and might help me narrow down what that giant crimson eye belonged to. It wasn't a dragon—everyone knew their eyes were iridescent—but it could be some other lesser-known beast that lived in the north.

I wouldn't do anything to jeopardize my sister's place in the competition while it was going on, but I needed to satisfy my curiosity.

A fire blazed pleasantly in the hearth, the sitting room comfortable and cozy.

A few plush chairs were set up in different seating arrangements, some meant for hosting acquaintances for drinks, some for enjoying meals, and the one I sat in now was perfect for curling up to read.

Which I tried desperately to do, but my mind kept wandering, bouncing from the incident with Axton to the dungeon and my own muddled feelings. I'd *sworn* Prince Envy had looked nervous. It wasn't an emotion I'd ever associated with any prince. That alone made me even more convinced something significant was happening, something they were all plotting.

It would sound mildly delusional, if Axton hadn't tried so hard to divert my attention in his private study directly after. And, despite how much it pained me to admit it, he'd done a very good job at it. I *had* been completely focused on him, on his so-called punishment, and had stopped wondering about the red-eyed creature he'd locked away.

But what would scare a Prince of Sin? Better yet…what would scare more than one?

I'd read the same paragraph on winged hell boars over and over, mind spinning with theories, until a knock sounded at the door, and I finally set the book aside.

True to his word, the damned prince had indeed sent toys to my bedchamber, along with ribbons and chains. He'd tucked an instruction manual in, complete with pictures illustrating how I might tie myself up and pleasure myself with a riding crop at the same time.

A note scrawled in his hand offered a few suggestions if I needed "inspiration" on how to ride the beast.

I upturned the box into the trash bin, seething at him.

Arrogant, no-good demon. I ought to tie the ribbons around the toy like a present and send the damned thing back with a message for him to respectfully use it on himself.

How dare he continue his rakish behavior while courting seven hopeful ladies. I ought to rejoice at slipping that noose all those years ago.

There was no world where Gabriel Axton, the Prince of Gluttony, would ever be monogamous. Which was one more reason he was all wrong for my sister.

I snatched my book back up, determined to read, but gave up again once I had to reread the same sentence several times and still couldn't retain anything. I was too on edge, too caged, to settle in and get lost in the history of hell beasts and their supposed start as hexed souls.

I paced around the private suite we'd been given, still in a dark mood. Just when I was certain I couldn't despise the prince more, he'd gone and proven me wrong once again.

On your knees.

His voice had been a silken purr despite the steely command. I highly doubted I was the only one who'd assume that tone indicated he had more than an apology on his mind.

Another knock interrupted me from thinking any further deviant thoughts.

A footman greeted me warmly. "I'm to escort you to dinner."

I hid my scowl. It was a polite way to let me know His Highness wasn't leaving me unattended. With a smile that promised retribution to my nemesis, I followed the footman into the corridor. If I didn't visit the apothecary soon and pay for some hex to—

I halted.

"Gods below. That's it!"

The footman turned, a crease forming in his brow. "Pardon?"

My pulse raced so hard I nearly took off sprinting. I was right on both counts.

"Miss?"

I blinked at the servant, trying to calm myself down and not give him any more reason to think I was behaving suspiciously.

I fanned myself, knowing it wouldn't be hard to make him think I'd become feverish.

"I'm dreadfully sorry," I said, out of breath. "I'm afraid I'm not feeling well."

Before he could encourage me to follow him anyway, I darted back to my rooms, slamming the door as I leaned against it, my mouth curving in wicked delight.

Hexed objects. They were the only things aside from ice dragons that gave princes pause. When I ran into Envy in the dungeon earlier, I'd thought of his recent game. Of Ryleigh's investigation that had led nowhere.

My intuition had picked up on the subtlety and I'd been too distracted by that crimson eye to sort through what had made me think of it.

I guaranteed, whatever was happening with the dragons, or whatever other darkness the princes were frightened of, had something to do with a hexed object.

Discovering which of the seven supposed objects was to blame was my new goal.

Ryleigh would be the best place to start since she'd done a decent amount of research on them, but she already thought I was wrong about the dragon attacks, and our friendship was suffering through a strange patch.

If I went to her now, she'd ask questions. Questions I didn't want to answer just yet. But she wasn't the only source of information about hexed objects.

I knew exactly where to find more information on them and still keep my secrets.

And it involved slipping out of the castle as soon as possible.

THIRTY-SEVEN
Prince Gluttony

*B*LOODY HELL," I cursed, staggering forward from the sudden impact.

Excruciating pain lanced through my back as five talons pierced my flesh clear to the bone. I gritted my teeth to keep from shouting. I'd taken plenty of talons to the chest and back, but this was pain unlike anything I'd ever experienced before.

I wrenched myself free of the dragon's claws, my dagger flying out of my hand, sinking into the snow several paces away.

I swore and rolled to the side, narrowly avoiding another hit. The wounds in my back tore open from the movement, the pain making my vision swim.

Teeth snapping perilously close, the dragon dove for my throat, its snarl rippling through the night as I dodged its next attack.

It knocked me to the ground again, all four legs crushing the breath from me as it drew back, preparing to unleash its unholy flames.

I wouldn't die, but I didn't like the idea of having my flesh singed off.

A horrendous amount of time would be needed to regenerate after an injury that intense, and our little farce to distract the realm with the competition would be for naught.

It would be rather hard to explain a prince who'd been scorched.

I growled and launched the dragon off me, muscles trembling from its massive weight.

Not a moment too soon. Icy fire slammed into the nearest tree, the snow-covered branches bursting into white flames. Gods' blood. That was far too close for comfort.

"Got it?" I shouted to Envy, eyes locked on the snarling dragon as it stalked closer. My wounds hadn't healed yet. And the dragon seemed to sense my weakened state.

"Unless you get eaten, you'll be the first to know."

Sarcastic prick.

I jumped to my feet, circling the dragon as it snapped its jaws at me. This was taking far too long. We should have been in and out of the dragons' den in seconds.

Our plan was clear—I'd cause a distraction; Envy would grab what we'd come for.

I chanced a look at my brother. Envy's head cocked to one side as he studied his opponent. We didn't have time for plotting. We needed to act. Swiftly.

The dragon fighting me launched itself at my chest; I avoided its talons by inches, each sudden movement making my breath catch.

"It's a gods-damned baby," I shouted. "Scruff it like a kitten and get out of there."

"Vicious little thing tried to take my hand off."

"I'll take your cursed head off if you don't hurry."

The dragon lifted its massive snout, snuffing the air.

Since ice dragons were extraordinary predators, it knew it had dealt a winning blow. Whatever was happening with my wound was already starting to fester.

If we didn't retreat soon, I'd be in serious trouble.

But I would stay here and battle as long as I could. We'd already lost two hatchlings. I refused to leave without saving this last one.

The wounds throbbed in time with my heart, indicating the dragon's talons might have been coated in poison or some other toxin that was impeding my ability to heal.

With little choice, I confronted the dragon head-on. Charging the beast, teeth bared.

It collided with me in a snarl, talons scraping down my chest. But my effort hadn't been in vain—the great scaled beast retreated from the impact, finally stepping into the snare I'd set.

In a whoosh, the dragon launched into the air, shrieking at the iron clamped around its hind leg. With its focus entirely set on escape, I rushed to Envy, plucked the damn baby dragon up by the scruff, then carefully tucked it into my cloak.

It burrowed against my leather, bleating softly.

"Let's go."

I didn't have the energy to call forth my wings or *transvenio*—I was severely weakened from the blood oath, vow with Blade, and whatever toxin was in my system—so we raced down the mountain, sliding over the mixture of snow and ice that coated the ground, the sounds of the furious ice dragon piercing the night.

Envy occasionally shot me a concerned look, his attention sliding to my leaking wounds, but I ignored him, pushing on through the treacherous terrain. The snare wouldn't hold the ice dragon for long. We'd be lucky if we made it to Merciless Reach.

We were close, though. A few more meters and the stone fortress would come into view.

My steps faltered a few times, but through sheer force of will, I put one foot in front of the other, my vision going in and out of focus like mad.

"Almost there." My brother dragged me alongside him. I had no recollection of Envy even taking my arm but realized through the haze descending that he'd taken most of my weight.

Finally, the fortress emerged like a fist punching the sky.

We staggered toward it, the roar of dragons echoing off the walls.

Envy's muscles tensed as he hoisted me closer and all but ran us into the enclosure.

White flames scorched the wall beside us as Envy tossed me inside, then kicked the door shut.

He reached down and pulled the little dragon from where I still clutched it to my chest, swearing he'd see to it. The little creature flapped its feathered wings, iridescent gaze locked on mine.

"Safe," I said, not caring if I was speaking to a dragon in a soft tone in front of my brother. It blinked down at me, tucking its wings in tight.

Then it looked at Envy and sank its teeth into his hand.

My brother cursing the old gods for creating tyrant baby dragons was the last thing I saw before the world went dark.

A stern face swam into focus. Helga. The royal healer shook her head, her short gray hair swinging with the motion. I blinked as more of the room came into view.

Stone walls, straw mattress. A tapestry tacked to one wall to help keep the draft out.

I was in my private room in Merciless Reach. I hadn't slept here in years.

I dropped my head back, closing my eyes as the wave of nausea passed.

Helga clucked her tongue.

"Taking a baby from its nest isn't your finest idea, Your Highness. You're lucky you didn't get hurt worse."

"Had no choice."

Helga hummed as she wrapped a bandage around my chest. "You could have left it."

I thought of the little dragons we hadn't saved. I would take ten more wounds if it meant they could have survived.

"Did anyone ever tell you you're as mean as you are talented with remedies?"

Her smile was sharper than the scalpel she used to cut the cloth.

I pushed up to my elbows, hissing at the searing pain. I glanced down at myself, hoping to see healed flesh at the parts uncovered by bandages, but the agony dashed that dream.

One bandage was wrapped tightly around my chest, covering the gouges in my back.

I had no idea what the wounds looked like, but the medicine soaked into the cloth stank to holy hell.

"Did Val already take the hatchling to the habitat cave?"

"Aye. She took the little biter there shortly after you arrived."

She sealed a jar of medicine and set it on the nightstand.

"Toxin or poison?" I winced as Helga helped me into a sitting position, stuffing an extra down pillow behind my back as gently as she could.

"Toxin from what I can tell. Nasty one." She nodded to the jar of suspicious-looking brown liquid on the nightstand. "You'll need to dress the wound twice a day for the next few days. Should heal up okay."

"I'll do my best. But make no promises." I rested my head against the wall, already tired. "I've got a competition to host. I can't smell like a rubbish bin. Lovers frown upon that sort of thing."

"Suit yourself. But having your flesh rot might be more of a deterrent to love."

"If they cannot love my fetid flesh at its worst, then they don't deserve me at my best. Isn't that how the mortal saying goes?"

Helga gathered her supplies and headed for the door, muttering the whole way.

She'd been nursing me back to health for decades and might be the closest thing to a mother I'd ever known.

Envy slipped into the room when she left, eyeing the bandage with distaste.

"You smell like a dead goat that's been baking in the sun for days."

"That's oddly specific. I'm sorry you've encountered that before." I closed my eyes for a blessed moment before opening them again. "How's the dragon?"

"Safe. Seems to like the habitat on your grounds. It's been chasing its tail and pouncing on moths. Little bugger bit Val, too."

I exhaled. At least the retrieval had been worth the pain. "Has any more news come about other offspring?"

Envy shook his head. "From what my spies gathered, those three were the only hatchlings born this year to their pack."

Not such an oddity. Ice dragons lived for a long time and often only produced a few offspring every hundred years or so. But to lose two-thirds of the new litter was unfathomable. I couldn't begin to consider the ramifications to my loss of power if they didn't recover.

I hoped the other packs were faring better. So far, we hadn't found evidence during our patrols that they'd succumbed to the same madness.

"At least we saved one," Envy finally said.

My jaws ached from clamping them together so hard.

Regardless of what was happening with the dragons, only saving one didn't make us heroes. It had been hours since I'd received the grim news that the dragons had potentially turned on their offspring, but I'd acted as swiftly as I could without raising suspicion.

Unless I wanted the scandal sheets to start looking into what I did when the competition wasn't going on, there was no way I could have left high tea to seek out Val and read the missive without speaking to each suitor. Then I had to address the Adriana-dungeon situation.

"The baby's eyes are iridescent," I said. "That means whatever's impacting the adults hasn't harmed it yet."

My brother looked like he wished to say more but turned his attention to the lone window set high in the wall. "Your oath with the journalist is a problem."

I'd been waiting for him to bring it up. Figured the bastard would choose the perfect time. I couldn't simply get up and leave and he damned well knew it.

"Bond or not, I've been saying she's a problem for a decade."

My poor attempt at levity missed its mark.

"You got hurt because you're not operating at full power when you're too far away from her."

I set my jaw. There had been some…discomfort. I'd expected to feel some slight pain but was surprised when it was much stronger than anticipated. I had a sneaking suspicion it was also worse because of the drain on my power I'd suffered by not sparring with dragons. I needed to fuel my sin another way, or we'd all be in serious trouble soon. I'd never sworn a blood oath with anyone before, and even if I'd polled my brothers, everyone's pain threshold was different.

Hopefully Adriana was in bed and hadn't noticed a phantom sensation.

"It's nothing I can't handle."

"Maybe this time." He exhaled. "But what happens when the dragons are farther north? You'll need to take her to Merciless Reach to avoid losing power next time."

"Absolutely not." I wouldn't bring Adriana anywhere near the dragons until the situation was settled. "I'll make do."

"To keep her safe or your secret safe?"

"Does it matter?"

He gave me a long look before staring back out the window.

"The frequency of the attacks has also increased over the last few days." Envy's tone was far too casual, indicating the comment was anything but.

"Your point?"

"Magic overriding magic gets messy."

"What the ever-loving fuck does that mean, Levi?"

"We'll find out soon enough." He finally dropped his attention back to me. "Rest up. Bathe. The first event is slated to start in a few hours. You need to give the performance of your life today. No one can suspect you're hurt. If they start digging, there's plenty of skeletons for them to unearth."

THIRTY-EIGHT
Adriana

I TUGGED THE hood of my cloak down over my brow, wiping snow from my lashes that collected in clusters. My gloves were soaked through, smearing the coldness across my cheeks.

I gritted my teeth and hurried along, my boots already so ice-cold and damp, the bones of my toes ached. Another brutal storm had blown in this evening, leaving a foot of snow in the streets, and the trek from House Gluttony through the city was miserable. And a bit unnerving.

This late at night, with only the eerie sound of snowflakes sizzling against the lampposts and the crunch of my own boots, it was easy to feel like you were being preyed upon.

By ice dragons, devious princes, or coin-snatching deviants, one could never tell.

I paused at the cross street, trying to get my bearings. The building signs were mostly covered, the streets so laden with snow it was hard to distinguish familiar landmarks. But that wasn't the only obstacle I was working through.

An uncomfortable feeling wound me up inside, like someone had started pulling a thread too tightly around my heart, wanting to drag me to their side. For some god-less reason, I wanted to follow it to its source. I rubbed at the knot in my chest, taking a moment to catch my breath as I peered at the street sign.

Roots and Remedies, the only apothecary shoppe run by an actual witch, was located several blocks away from the castle, almost bordering the night district. I was blessedly close. Blizzard, strange pain, or not, nothing would keep me from hunting down this particular lead.

I hurried along the street, thrilled to see the warm, welcoming glow of the apothecary. Sascha never closed; she claimed she didn't sleep either, but that wasn't substantiated by any information I could find.

Witches, true witches, weren't like humans who practiced spell work. These were supernatural beings descended from the goddesses, and, typically, mortal enemies of demons.

Why Sascha had chosen to align herself with House Gluttony was a mystery, but tonight I was glad for the peculiar decision.

I kicked the snow from my boots as I opened the door to her shoppe, the bell tinkling pleasantly to announce my arrival.

The scent of herbs wafted through the air, a lovely mixture of sweet and spicy and earthy. I glanced around at the shelves—on the far side were tonics and elixirs; on tables smattered throughout there were candles and incense and dried innards of gods knew what.

But at the very back of the store were wooden shelves filled with books. Spell books and hex books and remedies and potions and the standard curses and poxes.

Sascha came out from the back room, eyeing me with a slightly less hostile look than she reserved for most demons. "Still trying to hex the prince?"

Despite the increasing discomfort in my chest, my mood brightened. "Do you have anything new that would work without his true name?"

She snorted. "Glad to see you're as feisty as ever. What are you looking for?"

"Any information on hexed objects."

Her brows rose. "Thinking of going to war with Axton?"

"Not exactly." I kept my smile in place, unwilling to alert her to my true motivations. "Call it curiosity."

"Number one killer of cats."

"They do have nine lives, so I'll take my chances."

"Touché, Miss Match."

The witch scanned the shelves I'd been eyeing up, then disappeared into the back room once again. I made my way to the register, idly checking out the assortment of items she'd been tagging. A ledger was open that... My gaze sharpened. It wasn't a ledger.

It was a grimoire. It was the nosy reporter in me who wanted a better look. I'd seen plenty of spell books before, but a witch's grimoire was something special. More like a diary of personal spells often passed through generations of family.

My pulse pounded painfully as I rolled onto the tips of my toes, quickly scanning the words scribbled at the top.

Communico Dracones. It could be translated two ways, but each held the same meaning.

It was a spell used to communicate with dragons.

Sascha swept out from the back room with an ancient-looking book tucked beneath her arm.

"This book isn't for sale, but you're welcome to borrow it for a small fee."

She knew I didn't have much money to spare, and while she'd never admit to it, the witch could be kind when the mood struck.

"Thank you. When do I need to return it by?"

She looked me over. "I'll lend it out for three days. Agreed?"

"Yes, that will work." It would have to. I absently rubbed at my chest, watching as the witch cast a spell, then took the coins from my little purse. Magic sizzled and crackled across the book. "What was that?"

"The book will magic itself back to me in seventy-two hours from now."

"You ought to share that little trick with Prince Sloth. I've heard he gets irate if someone borrows a book and doesn't return it."

A devious sparkle entered her eyes. "I've heard he gets more than irate if someone crinkles the pages."

I glanced back at her grimoire. "Who was interested in speaking to dragons? Is that even possible?"

"Unless you'd like me to share your secrets, it's best to not try to pry others from me." She closed her spell book and narrowed her gaze on me. "You keep rubbing your chest. Are you in pain?"

There was little sense in lying. "Yes. But I can't afford a tonic."

She strummed her fingers on the table. "When did the feeling begin?"

"On the walk over here. It's been a stressful day."

"Describe the sensation. Sharp pains. Shooting, prolonged."

I eyed her warily. "You're awfully curious."

"Perhaps we're both a little feline in our ways."

I laughed softly. "It feels like someone's winding a thread around my heart, trying to lead me to them."

"I see." Any humor we shared slowly left her expression. "Hurry along, now. The clock is ticking on how much time you've got left with the book."

"Aren't you going to diagnose me?"

"Whatever you're suffering from, I can't address with a tonic or tincture." She seemed to consider her words carefully. "But the prince might have answers you seek."

"Why would he…" I cursed. The oath. I assumed this was an effect he failed to disclose. "I think I know exactly what's wrong. And it's six feet four inches of troublesome demon."

"It seems so." Sascha laughed softly. "You never disappoint, Miss Saint Lucent. I understand why you get under his skin."

I smiled sweetly. "Hopefully like an incurable rash."

I bade her good night and stepped back into the storm, cursing Gabriel Axton and his oath all the way to his wicked House of Sin.

THIRTY-NINE
Prince Gluttony

"GOOD MORNING, SUITORS. Thank you for joining me this lovely winter's day for our first public event."

I flashed my most charming smile at the group of potential brides standing before me, dressed in their thickest cloaks, ignoring the sharp pain radiating down my back. It had only been a few hours, and the dragon wounds still hadn't healed, not that I expected they would, given Helga's assessment, and each breath was more agonizing than I'd care to admit.

Though some discomfort was alleviated simply by being near Adriana again. At least my body wasn't fighting against the blood oath magic too.

My attention swept across the throne room—at my request, Val had had it decorated like a winter wonderland, leaning into the blizzards battering our circle this time of year.

Snow-covered bows arched down the aisle toward the throne, the little Fae orbs hanging from them offering a soft, flickering glow. Trees sculpted from thick slabs of ice twisted up toward the painted ceiling, giving the impression we were under a cloud-covered sky.

I'd even altered the temperature, so it felt as if we were all standing outside in an enchanted forest. The result was appropriately overindulgent and very House Gluttony.

Mugs of melted chocolate with brandy marshmallows and trays laden with pastries were passed around to the crowd, who'd been told to attend in their finest winter attire.

Despite the lavish setup for what promised to be an enjoyable event, today would be excruciating for me to get through. Though, given the nature of today's event, I wouldn't be the only one suffering. My sweet, devious rival would undoubtedly want to throttle me soon enough.

Which would prove entertaining for the papers. Thus far we'd done a wonderful job with keeping the scandal sheets busy, ironically, thanks in part to Miss Match breaking the story first, but that could change as swiftly as the next gust of wind.

I'd had everyone gather in my throne room—including Miss Saint Lucent—the chamber now filled to capacity with members of every House of Sin who'd scored an invitation to the grand event.

I wanted to lean into my public reputation, giving the realm everything they desired in their favorite rake.

I stood before my dragon throne, ensuring my voice carried over the excited hum.

"From now through the end of the competition, at least one suitor will be eliminated per week until the best match remains."

There was a polite smattering of applause from the crowd of courtiers.

My brothers stood stoically near their House members, watching the show with interest. All except Pride. He had declined the invitation at the last minute. A surprise to no one.

My brothers looked as eager as the rest of the crowd to find out what we'd be doing today. Rumors in the papers already hinted at it, and I was excited to confirm their suspicions.

My attention slid to Adriana. Our bond unexpectedly hummed as I took her in, and I wondered if she felt the corresponding sensation. I flexed my hand, wishing I had a weapon in it and was on the hunt, burning off whatever this growing hunger was.

No good would come from it.

I tore my attention away from her and settled it on much safer sights. My suitors. Vanity was resplendent in a gown and matching cloak that looked like spun gold. Eden stood beside her, wearing an amused expression that worried me.

She, like her sister, observed far too much.

Cobra played with a dagger, her expression set into one of pure determination.

Erudite sagged behind the ever-hostile House Greed and House Envy suitors, reading a book she'd snuck in, and Allure from House Lust eyed me up like I was on the menu today and she was rather hungry.

I'd chosen a lovely little test for today and knew Adriana would absolutely hate it. Perhaps enough to seek me out in private to tell me how much of a worthless rake I was.

An eventuality I shouldn't be looking forward to. We needed to stay away from each other, not keep tempting fate. I was already struggling to maintain control of my power while fighting a secret war at night.

"My brothers wanted each House of Sin represented as I decided on events, but as this competition is to find *my* match, I've decided to tailor each one to House Gluttony."

I scanned the suitors again, then settled my gaze on my rival.

I was very curious to see how she'd react to the news. The oath *had* to be impacting her as strongly. No matter how hard she'd pretended otherwise.

"Our first test will be kissing, in tribute to indulging sweet desires. Though I'm sure my brother will say it's secretly an ode to House Lust."

Excited shouts and catcalls went up from the House Lust section of the audience, my brother's whoop being the loudest. I'd decided, last minute, this "test" would be the easiest for me to withstand while I healed.

"But that's not all. The test begins now. Each of you will be given a chance to vote for your favorite suitor."

A lovely flush spread across Adriana's face and neck.

I would wager my crown she wasn't blushing from excitement. She was likely so angry she was contemplating joining House Wrath.

"In the spirit of keeping things fair, I'll be blindfolded. Whoever ignites the most passionate response with a single kiss wins. Everyone else will face possible elimination. Val?"

I motioned to my second-in-command, who strode up the dais, blindfold in hand.

Once it had been secured, I set my expression into my familiar mask. The crowd roared with approval. "All right. Val, please send the first suitor up."

With my eyes covered, the rest of my senses were heightened. I heard the light pad of her heels as the first suitor slowly ascended the dais.

I sensed her excitement and nervousness but also that she was oddly determined as she rolled onto her toes and ... gave me a chaste kiss on the cheek. My lips twitched. If I had to place a wager at one of Greed's gambling dens, I'd say that had been Eden Everhart.

The next suitor strode up to the dais, her steps ringing out like gunfire as her heels clicked against the stone floor. I had no guess at her identity as she gently nibbled my bottom lip.

Perhaps Erudite from House Sloth. It had been a slow sort of embrace. Book lovers made secretly devious bedmates. No wonder Sloth's House was a library.

The third potential match was before me, and with my eyes still damnably covered, my mind suddenly played a horrid trick on me. Instead of one of my suitors', it was Adriana's hands that were gently sliding up my chest, prompting my pulse to speed.

My face angled down to hers as if drawn by a magnetism we couldn't deny.

The moment our lips brushed, my hands settled on her waist, the kiss a slow, sweet greeting between lovers. I'd just been struggling to breathe, yet suddenly seemed fine now that it was my rival in my arms.

In the darkest recess of my mind I knew this wasn't real, that Adriana was across the room and would never kiss me so thoroughly in public—or private—but I didn't want to give up the fantasy just yet. My body hummed with new need as my hand idly stroked along her side.

My touch was so light, so tender, I felt her swaying closer, losing herself to our embrace. I slowly tugged her against me, needing to feel her heart beating in time with mine.

The kiss drew hoots and hollers from the crowd as we got lost in each other.

I ignored the building applause as I deepened our kiss.

Truth be told, I'd forgotten all about the competition. The other suitors. The many eyes glued to us. I wanted to fall back onto my throne with her on my lap and take her right there.

Adriana was all I—I abruptly stepped back, breaking the kiss.

Reality came rushing back in, nearly knocking me backward. I wrenched my blindfold off and blinked at the woman before me, the one whose eyes were a deep chocolate, not ice blue.

Vanity bit her swollen lower lip, then flicked her long golden locks over her shoulder, giving the crowd a slight curtsy that drove them into an uproar.

I glanced up, locking eyes with Adriana almost instantly. I expected to see her scorn, her disgust. The familiar look of annoyance at my public antics. There was none of that.

Her expression was impossible to read. No hint of fury or disappointment or anything else. It was as if she'd completely shut down.

A cold, dark feeling descended.

I took a step in her direction, propelled by our magical bond, and halted as Lust strode up to the dais, blocking my path.

He shoved the blindfold at me. "Finish the test, Gabriel. Everyone's watching."

My attention shifted to the rest of the room. All eyes were still fixed on me. Reporters, suitors, spectators—some already leaning in to whisper.

Now wasn't the time to falter or cause a scene.

I didn't look at Adriana as I snatched the blindfold. Instead of doing what I wanted, I gave the crowd a wolfish grin, and did what needed to be done for my court.

FORTY
Adriana

IT WAS SETTLED. I was going to the gallows for regicide. I couldn't believe Axton had sent a note—with obnoxiously neat handwriting—that *strongly suggested* I was to attend this grand public event.

He didn't say "or else I'll disqualify your sister and burn down your entire world including all your undergarments and perhaps steal your puppy if you have one" but I'm sure he would have if he had an attention span longer than that of a fly.

I wasn't sure what he was hoping to prove with this display, aside from knowing our magical oath would make this rather...uncomfortable.

Of course there was also his rakish behavior in his study last night, commanding me to my knees. And he wondered why I despised him? More the fool was I for thinking that things would ever be different, that he'd ever choose me in any capacity.

I stole a glance at my stepmother. She stood with the other parents of the suitors, her attention sharp on the competition. She'd barely spared me a second look when I'd taken my place near the back, thank the old gods for that.

Now I could seethe in private. I'd never felt territorial before; pissing contests ought to be reserved solely for dogs and ridiculous princes. Yet part of me wanted to march up to the throne and either slap or kiss Axton senseless.

Watching him gather Vanity up in his arms—kissing her like she was his favorite indulgence and he'd die if he didn't drink his fill of her—made me see a decidedly murderous shade of red.

It was, of course, proof that he would make an abysmal husband and my sister should run far and fast before getting swept up in his debauchery.

I pressed my mouth into a hard line as Cobra, the House Wrath suitor, strode up to the prince next, grabbed his lapels, and crushed her lips against his, taking his lower lip between her teeth in a punishing display of affection that made him wince.

The petty part of me hoped she made him bleed, but he'd probably enjoy it, the fiend.

I averted my gaze, trying to focus on the book of hexed objects I'd spent all night reading. The witch's book had been a wonderful starting point but wasn't as forthright as texts written by demons about the objects. Which meant I'd need to sneak into Axton's library and see what he had on the subject. Perhaps I might even delicately ask another prince if I could visit to see their libraries under the guise of research for my column.

Ryleigh was still the most likely resource for answering my questions about hexed objects, but I wanted to avoid going that route for as long as possible.

If this were any other time, if there wasn't any strange sort of tension brewing between us, I would feel differently. I hated that I'd stopped confiding in her—I hated it more that I'd kept so many secrets. One day soon I needed to sit down and talk with her, fill her in on everything that had happened these last few weeks.

Including my unintentional tryst with the prince I hated.

I stole a peek at the other Princes of Sin. Except for Prince Pride, all were in attendance. Each seemed wholly invested in the competition, their gazes alight with the need to win.

Even Prince Sloth was tense, watching from where he leaned against a column. My attention drifted over to Emilia, who stood beside her husband, Wrath, then drifted over to the silver-haired beauty standing with them. That had to be Camilla Antonius, the woman who'd beat Prince Envy at his own game.

My focus went back to the throne.

The next suitor pulled her shoulders back and marched up to the dais, looking like confidence made flesh in her flowing emerald gown. House Envy in all its jealousy-inducing glory. I ignored the languorous kiss now taking place between Omen and Axton, instead focusing on my own strategy to slip away to investigate.

Allure from House Lust flipped her long golden hair over her shoulder, then sauntered up to the prince, her entire aura exuding seduction as she tapped Omen on the shoulder and dismissed the House Envy suitor with a flick of her wrist.

Instead of yanking him to her or leaning in chastely as the others had done, Allure slowly circled him, trailing her fingers across his chest, his shoulders, his back.

I didn't know why I was still watching the scene; I ought to—

Axton grimaced. The look had been there and gone in an instant, but I'd been watching him closely. And I didn't think his reaction was because of pleasure.

He'd *flinched* when she touched his back.

There. It happened again. This time he'd winced.

I was suddenly very curious about his reaction.

Allure raked her nails down his spine, drawing him nearer. He stiffened, his chest barely seeming to rise with his next breath. I'd wager my soul he was injured.

Badly, if his actions were any indication. Princes of Sin normally healed within moments.

Allure didn't notice his reaction. But I couldn't help but stare as he slowly drew in a breath, the movement seeming to cause another bolt of pain.

What in the realm had he been doing to cause such an injury? But the better question was, how had he not healed yet?

Allure rolled onto her toes, her tongue teasing the seam of his lips.

Axton didn't deepen their kiss. I wasn't sure if he was in that much pain or if he simply wasn't interested.

Undeterred by his lack of participation, Allure moved her attention to the column of his throat, kissing her way up it. Axton's smile seemed to be stuck in place.

Lust catcalled from the crowd, encouraging more hoots to go up.

A diversion from a rival House of Sin. First Envy had been in the dungeons where that red-eyed beast was. And now Lust was making a scene.

How curious indeed. At least three Houses of Sin were involved.

This whole competition was growing more mysterious by the day.

I thought of the scandal sheets. The rabid excitement sweeping across the realm. Could it *all* be a clever distraction? If that was true, it would be an inter-court plot to fool us all.

I glanced back at Prince Lust, who continued to whoop and cheer, drawing the attention of the gathered crowd. If at least two of the other princes were involved, there had to be something big they were hiding. Something worth setting aside any inter-court rivalry.

Which meant they had to be scared.

While the final suitor staked her claim on Axton, I asked myself the same question I had the night before.

What would frighten a Prince of Sin?

Hexed objects and ice dragons attacking certainly. But what if it was more than that?

No one noticed when I slipped out of the throne room and hurried along the empty corridor toward the second floor. No one, that was, until Val stepped out from the shadows like some meddling ghoul from the Great Beyond. If only I had some holy water to banish her with.

I subtly patted down my bodice in case an errant vial was tucked away.

"Are you lost, Miss Saint Lucent?"

Her tone was pleasant, but the underlying feeling I got from our encounters was that she was mentally stringing me up and dicing me into little bites to feed to the dragons.

I didn't take it too personally. Val didn't care for most demons, vampires, witches, or really anyone—it wasn't as if her dislike was directed solely at me.

I had a feeling she'd prefer to stalk off into the woods and live her life peacefully in a cave, far from debauchery and anything else that annoyed her. Prince Gluttony very much included. Under different circumstances, I would rather enjoy spending time with the curmudgeon. I was sure she had a great many stories she'd like to vent after having to deal with him and his antics for so many years. Truly, she ought to be awarded some medal for her service.

"I was heading to the kitchens."

"Since your sister is one of Prince Gluttony's suitors, you needn't trouble yourself with fetching your meals. Simply call for service in your rooms."

"I only wanted a cup of tea. It's no bother."

Her smile never faltered. "I'm afraid I must insist. We wouldn't want anyone to report that our hospitality was less than extravagant. Would we?"

I studied the woman standing between me and the library, silently cursing. Unless I decided to barrel through her and thus cause a scene for Eden, I'd need to keep up my ruse of hunting down the kitchen and sneak out later.

"Very well."

I gave her a bright smile and silently hexed her firstborn to scream all night for months on end as I slowly made my way back to my family's guest suite.

I would rather sit on needles than return to the throne room and be forced to watch Axton swoon over anyone who'd have him while claiming it was done to help him find true love. None of the fairy tales ever said the prince had to kiss every maiden he saw to find his princess.

I made sure to stop and admire each painting I passed before returning to my chambers, wasting time in case someone was waiting there to escort me back to the cursed event to vote.

Unless I could cast a ballot to depose the prince, I wanted no part in deciding who kissed him best.

When I arrived at my family's suite, I wished I'd taken my chances with Val.

I glanced longingly into the corridor, debating if I should slip out again. One sharp look from Sophie decided my fate. I stepped in and closed the door with a quiet snick.

"You cannot honestly believe he'd think a peck on the cheek was the most passionate kiss, Eden. Do you have any idea how close you were to being sent home?"

Sophie towered over my sister, who sat primly on the edge of the settee. Eden's attention darted to me the moment I entered the room, her expression pleading. Despite the opportunity living in the castle provided for me to hunt down clues, and as much as I'd love for Axton to send us all home for personal reasons, I set my feelings aside and sat next to my sister.

Controlling my emotions was a monumental task, considering the aggravation that still burned through me from the whole miserable kissing contest.

Instead of showing any annoyance that would lead to questions, I pretended all was well.

"Do you think I ruined everything?" Eden asked.

"I happen to think he was amused by your kiss. It was the only one of its kind, therefore made you memorable."

Eden's bleak expression turned hopeful. "Are you just saying that to make me feel better?"

"Of course she is," Sophie snapped. "He's a Prince of Sin, not virtue. And if your sister had any clue how to snag him or any husband, we'd—Anyway, you'll need to do better."

I shot my stepmother a scathing look; she'd almost confessed my secret history with the prince.

"Did you see the corners of his mouth twitch after the kiss?" I asked. "Or read the way his body had angled toward her as she left? He was definitely intrigued. He didn't respond that way to anyone else."

Eden's brows rose. "I didn't notice that."

"It was fairly obvious," I said, not liking the spark of interest entering her gaze as she looked me over more carefully. "I've been watching him for a decade for my articles," I added, a touch defensively. "I'm used to seeing how he interacts with potential...suitors."

Before my sister could comment, Sophie tossed her hands in the air. "And none of it matters after Vanity's performance. Anyone could see he was the most passionate with her."

I had to mentally force my hands to remain unclenched at my sides.

Gods' cursed blood oath.

That had to be the sole reason for my surge of...unpleasant emotions. Except I knew seeing him act as rakish as ever after our encounter at the Seven Sins was stirring up old hurts. He hadn't cared one bit that I'd been standing there, watching the whole encounter. In fact, he never seemed to remember anyone else had feelings when his power-hungry sin ignited.

I would do everything I could to avoid him from here on out. For multiple reasons.

"Who did he end up choosing?" I asked, trying to thwart Sophie's next tirade about Vanity Raven and her supreme kissing skills. I could only play pretend for so long.

"He hasn't decided on a winner—they're still tallying votes." Sophie crossed her arms. "But he sent Allure Whitlock home."

"The House Lust suitor?" I asked, as if I didn't know. My stepmother shot me a look like I'd lost a few hundred brain cells in the last moment. "But that makes little sense."

"Why?" Eden asked, seeming genuinely curious.

I hadn't meant to say that out loud. I lifted a shoulder. "It's surprising that House Lust would lose the kissing contest."

A furrow formed between my sister's brows. It was the best excuse I could come up with and extremely plausible. Eden knew me well, though, and always spotted when I was diverting attention. She looked me over for a long moment before finally glancing away.

I exhaled quietly, then turned my thoughts inward.

If House Lust was involved in either covering up a dragon attack or preventing one, why in the world had Axton sent that suitor home? I would have thought he'd want to keep Lust close as a cover story. If that really was what was happening behind the scenes.

The plot had just thickened and the mystery lover in me was more determined than ever to fit the seemingly random puzzle pieces together tonight.

Rumors frightening enough to put the shadow network into hiding.

Ice dragons attacking.

Hexed objects.

Jackson's unconfirmed cause of death.

The realm-wide hunt for Prince Gluttony to find a bride.

Somehow, some way, everything tied together. And once I figured out *how*, I'd have a story that spanned farther than I ever could have imagined.

So far the picture being painted was bleak—the ice dragons had attacked, someone did die, and we were being fooled by our own press.

While Sophie and Eden argued over how to proceed in the competition, I excused myself under the guise of writing my next column and retired to my room, waiting until the castle had turned in for the night before putting my plan into action.

FORTY-ONE
Prince Gluttony

I SANK INTO THE steaming tub, my wounds screaming in protest. Today's contest had been a disaster for me personally, but the realm loved it, which was all that mattered.

Several scandal sheets hit the press within hours of the competition, excitedly claiming that Vanity Raven would win the crown.

Everyone from Ryleigh Hughes to Anderson Anders let it be known that House Pride would take the glory. Pride wouldn't be able to stay hidden from the events for long—he'd need to make an appearance after his suitor took an early lead. Or he'd start to suffer from the gossips turning their attention to him. Which would be a welcome relief.

Thankfully, because of that performance with Vanity, no one noticed when Allure ripped open my slow-healing wounds and I nearly passed out.

They'd been too busy scribbling notes and speculating about me and Vanity.

Little did anyone know, I'd been caught up in a fantasy involving my rival.

It had been so real, so vivid, I'd almost taken her on my throne. It was the first time one of my dreams had occurred while I was awake. I wasn't sure if it was a sign of my power dwindling from overuse or if the blood oath was causing another unseen complication.

Unease had my muscles bunching tighter despite the scalding bath.

Part of me still wanted to hunt Adriana down. I knew why Lust had interfered—and was grateful he'd stepped in before I'd caused a scandal. No matter that she didn't want me; I hadn't expected the kissing to get so heated during the competition today.

I might be a ruthless bastard when it came to certain things, but I wasn't cruel.

Adriana made it clear she'd never court me, even after our interlude at the Seven Sins, and I had several potential partners who I liked despite the deceptive start of this competition.

Maybe it wouldn't be the worst thing to allow myself to fall while still solving the dragon issue. Redeem my actions in some small way and forget my constant craving for the one person in the realm who would never have me. Maybe the dragon's fate was tied to mine.

If I could sort out what, exactly, that was.

Adriana's face suddenly emerged in my mind, forever taunting me.

The truth I so rarely admitted, even to myself, was that despite my reputation as a rake, I'd spent years turning away lovers, unwilling to pleasure them while I envisioned someone else.

It wasn't that hard to get away with, thanks to my court's insatiable need to overindulge. There were orgies on any given night, and no one realized I didn't *actually* partake.

This was my curse. To crave what I couldn't have.

And I couldn't tell if I was unable to break it or simply didn't care to because deep down I liked the pain.

Maybe magic wasn't involved, and I subconsciously chose to submit to the endless cycle of wanting what I could never have.

I closed my eyes, slipped under the water, and held my breath, allowing the herbs to sting my body into submission. We still weren't sure what had coated the dragon's talons to cause such a slow healing response, but at least the medicine was beginning to close the worst of them.

For the first time in what felt like ages, I began to drift, my mind going still and dark.

A knock at my bathing room door obliterated the serenity.

"Your Highness?" Val's voice accompanied her second round of knocking.

I broke the surface of the water, ran my hands through my hair to smooth it from my face, and considered abdicating my gods-damned throne.

"Enter."

Val grimaced when she stepped into the bathing chamber.

"Well? Did you come here to braid hair and bond in the tub or is there some crisis that needs my attention?"

"The hatchling escaped from the habitat."

I stared at her for a moment, trying to sort out if she was toying with me. When her expression didn't shift, I cursed.

"How long ago?"

"Five minutes. We think he's in the dungeon."

"How in the hells did a baby dragon make it from the habitat by the stables to the dungeon in five minutes?"

Val looked to the ceiling as if praying for someone to intervene. "It's fast and determined."

"And?"

"And the damned thing bites. Hard."

I stood from the tub, mildly amused when Val flung a length of linen at me to tie around my waist. As if anyone in my court cared a whit for modesty.

I quickly dried off and strode into my room, grabbing a pair of trousers and a shirt. Despite his momentary alertness with Adriana, Silvanus still hadn't roused from whatever gripped him, so the baby dragon should be safe.

A few moments later, we were making our way to the dungeon, hunting down a menacing baby dragon.

In a very princely manner, I dropped to my knees and crawled across the dirty floor, checking under the straw in the cells. Flipping over any stones the little beast could have crawled behind.

Val assembled a few hunters, and they were all in similar positions, softly cooing and clucking their tongues to lure the hatchling out.

I shook my head at the sight. Here stood some of the most fearsome members of my court, crawling around the dungeon, hunting a baby dragon.

It felt good to find some levity after the disastrous day.

I'd been about to make a joke when a roar erupted from Silvanus's cell, followed by a panicked bleat.

Of course the damned dragon would come to now.

I jumped up from the ground and raced to the end of the dungeons, skidding to a stop in front of the dragon's cell, dreading what I knew I'd find.

I wrenched the door open and halted.

Silvanus's jaws were clamped onto the hatchlings neck, his eyes glowing that violent, bloody red. I took a careful step into the chamber and froze as he shook the baby dragon.

"I'm unarmed, Sil." I held my hands up. I sensed Val moving in. "Stay there," I commanded. "No one else comes near him."

I didn't want the dragon to feel like he'd been cornered or overpowered. There was no telling what he'd do then. I kept my attention locked on him, watching for any flicker of recognition. There was nothing to indicate he was aware of anything but plotting his next move.

"Set the hatchling down. You want to fight me."

I took another step toward him, stopping when his next growl rumbled the floor.

The baby struggled in his grasp, bleating. Its panicked cries pierced my own cold heart.

If I didn't act soon, it would die. After losing the only other two babies this year, I wouldn't allow that to happen.

Sil reared back, his eyes going vacant. I unleashed the only magic that might work.

"Set the hatchling down now."

My voice echoed with the full power of a Prince of Hell.

Silvanus wrenched his head back and forth, his pupils dilating as he fought the magic command. In some strange twist of magic, I was in *his* head, seeing through his eyes. His mind.

Red tinged everything and as I stared at myself through his eyes, feeling off-kilter and disoriented, I was suddenly in a memory. At first all I saw was a shadowy figure.

Then the color blue.

It seemed like the disjointed ramblings of madness, but it gave me excellent insight into how his mind was working. Perhaps it could be something we could study.

I was about to wrench myself out of his head when the shadowy face finally came into focus. Everything in me stilled. Adriana. Silvanus was fixated on her as if under some primal command to seek and destroy.

Suddenly, he ducked his head and charged, ripping me from his mind.

I dove forward right as he jumped, clearing my body as I rolled to the ground and pivoted, never turning my back to him.

Silvanus roared, the sound loud enough to wake the whole gods-damned castle. He barreled through the open cell and into the hall, the hatchling still locked in his jaws, then took off for the end of the corridor.

I bolted after him. "Take him down! Protect the baby!"

Val unleashed her throwing knives, aiming at his flank, his wings. She struck true, but it had little impact on the massive dragon and his tough hide.

The other hunters raced after him, tossing chains at his feet. He jumped at the last moment, avoiding them as they clattered against the stone, flying past the dragon.

I unsheathed my House dagger, my wings snapping open.

He was heading directly for the window I'd had painted over with a strong illusion. It was meant to look like stone, but somehow the dragon had detected what it was. Not even the most skilled magic wielder had sensed the truth of the illusion.

I used my supernatural speed, reaching for him just as he shattered through the wall and glass, the stone breaking easily at the impact.

Wings out, I jumped from the window, flying after him, my focus on the baby, which still bleated for help. Our flight was not a silent one.

I could only hope my suitors were occupied at the other end of the castle.

Silvanus careened toward the garden, headed over the stables, then banked toward the mountains beyond Merciless Reach.

Incredibly, despite the vacancy in his gaze, he knew where to go.

His mighty wings flapped with brutal grace as he aimed upward, catching the tailwind and increasing his already impossible speed.

I pumped my own wings as hard as I could, catching the same powerful gust as we sailed past the fortress, ignoring the hunters racing for cover below.

We were heading toward the barrens. But first we needed to pass the mountain range that separated us from them. My pulse pounded. If Sil flew us over the barrens and found his pack, I was going to have trouble retrieving the baby dragon by myself.

Too soon the first mountain veered up in front of us, the cliff face rocky and unforgiving.

I raced after him, nearly catching up, my dagger aimed at his chest. I'd—

He whipped his giant head back and forth, launching the baby dragon toward the side of a mountain, in the opposite direction from where he continued. The hatchling was still too small to fly on its own.

I cursed, diving toward the baby, leaving Sil as I raced gravity, praying I'd be victorious. At the last moment, I snatched the baby into my arms, tucking it against my body as I braced for impact. I'd been going too fast and was too close to the mountain to avoid hitting it.

At the last moment I turned, my back slamming into the ice-covered rock, the wind getting knocked out of me so hard I saw stars. I slid down the mountain, keeping the baby in the cradle of my arms as I sank to the ground, breathing hard.

I sat that way for a few moments, allowing the full impact of Sil's escape to sink in.

The tiny dragon crawled up my neck, nuzzling me, its icy snout causing a slight shudder. I tipped my head back, looking up at the cold night sky as I petted the dragon.

"Well," I said to it. "Your name is Vexus. You little vexing troublemaker."

He bleated excitedly from his grand adventure, the heathen. He belonged to House Gluttony through and through.

I stared at the sky for a few more moments, hoping for a glimpse of iridescent scales glinting in the moonlight. All remained quiet.

There was no use in trying to track Sil tonight; by the time I brought Vex back to the castle and assembled a search party, he'd be long gone.

I pushed myself to my feet and stretched, thankful for my ability to swiftly heal.

Unlike the anomaly that happened during the dragon attack when we'd rescued Vex, my body was unharmed now. Except for the cursed dragon wounds that were still taking their time to heal.

I held the dragon close and launched us back into the air, my mind already spinning in several directions. Once I took the hatchling back to its temporary nest, I'd spend the rest of the night researching any information I could find on dragon fixations.

That Silvanus had been thinking of Adriana nonstop was a troubling revelation.

The simple explanation might be that he'd seen her in the dungeon and she had somehow imprinted on him. Or maybe it had something to do with the blood oath we'd sworn.

There was another reason I couldn't ignore.

I couldn't stop from wondering, once again, if this was all tied into my private curse.

If I even had one at all. I still couldn't tell what it was, or if I was simply unlucky.

FORTY-TWO
Adriana

ONCE ALL WAS quiet, I rose and donned a black dress—since that seemed to be the first rule in any good spy novel—then tiptoed into the corridor. After waiting a few beats, I raced toward the royal library. Honestly, it was a blessing that I didn't run headfirst into a wall or get a neck cramp from craning my head back and forth so often to check that I wasn't being followed.

I kept to the shadows, praying I could emit an invisible shield if I believed hard enough, and silently whooped with victory when I made it to my destination without running into a soul.

Namely, Val and her cursed ability to track me down.

I shut the door behind me and scanned the room.

In typical House Gluttony fashion, it was a feast created for any book lover to indulge in.

I took a moment to soak it in, hating that I loved it so much.

Dark, gleaming shelves were filled with leatherbound books, the spines embossed and gilded. The floors were layered with woven rugs, and an excessive number of overstuffed chairs and couches were grouped around a grand fireplace.

Except for one low-burning lantern in the back that I prayed was left on by mistake, the cathedral-sized chamber was dark and empty. It was the perfect place to curl up with a mystery novel and lose yourself in pages that crunched like dry leaves each time you flipped them.

Alas, the only mystery I needed to solve was the one surrounding the dragons.

I listened for a few beats but didn't hear any sounds—no turning pages, no soft inhales or exhales or creaks of someone moving around in a chair—and hoped that meant I was correct: whoever had been here simply left the lantern on, the careless fiend.

That settled, I peered up at the plaques located at the end of each shelf, thankful for the golden gleam that allowed me to make out the words etched onto them.

The library was organized into sections that were easy enough to find, so I made my way to witches, spell work, and potions. My victory was short-lived when I rounded the corner and stumbled upon the prince bent over a book...reading, of all unnatural things.

Everything in me seized at the sight of him. He was the one cursed being in the realm I'd hoped to never encounter again. I swore he knew it and put himself in my path just to irk me.

I glared at his broad shoulders, his ruffled hair, the chestnut strands gilded from the lamp's warm glow. Instead of a lover running their hands through his hair making the locks unruly, it looked like he'd raked his hands through it.

A sign he was worried or that the book he was reading was giving his tiny brain a cramp?

One could never tell when it came to him.

Since his back remained turned to me, I peered at him for a few more beats. I was hoping to sort out what he was doing, but my attention drifted over the suit jacket he wore, the material straining against the muscles I knew were hidden beneath.

He had no right to look the way he did—like the universe's most tempting mistake. He was all harsh lines and hard angles except for his cursed mouth; that was all curved, soft wickedness. And he certainly knew how to use it.

I burned just thinking of our most recent night together and immediately wished a window would blow open and let in an arctic blast of air.

He was entirely off-limits, even without his competition raging on.

A flash of him kissing Vanity sent ice rushing through my veins. *Ruthless Rake*. And there I was, staring like all of his doe-eyed acolytes.

I made to quietly step back when Axton suddenly glanced over his shoulder, his attention sliding along my frame as if he'd known all along that I'd been standing behind him.

His eyes darkened as he drank me in, and for some reason, I held my breath. I wasn't sure if I craved an apology, or some sign he knew he'd hurt me earlier. I hesitated from retreating, even knowing it was the safest move for my heart and sanity. Maybe he would surprise me.

"You have no idea how tempted I am to cuff you to my bed, Miss Saint Lucent."

And just like that I returned to my senses. "Are you wholly incapable of uttering a sentence that isn't rakish?"

His smile was a quick flash of teeth. "Thinking filthy thoughts again?"

"I'm not the one dreaming of tying you to my bedposts."

"Truly a shame. You might have some fun living out your darkest fantasies. I'm sure I'd look rather dashing in your bed." He sighed when I didn't take the bait. "I want you where I can see you. It's either my room or the dungeon. My room would be far more convenient and less drafty."

At that I smiled sweetly. "Will I be sharing a suite with the crimson-eyed creature, or will I have my own accommodations there? Unless of course that's what injured your back. Then I'd like my own dark, dank cell."

He stilled for a moment, his body tense. In the next moment, he was relaxed again, making me question what I'd seen.

"How do you know I'm injured?"

"How anyone else *didn't* notice is the true mystery. I've seen you kiss plenty of people and you never once winced."

"Perhaps I *should* send you into the dungeon," he muttered.

I made my way over to the little table he was sitting at, attempting to see what he'd been reading. It hadn't escaped my notice that he was in the same section I'd sought out too.

Maybe he *was* searching for hexed objects and all my theories were correct.

The rake closed the book and leaned an elbow across it, hiding the title, the perfect image of casual interference. He grinned, knowing I knew exactly what he'd done just as he'd figured out what I'd been up to. Curse him. We were two opponents circling each other again.

I dropped into the chair beside the prince, earning a look of surprise.

"What? Am I not permitted to sit with your spectacular royal self?"

"You and I both know you're scheming."

"And we both know you love thwarting my efforts, so we're evenly matched." He raised his brows and I quickly added, "In our attempts to outwit the other, obviously. We'd never suit otherwise. Not that I think about you in that capacity. Ever."

Internally I strangled myself.

Axton scanned my face, and an unusual seriousness entered his expression. "Why do you hate me so much?"

No one could ever accuse him of not being direct.

"I'd really rather not discuss it."

"I'm afraid that excuse won't work again."

He stared at me so intently I started to wonder if he was somehow using magic to see through my emotional walls. Or maybe, upon further inspection, there was a different reason he wanted to know. But why?

"The other night you mentioned the All-Sinners Ball," he said. "It seems we have very different recollections of that event."

"The past is not something I wish to revisit."

He raked a hand through his hair, his jaw straining.

"I'm afraid I must insist." His tone indicated I was correct; this was about more than our differences in memory. "I'll start. When you walked into the ball that night, I remember exactly where I was. At the bottom of the stairs, ready to ask someone to sneak off to the garden."

"How romantic."

"Then you paused at the doorway, and I lost all sense of time and place. I *had* to know you."

My gaze sharpened on him. "Why are you telling me this?"

"Because." He held my stare. "I thought you were the most devastating thing I'd ever seen. A comet speeding directly at me. And I was so lost to your splendor, I didn't care if you wiped me clean out of the realm, so long as I got a chance to admire you, even from a distance."

My stupid heart fluttered despite my brain screaming for caution. Axton was known to charm all he met. I knew that more than anyone. This was likely another scheme.

"I don't understand what you're getting at or why it matters."

"You wore the most beautiful blue and silver gown. I remember vividly the way the candlelight glinted off the jewelry you had on—some matching earring and bracelet set. Nothing was overdone or extravagant, nothing to excess. Yet I wanted to indulge in everything you had to offer. Conversation. Stolen kisses. Simply listening to you speak as we danced."

My eyes burned. He couldn't lie outright, so he must believe his story, but none of that actually happened that night. Except for the fact that I'd been wearing an earring and bracelet set. It was the night I'd lost my mother's bracelet, and that stung more than Axton's cold dismissal.

"Axton, please—"

"I watched from the sidelines for a long while, trying to hunt down clues to what you liked. I wanted to find common interests, impress you. You were surrounded by suitors, and I was plotting clever ways to steal you away to the garden. When I approached you, all my plans vanished. The look you gave me—it was like I'd drowned your pet."

His voice turned soft, quiet. "You hated me then, before I even had a chance to win you over. So yes, Adriana, I think we need to discuss that night. Because in my version, I wanted a much different outcome for our story. I wanted to give you my royal mark."

A royal mark was no small thing.

Princes rarely gave them to anyone, they were a show of high honor, of rank. They were similar to tattoos but very small and easily hidden.

A royal mark allowed the prince to sense the whereabouts of the one he'd marked, but it also allowed the one marked to summon the prince at will.

Other rumors suggested it also granted someone immortality after a small ceremony or spell was cast. That part was even more rare, so I wasn't sure how true it was.

How could Axton honestly believe that was how strongly he felt when his recollection was entirely false?

"I—" Frustration built in my chest as I inched closer, as if proximity to the prince would spark a memory. "That's not how that night went. You and I—you and I *did* go to the garden. You told me everything a young, hopeful romantic could ever want to hear. Made all sorts of declarations and promises. You charmed me so thoroughly we made love right there and everything was incredible. Up until you left me directly after to sleep with the viscountess. The same one who'd been calling me a social climber all evening and attempted to have me tossed from the ball for being *common scum*. I was mortified. You discarded me like I meant *nothing*."

I exhaled, my breath hitching slightly. "It was the first time I realized how much you used your charm to get whatever you desired. Then once you had your fill of whatever you'd been after, you moved on to the next thing you hungered for."

His gaze narrowed on me. He leaned on his elbows, his face perilously close to mine as he searched my face. "That never happened. Yet I don't detect a lie."

I had no answer to the question I saw burning through him. His frustration matched mine in equal measure. How could we both have such different memories of that night?

Either the prince had been in some wildly delusional stupor, or there might be something worth investigating. Memories didn't just alter so drastically.

My emotions churned like a stormy sea as my mind spun with theories. Magic? Stupidity? Or good old-fashioned intoxication? Could *someone* be responsible for our animosity?

It seemed too far-fetched, but stranger things were known to happen in the Underworld.

A lock of my hair fell forward, but before I could tuck it back, the prince reached over and smoothed it away. His hand lingered, angling my face up gently.

I should knock his hand away. Lean back. *Anything* to avoid his touch.

We shouldn't be here together. I should consider my mission to unearth clues about hexed objects a failure and try again tomorrow. Far from his too-charming ways. I'd gone a decade without succumbing to his seduction and I blamed our oath for blurring those lines now, even knowing that was false and it had nothing to do with my emotions.

His thumb stroked along my jaw, the motion soothing and so very tempting.

"I have another confession to make," he whispered. "During the contest, I convinced myself Vanity was you. Once I realized my mistake, I wanted to apologize. Right there. In front of everyone."

My heart thundered. "You didn't, though."

Axton tipped my chin up, watching me as he slowly brought his mouth to mine. "Forgive me, Adriana."

His lips hovered a breath away while he waited for my reaction. When I didn't pull back or demand he unhand me, he closed the distance, taking my mouth in a sweet, chaste kiss.

It was filled with yearning, apology...a wordless plea for forgiveness.

I could break away from the embrace, refuse him and his advances. There was no pretending this was my stranger now; I knew exactly who was kissing me and I didn't hate it.

Maybe it was his confession about what happened that night ten years ago, or the complicated emotions it stirred, but I kissed him back as sweetly, my fingertips tentatively sliding up his arms, grounding me in the moment.

This tenderness was so at odds with the male who'd wanted to bend me over his knee, promising a sinful punishment if I'd consented to it.

The male who'd also sunk to *his* knees in a rooftop garden and made me soar with his wicked mouth.

This version of Axton was truly dangerous.

He was the sort of prince people dreamed of. Dark, charming, completely infatuated.

Someone worth falling for.

He kissed me a little harder, like he couldn't stop himself from fully tasting my lips.

For a moment, I forgot who we truly were to each other. The years of back-and-forth, the animosity. There was only the here and now. And this kiss that was bringing all my walls crashing down. His lips parted on a groan, his tongue sweeping in to claim mine.

He tasted like my favorite mistake.

The next thing I knew, he was pulling me onto his lap, and I was happy to give in to this craving, even knowing it was forbidden.

My hands framed his face, our kiss turning from sweet romance to ravenous desire, our need to be close, to feel everything, taking over.

He leaned back, and the pain I'd seen earlier in the day was the last emotion playing across his features as he ran his hands up and down my body.

"You're going to be the end of me." He dragged me along his length, and I forgot how to breathe. "And I fucking welcome my demise."

"Gabriel, wait." His name came out much too softly. "Your back."

He kissed me hard, his lips owning mine over and over.

Here was the male from the Seven Sins who craved dominance in his pleasure.

The one who'd bring me to the brink and yank me back, sweetly torturing me until I'd crawl to him, begging.

I gasped and drew back; his hooded gaze was filled with the same need I felt as he watched me fall apart right there.

I didn't care about his competition, or our history, or any other complication.

I wanted him. Right this instant.

His eyes darkened, his powers alerting him to my every emotion.

He swore and hoisted me up, deftly undoing the button of his trousers.

"Are you sure?" he asked, hips grinding into me.

Maybe I wasn't the only one who'd get on my knees and beg. His intense gaze locked onto mine, his emotions as heightened. He would stop if I said no.

No matter how much he'd want to take me right there, he'd walk away the instant I said to. Between that and his very different recollection of the All-Sinners Ball, it made my decision easy. Perhaps it was time to try again.

"I'm sure. Are you?"

"Is there any doubt?" He dragged me over his arousal again.

"Your injury..."

"I've never felt better."

"Liar." I captured his mouth with mine, lifting myself up as he fumbled with my skirts.

Before I could process what happened, we were somehow across the room and I was pinned against the shelves in a dark alcove partially hidden by a potted fern, and the prince's entire front was pressed to my back.

"What are you—"

He gently placed a hand over my mouth, then brought his lips to my ear. "When I take my hand away, remain as silent as you can. Someone just entered the library."

He didn't have to say anything else; fear gripped me tightly. We were close to being caught. In a *very* precarious position. He had me up against a wall, very clearly aroused.

If anyone found us together...it would be disastrous. For him, for me, for my sister—I could only imagine Sophie's response if she discovered our indiscretion.

A strained moment passed before I heard what his heightened senses had picked up.

Voices carried over, hushed whispers that made my pulse race harder.

I went as still as possible, praying for whoever had entered the chamber to get their books and leave. Another moment passed by in the span of what felt like a decade.

Then I heard the unmistakable sound of fabric rustling. A sound that was not made from someone coming to fetch a book to read in bed. Soft giggles followed.

Another couple had decided to use this room for a secret midnight tryst.

I closed my eyes, trying to force the sound of kissing from my mind as the prince's arousal pressed into my backside. Axton moved closer as if to shield me with his mass, and I listened helplessly as the lovers moved to the aisle next to ours.

"Wait, what if someone walks in?" one of them asked.

I froze.

It was nothing more than a low whisper, but I recognized that voice immediately.

I glanced over my shoulder at the prince. He was watching me closely and hadn't reacted at all. Which meant he didn't know who the secret lovers were. Or he was too preoccupied at the moment to really pay close attention.

I couldn't hear who the second person was — they were speaking much too low — but I knew with certainty who one was. My sister.

I thought she'd had a crush on Prince Gluttony and hadn't known her to show interest in anyone prior to being chosen for the competition.

Questions swirled in a maelstrom as I tried to seize one to focus on.

Who was her lover? When had it begun?

Was it just a passing romance or something more serious?

And why in all the realms hadn't she confided in me?

That, I suspected, was due to the fact that I'd been absent a lot. Either working or hunting leads in the shadow network. We hadn't been spending a lot of time together.

Still, it hurt to know she had a whole secret life I wasn't a part of.

I would have to choke all the questions down and let them go for one very good reason. There was no way for me to confront Eden about her midnight rendezvous without giving up my own secret in return. Axton and I had already had our moment in the scandal sheets, and I refused to end up there with him again, intriguing midnight interludes or not.

Axton leaned forward, his fingers skimming the shelf above my head. For one intense moment, I thought he was going to finish what we'd started, despite an audience.

A moment later, a latch clicked. My pulse pounded furiously at the small sound, but no one seemed to notice. They'd resumed their kissing and were completely unaware that anyone else was in the chamber.

Axton jerked his chin toward the hidden escape, indicating I should step through and leave the library. I wasn't sure if he planned to follow me or if he was going to confront the lovers. I couldn't let him find out Eden was involved.

To keep the prince from focusing on who the other couple was, I tugged him through the chamber with me and prayed I wouldn't get swept up in his charms once again.

FORTY-THREE
Prince Gluttony

OVERS SLIPPING AWAY for a midnight tryst in my library wasn't
normally in fashion. House Gluttony was infamous for putting on
a show, allowing an audience to feast on their passion.

Which was why I hadn't worried about getting caught with my lovely
rival.

Now my pulse pounded, my cock ached, and the demon part of me
wanted to curse it all and finish what Adriana and I had started right
then and there.

It would be so easy to slide her silk skirts up, to stroke the soft skin
of her thighs above the lace-edged stockings, to take the lobe of her ear
between my teeth as my fingers found that secret haven to ensure she was
ready before I buried myself deep.

I'd clamp my hand across those full, perfect lips to stifle any errant
moans, even knowing no one would hear us. Just to play into her fantasy
of being caught.

The magic bond between us sizzled, only too happy to fuel the flames
of our desire.

When I remembered my hidden exit, I praised every power that be
that it hadn't been far from where we'd been sitting. I followed her into
the small corridor, closing the bookcase door behind us. No light seeped
under the door. No sound or interruptions.

Magic I used to ward it from intruders meant it remained as silent as
a crypt.

We were once again blessedly alone. I placed a palm at the small of her back, guiding her deeper into the passage. We'd only gone a few paces when she stopped.

I felt her attention shift to me as she pressed closer to the wall.

When she spoke, she barely made a sound. "Can they hear us?"

"Magic keeps all sound from entering or leaving."

Saints curse me. I sensed her emotions shift back to arousal now that she knew we were alone and wouldn't be heard. She took a small step backward, bracing herself against the wall and the curve of her lips let me know it was by design.

Adriana wanted *me*. There was no glamour this time, no masks, no excuses to hide behind. It thrilled me enough to spark my power.

I moved until I stood in front of her, then leaned in. This close, there was no hiding how much I still desired her too.

Gently, quietly, I pulled her hips against me, ensuring I hit all the right places, even hindered by our clothing. Her quiet gasp encouraged me to repeat the motion.

"Do you want me to stop?" I asked.

She hesitated, then shook her head. "No."

That same dark thrill filled me again, feeding my magic. I still couldn't quite believe she was knowingly in my arms, just as attracted and wanting.

Ten years. I'd hungered for this moment for an entire decade.

I slid my palm down the front of her bodice, teasing her stomach before dropping lower. I wanted to take my time, to indulge in every sensation, savor it. From the feel of the smooth silk of her dress to the rasp of her breath—it was decadence and I wanted to commit it all to memory.

I slowly stroked upward, skimming her ribs, moving until I caressed the underside of her breast. Her chest rose and fell against mine. For once, Adriana Saint Lucent had no critique.

The moment felt fragile. Tender. Like one wrong move could destroy it all.

Our conflicting confessions about the All-Sinners Ball had my emotions spiraling.

My thumb brushed across her nipple, the taut bud already hard from her arousal.

I shouldn't be touching her, craving her when I had research to do. But I couldn't bring myself to stop. She was a feast I couldn't help but sample from—her mind, her body, the way she made me feel a hundred emotions at once.

I cupped her breast, noting the way she gripped me tighter, her breath hitching slightly.

I finally reached down, slipping one hand under her skirt then dragged the material up, tracing little patterns as my fingers drifted higher.

Her skin was smooth and warm, and I wanted to strip us both down and spend hours tasting every inch. I quickly realized she wasn't wearing undergarments.

I swallowed hard, my attention fixated on that glorious detail.

If I didn't have a competition, if there weren't two sinners already making use of my library, I would take her back and make her come against the shelves. She was here. She was safe. And I wanted to keep her where I could ensure Silvanus didn't find her.

Adriana had been so adamant about the All-Sinners Ball, about us getting intimate in the garden. She didn't know I dreamed about it, that it was something I'd desired since that first meeting. That no lover had ever sated me, no matter how wonderful they were on their own.

That I'd eventually given up taking anyone to my bed, abstaining for years because all I wanted was *her*.

There was no way in any of the hells that I'd forget making Adriana mine that night.

Not when it haunted me. Now, with her in my arms, arching into me, willing and aroused in our own private chamber, it felt like the worst sort of punishment to end our evening early.

"Gabriel."

It was close enough to my true name that my sin ignited.

I wanted to indulge her every desire.

"Please. Touch me."

I finally stopped teasing and slipped two fingers inside her. She released a breath as I slowly withdrew them, then thrust back in, fucking her softly with them.

Adriana arched into me, giving me leave to tease her breast with my other hand, wanting to ignite all her passions. While I obliged, she rocked against my hand, seeking her own friction.

I would never get over how good she felt, how right. I could spend decades exploring her body, discovering what she liked most, what drove her feral.

I settled on giving her all I could now, wringing as much pleasure from her as possible.

"Don't stop." She tossed her head back, panting as I continued to pleasure her in slow, taunting strokes. In this moment, in our own secret hiding place, it didn't feel like she hated me.

It felt like she craved my touch as much as I craved hers.

I took her mouth in a punishing kiss, my fingers working her faster and harder until she finally shattered in my arms, her body submitting to my ministrations.

I closed my eyes, allowing the moment to stretch.

I wanted to take her to my bedchamber, tie her wrists to my bedposts, and pretend the world wasn't in chaos as we lost ourselves in each other.

I was contemplating doing just that when she straightened and pushed herself off the wall.

"Oh, my gods."

"It's a little late to be praising them, darling. But I'll accept your compliments."

"Not you, rake." She playfully slapped my chest. "I think I know exactly what's going on."

Everything in me stilled. "Regarding?"

Adriana adjusted her gown and stepped away, biting her lower lip as if to keep from answering before she thought her response through.

She'd put more than physical distance between us. I felt the emotional wall slam into place, keeping her innermost thoughts and feelings from me once again.

"Nothing," she said, taking another step from me. "I don't know why I said that. It's late, and I haven't been sleeping all that well. I really should get back to my chambers before anyone notices I'm gone."

"You do realize I sense when you lie, correct?"

She ran her gaze over me, a furrow forming between her brows.

"You gave me an orgasm, Axton. Did I somehow miss the part where I now owe you my innermost thoughts in return?"

"I should like to think we made some breakthrough here tonight. You clearly harbor anger about the All-Sinners Ball—we've proven that false. We can start over, call a truce."

"One conversation doesn't erase a decade of our past."

"And the intimacy we've shared? That doesn't count for a bit of honesty between us?"

She looked at me like I was some curious specimen from a distant realm.

"Tell me what happened with Jackson."

Of all the cursed questions I thought she'd ask, that was the last one I expected. "You honestly wish to discuss that after what just passed between us?"

She shook her head. "If you aren't willing to share your secrets with me, how can you possibly expect me to open myself up to you?"

"You have spent the last decade trying to ruin my court in the press. I would be a fool to share classified information."

"Proving my point wonderfully," she said, not unkindly. "The past can't simply be forgotten because you declare it should be."

I balled my hands into fists. No matter what passed between us, Adriana and I were destined to never trust each other, it seemed.

I offered her my arm and contemplated how the hells we could ever find peace if neither one of us took that first, vulnerable step into the unknown.

❄ ❄ ❄

Dawn came much too soon, and with it more headaches.

Once I'd escorted Adriana back to her rooms and secretly placed guards on the ground floor below her chambers to avoid detection, I'd returned to the library. Thankfully it had been empty. Unfortunately, that was where my luck ended.

I hadn't found a single bit of useful information on what would break a dragon's fixation on someone. I sent a missive to House Wrath in the predawn hours requesting his help.

Adriana and I had shared intimacy, but just as she couldn't confide whatever she'd sorted out last night in me, I couldn't tell her about the dragons. At least not until it was necessary. For now, I'd have to hope my guards were enough to keep her safe.

Tension radiated around me as I climbed the stairs and entered the war room tower.

Val was waiting with Wrath. Their mugs of steaming coffee sat untouched, the breakfast trays still covered.

"No sign of Silvanus, I take it?"

Wrath indicated a negation with a shake of his head. "There are signs of where they passed through—mostly bones and viscera. I also spoke with a few solitary demons who claimed to have seen the pack tearing into each other before they escaped a massacre."

I paced in front of the arched window, my gaze scanning the mountains in the distance. I wanted to put my leathers on and take to the skies, tracking the dragons. But duty called.

"The suitors were scheduled to take part in a sword fight in an hour but will be showing off their cooking skills today," I said. "I don't want anyone lingering outside the castle if it can be helped. We're spinning it in the press as sharing their favorite indulgence for House Gluttony in honor of my sin. I want extra hunters stationed around the grounds. Get Lust and Envy here but keep them hidden. I want them skyward at the barest hint of a dragon."

I pivoted to face my second and my brother.

"I also want someone watching Adriana. Sil may be fixated on her." And she was certainly up to another scheme. I didn't point that out, not wanting to create more tension with Val over how to handle Adriana.

Wrath's gaze narrowed. "What do you mean *fixated* on her?"

I quickly debriefed my brother on the strange images I'd seen, the feelings associated with them stemming from the dragon himself. I shared my new theory of it somehow being connected to the blood oath we'd sworn. That Sil had somehow sensed it.

Wrath cursed.

"Maybe it's time to call off the competition," he said. "Lock down our circles. Come up with an inter-court strategy to hunt and track the dragons."

He meant hunt to kill. Which would be the last option I'd explore for several reasons.

I glanced at the clock. "Reporters are arriving soon for the next event. We move forward as planned until that's no longer possible."

The kitchens had been rearranged into six separate stations for the remaining suitors. Eden practically bounced on the balls of her feet as she checked over her basket of ingredients. Vanity's table was next to hers and she shot an amused look the other girl's way.

It was nice to see the suitors getting along.

I stepped into the middle of the chamber, offering each suitor and the reporters lining the wall my most charming smile.

Inside, my emotions churned. I wanted to be on the ground with my hunters or in the sky with Wrath, tracking Silvanus. Outwardly I didn't give any hint of my inner turmoil.

"Welcome to the next event—your favorite indulgence." I glanced at the door. Adriana was noticeably absent. Which was for the best. "Today I'll be sampling *your* favorite dish. It can be savory, sweet, sour, a combination of all, or a drink you enjoy."

Erudite set her journal down. She'd been studiously scribbling notes. "What if our favorite indulgence includes food and a beverage?"

"By all means, if you've got the ambition to make both, please do. There are no rules for this event. I do want to know the story behind your dishes, though. Something to give me a clearer sense of who you are individually."

"How long will we have to complete our dish?" Ava of House Greed asked.

"Thirty minutes. We have a clock that will count down your time."

Omen from House Envy glared at Ava. "If someone is only making a beverage, that hardly seems fair."

My smile was getting harder to maintain. These would be the longest thirty minutes of my existence. I exhaled, forcing myself to think of the realm. And the reporters who were watching my every reaction much too closely from the sidelines.

Anderson Anders and Julian Wren leaned in, their quills flying across their notepads. No matter how I felt inside, I would need to give another stellar performance. Thankfully Ryleigh Hughes wasn't in attendance. As Adriana's friend, she seemed to hold a grudge against me.

I clapped my hands together once, then nodded to Jarvis, who set the clock to begin its countdown. "Your time begins now. I *so* look forward to tasting your...offerings."

Deep inside, something uncomfortable knotted in my chest. A Prince of Sin couldn't lie, but we found clever ways to omit the truth.

My flirtation was expected, but it was getting harder to play pretend.

I hadn't been thinking of my suitors. If I had, the teasing words never would have left my lips, even if I'd desperately wanted them to.

Do I Secretly Belong to House Envy or Is He Just a Rake?

Special Miss Match from the Royal Suitors

Dear Miss Match,

I started courting someone with a reputation that rivals that of our dear prince. At first, it was all terribly exciting. He had a lover for every day of the week. Initially, I found that somewhat of a thrilling challenge, especially when I successfully captured most of his attention. But now my feelings have gotten the better of me and when he's not in my bed, I wonder who he's with instead. I'm not prone to envy, so it's disconcerting to experience that sin.

What would you do if the person you love loves someone (or several someones!) else?

Yours in scandal,
Uncomfortably Jealous

Dear Jealous:

Dating a rake certainly has its merits. Though I personally prefer to find a reformed playboy, if such a rare creature exists. To answer your question thoroughly, I've compiled some quotes from our most popular remaining suitors.

Miss Vanity Raven, House Pride: Have confidence in yourself. You are the most beautiful, interesting, intelligent, of his suitors. No one else compares to you, and if he forgets? Date a smarter rake.

Miss Omen Seagrave, House Envy: Why aren't you dating all the lovers you want and flaunting it? Try ignoring your lover at the next event and showering someone else you like with attention. Inspiring a bit of envy in a potential mate is fair game.

Miss Eden Everhart, House Gluttony: I believe that true love always finds a way. It might take time, it might take the fear of loss, but if it's meant to be, it will work out.

There you have it; jealousy is perfectly natural, and the best advice is to focus on you and your needs first. If your lover no longer suits, find a new suitor who does.

Until next time, stay scandalous, sweet sinners.
Miss Match

FORTY-FOUR
Adriana

WHILE EDEN AND my stepmother attended the next event, I took a hired carriage back to our little house with my borrowed spell book from Roots and Remedies in hand. I'd spent the morning avoiding my sister as much as I could, not wanting to alert her to the fact I knew she had a secret.

The few times I did engage, she'd asked if I was feeling well. I had a great many skills, but acting was sadly not one of them. I still couldn't quite believe Eden hadn't confided in me. Which was admittedly a touch hypocritical since I'd kept my history with the prince from her.

But I'd only done that to protect Eden from the scandal it had caused.

After spending so much time at the castle our home felt incredibly tiny, but familiar and welcoming.

Most appealing of all: it granted me space. From Axton. From my sister's secret. From my own complicated feelings. And most of all from the many threads all whipping around untethered in the growing mystery surrounding the prince's competition and the dragons.

If I just escaped my emotions regarding Axton, I might crack the story. It wasn't about the desire to see the prince's reputation in ruins anymore; it was about the safety of us all.

My intuition was buzzing with insistence. I was close to unraveling the knot that loosely tied it altogether. I'd heard of postcoital stupor, but after I'd orgasmed, I'd had a revelation I couldn't shake. Memories didn't simply cease to exist. Even after a decade.

I turned the key in the lock and screamed when a cloaked figure yelped back from inside our tiny home, crashing onto our settee.

"Ad?" a familiar voice screeched. "Warn a demon, will you?"

I hadn't realized I'd hefted the book like a bat until I lowered the tome. "Ryleigh, what on earth?"

My coworker let the hood on her cloak fall back, her hand clutching at her heart as she caught her breath. "You scared the life from me."

"Yes, I imagine it was quite the surprise to break into *my* home and find me here."

I stared at my friend as I shut the door. It had been several days since I'd last seen her. I'd been sending my articles off with a courier and hadn't gone into the office. I missed the days when we could simply talk about everything and nothing and not feel so...strained.

"Why are you here?"

She gave me a sheepish look. "Your sister asked me to retrieve some of her hidden recipes. Apparently, there's going to be a cooking contest tomorrow. His Highness wants to sample their most lavish dish."

"That's happening right now, actually."

"Today a sword fight is scheduled."

"Axton probably changed his mind on a whim." I lifted a shoulder. It was the least concerning news of the day. "When did you see Eden?"

Ryleigh paused. "This morning."

I wasn't sure when Eden had snuck out of the shared suite but I *had* been doing my best to hide from her, so I let it go.

I'd been locked in my private room most of the morning, trying to make sense of everything that I'd learned from the prince last night. That Axton couldn't lie complicated the story he'd shared about his version of the All-Sinners Ball.

I tried to focus solely on that confession. But I'd failed miserably each time my thoughts returned to how that conversation ended.

When his hands had begun that slow, decadent descent over my body, I'd given myself over to my traitorous heart.

It had taken until morning for me to realize that he hadn't tried to bring me to his bed. He'd pleasured me, then stopped.

I wasn't sure if he was simply using his charm on me like he'd been doing on the circle and his suitors, or if he genuinely felt attraction.

Given all the secrecy in his court, and the fact that I'd caught him in the library researching, I'd wager it had less to do with infatuation and everything to do with his scheme.

I'd fallen for his seduction and couldn't tell if I was more upset at that or at the fact that he'd been so talented with his fingers I'd make the same damned choice again.

Confession about the All-Sinners Ball notwithstanding.

I considered sharing the strange events with my friend but somehow couldn't find the words. Ryleigh had spent years counseling me to stay away from the prince. Reminding me why I hated him so thoroughly. She'd been there through the tears and heartache.

If she found out I'd been meeting with him in secret and giving in to temptation...it could be the end of our friendship.

I shoved that aside, focusing on the here and now. Ryleigh had my father's ledger book in her hand and was tucking one of Sophie's feathers back into it to mark her place.

A prickle of unease rolled down my spine.

"Eden's recipes are under a floorboard under her bed."

She glanced at my father's ledger, a crinkle in her brow. "This isn't it?"

I shook my head and her frown deepened. She set it down next to her, still looking confused.

"What's wrong?"

"Your sister said they were in the ledger. She never mentioned anything about the floorboards. That's odd, isn't it?"

It was peculiar, but Eden might have simply been distracted by her big secret.

I kept my expression perfectly neutral. I loved Ryleigh, she was like another sister, but given how strained our relationship had been recently,

I couldn't exactly say I trusted her to keep this between us. She was a scandal sheet reporter assigned to cover the romantic competition of the century.

If she caught one whiff of Eden's midnight adventure, it would be the end of my sister remaining in the competition and free of scandal. No one would pass up the money or fame that would come on the heels of breaking that story. Not even my friend.

Even if Eden was carrying on with someone in secret, I still couldn't rule out the fact that she might want to win.

"She probably wrote them in code in the back." I smiled. "You know how much Sophie despises for her daughter to 'whittle the day away like a commoner.' I'll take it just in case."

Ryleigh's grin was back in place at that, though it seemed a touch brittle.

"Your stepmother is quite the personality, considering she gave up her title when she married your father."

"Coins can buy a great many things, except for good sense."

Ryleigh nodded to the book I held. "Just some light afternoon reading?" She squinted. "Is that a book on hexes? Ad. Please tell me you're not trying to interfere with Prince Gluttony's competition. I support your rights and wrongs, but this might be crossing a line."

I set the book on the small table in our kitchen.

"It's not for the prince. Just a hunch I'm working on."

Ryleigh stood and drifted over to the book, flipping it open. "Are you still convinced the ice dragons are attacking in secret? I thought you gave that up weeks ago."

"I told you, it's probably nothing. Don't you have some reporting to do?"

She sighed. "Unfortunately, it seems I'm late to the event. Mr. Gray wanted me to attend the sword fight. He's convinced some scandal will happen with weapons in the hands of ruthless lovers. Now I'll need to see if I can catch the end of the cooking competition."

On the slight chance she didn't already miss the event, I sent her off with a few of Eden's hidden recipes, then mulled over the encounter.

Eden *must* have sent Ryleigh; otherwise she wouldn't know about the recipes. And yet, the whole situation was odd. Even being a close family friend, it was strange that Ryleigh would come fetch recipes and not Sophie or one of the maids assigned to my sister.

Had Ryleigh lied?

I flipped through my father's ledger, heart aching at his familiar scribble.

Quill
Dagger
Throne
Paintbrush
Jewelry
Crown
Wings

All items he'd sold in the week before his death. I closed the little book, feeling his loss all over again. It was almost enough to—I snatched it back up, scanning the last entry again.

How on earth had he sold wings?

My pulse began to race as I read each item again. And again.

A pattern started to emerge. Seven items. Some of which I knew represented hexed objects. I read the list over, mind churning. After he'd died, I'd heard whispers that he'd been dealing goods to the dark market. It wasn't unusual for a merchant with his connections to trade such objects. I knew he'd made his fortune through the sale of goods demons couldn't easily get.

Could one of these items he'd sold be the answer?

The more I read the list, the more my attention snagged on one detail. The quill.

My entire body froze as puzzle pieces clicked into place. I was almost entirely sure I had my answer to why Axton and I had very different memories. Before I shared my findings, I needed to get some better answers. Ryleigh was not an option, especially after today.

But I suddenly had a very good idea how to get the answers I needed from someone else. I just had to convince Axton to assist in my investigation.

I grabbed a piece of parchment and my quill and sent a note to the castle.

Hopefully the prince would meet me as soon as the event ended. Though, given the nice little threat at the close of my letter, I imagined he would show up right on time.

Prince Gluttony stole a glance at me that I pretended not to notice. I couldn't risk being distracted by his ruthless seduction tactics. Especially while we were in a rival House of Sin.

House Envy was everything one expected from a grand estate ruled by the sin of jealousy.

The winter gardens were immaculate, the house a work of craftmanship that was so exquisite it made you ache with want.

Inside was where the true magic happened. Prince Envy was a well-known lover of art, and his fiancée was an artist with a rare talent. They were well suited.

And they were currently staring politely as Axton and I entered a private chamber deep within Envy's castle. I'd requested that our meeting remain secret, given the delicate nature of what I was about to unleash on these cunning Princes of Sin.

My nerves almost got the better of me—I briefly considered turning right back around and hunting down answers on my own. But that wouldn't help our realm if my hunch proved true.

It would be the first time I'd ever set my differences with Axton aside and brought him in on an investigation. But this story was bigger than our rivalry. And somehow, the two felt tied together.

I glanced around the meeting room. Artwork in gilded frames hung tastefully on paneled walls; sculptures sat regally on columns designed to show them to their best advantage. And sitting at an intimate table set with food and drink were the prince and lady of the House.

Miss Camilla Antonius, soon to be Princess of Envy, offered me a warm smile.

Her silver hair was unbound, the loose curls looking a little wild and untamed.

"You must be Miss Saint Lucent," she said, standing to greet me with a hug. "It's a pleasure to make your acquaintance. My fiancé has told me a great many things of your beauty. I can see he wasn't exaggerating."

Axton's palm suddenly found its way to my lower back, where it remained. I hid my smile. I was certain Envy had only said that to needle her—the jealous game-playing fiends.

"Thank you, my lady. You're too kind."

Camilla's silver eyes sparkled devilishly as they shifted to the prince looming behind me. Axton's hand remained stubbornly in place. He was feeding his brother's sin and couldn't seem to control himself.

"Well?" Envy swirled a goblet of wine before sipping it. "Let's hear what the big revelation is."

If he was trying to unsettle me by being brash and direct, he was in for disappointment. I ate those obnoxious royal traits with a dessert spoon.

I glanced at Axton, then back at Envy. It was no mistake I'd wanted to come here first. The Prince of Envy had quite the reputation when it came to hexed objects.

"Have either of you heard of the Hexed Quill?" I asked.

Tension descended like an unwanted army. It was as if all the air had been sucked from the room with my question.

Camilla's lips twitched; she understood and appreciated my move. I decided I liked her very much. I sensed she and I were cut from similar cloths.

Envy leaned back in his chair, his eyes narrowed. "Of course. It's rumored to be one of the first objects created of its kind; therefore, it's highly potent."

There were supposedly seven hexed objects missing throughout the realm, but no one knew the true number. There could be dozens for all anyone knew.

In hopes of destroying the demon princes, the First Witch, an immortal being descended from a goddess, had cursed several items using the darkest sort of magic, which gave the hexed objects sentience over the years.

Their powers were often twisted; what was once a throne could be a dagger. Or what was once a quill could take over the mind of anything it desired. Or so the stories went. There were even stories of the hexed objects taking over a mortal's life before discarding their bodies.

I'd never actually encountered a hexed object before, making it hard to know truth from fable. So much of our history was based in myth, spanning thousands of years and often getting lost to the passage of time and faulty memories. But Envy had just played a game where hexed objects were involved. If anyone aside from Ryleigh had any idea about them, it was him.

"Several years ago I heard from a trusted source that the Hexed Quill can rewrite history," I said, watching Axton as I spoke. He'd grabbed a bottle of demonberry wine, feigning casual interest. But I noticed the white-knuckled grip he had on his goblet. "But only in small ways."

Envy steepled his fingers. "That's true as far as I know."

I was relieved he confirmed that small fact. Given Ryleigh's research into the quill, I had the basics of what it did. Now I knew Envy was willing to share correct information.

"Would you mind elaborating?" I asked, excitement thrumming. "For example, let's say someone attended an event. Like the All-Sinners Ball. Would the Hexed Quill be able to change the outcome of that night?"

Axton set his wine down, his casual mask gone.

"What does the Hexed Quill have to do with the All-Sinners Ball?" he asked, his tone taking on a slight edge. He certainly was sensitive about that night. Though maybe his voice also sounded like it held the slightest hint of hope.

"If the quill can rewrite events, that's what I'm trying to figure out.

However, like all magic, it's got limits. And it also has a price." I turned to Envy. "That's correct, isn't it?"

There was nothing more ominous sounding than dark magic demanding a price.

Envy nodded. "All magic has limits or else it would overtake the realms."

I shuddered at the thought, my imagination sparking in a hundred directions despite my best efforts to not be intrigued.

"You think the Hexed Quill was used at the All-Sinners Ball?" Axton asked. "Why?"

The intensity in his gaze gave me pause. It was time to tread carefully before he shut the meeting down and whisked us back to House Gluttony. I had a feeling his secret was getting closer to being exposed. And it *did* tie into the night our world went astray.

"From what I've observed of our stories not aligning, I think it might have been used. What else impacts memories like that? You believe your version as adamantly as I believe mine. Either we both forgot, or one of us is lying. You didn't detect deception from me, and unless you've figured out how to lie, you cannot tell me something that isn't true."

Axton's expression was impossible to read. But I swore there was a flicker of excitement.

"If neither one of us is lying," I pressed, "then how do you account for that discrepancy?"

"Elaborate," Envy demanded. "And don't spare any detail."

"Very well." I recounted everything I could about the All-Sinners Ball first, then Axton followed up with his version of the event.

When we finished, Envy shared a long look with Camilla.

"I didn't detect lies from either one of you," Envy admitted, his expression turning dark. I had a feeling a Prince of Sin didn't appreciate his powers being thwarted.

"I wasn't present at the ball," Camilla said, "but memories are easily manipulated and one of the signs a hexed object might be at work."

It was what I'd thought too. *Finally*, some of my theories were seeming less impossible.

"If magic like that was used, what might the price be?" I asked.

Envy seemed to consider his answer carefully.

Which meant there were details he didn't want to give away.

I tried to keep my expression and my emotions from betraying how much I wanted to hear his answer. This was it. I *knew* it. We were straddling the line of what the princes were keeping from the realm. I was certain my pulse was pounding so loud they'd hear it.

"Memory magic often creates a...rift...somewhere," Envy finally said. "It might take years to manifest. But it always catches up."

Axton ran a hand over his face. "Why would someone use the Hexed Quill on me that night? To ruin my relationship, for what purpose?"

"You and Adriana never married or courted. Maybe that was the goal. Maybe they were envious, or covetous. Or any other sin—all were present that night," Envy said. "Or maybe it had nothing to do with you and her and that was an unseen result."

A rift...I wasn't sure what that entailed, but it sounded like something powerful enough to make the princes all work together. I was almost certain the bridal competition was a farce.

"Let's say this is true," Axton said. "What does it matter now? It's done."

"Not quite." Envy's attention shifted to me. "Unless the past is restored, the hexed magic will continue to feed off the next-strongest being in your circle to fuel its power."

Axton went preternaturally still.

"Wouldn't the strongest being in our circle be Axton?" I asked. There wasn't anything more powerful than a Prince of Sin in this realm.

Envy shook his head. "Since he's the subject of the magic's focus, it draws from the next-most-powerful creature."

I stopped breathing.

Oh, glory be to the wicked. I was on the right trail! Ice dragons were the second-most powerful creatures that were in our circle. The rumored attacks, Jackson's untimely death, the injury to Axton's back that didn't heal a few days before…

I swallowed the sudden lump in my throat. I found the thread that bound it all together.

"The magic used is still in effect, then, correct?" I asked.

"Yes. Right now, there's probably a low level of magic constantly working to alter everyone's memories—you, Gluttony, the other princes, and every other guest present during that time frame," Envy said. "It's a lot of power to sustain every day, for the last decade."

I searched my emotions for any hint of truth to magic being used on me. But I hit a wall too impenetrable to crack. Was that dark magic at play?

I'd always believed it was my own wall of protection I'd built.

If it was magic…it would be a violation too large to grasp. Someone would have changed the trajectory of my life with one swipe of their magic pen.

I rubbed my temples as a sudden headache came on. I'd been so concerned about hunting down the lead, I hadn't considered how the truth would make me feel.

I finally looked at Axton; he seemed as skeptical as I was. It was a lot to take in.

"Assuming Miss Saint Lucent's correct, I imagine we need the quill to rewrite our story," Axton said. "Any ideas where to find it?"

"Not the quill, exactly," I said. "According to my source's research, we need to find the journal or paper where the new outcome of the ball was written. Then we'll need to burn that to release the dark magic. Time won't be rewound, but our memories will be restored."

Axton's gaze locked onto mine. There was a storm of emotions in his, though I couldn't quite figure out what he was feeling the most above all.

I didn't think hope. Maybe disbelief. Or anger.

"Who is your source?" he asked. "Maybe they have the quill and the parchment or journal or whatever they used to re-write the event on."

I might be sharing my theory with him now, but wouldn't give him

Ryleigh's name. I knew that she'd never found the quill; I'd commiserated with her on her perceived failure.

That story had been her life's work and I understood how it felt to be forced to let it go when the leads died.

"I'm afraid that's confidential. But I know for certain they never located the quill, so there's no chance of them having re-written the All-Sinners Ball."

The princes exchanged looks, their displeasure chilling the air around us.

"Well, this has been most illuminating indeed." I stood from the table. "Thank you for your time, Prince Envy." I turned to Camilla. "And thank you for your insight."

Axton rose, but I stayed him with a hand to his arm. "I'd like to travel back alone, if you don't mind."

"It will be hours by coach," he said. As if I was unaware of the distance.

"All the same, I'd prefer to be with my own thoughts."

"Very well." He turned to his brother. "Send for your coach."

I felt his attention on me as I left the room with a footman, but I didn't turn and look back.

My mind and heart raced from the implications of everything I'd just had confirmed, and I had no idea what my next move should be.

The Hexed Quill was most certainly the cause of the dragon attacks.

In theory, that meant it was imperative to locate the original hex and destroy it. But who had motive? To solve that mystery I'd need to put my investigative skills to the test.

It was time to go over every detail of the All-Sinners Ball.

I'd scour guest lists and hunt down any leads, then hope to the old gods I'd break the case before the Hexed Quill's chaos destroyed us all.

FORTY-FIVE
Prince Gluttony

*T*wo hours after Adriana's departure from House Envy, and as soon as I'd gotten word that she'd arrived back at my castle safe and sound, I stood on the roof of my House of Sin.

Envy accompanied me to brief Lust, Greed, and Sloth on the details of our meeting with Adriana. With the new information we received, we had to re-strategize.

Pride was busy with his own issues once again, and Wrath was patrolling the northern territory. I'd fill him in tomorrow.

"You think she figured out the ice dragon connection, too?" Lust asked, leaning against the balcony's railing. To the casual observer he looked at ease, but the tension in his gaze said otherwise.

I dropped onto one of the chairs in the rooftop garden of House Gluttony. "Most certainly."

Greed exhaled. "Did you offer to pay her for her silence?"

"Of course not." I pinched the bridge of my nose. Leave it to Greed to think everyone suffered from his same sins. "She's got morals."

Sloth gave him a look that called him incompetent and slunk to the opposite side of the balcony, as if idiocy could be catching.

One thing I had no doubt about: Adriana Saint Lucent was brilliant, and it wouldn't have taken long for her to piece together the part about the magic seeking out the next-strongest being.

She knew the dragons were restless. She knew a prince had been attacked.

Now she had a reason to hunt down the story.

For all I knew, she could be sitting in her chamber now, drafting up my demise.

Envy poured each of us a generous serving of the blackberry bourbon he'd brought, then set his attention on the horizon. Another storm was approaching, the visibility swiftly dwindling.

Soon we wouldn't see the mountain range where the dragons dwelled.

We'd come up here to discuss our next steps while my scholars pulled old guest books. I wanted to watch for signs of any dragons roaming too far from their territory.

Knowing what we did now, an attack seemed not only certain but inevitable.

"Not wiping her memory is going to be a problem, Gabriellis." Envy shifted his attention to me. "She'll write an article eventually, even knowing magic is at play."

"You're the one who decided to share more information with her." I downed half my drink. The burn felt good. "I'm not sure what you were thinking."

"She already unearthed more than we had. Do you think it mattered if I confirmed her theories? Better to give her some answers rather than have her asking around where we can't monitor her."

It was a good point. I was simply too on edge to appreciate it and wanted to fight.

It wasn't the fact that Adriana had figured out the answer to the problem that we'd been hunting for. In fact, that made me appreciate her even more. It was the fact that my recurring dreams...they'd been real. And I hadn't known magic was at play.

Envy watched me over the rim of his cup.

"Did you tell her you loved her at the All-Sinners Ball?" he asked, startling me. I thought he was attempting to joke. None of our brothers laughed. To have magic used on us was a serious threat. That I hadn't detected it made them all consider their own vulnerability.

"I have no recollection. Why?"

I waited for him to elaborate. Apparently, he felt no need to.

"Get to the damned point, Levi. Why does that matter?"

Envy scowled at the nickname. "The point is the magic didn't make you hate her. Which makes me wonder how intact her memories are. From what I gathered from her tonight, she remembers sleeping with you. It's a wound that's festered each time you tried to get her attention over the last decade with your abysmal courting antics."

"It's not as if I set out to hurt her." I sighed. "If I knew she was mine, I would have acted differently. I'm not a complete fucking monster."

Greed's mouth lifted in amusement. "No, you're just a prick."

Lust snorted. "Watching her chew your ass out after each failed attempt to impress her has been entertaining, though."

I opened my mouth to snap that I hadn't been trying to impress her, then shut it.

They began to mock my many denials over the years, suddenly claiming they knew—dark magic or not—that we secretly loved each other, and I tuned them out until Sloth taunted me. "Anyone with a modicum of common sense could see you wanted her."

"Did you just call me an idiot while boasting of your intelligence in that high-handed, bookworm way of yours?" I asked, feigning being wounded. "You truly are a well-read prick."

The levity between us was short-lived. I really considered what they were saying.

Putting myself in Adriana's position, knowing what I knew now, entertaining would be the last thing I'd feel. She'd watched me indulge my sin with countless lovers.

My reputation for being a rake was well earned—at least as far as I'd led everyone to believe. She didn't know it had all been an act, a way to fuel my sin without actually indulging in carnal desires. Each time it must have twisted the knife, reminding her of that first night.

She'd accused me of discarding her. That couldn't be further from the truth.

"I have no recollection of taking Adriana to my gardens," I admitted once they'd finished rehashing their favorite blunders of mine. "Only my attempts to engage in conversation."

And they hadn't gone well. A lie, apparently.

My jaw strained as I considered how far the deception went. Not only had the perpetrator put my court in danger; they'd ruined my life. Had that been the goal, or was it simply a casualty of their secret war?

"Another indication the quill was used," Envy said. "It seems like your relationship might have been the target."

"*If* that's the reason, then someone worked hard to ensure she didn't remember you in a fond light," Lust added. "Who'd you piss off?"

"Did you flirt with anyone else?" Sloth asked.

"Who's asking dumb questions now?" Lust quipped.

I raked my hands through my hair, my attention shifting back to the sky. "Maybe they hoped to weaken my court."

Val's worries didn't seem so far-fetched now.

Adriana's scathing articles could have turned the tides of my sinners. If they aligned with different sins, my court would eventually collapse.

Whoever used the quill made sure Adriana hated me and that I wouldn't remember making her mine at all. There was an answer in that little detail, one that would solve it all.

My attention turned inward. I tried to focus on any particulars of that night and drew a blank. "I'm not sure we can trust my memories even if I did remember anything."

It felt like the worst sort of violation, to have my mind tampered with. My life. When I discovered who dared to thwart my happiness—and Adriana's—I'd feed them to the dragons.

I finished my drink and motioned for my brother to refill my glass, my mind turning over all the information I'd learned.

Envy gritted his teeth at the order but obliged, pouring another knuckle of liquor.

I trusted my brothers enough to know that if they believed Adriana was correct and the Hexed Quill had been used against us, it was true.

Logically it made sense. But it was still hard to reconcile.

I tossed back the second bourbon, the burn grounding me in the here and now.

"Even if my memory comes back, the damage is done."

"How very defeatist of you." Envy sipped his bourbon, eyes glinting. "With your thirst for adventure, I would have thought you'd fight for her."

I had a damn House of Sin filled with potential brides and a hexed object still at large. If the realm discovered the truth about me and Adriana... *scandal* was too mild a term.

I couldn't risk discovery yet.

But maybe I could begin to rebuild what we'd lost. An idea slowly formed...

A ball might be the perfect way for me to not only continue to distract the realm but to sneak a dance with her too. Make up for some mistakes.

My attention shifted to the sky. No dragons to be seen. "I assume I don't have to tell any of you to keep this information between us. The last thing I need is for the scandal sheets to find out." I glanced at my brothers. "Did you give Wolf my message?"

"Of course." Envy moved to the railing, staring out at the darkening clouds. "If anyone can track down a hexed object, an Unseelie hunter can. He's scouring his network."

An unsettling suspicion crossed my mind, too preposterous to be true. Still, I couldn't immediately dismiss it. "You don't think Adriana wielded the quill, do you?"

Envy straightened from where he'd been leaning against the railing, brows raised as he looked at me, then Sloth. "She *is* a writer."

Sloth was silent for a few moments, his gaze turning inward. That he didn't immediately call us both idiots set me further on edge.

Eventually, he lifted a shoulder. "It's possible. Maybe you did something that made her want to forget. If she did use the quill, she might not be aware."

"Wouldn't she know if she had the quill?" Greed asked. "Or the journal or parchment?"

"Not necessarily." Envy's expression turned dark. "She might have hidden them and forgotten or tossed them out after she'd left the ball. Anything's possible."

"Maybe someone coerced her into writing it and she had no idea what it was," Sloth added. "It stands to reason it had nothing to do with you, and maybe it was about someone wanting *her*. Perhaps she ignored someone's pursuit who didn't take kindly to that."

We were all quiet for a while, lost to our own thoughts and suspicions.

I'd been arrogant enough to believe *I'd* been the target and prize. And the magic that bound us...it didn't like the idea of someone taking Adriana from me.

Shoving that territorial aspect aside, she *had* been attracting attention from many suitors that night. Perhaps someone was jealous and wanted to ruin what we had so they might steal her one day. That theory invited in a whole new slew of suspects.

And that made me want to hunt them down and do unspeakably dark things. If another sinner from a different court thought to undermine me in my own circle, I would go to war.

I ran a hand through my hair and heaved a sigh.

"Return to your circles and see what you can find out about the attendees of the All-Sinners Ball. I'll try to unearth more clues about the quill—there's got to be some trail of owners to follow. Tomorrow I'll try to flush out the culprit."

"How do you plan on doing that?" Sloth asked.

I strode toward the door. "I'm going to throw another ball."

After spending the rest of the night planning the ball and sending out invitations, I was eager to meet my nemesis at the stables the next afternoon. Adriana's expression shuttered the moment she saw the hell horse. As in singular.

We were about to get very comfortable. In light of her discovery of the

Hexed Quill, and also what happened when we were in the library, it had been a battle to get her to come for the ride today. She claimed we needed distance while we sorted this out, especially when I'd asked her to dance with me at the ball tonight. I politely disagreed.

The competition might still be on, my suitors and court wildly excited by the announcement of the sudden ball, but solving this mystery took precedence over all.

One way or another, I would find out if Adriana had wielded that quill. My gut told me she hadn't. And there was another, more personal reason for our little early afternoon excursion.

I adjusted my leather gloves.

"Is there a problem, Miss Saint Lucent?"

I stroked Magnus's neck, the giant black stallion impatiently toeing the dirt. It had been nearly a week since I'd taken him out. He was ready to run.

Thankfully my dragon wounds from the incident days before had finally healed. The ride wouldn't be too bad. For me.

Adriana looked like she was stepping into a new nightmare.

"Where is my horse?" she asked.

"Do you know how to ride?"

Her attention drifted between me and the horse. "No."

"Well, then. Let's get you up."

A stable hand took the reins while I lifted Adriana onto the horse, her breath catching as she settled at the front of the saddle. I launched myself up, settling comfortably behind her.

She stiffened, doing her best to lean forward, avoiding any unnecessary touching.

As if we hadn't been ready to tear each other's clothes off a couple of nights before and I hadn't brought her release in the hidden corridor.

I grinned at her back, then spurred Magnus into a canter, guiding him out of the stable and into the softly falling snow.

Adriana tugged the hood of her navy cloak up, a shiver rolling down her spine as we began a slightly faster pace. Her grip on the pommel tightened as we began to bounce, her bottom lifting off the saddle with each of our steps.

"Stop squeezing with your thighs; you want your calves close to the horse. Angle your heels down and roll into the movement," I said. "You'll keep your seat better."

I pulled back on the reins, slowing Magnus as a protective surge rose in me. It wouldn't do to have Adriana flying off the horse.

"Here." I handed her the reins. "Rest these against the pommel. Lean into me."

I placed my hands on either side of her body, pulling her hips into mine. Tension radiated through her, and Magnus whinnied, his head tossing from side to side.

"You need to relax, or Magnus will buck. A horse senses when a rider is anxious."

"I'm not sure how relaxing is possible at the moment."

"Close your eyes. Don't think about how good I feel. Think about the horse. Let your thighs clasp its sides lightly but hold on a bit more with your calves. With your heels angled toward the ground, it helps maintain your balance."

She took a deep breath, then slowly adjusted her body, her legs now curving around the horse's middle.

"Good. When we start moving again, roll your hips in time with the horse's gait. The motion won't be as jarring, and you won't lose your seat. It's all about finding the rhythm."

I took the reins back, holding them lightly in one hand and clamping my other around her hip to ensure she stayed in the saddle. It might have been a touch unnecessary to hold her so closely, but I *was* a rake. At least where she was concerned.

"We'll start slower. Ready?"

She exhaled, the plume of breath coming out in a cloud. "I think so."

"If you start to tense, lean into me, move with my body. I won't let you fall."

I clucked at Magnus and urged him into a canter once again, ensuring we stuck to a well-trodden path that curved around the perimeter of House Gluttony.

Adriana's body was still too stiff, but she'd started to find her rhythm with the horse. Eventually, she relaxed against me, her back molding to my chest as we entered a full trot.

Magnus neighed, chomping at the bit; he wanted to unleash himself. Galloping through storms was his favorite pastime. And I could deny my horse nothing.

Once I was certain Adriana wouldn't go tumbling off, I kicked my heels into his flank, giving him the signal to fly. He needed no further encouragement.

Magnus raced along the path, the trees on either side of us blurring into an indistinguishable mass of dark green.

Adriana shrieked and my arm immediately circled her waist, banding her tightly against me as we tore down the path, then darted into the woods, her body moving with mine.

She felt good in my arms. Right.

I tried to focus on my mission, thinking of how to interrogate her about the quill without causing a bigger rift between us, but the more she bounced against me, the harder that became.

Almost quite literally.

I gritted my teeth. Perhaps this wasn't the best plan.

The old gods had an abysmal sense of justice—I was the one fully being tortured now.

And I'd *swear* the hellcat in front of me sensed it. Adriana suddenly moved a little too enthusiastically, her bottom all but gyrating against me while her breasts bounced on my arm.

By the time Magnus drew to a halt near the falls, I was downright ornery.

I dismounted and helped Adriana down, noting the gleam in her eyes as she swept her attention over me, found proof of my reaction to her taunts, then flicked it away.

She'd known precisely what she'd been doing.

If I wasn't so bothered, I'd be impressed with her victory. She'd certainly turned the situation in her favor. She didn't spare me a second glance as she strode forward, following several hundred candles that illuminated the path that wound behind the waterfall.

I followed on her heels, noting with pleasure that all had been done to my specifications.

A small table and chairs were tucked behind the raging waterfall, the sound a dull roar as water rushed into an icy blue pool, the surface a frothy white.

I'd sent my staff ahead earlier to set up a romantic picnic at one of my favorite locations on the property's grounds. Behind the flowing curtain of water was a natural cavern made of thick slabs of ice, the walls taking on a beautiful pale-blue tint from the frozen water.

In the next cavern over was a hot springs lagoon that I opened up to the public, making it a popular location for my court and circle who wished to indulge in nature.

It was a winter dreamscape. Even a cynic like Adriana felt the awe. She turned in place, taking in every inch of our surroundings, an expression of wonder on her face.

I'd never seen such a look on her before and caught myself before I did something foolish like trace the curve of her cheek, memorizing the shape of her joy.

I cleared my throat and pulled out her chair. "Please. Have a seat."

She settled onto the chair and flipped the hood of her cloak back, her attention still riveted to the scenery. She didn't trust my motives.

I pulled one of the baskets of supplies out from where the staff had left it, then popped the cork on the sparkling wine. I filled our glasses to the top, then set the platters of cheese and fruits and cured meats on the small table, arranging everything just right.

Adriana watched me the way someone might stare at a dog that suddenly began speaking to its owner in their native language.

I quirked a brow. "It's hard to tell if you're impressed or horrified."

"I didn't expect you to serve yourself."

"Actually, I'm serving you first. To save you from swooning too hard, I also muddled the lavender and lemon and bottled the wine."

She gave me a flat look and sipped her drink, her gaze flicking back to mine. "You're serious."

"You seem to have forgotten I can't outright lie."

"You and your brothers are well versed in lies of omission and word-play."

I smiled politely. "True. But you are free to lie whenever you please."

"And you would sense when I did, so I don't see any point in holding my tongue."

It was the perfect segue into what I'd brought her here for. Well, one of the reasons.

I fiddled with the stem of my flute, watching her carefully. "Who do you think used the Hexed Quill?"

She looked me over carefully.

"I'm not sure. I've been trying to think of anyone who had the means to pull it off. Or the motive. Why target your court?"

If she was trying to get me to admit to the ice dragons, I would disappoint her there.

"I'm curious why your memory wasn't impacted the same way as mine."

She searched my face. "Is there something you're getting at, Axton?"

"You write."

There was one tense moment of silence before she reacted.

"Unbelievable." Her mouth pressed into a hard line. "You believe I used the quill. To ruin my own life?"

"It's possible you don't remember using it." I thought of her friend, the other writer. "Or maybe it's someone you know. The columnist who wrote about us. There were rumors she was interested in taking your position as top reporter, were there not?"

If looks could kill, I'd be in the Great Beyond.

"I wasn't top anything at that time, especially after our scandal hit the press. And Ryleigh is like family. She would *never* betray me."

Annoyance prickled at her fierce defense of her friend. Mostly due to the look of pure loathing she tossed my way. "Just like how she didn't allude to you to sell more scandal sheets."

"How can you be certain you didn't regret your choice and decide to rewrite your story? Maybe that's why your memory of us sleeping together is gone and mine is not."

"I do *not* regret it."

"Of course you don't." She gave me a flat look. "You don't even remember it."

The air in the cavern suddenly felt too warm, my heartbeat too fast. Tension crackled between us as I finally unleashed my greatest secret.

"I have *hungered* for you in ways you cannot comprehend. I've craved you. More than my sin. You haunt me, Adriana." I nearly shook from the confession. "My dreams are the only time I get to worship you. Do you have any idea how many careful lies of omission I've told over the years? The role I've played this last decade. All to hide the truth of how deeply, wholly lost I am to you?"

She tossed back her sparkling wine in an impressive gulp, then stood.

"If this meeting is done, I'd like to go home. I still have a column to write and turn in."

I rose, noting with satisfaction that it wasn't fear I sensed coming from her as I leaned across the table, dominance rolling off me in waves. "No."

Her pretty eyes flashed like daggers. "It's not up for debate, you oaf."

"You're right, it's not. Now sit."

I hid my grin as her arousal nearly knocked me backward.

She wanted to hate my arrogant command, but her body felt otherwise.

I knew if I dropped my attention, I'd see the hard buds of her nipples outlined through her silk bodice, begging for my wicked mouth.

Adriana liked when I dominated her in this manner only.

It was one battle we could happily agree on.

We stared at each other, our faces mere inches apart, until she finally dropped back into her seat, her expression thunderous.

"Well?" she asked, voice clipped. "What falsehood do you wish to confess to now?"

"The truth is, sweet nemesis"—I lowered my mouth to her ear—"I have not fucked a soul since the All-Sinners Ball. But I have made love to you a thousand times in my dreams. And I have never *once* yearned for anyone else to visit my bed."

I stepped back enough to watch the truth of my confession settle in. She searched my face, her eyes glimmering with unshed tears.

"What do you want from me now?"

To do all the unspeakably depraved, wicked things you and I both desire.

"The same thing I've wanted for longer than I'd care to admit."

I might not remember sleeping with Adriana, but the dark magic hadn't been the only thing keeping us apart this past decade. My actions were equally to blame.

After her first scathing article had been printed, I'd gone on a public rampage to indulge my sin; the more Adriana skewered me in the scandal sheets, the more I tried to prove her wrong.

It turned into a vicious cycle, and I'd ultimately only succeeded in proving her right.

The more we fought our private war, the less chance there was of winning.

I tried to recall the All-Sinners Ball in detail. It was fuzzy at best. But one image I'd held on to with stark clarity had always been the first moment I'd seen her enter the ballroom.

I might not remember much from that night, but I would catalogue every detail from this point forward. My sin ignited, my hunger for her all-consuming.

I dragged my gaze from her frosty eyes down to her toes, then slid it back up, leaving no question about what I starved for. This was House Gluttony, and I was more than ready to indulge. Her bodice strained against her quick breaths.

My sweet enemy was about to surrender to her future; she just didn't realize it yet.

Someone stole her from me once. And, unless she told me otherwise, she would be mine.

Tonight.

I leaned closer, brushing my lips against the shell of her ear, satisfied by the shiver of pleasure that rocked through her at the small contact.

Her slight gasp would be the first of many.

Beginning now.

"I want to give you my royal mark. Then spread your thighs and feast."

FORTY-SIX
Adriana

HEAT FLAMED THROUGH me as Axton's focus drifted over each curve of my body, his expression hinting at all the wicked plans he was devising.

Perhaps *hinting* wasn't the right word. He looked ready to devour me whole.

And try as I might, I didn't hate it.

If I was annoyed with him a moment before, I couldn't recall why.

He hadn't done anything more than lean across the table in a show of male dominance and my knees practically gave out from the sight.

Traitorous knees. They clearly couldn't be bothered by our years of friction with the prince. In that moment all they knew was he was an apex predator on the hunt, and they very much wished to be caught in his sinful clutches.

Or maybe I was simply recalling how it felt when my stranger had gotten on *his* knees earlier in the week. Or how Axton himself had felt when we were pressed against that wall in his hidden chamber off the library. Blast it all. It was his cursed confession, and I knew there would be no going back from it, especially if I accepted his royal mark.

I couldn't quite process everything he'd admitted. But I knew how I felt.

And his searing look burned away any remaining fears. The Ruthless Rake hungered for me. Enough to forever mark me as someone he held in the highest regard.

There was no undoing a royal mark that I knew of.

It seemed impossible that he truly felt that way until he settled that intense gaze on mine.

My pulse raced in anticipation; he could melt a glacier with that heated stare.

I subtly glanced around the ice cavern to make sure the walls hadn't thawed.

"First, I'm going to give you the mark right here."

He reached over and traced the expanse of skin along my bodice to the right of my heart. My chest heaved from the light touch.

"Then I'm going to bind your wrists with my belt, tie you to the chair, and kiss every inch of your skin."

My focus shot to him and remained there. He waited, brow quirked, for my response. But I had no quip. No argument. Only a steady throbbing that was growing more insistent.

His mouth curved. He knew he'd succeeded in gaining my full attention.

Or maybe he knew I'd have no desire to fight him on this. He *was* my stranger from the Seven Sins. He knew the secret longings of my heart. And I knew his.

Filthy, filthy Prince of Sin.

"Then, once you're begging for my cock, I'm going to bend you over this table." He traced a line across the small table before us, slowly pushing the food aside. "And pound your pussy so hard you won't care if I'm the devil himself so long as I make you come again."

I closed my eyes, trying to quell the hollow ache steadily building from his words.

There was no use denying how aroused he made me. If he didn't touch me soon, I'd ease my own need and I didn't care if he stood there and watched.

In fact, I had a suspicion he'd rather enjoy the show, knowing it was all for him.

I shook those thoughts away. "We can't."

"Why?"

I blew out a frustrated breath. "Oh, I'm not sure. Perhaps it has something to do with your competition to find a bride? Or my sister being one of your suitors?"

His gaze narrowed. "Your sister is lovely, to be certain, but I think you and I both know I'd never choose her."

And, knowing what I did of Eden's secret lover, I didn't think she'd wish to choose him. Still. "Even if you don't choose Eden, you still have other suitors to consider."

"Fair point. We'll do exactly what we swore an oath to do—court in private until the press finds another story to focus on."

I laughed softly, shaking my head. "You are the royal favorite. I doubt anyone else will hold the same appeal for the papers."

His mouth curved. "With enough motivation, I'm sure Lust might give them a few scandals to report on. Maybe he can step in and take over the competition."

I couldn't believe we were sitting together, calmly devising a plot to carry out a secret romance. I'd blame the damn magical bond we shared but knew it ran deeper than that.

Much deeper.

My mind kept repeating his confession, as if I'd ever forget a single word. It felt too much like a fantasy, knowing Gabriel Axton had secretly hungered for me the same way I'd hungered for him.

Part of me still worried this was too good to be true, that I was falling into the same trap I had ten years ago. That this would all come crashing down once more.

I didn't know how I'd survive another scandal or another heartbreak. But wasn't love about trust and faith? Maybe it was time to put the past aside and live for today.

"If we agree to this, no one can find out," I said. "I need to find a way to tell my sister."

"Your secrets are mine, darling. I'd never betray you." He leaned in again. "Are you amenable to what I have planned for us now?"

Gods, I shouldn't be, but I was. "Yes."

"Wonderful. But first. The royal mark."

The prince came around to my side of the little table, offering his hand to me, palm up. I took a steadying breath as I rose, taking his hand. His other arm snaked around my waist, slowly reeling me in. I inhaled sharply. I wanted his mark, wanted the confirmation that he felt the same way I did, but it was all happening so quickly. It felt a little like a fever dream.

Though I supposed it *really* all began ten years ago. Our happily-ever-after had been stolen and we were now about to reclaim it.

"Nervous?" He grinned down at me as he placed my hand on his shoulder, then gently brushed my hair back, granting him access to my skin.

"Will it hurt?" I asked, gripping him a little tighter.

"Not at all." His smile turned wicked. "It will feel like a kiss. Ready?"

"To enter an unbreakable bond with a Prince of Sin and basically sell my soul? Who wouldn't be?"

His chuckle was dark and deep and made my toes curl. "Sweet nemesis. You act as if your soul hasn't already been mine from the start."

"Arrogant demon."

"Confident prince."

His gaze suddenly dropped, the reverence in his eyes letting me know the teasing was over and this was no longer a joking matter to him.

My eyes fluttered shut as he brushed his knuckles along my jawline, then slowly followed the curve of my neck down to my shoulders. He slipped his fingers along the inside of my bodice, gently drawing the silk back to grant him more access to my chest.

His touch was so intimate, so caring. If my heart wasn't already in danger, it would be.

Once my gown was off my shoulder, he leaned in, starting the process with a chaste kiss to my pulse point then continuing lower, his lips gliding softly along my skin. When he finally reached the place he planned to mark me, his tongue traced a small pattern over my flesh.

It tingled at first, then his tongue swept over me again, tracing the same design and a heat ignited that seemed to set my whole body aflame.

Axton was right: it felt like he'd kissed me and I wanted more.

He drew back to admire his work. "Do you like it?"

I glanced down, trying to make out the small mark in the dim light. It was so pale against my skin it was hardly noticeable. Just a baby blue shimmering mark that looked like the outline of a dragon. No one would really see it unless they knew to look for it, but I felt the slight buzz of magic beneath my skin, almost purring with pleasure.

"It's beautiful," I said, glancing up.

"I couldn't agree more."

Axton began to unbuckle his belt, watching me the whole time, his movements slow and torturous as he slid it from around his hips. He'd promised to mark me, then tie me up and kiss me *everywhere* and he was nothing if not a demon of his word.

My pulse began thrumming in excitement as I sat back down.

He wound each end of the belt around his fists, holding the strap of leather taut between us, much like the growing tension. Tension that had nothing to do with the new magic binding us and everything to do with our emotions.

The prince suddenly drew the leather close then wrenched it back, causing it to clap loudly in the ice chamber.

My knees pressed together, the anticipation driving me wild with want already.

"Do you wish for me to stop?"

I'd give him an incredulous look if my gaze wasn't fixed with complete fascination on where he stroked the leather with his thumbs.

I realized he was still waiting for a response. "No, I don't want you to stop, Axton."

He walked around the table, his attention locked on mine.

"Clasp your hands behind the chair and twine your fingers together like you're praying."

I couldn't help the tiny snort that escaped. "Highly inappropriate comparison."

A devilish gleam entered his eyes. "You won't think that when you're riding my face and shouting for all the gods to come to your rescue."

I'd call him arrogant but knew from experience I'd be doing just that within moments of his tongue flicking over my body.

He prowled around my chair, swiftly tying me into position.

The leather was cool and a little rough against my skin, the strap pulled tightly against my wrists as he wound them, then looped the rest through in a tight knot so I couldn't pull free.

My heart raced as I tested my bindings. I truly was at the prince's mercy.

As if sensing my slight panic, he knelt before me, a serious expression on his handsome face.

"One word and I'll stop. This is about pleasure, not pain. If at any point you don't wish to continue, that is completely fine. I will be controlling your pleasure, but you ultimately control *me*. Understand?"

I flashed him a rather saucy smile. "Do you honestly believe I'd bite my tongue?"

"That wicked tongue is only one of the many reasons I love you."

A thrill raced down my spine and I shuddered against the emotion. Telling me he hungered for me was one thing but hearing him say he loved me was something else entirely. We both seemed to unravel at the confession, our need becoming all-consuming.

He leaned close and took my mouth in a kiss that stole my breath, the ferocity of it nearly knocking us both backward.

I strained against my bindings, wanting to run my hands through his hair.

Axton pulled back, a wicked curve tugging at his lips.

"The cavern next to us has one of the most popular lagoons in my circle. And today is the day I open it to the public. Anyone might happen upon us."

My chest heaved against my bodice, my breathing turning sharp and too quick.

Axton had brought us somewhere we might get caught. All to play into my fantasy.

"We just agreed to keep this a secret. Are you mad?"

He flashed me a wolfish grin as he approached. "Trust me."

It was a monumental task, especially when he began drawing my skirts up to my hips, slowly exposing me to anyone who might come by for a swim.

My knees locked together, even as I felt the heat building deep inside me.

"Spread your thighs."

I craved his touch, but I wasn't sure I could cross the threshold from fantasy to reality with so much at stake. If we were discovered now...

Axton circled my chair, then leaned across my shoulder, his mouth pressed to my ear the exact moment he touched between my thighs.

I drew in a sharp breath from the shock of unexpected contact. It took everything in my power to not grind myself against him, seeking relief from the growing arousal.

"Axton, I don't think—"

"We ought to hurry. Or else anyone who arrives will have quite the show. Because I don't plan on stopping until you're begging for mercy."

He took the lobe of my ear between his teeth, then swirled one finger through my slickness. I moaned from the pleasure.

"This is *mine*."

He withdrew his finger, then slapped my clit, the sensation sending a heady rush through me as he cupped me again. The move was pure possessiveness and shouldn't be attractive, but my body disagreed. I was so wet and swollen with need from his savage claim, it almost hurt.

"And I will not share you with anyone."

"Gabriel, please."

I struggled against my bindings, wanting to touch him in return.

He nuzzled my neck, then the royal mark, his fingers exploring the entire time.

A pebble fell from the chamber, making me tense in all the right ways. It was only a rock, not a person. This time.

"From here on out, I'll indulge your fantasy but will never invite anyone into our bed."

He stroked my body with slow, sinful swirls, spreading my wetness before finally thrusting two fingers deep inside me. He pumped in and out a few times, then abruptly stood, my body bereft at the loss of his.

"When the competition ends, you will move into my chambers."

"Shall I roll over and fetch next?"

Axton loomed before me, removing his jacket, then undoing the buttons of his shirt, his gaze running over every inch of me while he undressed.

"Your mouth is my greatest fascination. Never stop challenging me, darling."

I watched, rapt, as he shucked his clothing off, leaving only his trousers slung low on his hips.

He truly was a dark god. His abdomen was all ridges and hard muscle, soft skin pulled over a warrior's body. His tattoo...it made me want to run my tongue all over him.

"Keep your thighs spread."

There was a delicious threat left unsaid, and part of me wanted to disobey him just to see what he'd do to punish me. I had a feeling I'd rather enjoy it.

But I also enjoyed when he was on his knees before me, so I slowly heeded his demand.

Once I'd bared myself to him, he dropped before me, his large hands stroking up the back of my legs, wrapping around them until he dragged my bottom to the edge of the seat.

With a dark gleam in his gaze, he slowly hoisted each of my legs over his shoulders. My dress was going to be completely crinkled but I didn't care.

It was an awkward position, my hands bound behind me, my bare bottom hanging off the seat, but Axton's attention was wholly fixed on the wetness at the apex of my legs.

"You are my favorite indulgence, Adriana Saint Lucent."

He leaned forward then licked my slit. I arched up as high as I could, but Axton controlled the movement of my body. His big shoulders made me spread wider for him, and he took full advantage. His tongue flattened, ensuring the next stroke covered all of me.

I cried out, the restraints both perfect and horrid. I wanted to thread my fingers in his hair, tug him to me, and ride his face as he'd so crassly said before.

Instead, I could only sit there, squirming, as he feasted, choosing how best to torture me. The prince was in no hurry. He took turns alternating between filling me with his tongue, then swirling it against my clit, nibbling and sucking and driving me to the brink, before sitting back on his heels, blowing a slow stream of breath against my swollen flesh.

He'd said we needed to hurry, that anyone could come upon us. I couldn't remember why I cared. Now all I wanted was for him to end this sweet misery.

"Axton, please," I begged. "Stop playing."

The cursed prince would do no such thing. His wicked tongue traced the seam of my body before he thrust it deep inside, penetrating me in a way that made me call out to the gods.

His chuckle vibrated along my body, and just when I was certain I'd fall over that glorious cliff, he pressed a chaste kiss to my inner thigh.

"Forget the ball later. I'm going to stay here all night."

I thrashed against my restraints. I loved them and hated them and wanted to take back control while also secretly loving this torture.

Axton continued his languorous tasting, bringing me to the edge and back so many times I thought I'd gone mad. He cupped one of my breasts, flicking a nipple, and my body thrust forward, hoping for another delightful sweep of his tongue. I leaned back, praying out loud for mercy, for an orgasm, for the gods to strike the prince down for being so wicked.

"Eyes on me. Or I stop."

I was so frustrated I could scream, but I locked my attention on him.

When Axton brought his mouth to me again, I nearly cried with relief, sensing his torturous foreplay was over. His fingers dug into my thighs where he held me aloft, his tongue increasing its tempo across my clit. I wanted to watch him, but my attention drifted to the lagoon.

It was heady, imagining someone coming upon us now. I found my legs spreading impossibly wider, safe in knowing no one was really there to see the prince pleasure me.

I hadn't realized I'd been gyrating against his face until he growled low in approval.

I was so close, so ready...he sucked my clit, hard, then thrust two fingers into me.

I cried out as my orgasm finally released and Axton lapped every last drop of it up.

I'd barely come down from the feeling, my bones all but liquid in the aftermath, when Axton lifted me from the chair, then gently placed me on my knees.

I licked my lips as he shucked his pants down and let his giant, thick cock spring free.

He looked utterly delectable standing there before me, naked and proud, and I was more than ready to indulge.

FORTY-SEVEN
Prince Gluttony

*A*REN'T YOU GOING to untie me?"

My sweet, sweet nemesis couldn't hide the desire from her face. Adriana *wanted* to run her hands all over me. Which made torturing her even more fun.

"No. I'm going to fuck that pretty mouth all on my own." I traced the seam of her lips. "I need you to take me. *All* of me, darling."

Her arousal hit me so strongly, I nearly came before she touched me.

I thought the first flick of her tongue over the head of my cock was a spiritual experience.

Until her wicked mouth closed around my shaft, and it was the closest thing to heaven a sinner like me had ever known. She nearly took me to my knees with the next stroke, and the sharp gleam in her eyes told me she knew it.

"*Fuck.*" I wound her hair around my fist, guiding her deeper. She kept those beautiful, bottomless pools of blue trained on me, watching me drown in her.

Adriana kneeling, hands bound behind her back, taking me fully and being equally turned on was the most erotic sight I'd ever seen. A primal need to claim her overtook me.

I pumped into her mouth a few times, but it wasn't nearly enough.

I wanted to be inside her.

I had every intention of bending her over the table and giving us both what we desired but craved more intimacy. She might recall the first time we'd been together, but I didn't, and I wanted to watch her unravel from pleasure. Perhaps I was sentimental.

At least where she was concerned.

I untied her wrists and scooped her up, gently laying her down on a pile of furs, wanting to indulge all her senses as she writhed along the soft bed.

I kissed her softly before our hunger took over.

I tugged her bodice down, heedless of the fragile silk and lace. I needed to get my mouth on her. In a move that impressed even me, I yanked her gown off without destroying it and tossed it aside then turned my attention back to my beautiful rival.

My royal mark shimmered, filling me with a sense of gratification I'd never known before. It was the most pleasure I'd ever felt, knowing she'd chosen me in return.

Adriana arched into me as I lavished her breasts with affection. My cock teased her entrance, and it was the most magnificent sensation in the universe.

With one hard thrust I was seated inside her.

I paused, taking my time to kiss along her jaw, down her neck, tracing the royal mark, then drawing the peaked buds of her breasts into my mouth, sucking until her hips bucked upward. She felt too damned good to be real, especially when she ran her hands along my body.

"Is there something you'd like me to do, Miss Saint Lucent?"

Her scowl was the most delightful thing I'd ever seen. "If you haven't figured that out yet, perhaps my previous claims regarding your cleverness hold true."

I laughed softly, then rolled my hips forward, rewarding her for the quip. If I thought Adriana would follow my lead here, I was wrong.

Whenever I slowed down, she met my thrusts with her own in a glorious rivalry of who might inflict the most pleasure on the other.

Soon we were both panting, her legs locked around my hips as we raced to the finish line.

"I'm close." Her voice was soft, seductive.

I slipped a hand between us, pressing a finger to her clit, and she cried out in rapture, shattering beneath me as I found my own release.

I kissed her thoroughly, deeply, my cock still buried inside her. I hadn't been entirely joking earlier—I could spend the rest of the day and night here with her and be perfectly content. I drew back, brushing the strands of damp hair from her face.

"I adore you in obscene ways."

Her smile was soft, almost shy. "Likewise."

I twined our fingers, pinning her hands above her head. I was ready to go again and so was she. I slowly pulled out, then rolled my hips, kissing her deeply as I filled her.

I paused to focus solely on ravishing her mouth, my tongue stroking hers until I felt her clenching around me. Only then did I pull out and thrust in again. Loving how she reacted to each slow movement. I held her hands up, bringing my attention back to her breasts.

Adriana bucked against me, setting the pace of her own pleasure. I brought my mouth back to hers, too willing to let her fuck me for a while.

"Gabriel."

"Close," I whispered, taking her earlobe between my teeth. "My true name is Gabriellis."

She stopped breathing for a beat, then kissed me like I was the only real thing in her world. "Harder."

I needed no further instruction—I pounded into her until her soft moans filled the chamber, drawing me to my own release as we came again.

She whispered my true name like a curse, and it might have been the only time I'd ever welcomed a hex. I dropped my head to her chest, kissing her heart.

"Your Highness!"

Adriana's entire body tightened beneath me, and it took a moment for my brain to catch up. It hadn't been her crying out. Dread swept over me as the sound of footsteps grew closer.

There was no time to act, to hide.

We'd been caught. My focus snapped to the mouth of the cavern, where Val burst in.

For one horribly taut moment, no one moved.

My second froze, her expression one of pure shock as she took in the scene, trying to make sense of it. Adriana faced me, but her ice-blue hair was in full view of our unexpected guest. Her fantasy of being caught had been just that—a fantasy. The horror she felt slammed into me so hard I almost scooped her into my arms and sought cover.

There was no hiding who my lover was. And, given our very public feud, finding us together was quite a surprise. Val blinked rapidly, as if her eyes deceived her.

Her attention dropped to Adriana, and it was impossible to read her thoughts.

"Val," I snapped, doing my best to shield Adriana from view. "Give us a moment. Now."

Val gave me a look of regret. "I can't. We located where Silvanus has been hiding."

"Shit." I shut my eyes, then opened them, heart pounding as I sorted through ten different action plans in seconds. "Take Magnus back to the stables. I'll meet you at the castle soon."

Val gave Adriana another long look. "We might need her help."

I glanced down at my lover, indecision warring in me like two great enemies. Val was really asking if I trusted Adriana with this court secret. My pulse pounded. If Silvanus was planning something, he wouldn't stay in any camp for long. A day, maybe less. I needed to track him now and try to incapacitate him with slumber root.

If I was ever going to place trust in Adriana, it was time.

I'd already given her my true name and my royal mark; there was no reason to keep anything else from her now. She had the power to destroy me in more than one way, should she choose. And after our meeting with Envy, there was no chance Adriana hadn't already figured out that the dragons were being targeted by the hex.

"What are you thinking?" I asked my second, granting her permission to speak freely.

If Val was surprised, it didn't show. "Take Miss Saint Lucent back to the castle. Create a scandal worthy of all the gossip sheets. We'll need a diversion if anything goes...wrong."

Adriana peered up at me, her expression hard to decipher. "Is Silvanus a dragon you've been hunting?"

I inhaled deeply. "Yes."

"And the Hexed Quill has impacted them, enough that they've attacked?"

Val watched us curiously. I realized why: I was still shielding Adriana with my body, completely forgetting we were in a highly scandalous position.

"Go. Take Magnus to the stables and we'll see you soon."

"Is there anything I should prepare for when we meet again?"

A plan formulated quickly. "You'll burst in and tear me from the castle, drawing attention to our arrival if it goes unnoticed."

Without another word, Val bowed and left.

"You don't have to take part in this distraction if you don't want to," I said, my attention fully on Adriana. "I'll find another way that won't involve you."

Adriana's fingers dug into my arms.

I couldn't tell if she was gripping me so tightly to keep me close, or if she was trying not to strangle me for suggesting she participate in a public scandal.

Determination entered her features. "What's the full plan?"

"If we're caught together, all eyes will be on you, hungry for any morsel you feed them. You'll simply play up our arrival, give them reason to believe we're secret lovers."

"Because we are."

"Only for now." I kissed her softly. "While they're trying to get the details of our affair, I'll hunt Silvanus and stop him before he has a chance to round up the rest of the pack or find allies in other packs.

Hopefully all will go smoothly, and I'll return in time for the ball, call off the competition there, and declare myself to you, ending the scandal as soon as I'm able to."

A small smile crossed her face. "Let's go cause a scandal."

With our blood oath, if I left her here and traveled too far, there would be pain. For both of us. I wasn't concerned about me, though.

"There's one more aspect to consider."

She pushed at my chest. "The blood oath discomfort? I'm well aware. You've been a pain in my ass for a decade. I'll live."

I wanted to smile but couldn't.

"Are you ready?" I asked instead.

She nodded.

I launched myself off her and was in my trousers in the next beat, using my full power to bend time. Adriana quickly slipped her gown over her head, cursing at the crumpled fabric and torn lace. There was no way to disguise what we'd done. Not that we were trying to.

I wrapped my suit jacket around her in an attempt to hide the state of things, knowing it would draw further scrutiny.

I took her hand as we raced for the mouth of the cave. Once there, I swept Adriana up in my arms and took to the sky. Within moments we touched down outside my House.

I placed a possessive hand on her lower back, needing to feel her whole and healthy and alive, not simply for the sake of causing whispers, as I walked her up the wide stairs leading into House Gluttony. We'd just stepped into my receiving hall when someone gasped.

I glanced up. As far as fate went, I supposed this was the best demon to run into first.

Ryleigh Hughes stared, unblinking.

I ought to be relieved that our plan was already spinning into place.

But it didn't feel right. It took all my power to forge ahead and not claim Adriana as mine right there, damning all consequences.

"What in the hells happened to your dress?" she asked.

"I can't talk now." Adriana's voice was meeker than I'd ever heard it before. She was playing her role stunningly well. Now it was time for me to do the same.

I wrapped my hand around Adriana's, drawing more attention to our connection. She squeezed my hand back, a silent signal that she would still play her part, that it was okay.

Movement caught my eye, and I looked up. Courtiers and the suitors from House Greed and House Envy now stood on the stairs, whispering. This was a disaster in the making.

Ryleigh glanced between us, and I could see her fitting the pieces together.

"Have you lost your senses?" she asked, stepping back. *"The prince?"*

It was difficult to not bristle at her tone. Instead of reacting to the less-than-flattering reaction, I leaned in and brushed a chaste kiss to Adriana's lips, sealing our fate.

"Your Highness!" Val burst into the room, right on time. "You're needed."

I turned a haughty glare on the reporter.

"Miss Hughes. Please see yourself out. The castle isn't entertaining reporters until tonight." I gently tugged Adriana, drawing her near. That part wasn't an act. "I'll escort you to the gardens."

"Go, please. I need to get to my chambers before anyone else notices."

She was a cunning liar. I might be irrevocably in love.

"You're certain?"

"Very."

With one final look over my shoulder, I followed Val out of the castle.

"You got the transportation spell from Sascha?" I asked. She nodded. "Good. We'll meet at Merciless Reach, compile a retrieval team, and head out from there."

I was airborne in the next breath, racing toward the fortress.

Moments later, I touched down in the courtyard of Merciless Reach, Val appearing seconds behind me. We strode toward the building, readying for the hunt, before drawing up short at what greeted us.

Two dragons circled the fortress's towers, streams of icy fire blasting against the walls, covering it in a sheet of ice. Windows cracked from the sudden shift in temperature, the dragons beating their tails against the walls, trying to tear them down.

The fortress was warded by magic, but that kept the dragons out and the stone protected. The windows were a weak spot, which was why we only had them placed strategically throughout the compound—mostly where we could fire arrows and bolts.

Inside, shouts bellowed out from the windows that were already blown out. Hunters were already fortifying the places breached. My guild was well trained for any attacks.

I scanned the sky, searching for Silvanus and his familiar scales. He was noticeably absent. I strode inside the fortress to where Felix barked orders at a line of hunters.

"Is the slumber root ready to be shot at them?"

"Yes, Your Highness."

"Good. Cover the arrows and weapons in it. Any little nick in their scales will be enough."

I watched the dragons soar through the sky, narrowly missing the tallest tower, where archers normally patrolled.

"Is everyone in the fortress?" I asked Felix.

"Yes, Your Highness."

As I studied the dragons, I realized they were flying in loose knots.

There was something about the formation, something that didn't feel right. Felix reported on damage sustained and I half listened as I focused on those two dragons.

They weren't attacking...it was almost as if they were—

"It's a distraction." My heart pounded furiously. "Does anyone have eyes on Sil?" I glanced at Felix, Val, and the hunters who'd gathered around me. "Is he still in the barrens?"

"We lost him moments before you arrived," Felix said. "He was headed due west. Then these two showed up and we had to focus on securing the guild."

I cursed. "What's due west of here? The Sin Corridor?"

"Could be another pack," Felix said, pulling out a worn map. "Silvanus was our contact with his pack. It stands to reason he was also sent to other packs for his alpha."

Gods-damn it all. If Sil was seeking out another pack, he was trying to gain allies. How in the seven hells was a mad dragon able to plot battle when he'd only been thinking of killing?

I had a growing suspicion that we were about to discover what the dragons were plotting, and no matter how hard I tried, we were always one step behind the cunning beasts.

An attack was imminent. But would they hit all Seven Circles like last time in a coordinated strike? Or would they surprise us by targeting one House at a time?

My gut said they'd be coming for my House first because of the hexed magic.

"I want hunters and archers in place at House Gluttony now." Silvanus might not know where Adriana was, but given his murderous fixation, I didn't need him getting close and scenting her. "Has Shayde sent word yet?" I asked.

"Yes." Felix looked relieved to report on something good. "He'll be here soon."

Thank the gods for that. I moved onto the parapet, arms crossed.

Tonight had been a glorious disaster.

Glorious with Adriana in the cave. Disastrous for everything that followed.

Silvanus had slipped the noose, and everything I'd been trying to keep quiet was about to explode in the biggest scandal to hit the Seven Circles. One I had a hand in creating.

The ball was certainly going to be an event no one would miss. Hopefully Shayde would have the information I needed to end this all.

Several minutes later Val stepped onto the narrow outdoor pathway, shivering from the cold. She was quiet, no doubt working out the best way to approach an uncomfortable topic. And it didn't take a genius to know who the subject would be about.

"If you're about to counsel me on Adriana, I suggest choosing a different time."

"It's going to be in all the papers" was all she said. As if I was unaware of our plot. "We can get ahead of the story to minimize damage to your image. Let Adriana take the fall."

"Absolutely not," I said, annoyed it was even being suggested. "I'll call off the competition and tell the truth at the ball tonight. Just like I planned with Adriana."

"Sometimes plans change, Your Highness." Val kept her gaze trained on the sky. "If you reveal the truth—that the competition has been a distraction—the entire realm will turn on you."

I said nothing to that. She was correct.

"Now is not the time to lose sinners and weaken your court because you promised Miss Saint Lucent otherwise," she pressed. "Do what you need to do, Ruthless Rake."

She bowed and went back inside, leaving me.

To go back on our plan, to choose the realm over Adriana, would mean giving her up forever. I'd felt the trepidation in her tonight, the fear that my confession hadn't been real. She still hadn't quite believed me even after I'd marked her.

If I didn't follow through with my promise to publicly declare myself to her, there would be no Hexed Quill to blame. Adriana would hate me all on her own.

I would be the villain she believed me to be, and I'd deserve it.

Heroes made sacrifices. And it had been a long time since anyone confused me for someone who took the moral high ground.

Val had issued it like a dare.

My grip on the railing tightened as I watched the dragons get farther away.

A good leader would do whatever they needed to for their court and their people.

I was lost in thought when Felix found me. "They're here."

FORTY-EIGHT
Adriana

I HURRIED THROUGH the main corridor, clutching Axton's suit jacket to ensure that anyone passing by noticed it—and my state of dishevelment. I might have also run my hand through my loose curls, ensuring they were a bit wilder than normal. It wouldn't do to only have a few witnesses.

If we were going to cause a scandal, it needed to spread quickly.

Footsteps rounded the corner I'd just turned off of, racing along the marble. I knew it would be Ryleigh before she called out.

"Are you going to explain the state of your gown, Adriana?"

Something in me bristled at her tone. I wasn't the only one keeping secrets.

I paused, glancing around the hallway. No servants or staff or courtiers. That could change without a moment's notice, though. I spun around.

"Would you like to tell me why you used the Hexed Quill?" I asked, keeping my voice low. "What exactly did you hope to gain from using it on me?"

Ryleigh's expression was almost as frosty as the walls in our cavern had been.

She stared at me like she didn't recognize me. "You think I used the Hexed Quill to help you make the same mistake with the prince?"

"No. I think you used the quill at the All-Sinners Ball and destroyed my life. Then carried on every day as if nothing was wrong. I deserve to know why."

"Have you and the prince been lovers this whole time?" she fired back, her voice ringing throughout the hallway.

I stared at her for a moment. She very clearly hadn't answered either question.

A deep hurt twisted inside me. All this time my friend had known, had wielded the weapon that ripped my heart apart. And she could not care less.

"That's all you care to ask? No apology for the hurt you've caused me? No admission of guilt?"

"Did the prince plant this ridiculous notion in your head?"

There was such vehemence in her tone, I drew back. "I need to hear you tell me it's not true."

She crossed her arms, her expression filled with disgust.

"I will not. I won't entertain something so insulting. You ought to know I would never harm you. Have you ever even hated him, or has it all been a lie?"

"Why won't you answer me? It's a simple question. Did you use the Hexed Quill or not?"

Ryleigh could be wildly stubborn when she wished to be. And her expression indicated she would not answer me unless I gave her something first. If that's what it took, so be it.

"Not everything's been a lie," I said. "Unlike the secrets you've kept from me for the last decade."

Ryleigh narrowed her eyes. "You truly believe I could look you in the eye every day, knowing what I did? Is that what you think of me? What motivation would I have?"

She seemed so adamant, so hurt. It didn't ring false. I suddenly wasn't sure what I believed. Ryleigh was either the best stage actress the realm had ever known, or she was being truthful. And one thing I knew for certain: she did not care for the theater.

Still, the evidence pointed to her.

"You are the only one I know who sought the quill. Not only that, but you were also searching for it before the ball, then suddenly gave up." I searched her face. There was nothing to be read in her expression. "What would you believe? The evidence is damning, Ry."

Her eyes shimmered with unshed tears. "I would believe in our friendship. No matter how damning the evidence. In fact, I would have gone directly to you the moment I heard such a rumor. I don't keep secrets from you, but it seems that's not reciprocated."

I exhaled, most of the fight going out of me. Along with the sense of betrayal.

Unless she'd used the Hexed Quill on herself and rewrote her own memories, I didn't think she was to blame. I softened a bit more.

My friend was right—I *had* been keeping a lot of secrets, and if we hoped to move forward from this entanglement, it was time to answer one of her earlier questions.

"Axton was my stranger from the Seven Sins. We only discovered the truth recently. I didn't tell you I kept seeing him because until tonight I hadn't figured out how I felt or what to do."

Ryleigh's expression darkened, and it took me a moment to understand why the explanation caused more strife. I hadn't exactly been forthcoming about visiting my stranger on several occasions. In fact, I'd kept that information very close, not wanting to share it.

If I thought the realm finding out the truth was going to be bad, this was even worse.

It felt as if a line of gasoline had been lit on fire and little explosions were going off in quick succession.

"And what dark magic is at play here?" She motioned between us. "Causing you to lie to your friend? Or is that simply a character flaw I never knew you possessed? Regardless of my personal opinions on the matter, I would have been there for you. Like I've always been."

I drew in a deep breath.

I hated how hurt she was, I hated that my actions and secrecy caused it. Everything was a mess and I had a feeling it was going to get much worse before it got better. And I owned that. This was my fault. I made the mistake and I hoped one day she could forgive me.

"I didn't tell you about seeing my stranger because I didn't want to admit that I cared. Everything was already so complicated. It had nothing to do with trusting you or not. I swear it."

"I kept wondering why you'd grown distant." She looked ready to either stab me or cry. I wasn't sure which was worse. "And it wasn't about me at all. It was you making the same mistake you've spent a decade trying to get past. Have you suddenly forgotten how much you hate him? Magic or not. You were heartbroken. That was real."

"Ryleigh..."

"I was there. Every day, Ad. Every day, watching you try to emotionally rebuild, hating how deeply you'd been wounded. I've always supported you. And after years of friendship, you simply throw it away for what? The thrill of a secret romance? Or were you too ashamed of sleeping with someone who is very publicly searching for a wife?"

It felt like I'd taken a punch to my center. I drew in a slow breath and released it.

"It's different this time; he's different. It was never his fault. The Hexed Quill—"

I cringed. I knew how that sounded. How it always sounded to an outside observer.

But it *was* different. He'd trusted me with his royal mark and his true name.

I still couldn't quite fathom the casual way he'd told me one of the biggest secrets a prince possessed. That action alone made me trust him now.

"Of course. The Hexed Quill. It's to blame for everything and your prince is absolved of all wrongdoing. Do you honestly believe this time is different?" She was practically yelling now. I'd never seen my friend so upset. "Was the quill responsible for the way he treated you these last ten years? The way he barely acknowledged you or taunted you at every event? Where is he now, Ad? You come back to the castle, clearly from a tryst, he kisses you in front of his suitors, and he leaves. The circle will tear you apart and drink you dry."

I had no defense for that. It was all true.

Ryleigh tossed her hands in the air and shook her head.

"I cannot stand by and watch you make the same mistake. He hasn't changed, Ad. And when he breaks your heart this time, don't say I didn't warn you."

"I'm so sorry," I said, hating that we'd ended up here. "I truly am."

"I am too. You will not come out of this scandal unscathed. Everything you've worked and sacrificed for will be destroyed. I hope your little secret adventure was worth it."

Without another word, Ryleigh turned on her heel and strode from the corridor, finished with me and our conversation.

I blinked tears back, refusing to let them fall in public.

"How utterly pathetic." Omen stepped out from around the corner. "You didn't really think he'd choose you, did you? The prince hunts. You were simply prey he couldn't pass up."

I swallowed the sudden lump in my throat.

I only had to endure their taunts for a few hours. Then Axton would make his announcement and everything we'd suffered through for the last decade would be restored to how it always should have been.

My emotions warred with one another—I believed Axton when he said this was different, that we were in this together. But I'd believed him once before too. He hadn't given me his true name or royal mark back then, but he'd also gotten better at playing the part of charming rake.

Was I really the fool in this scenario? Maybe Ryleigh was right—maybe the quill was only the catalyst and all the hurt that came after was not because of any hex.

I started to walk away, needing air and a few moments to breathe. I refused to engage with Omen and make the situation worse for myself.

"There you are."

Sophie's voice drew me up short.

I slowly pivoted to face her. My stepmother's expression was a mask of forced indifference as she scanned me. My unkempt hair, my wrinkled gown. The prince's jacket hanging around my shoulders like a victory flag. I wanted to crawl into a hole. Of all the demons in the realm, I did not want my stepmother to see me in this state.

"Get to our suite. Now."

She started walking in the direction of our private quarters, her pace punishing. I hurried after her, leaving Omen and whatever rumors she'd spread behind me.

"Is Eden okay?"

Sophie shot a look over her shoulder that silenced any further questions. We sped along decadent corridors until we came to our extravagant suite. I followed my stepmother inside and she rounded on me, finally unleashing the fury I'd sensed.

"How dare you ask if your sister is all right when you have been scheming in secret."

My blood ran cold. "What do you mean?"

"What do *I* mean?" Sophie's nostrils flared. "I mean that despite the ball he's hosting for his suitors tonight, all the servants could whisper about was how the prince was caught in a very interesting position with his public rival."

I dropped onto the settee in our living room, burying my face in my hands.

If the servants were already passing the news around, it meant the scandal sheets would catch on to the story soon enough. Our ruse had worked, brilliantly.

We'd planned for it, but still…the reality of facing the consequences alone started to weigh heavily, especially as my stepmother paced in front of me.

It was for the safety of the realm, the court. I knew that, but my family didn't.

I drew in a steadying breath, then looked up at my stepmother.

"Does Eden know?"

"Not yet. She's off with Vanity getting fitted for her gown and has missed all the gossip. But you better pray to whatever old god you can that this remains a secret until after the ball. Do you have any idea what a scandal of this nature will do to our family?"

"We live in a realm of sin. It's hardly—"

"Sin is one thing. Fornicating with the prince of our circle, while he's hosting a realm-wide competition to find a princess, of which your own blood is vying for that coveted crown, is reprehensible behavior. Have you no honor or loyalty to family? What would your father think?"

My eyes suddenly burned. "You've crossed a line, stepmother."

"Have I? Because I'd argue you crossed a line when you spread your legs *again* for a male who is clearly uninterested in taking you to wife."

I flinched as if she'd struck a physical blow.

Sophie watched me closely, her cruel mouth twisting into a sneer.

"Stupid girl. Nearly thirty and still unable to see the truth. The prince doesn't care about you. If he did, he'd call off the competition right this moment, publicly declare himself to you, and prevent any rumors from spreading."

If she only knew, that was precisely our plan.

I kept my mouth shut, unwilling to share the truth. In a few hours everyone would know.

Sophie glanced around our empty sitting room.

"Do you see him here? Hunting you down to make sure you're all right? Ensuring no one speaks ill of his beloved?" She shook her head. "Do not be surprised when this explodes across the realm and he does nothing. Once again."

Despite my best efforts to will the tears away, a few spilled down my cheeks, dripping onto my silken gown. I hated my stepmother in this moment. Not because she was cruel or cutting as usual, but because I knew she was trying to protect me in her own twisted way.

She had been there when Axton ran off with someone else at the All-Sinners Ball.

We'd gotten caught in the garden and he left me directly after we'd been together to feed his sin, and the papers had gone wild with how foolish I'd been to try to go up against a noble.

Maybe he never really went off with another; maybe none of it ever happened before the magic came into play; maybe the Hexed Quill simply made us all believe it; but the vicious rumors and gossip about me that were printed for the realm to laugh about were very real.

The backlash of that night *did* impact me and our family. Eden had been young, so we'd shielded her from most of it. But Sophie and I had borne the brunt of the scandal.

Now my stepmother believed we were standing on the precipice of the same mistakes. If I could only confide in her, maybe she would understand. But I promised Axton I'd play my role.

"It won't simply be your life that's ruined this time," Sophie continued. "Eden will not come out unscathed. Who will have either of you? To work or to wed? Did you even consider what the consequences would be for us all?"

It had been difficult to find a paper that would hire me. And now, as much as I hated to admit it, Sophie was right. Once the scandal sheets reported that Axton and I had been intimate again while his competition was heating up, *he* wouldn't be the one scorned across the realm.

I knew that. And yet I'd still make the same choice.

There was so much more at stake. If the realm found out about the dragons, the Hexed Quill...chaos would break out. And if the dragons finally attacked? Countless lives could be lost.

"He'll do better this time," I said, hoping to will it into existence, even if doubt crept in.

Sophie gave me a pitying look. "We'll see soon enough."

Secrets and Scandals
The Rake of Rakes Continues His Infamous Ways

By Julian Wren, The Wicked Daily

Dearest Sinners,

We here at the *Wicked Daily* have the most delectable story for you to indulge today. The Prince of Rakes has truly shocked the realm with his latest indiscretion. Rumors are flying across the Seven Circles about a delicious scandal that took place on the grounds of House Gluttony with none other than our own Miss Match. Talk about staying scandalous!

For those unaware of her true identity, allow me to exclusively reveal it here: the prince was found with his sworn nemesis, Miss Adriana Saint Lucent. The pair of secret lovers were caught post-tryst trying to sneak into the castle. Witnesses report he kissed her before dashing off.

We've reached out to Prince Gluttony for comment, but he's not speaking to the press at this time. Adriana Saint Lucent is also staying unusually quiet — if she had hopes of becoming the true victor of the prince's heart, they must be dashed now. Prince Gluttony has made it clear through his silence that he will choose to tie himself to another.

When asked about the scandal, her sister and favorite suitor to the prince, Eden Everhart, simply stated the ball ought to be the focus of the day. We disagree. One thing all the scandal sheets and contestants can agree on is how impressive it was for Miss Match to fool us all with her romantic advice, all while trying to steal the prince for herself.

A report from the palace suggested the winner of the competition will be crowned at midnight, so it seems her scheme failed. One thing is certain — the ball should be a thrilling event.

Until next time.
I'm Julian Wren, signing off.

FORTY-NINE
Prince Gluttony

I STRODE DOWN THE upper corridor at Merciless Reach and paused outside the chamber where my best spy waited. If my luck had turned, he'd be joined by a guest of honor. I opened the door and thanked the wicked powers that be. Shayde had done exactly what I'd asked. He'd worked with Envy to bring in reinforcements.

Standing beside my spy was the legendary Unseelie hunter known simply as Wolf.

His hair was snow-white, and his eyes were the gold of the creatures he'd taken his name from. He always looked like he was plotting some deviousness and trickery.

"Wolf. It's nice to see you again."

The Fae smirked. "It's rather fun to be owed a favor by a demon."

"Shayde, have Val triple your reward."

Shayde bowed. "How generous."

I eyed the Unseelie male, who lounged casually back in his chair. His reputation for sleeping his way across the realms was worse than that of any of my brothers.

The Fae looked exactly like the sort of danger he posed—a male who'd turn a lover inside out and make them hunger for more.

I understood why he got under Envy's skin. If he turned those half-lidded eyes on Adriana, I might rip out his throat.

Wolf removed an envelope from his jacket pocket and held it out to me. "This wasn't easy to find, but it's a strong lead."

I removed the contents and read them carefully.

The last will and testament of a noble I'd rarely interacted with since he'd spent most of his time in his country estate and not the castle—the Duke of Oleander.

His obituary.

And a rather curious letter addressed to a reporter.

I read through the findings carefully. The duke had apparently been in possession of the Hexed Quill and had a secret relationship with none other than Miss Ryleigh Hughes.

Adriana's coworker and friend.

"The Duke of Oleander died days before the All-Sinners Ball. And he bequeathed something with the initials of HQ to Ryleigh." I glanced up. "Where did you find this?"

Wolf's face split into a grin.

"I scoured any last wills and testaments for the last decade like you asked. Breaking into any barrister's office that was in business then. I started with nobility; the duke was of interest because of his rumored penchant for trading in dark market objects. I traveled to Waverly Green and confirmed with several dealers there that the duke was a regular client."

I paused at this delightful break in the case. The barrister had marked that Ryleigh picked up her item the day of the ball. It was exactly the information I needed.

I didn't have to worry about locating Sil. I could destroy the sheet the Hexed Quill had been used on and end this madness once and for all. Ryleigh had the quill. And that meant the parchment or journal or whatever she'd used to change our fates that day was close by too. I would send a team into her home immediately.

Relief flooded through me.

"Well done." I folded the will back up and tucked it into my suit, then turned my attention to Shayde. "I want eyes on that reporter. Send in a team to retrieve the quill and locate where the hex was written at once. Bring everything to House Gluttony undamaged."

"Of course, Your Highness." Shayde bowed low. "I'll return soon."

"Tonight," I said. "I want them both in my hands before midnight."

Shayde inclined his head, then disappeared into the darkness from which he'd chosen his name. I glanced at the clock, wanting to hunt down the Hexed Quill myself, but I refrained.

There was still a role I needed to play in public for a little while longer.

I had a ball to prepare for and a terrible wrong to set right.

It would be the perfect ending to a twisted tale—setting the past on fire and watching it burn so we could rise from its ashes anew.

One way or another, tonight would see the dragon curse ended, my court's future secured, and my life restored to what it ought to have been before Ryleigh meddled.

Tension radiated through me. We were close to ending this, yet I couldn't quiet that innate warning system. It was almost too good to be true.

I didn't have to find Silvanus, but it would be nice to know where he was just to be sure he stayed far from the castle. I only needed a few more hours. If I burned the hex, then my court and circle would never need to know how close we'd all come to disaster.

Wolf sauntered over to where I had a decanter filled with bourbon. He splashed some into a cut-crystal glass and swirled it before tossing it back.

His eyes gleamed. "What time's the ball?"

"Have all the arrangements been made?" I asked, inspecting the ballroom. The marble floors were pristine, flawless. Not a speck of dust or smudge to be seen. They would gleam under the soft glow of the candles I'd had strung up at different intervals from the ceiling.

Val checked items off on her list. "The dress arrived an hour ago."

I exhaled, then continued around the ballroom, ensuring each corner of the room was as enchanting as it could be. I'd had flowers and hedges brought in, along with an oversized stone fountain to emulate the gardens where I supposedly made love to Adriana for the first time.

I wanted to show my former rival that I might not recall that first evening, but deep down I'd never truly forgotten her.

"Are you sure you don't want to issue a public statement?" Val asked.

I stopped before the fountain, the marble dragon spitting icy water instead of flames. It was a dangerous gamble to host the ball tonight before I had the hex in my hand to destroy, but I needed to put out one proverbial fire and trusted my spies would bring me what I needed soon.

The scandal of finding me with Adriana was all anyone could discuss.

The suitors hadn't been put off by the fact that I'd been engaged in a secret affair. They felt it fed my reputation and helped to shine a spotlight on them.

There were no losers in this scandal.

Except for Adriana, though that wouldn't remain true for long.

I glanced at Val. "Is she here?"

My second didn't need to clarify. "Of course. She's in her suite."

If I hadn't needed to personally speak with the remaining suitors before the ball started to let them know the competition had ended, I'd go to her at once. But I owed them the chance to hear directly from me what had transpired and how sorry I was to have carried on, knowing my heart was elsewhere.

Val had made her feelings known about the potential damage to my court, but I knew what I wanted, and Hexed Quill or not, there was at least one thing I had the power to fix.

"I want this to be the event to end all events." I strode toward my suite. "Tonight, the realm will have a new story to focus on."

And it all hinged on whether she'd say yes to the most thrilling adventure of all.

FIFTY
Adriana

THE NEXT CARRIAGE rolled to a stop in the courtyard, the trumpets blaring loudly in welcome. It was black and gold, indicating House Wrath had arrived.

"Will they do that each blasted time?" I muttered to myself, pushing off the windowsill I'd been perched against. My nerves were getting the best of me.

As was Sophie's constant stream of admonishments.

Every hour on the hour she paced through our suite, reminding me that I was a fool. If I didn't rip my hair out by the end of the evening it would truly be a miracle.

From her endless ranting, I discovered that her maid had informed her that Axton had returned hours ago and he still hadn't deigned to come see me or even send a note.

That more than anything else stung. I had no idea if he'd successfully subdued Silvanus and the dragons, or about anything else that happened in the north.

He'd simply sent me a royal invitation for tonight's event an hour ago, along with Eden's, and that was that.

We were supposed to be a team and I felt like I was once again tossed to the sidelines, watching him make up the rules of play as he went. I'd been doing my part to keep the castle and gossips focused on me, and he couldn't even be bothered to see if I was all right.

I positively *hated* surprises. And without hearing from the prince directly, I had no idea what role I should play when entering the event. As far as I knew, the competition was still on.

Sophie certainly would have reported if she'd heard otherwise.

After everything we'd been through, I couldn't fathom how he would think leaving me in the dark while danger loomed *and* while I was keeping his secrets was a good idea.

He truly must not take me seriously as a partner or equal.

And that was one quality in a romantic interest I would not abide.

My opinion was valuable, and at the very least, I deserved to know I could trust he'd confide his plans with me before being heavy-handed and enacting them on his own, assuming I'd simply go along with whatever he'd decided.

He clearly hadn't learned from his previous error, when he'd had me fired from the *Wicked Daily* because he'd seen fit to offer me an obscene salary and tried to force me into being his personal reporter. As if my fate was his to dictate and not my own.

I couldn't believe I'd fallen for his confession.

I have hungered *for you in ways you cannot comprehend.*

Apparently not. Though he was correct on one count: I couldn't comprehend how he could say something so passionate one hour, beg for me to join his cause, then forget I existed the very next, once I'd done his bidding.

By now Eden knew of our indiscretion and she'd pretended otherwise. Though I had barely seen or spoken to her once she'd discovered the truth.

I wasn't sure if that was by her design or simply coincidence.

She had her own secrets, and no matter what, I would never reveal that she had someone she was privately courting, too.

"You need to finish getting dressed. You're expected downstairs with your sister soon," Sophie said from the door, startling me. "A footman will be waiting for you in a few moments."

"I'll be down shortly."

She looked me over critically. "Don't be late. The last thing we need is to cause another scene tonight."

With that lovely little speech, she left.

I glanced at the gown sparkling from its velvet hanger, its silver skirts trailing along the floor, the diamonds and aquamarines sewn across the bottom glinting like freshly fallen snow.

The dress looked like it was taken straight from the pages of the most decadent romance.

Too bad it felt like I'd be wearing it to my own social funeral. Or perhaps it was the death of my dignity, seeing as I was forced to show up alone and face his snickering court on my own.

The scandal sheets would be watching my every reaction, hoping for a hint of drama to report. Perhaps I could pry some of the jewels off the gown and pay for their silence.

It was wishful thinking.

Whether it was fear or bad milk, my stomach twisted into knots as the hour chimed eleven. It was almost time to face the world post-scandal. I would do so with my head held high, even if I wished to dry heave into a bucket.

There was no hiding from the rumors about me and the prince. Tonight, I would be on display for the whole realm, and either Axton would hold up his end of the bargain, or he wouldn't. There really was only one way to find out.

I'd been hoping to see Carlo one last time; his makeup and styling always made me feel like I was dressed in armor. But a lovely maid entered and helped me into the dress, adjusting my hair and painting my lips a pretty shade of pale pink. I slipped my crystal shoes on.

I looked myself over in the mirror one last time. It was incredible that outwardly I could look so serene while inside I felt turbulent. I allowed myself a moment to breathe.

"Oh, we forgot the most important adornment, miss."

My maid rushed over to a little box and flipped it open. An aquamarine and diamond tiara was placed on my head, the pale blue gemstones looking splendid with my hair.

I stared at my reflection. No one would guess my insides were thrashing with worry. Over dragons, the prince, my tattered reputation. I looked ready for court battle.

When the knock came at the outer door, I was ready for whatever happened next.

I strode into the corridor, smiling at the footman. "Lead the way."

My heart was in danger of beating itself straight out of my body as I stood at the top of the stairs overlooking the ballroom. Axton had once again fed his sin by overindulging. Or maybe he was a secret romantic. The room had been transformed into a garden, a replica of the one found here, in fact. It was the place our story began before everything went horribly wrong.

My gaze skimmed over the crowd, some already dancing across the floor. Some mingling near towers of food and pastries. A waterfall of sparkling wine flutes dazzled as demonberry wine flowed like a stream into the waiting glasses. It was beautiful.

On a dais Eden and Vanity clinked glasses with the prince, laughing at whatever he'd just whispered to them. I drew up short. I hadn't expected to see his suitors gathered around him.

It was all so...familiar. Him shamelessly flirting with anyone who'd give him attention, me lingering in the shadows. All while everyone ate up the sugary charm he served on that royal platter, never seeing him for what he truly was. My stepmother and Ryleigh were right: Axton wouldn't ever change. A pain began in my chest.

Suddenly, I wasn't sure I could go through with this. Whatever he'd planned, it didn't look like it included me. Before anyone noticed my arrival, I turned to leave.

My exit was thwarted when the herald stamped his staff on the marble floor, drawing all eyes upward as he called out my name.

"Miss Adriana Saint Lucent."

I twisted back around, swallowing the lump in my throat.

Silence fell on the crowd. It looked like a witch had cast a spell, freezing everyone in place. Except for the prince. He drank me in as if he and I were the only two in the room.

A familiar ember sparked to life deep within me before I stamped it out.

Cursed rake. I needed a few moments to gather my thoughts, far from his stupor-inducing charm. I wasn't sure it would be a good idea to talk now with so many witnesses, but he was once again taking that choice from me. If I left now, the gossips would go wild.

I set my jaw and began my descent into the social hells, holding my skirts in my fist like they were wrapped around Axton's neck.

I prayed to every god there was that I didn't trip on my gown and go sprawling to the floor. I could not begin to imagine how I'd survive that level of embarrassment.

Blessedly, I reached the bottom of the staircase without incident.

Axton was suddenly there waiting, his arm held up for me, looking like the perfect image of royal manners. He didn't have any idea I was upset. In his world, all was blissfully well.

With all eyes still burning into me, I dropped a polite curtsy.

"Your Highness."

I stood and began to move past him, pleased I hadn't made a scene. Public murder of a monarch would be rather hard to talk my way out of, especially with so many witnesses.

Axton must have been hitting the bottle before I arrived. The prince mirrored my movement, blocking my path. I drew in a steadying breath.

Now really wasn't the time for this discussion.

I would not commit regicide. I would not accidentally jerk my knee upward and remove the possibility of him procreating.

I would definitely make a sacrifice to the old gods if I didn't succumb to either urge.

Out of the corner of my eye, I noticed nobles leaning in to whisper to one another.

Wonderful. Thanks to the prince, I hadn't gone two minutes without drawing their scorn.

"What, exactly, are you doing?" I asked, keeping a polite smile in place. "You're causing a scene. And I should like to have a few minutes to collect myself."

He gave me the sort of devastating grin that felled even the worthiest opponent. Too bad I was completely immune to his charm. I stared coldly until the smile slipped from his face.

"Are you quite well?" he asked, looking me over more carefully.

If surviving a scandal, a broken heart, and public scorn was considered well, then I was positively peachy. "Would you mind moving? I really do need some air."

A spark of challenge ignited in his gaze.

"I would mind very much. Since I'm asking you to dance with me."

"I'm sure your suitors will occupy all your time."

He moved closer, either unaware or uncaring that the crowd had seemed to step in as well. "We had a plan, remember?"

"Did we? I can't seem to recall any details of how we're to proceed tonight. Oh"—I gave him the sort of smile that was anything but friendly—"perhaps it has something to do with the fact that you didn't bother to consult me."

"You're mad."

"Upset."

He tilted my face up, and for one fleeting moment, I thought he would kiss me right there in front of his whole court. He dragged a thumb across my lower lip, then set those multicolored eyes on mine as I put distance between us.

"I would have come to you earlier, but I was delayed."

"I took the brunt of the scandal while you rode out to save the day. The least I deserve is to know if you succeeded."

He understood what I was asking. "I was successful in one way. We found an interesting connection regarding a note written long ago."

The Hexed Quill. He'd found a lead on it. And he hadn't bothered informing me of such a huge break in the case. If I'd been upset a moment ago, I was furious now.

"If you didn't have five minutes to spare to write to me yourself, you could have dictated a note and sent a missive."

"You're right," he said simply. "I could have and should have done so. I had much on my mind and suitors to send home."

I glanced at the dais where Eden and Vanity lingered. "Apparently, not all the suitors."

His mouth quirked up on one side. "Stay clear of Envy tonight, or he'll try to tempt you to his House of Sin."

"I am not jealous, you ass. I'm annoyed. You haven't even apologized."

"Forgive me." He bowed low over my hand, then brushed a chaste kiss to it. "Save a dance for me before midnight. I promise you won't be disappointed."

FIFTY-ONE
Prince Gluttony

*Y*OU LOOK LIKE it burns when you piss." Lust clapped a hand on my shoulder, grinning wide. "No wonder she won't agree to dance."

"She didn't say no." And I was fortunate for that. Unintentionally or not, I *had* been a royal ass. Hopefully Adriana would allow me to make it up to her tonight when we were finally alone.

I stood on the terrace overlooking the ballroom, strumming my fingers on the cool marble railing. The suitors who'd been sent home all spun around to a country dance, having found fame and no shortage of suitors themselves now.

I glanced at the clock. Midnight was moments away.

After this song, I could finally end the competition publicly. The sooner I made the announcement, the sooner everyone could go home. I'd quietly had each of their rooms and houses warded, weakening myself a little more than I already was, but their safety was worth the drain on my power. My brothers were in attendance, so I had help should I need it.

I hoped to the old gods I wouldn't need it.

My attention swept across the dance floor, then searched the shadows and corners.

Shayde and Wolf still hadn't returned with the item we needed to burn to end the hexed item's magic, and Silvanus hadn't been found either. When I'd left Merciless Reach earlier, the end had seemed imminent. Now it felt like it was slipping from my grasp.

"Why aren't you out there dancing and making enemies of some husbands or wives?"

Lust grunted but didn't respond. "Any word on the dragons?"

My brother wasn't helping to defuse the growing tension.

"I sent a team after Silvanus. Still no sightings from when he went west." I tore my attention from the dance floor. "I found a promising lead on the Hexed Quill, though."

Lust's grin vanished as he straightened. "Who?"

"The reporter. Ryleigh Hughes. She was at the All-Sinners Ball."

Any excitement in my brother deflated. "So? By that count we could all be guilty."

I grinned. "Always follow a paper trail, dear brother. Ten years ago she'd been researching a story on hexed objects and interviewed a certain duke who'd been rumored to have the quill in his private collection. Her story posed the question of if a writer used the Hexed Quill, would it grant their stories a bigger audience."

"Gods damn, Gabriel." Lust looked impressed. "That *is* promising."

"But the evidence trail doesn't end there. She was also rumored to have had an affair with the duke—something substantiated by a letter I recovered from him to her. The duke gifted her with several items from his private collection. Much to the fury of his wife. There was a public feud that sparked between Duchess Oleander and Ryleigh, but it was overshadowed by a bigger scandal."

Mine and Adriana's. Which seemed like motive enough for Ryleigh. She'd taken the attention and scorn off herself and placed it elsewhere.

I glanced back down at the ballroom. There were so many jewels, I nearly had to squint to see the dancers through the glinting in the candlelight.

"How do you know his wife didn't use the quill to get revenge on him?"

"The duke passed away days before the All-Sinners Ball, and there was a slight notation in his will. Ryleigh was named and the letters *HQ* were marked for her among other items less intriguing. Documentation proves she received the quill before the ball, which means the duchess didn't have access to it."

"Talk about deception." Lust let loose a low whistle. "She's friends with Adriana. Seems ruthless to ruin her best friend's happiness."

"Maybe she was testing the quill and hadn't intended the consequences. Or she was hoping to create a bit of drama to overshadow her public battle with the duchess. Until we interrogate her, that is pure speculation."

None that would excuse the pain or the danger to the realm. But mortals had a saying that was eerily close to the truth: the road to hell was paved with good intentions—something most said, never truly considering what it meant.

I watched Adriana slink into the shadows of the chamber, trying to hide from the reporters who'd swarmed in, right on time. She didn't know I had called them here. I wanted every scandal sheet reporter in the Seven Circles present for my announcement.

A moment later, Shayde made his entrance with Wolf.

I held my breath, trying to determine what their stoic expressions indicated.

I couldn't tell if they seemed victorious or if they'd been unsuccessful in their hunt.

I released my breath. It didn't matter. I had enough to confront Ryleigh now and force her to hand over the objects.

Her betrayal would be especially hard for Adriana to handle on top of the latest gossip, but I couldn't delay ending this. Especially as the dragons grew bolder.

But first it was time to do what I should have done all those years ago.

I glanced at the clock on the far wall. It was time.

"Wish me luck."

Lust swiped a glass of demonberry wine from a passing tray and saluted me. "To an eternity of blissful hate sex."

Eden and Vanity caught my eye as I made my way down the stairs and

carved a path to the dais. They exchanged a secret smile, already knowing what I was about to do.

I strode up to the small platform and motioned for the quartet to quiet.

The assembled gathering turned their attention to me, the reporters
holding their quills at the ready. Ryleigh Hughes was among the crowd.

They expected a winner to be announced. And I was not one to disappoint.

"Thank you for joining me here tonight as I retire my bachelor's crown
for good." Chuckles went through the ballroom, but my attention was
fixed to one corner. "Before I confess who stole my heart, I have one
matter to tend to."

Val emerged from the back of the nobles and quietly made her way
over to Ryleigh. She would ensure the reporter didn't flee. Once she was
in place, I continued.

"I have not been entirely forthright regarding my reasons for hosting
the competition." I paused while murmurs went around the room. "A
secret threat to our realm has been the catalyst behind the deception.
One I hope you'll forgive me for. Tonight, I spoke with each suitor personally, letting them know before it hit the scandal sheets. My goal has
always been to protect my circle, my court, and my people."

"What threat, Your Highness?" Anderson Anders shouted from the
back. "Is it the vampire rumors circulating from Malice Isle?"

"Due to the ongoing investigation, that information is privileged.
What I can reveal now is the cause. I, along with each of my brothers,
have had private teams looking into the matter, night and day. Within
the last few hours we've finally found the link we've been searching
for."

My attention flickered over the crowd until it stopped on Ryleigh.

"Ten years ago, at the All-Sinners Ball, Miss Ryleigh Hughes used a
hexed object on my court. At this very moment, a team of hunters is
swarming her town house for the evidence we need to destroy the dark
magic at play."

Ryleigh's face drained of color. "I don't have any hexed object. I swear on the Crown."

She stepped back as if to rush into the shadows, but Val was waiting. My second's hand shot out, tethering the reporter to her side.

The smile I gave her was far from friendly. It sent the reporters' quills aflutter. I was affable until I wasn't, and it seemed to delight those who craved scandal.

"Miss Hughes, the Crown would consider your cooperation a boon when it comes time for doling out punishment. Lust. Envy." I motioned to my brothers, who moved in beside her and Val. "They will begin the interrogation while I tend to one more matter tonight. I suggest telling them where the Hexed Quill is and the place you wrote the new outcome of the ball. They will sense any lies."

Adriana stepped forward, reaching out as if to defend her friend. She seemed conflicted, but the crowd closed in around Ryleigh, cutting her off from getting closer.

My brothers were the most debonair-looking guards as they escorted Ryleigh to the dungeons.

Eden seemed to stop breathing. But Vanity was highly intrigued by the turn of events.

I clapped my hands, gaining the attention of the room once more.

"Now, hopefully, you're interested in one more announcement this evening."

I scanned the crowd, finding Adriana once again lingering near the wall. I kept my attention on her, speaking to her and her alone.

"The competition to find a perfect match might not have gone according to plan. But I have found love. And it has been one of the most frustrating, thrilling adventures I've ever embarked on."

Adriana's expression was impossible to read.

I wished to be next to her, to sense her emotions.

"Miss Saint Lucent, will you please step up to the dais?"

She slowly shook her head. "No, Your Highness. I'm afraid I cannot."

Sharp gasps erupted from my court. I silenced them with a ferocious look.

They might be deterred, but I was not. If Adriana wanted us on equal footing, I would go to her, crawling if I must.

"Very well."

I hopped off the platform and carved my way through the crowd. Whispers followed in my wake, but I ignored the snickering gossip. There was only one opinion I cared about.

Once I reached Adriana, I slowly dropped to one knee.

A hush descended from the double meaning of my action. No one dared to mock her now. Not when their prince kneeled before her.

"I choose you, Adriana Saint Lucent. From the first moment I saw you, a decade ago, you have haunted my dreams. It has always been you."

I remained on my knee, ready to remove my heart from my chest and hand it to her if that was her request. Adriana looked...horrified.

"I am, and always have been, irrevocably in love with you. Therefore, I cannot pretend to court anyone else. The competition is over. And if I'm being honest, it always has been because there is no one better suited for me than you." I inhaled deeply. "Adriana Saint Lucent, my sweet nemesis, will you marry me?"

The silence that spread throughout the room was all-consuming now. No one seemed to draw breath for fear of missing a single word.

Adriana kept staring at me like I'd somehow managed to grow a second or third head. She certainly knew how to keep my ego from over-inflating. She slowly took her attention from me and glanced around the room. Reporters moved in like sharks scenting blood in the water.

I inwardly cursed. I'd wanted them here to spread the word that I'd very publicly chosen her. That she would be mine for the realms to see if she'd accept my suit.

Being near her now, I sensed her emotions clearly. Hurt, distrust.

I hadn't considered that she might see this as another strategic move, even though I was doing exactly what I'd promised. She felt like I hadn't treated her as an equal. That I'd simply discarded her opinion once I returned from Merciless Reach.

I needed to act swiftly. Prove to her that I—

"Your Highness!"

I glanced around. The crowd turned, seeking out whoever had shouted.

Footsteps pounded in the corridor outside the ballroom, the frantic pace drawing my attention to the door. A second later it burst open and a messenger rushed into the ballroom, bending at the waist, panting. He looked like he'd been running for hours.

When he finally regained his breath and stood, I noticed what I'd missed at first.

His tunic was splattered with blood.

An icy chill raced down my spine, my senses prickling in warning. They were close.

"Dragons are heading—"

The glass doors leading out to the gardens exploded, shards flying through the crowd, slicing through skin and silk indiscriminately. Nobles froze as blood slowly seeped out and stained their finery, staring down as if they couldn't make sense of what had happened.

I lurched to my feet to shield Adriana with my body as the first dragon shoved its head into the opening it just made. A fierce, protective rage descended—so ancient and primal I couldn't fight it if I tried.

I would burn the world down and dance in its ashes if anything happened to her. "Wrath! Get airborne. We take the fight to—"

Several ice dragons bashed at the garden doors, spewing their icy-hot flames. Crimson eyes peered into the room, taking in the terrified shouts, which stirred them into a greater frenzy.

"Everyone, out!" I shouted, keeping Adriana behind me. "Get to the basement level!"

No one seemed to breathe as Silvanus emerged from outside, bashing his large tail against the door. It flew off its hinges, leaving a wide, gaping hole.

All at once, the nobles seemed to realize they were in danger. The entire ballroom erupted in chaos as everyone shoved their way to the exit.

I pulled Adriana toward the door, pushing a path through the crushing bodies.

I would sacrifice my court for her and not regret a wretched moment of the decision. I'd made peace with my moral compass long ago. If I had to choose between her and the realm, it would be her. Always.

"Get as far from here as you can," I shouted to be heard over the screams and shrill cries of the dragons. "I'll come for you when it's safe."

"Wait." She tugged back on my hand, digging her feet in. "My family."

If I had to fly her out to the most desolate region to keep her safe, I would. Silvanus was here and he would be coming for her, if only to feed his obsession.

"I will send guards after them."

I was about to unleash all my power when Wrath's shout rose above all else.

"They're coming for you!"

I turned, dagger drawn, as the dragons stalked forward. There were plenty of options for them to hunt, but they ignored easier prey in favor of me. Or Adriana.

My brother was right. I swallowed hard, then crushed my mouth to Adriana's before shoving her through the doors. If they didn't see her, hopefully they'd focus solely on me.

"Go!"

I didn't wait to see if she heeded my command. I made myself a tempting target as I twisted on my heel and dove toward the dragons, ready to end this once and for all.

FIFTY-TWO
Adriana

AXTON'S AND MY love story was doomed to never to be written. What had seemed to be the most lavish winter garden turned unexpected proposal was now a scene straight out of the Underworld.

Ironic, given that's precisely where we were.

I forced my way back into the ballroom, watching as Axton unleashed himself on the dragons, his House dagger glowing as it drank up blood.

My heart seized for a moment as jaws snapped perilously close to his throat. He'd thrown himself into their path without hesitation, forcing them to come for him instead of any of his court. It was courageous and fearless. And I wanted to slap him for being so reckless.

He was immortal, I reminded myself, and no stranger to fighting dragons.

He would survive, but my family might not.

With one last look at Axton, I shoved my way through the fleeing, hysterical crowd, jumping in place to see over the heads of the masses.

Tables were upturned, glasses of sparkling wine shattered, and everywhere I turned, demons were battling to get out of the chamber.

Eden and my stepmother were nowhere to be found.

Lust charged into the room, his dagger landing a blow to a dragon that sent it reeling back. Word must have already spread through the castle about the attack. Hopefully everyone else had taken cover. The cries of everyone still running for their lives would haunt my nightmares should I live through the battle. For every step forward I took, I lost an equal distance back. The crowd raged forward, shoving me along with them. I nearly lost my footing.

If I went down now, I'd get trampled to death.

With that constant fear driving me forward, I tried to see over heads and shoulders, bobbing my way across the room. I needed to get to the edge and wait.

A feat that was proving impossible.

Suddenly, the crowd paused for a moment, giving me a break to duck and run through an opening. I glanced back to see what had distracted them: Sloth and Greed had arrived in a burst of flame and smoke, immediately flinging themselves into the fray.

For a moment, I stood frozen along with the court, watching the battle rage.

Five of the seven princes fighting with all their strength was an image crafted of pure terror. I could not imagine fighting a dragon.

Nor would I want to end up on the wrong end of a demon's blade.

The princes were rakish, wicked things...until challenged. Then they showed what they truly were underneath the courtly charm and polished veneer.

The temperature dropped significantly, the floor slowly being coated with ice. Soon it would be impossible to run without falling. The realization made the courtiers panic more. I tried to gather myself, looking for Eden's pale blond hair. A flash of silver caught my attention.

"Camilla!"

I spotted her at the same time she found me, and we fought to get to each other as the chaos grew unhinged.

Dragons shrieked as they descended upon the ball, stampeding through the flowers and hedges. Icy flames spewed across the room, covering everything in their path in ice.

Cries of agony followed a blast of frozen fire. Someone hadn't gotten out of the way.

I shuddered at the cold and the fear coursing through me. I'd always thought the ice dragons were beautiful, but they were equally wicked and ruthless.

Incredibly, Anderson Anders was furiously writing with his quill, hiding near a column that was half torn out. The idiot was perilously close to a dragon.

I lost Camilla and prayed Envy would race up from the dungeons and find her. That he wasn't here yet made me think more dragons were hunting the corridors. If my sister and stepmother had gotten out of the ballroom, that meant they still might not be safe.

"Adriana!"

Eden's scream yanked my attention toward her. And the threat. Several paces away, an enormous dragon locked eyes with me. An innate warning sounded as I took an unsteady step back. It was the wrong move. I made myself look like prey.

The crimson-eyed dragon roared as it charged me, marking me for death. The ground rumbled so hard I nearly lost my footing as I turned and ran.

I shoved Anderson Anders out of harm's way and raced against the dwindling crowd, hoping to draw the creature as far away from my sister as possible.

I'd just bolted out of the destroyed wall and onto the veranda, sliding over a thick sheet of ice, when the prince appeared, suit splattered in blood, his expression dark and unforgiving.

His cravat was gone and along with it any trace of civility. He looked wild, untamed. The legendary hunter who ran headfirst into danger and adventure.

His attention swept over me before settling on something just above my head.

I didn't have to turn to know the dragon had followed me out.

The roar that erupted from *much* too close behind me shook the ground, knocking me off-balance as the air from its lungs froze strands of my hair. The ice coating the stone made it impossible to stay on my feet in the cursed heeled slippers, I was no better than a baby fawn attempting its first steps. I fell forward right as the dragon's jaws snapped at my back.

"Axton!"

The prince's wings erupted in a show of pure, overindulgent rage as he flung himself between me and the bloodthirsty creature, his body taking the hit meant for me.

He pivoted and kicked, launching the dragon back several feet.

Blood dripped down his arm from where the beast's teeth had torn into his flesh. The dragon tried to dodge around him, its glowing red gaze fixed on me.

I glanced behind the prince, staring at the monster stalking forward, my heart seizing. It was no longer alone. All the dragons were storming the terrace, heading our way.

The ice and frigid temperatures preceded them, the white flames slamming into the ground at our feet.

Chills that had nothing to do with the mighty creatures raced down my spine.

All their bloodthirsty gazes were locked on me.

Unholy gods below. The entire pack was coming for me.

I didn't need to have any previous experience with them to know they would tear through the prince and anyone else standing in their way.

"Axton!" I shouted, a plan whirling into place. He narrowly avoided the next strike, spinning to face me as he kept the dragon in his sights. "Take me north to draw them away. Once we're at Merciless Reach, you can take the fight deeper into their territory."

He flashed me an appreciative look.

"Have I mentioned how much I hunger for you?"

I couldn't stop the shocked laughter from spilling out. Leave it to the rake to flirt as several dragons closed in all around us. Axton landed another solid kick to the dragon's center, sending it flying backward into the rest of the pack.

"Hurry!"

I launched myself into Axton's arms and he had us airborne in seconds, the dragons shrieking as they took the bait and pursued us. Their wings flapping against the night was the single most terrifying sound as they slowly gained on us.

Axton's heart pounded furiously against mine and I hugged him tighter.

A blizzard raged around us, in part from the dragons' icy nature and in part from the winter itself. Soon I couldn't see my hand in front of my face, and if it wasn't for his supernatural powers, I'd be worried about how Axton was navigating us to the outpost.

He ran a hand up and down my spine, trying to warm me.

"We'll be there soon. If I didn't need them to follow us, I'd magic us there."

"I know." I nestled against him, teeth chattering.

Leave it to the prince to be more concerned with my comfort than the raging dragons pursuing us. He was positively ridiculous and I couldn't love him more.

Moments later, lashes coated in snow, I blinked at the towering wall that ran along the entire northern border. Snow covered the top of it, a frosted layer that glinted dangerously in the moonlight. A large stone building rose behind it, almost daring anyone to bring a fight to it.

Axton aimed straight for it, his flight a punishing momentum that defied any laws of nature. He was a force unto himself. All I could do was hold on as he tucked his wings in close and dove toward a narrow opening on the upper floor.

We landed with a soft thud and Axton set me down.

"You all right?" he asked, scanning me as if dragons weren't swarming the fortress.

"Yes." I swallowed thickly. "You?"

"I'd be better if you agree to marry me." He gave me a wolfish grin. "But, yes. I'm fine."

The levity was gone the next instant. A dragon thundered past the opening we'd come through. Axton took my hand and guided me deeper into the room, far from the opening that was too big to be a window but too small for a door. Perhaps it was used for a demon prince in flight.

"Don't let them see you." He took a dagger from his ankle and placed it in my hands. "Strike for their eyes if necessary. The fortress is warded; you'll be safe if you stay within it."

He stalked away then cursed and rushed back.

"I swear to the old gods if you put yourself in danger, I will tie you to my bedposts and make you regret scaring me for hours on end."

I yanked him close. "Make sure you come back and punish me soon. Or I will hunt *you* down."

He laughed softly and without another word, he was off and back into the battle, which already raged on here, twice as brutal as the one we'd just fled.

My pulse pounded as I lingered by the interior wall. It was far worse to hear the sounds of attack without seeing it. My imagination always was a bit too wicked.

Had the dragons somehow found a way to end an immortal? Was Axton hurt?

I inched closer to the opening we'd flown through and noticed a door a room over that led onto a parapet. Carefully, quietly, I moved just inside the doorway, watching as hunters and dragons and princes fought with brutal grace. It was unlike anything I'd seen.

The sheer majesty of the background—the mountains towering in the distance, the ice-covered building and stables—it was the most beautifully macabre location.

If it wasn't for the war taking place, I could understand why so many wanted to join the guild. Up here nature reigned supreme, the rules of court and society far away.

And nature was a ruthless leader. Dragons clawed their way through bodies, never looking back at who they felled as they raged toward Axton. Blood splattered across the snow, the sight as ghastly and as unnerving as the shrill cries of the beasts.

It was a battle that shouldn't be happening; the dragons hadn't done a thing to deserve the madness. They'd been pawns in a game none of us knew someone had played.

If the Hexed Quill hadn't been wielded, they would be continuing to live as they had for the last one hundred years, content in their northern playground. My senses were struggling to piece it all together—the mystery didn't feel solved. It felt like we were missing something.

Something that could truly end all this. But what...?

Ryleigh. Strained friendship or not, my intuition was having a hard time accepting the evidence the prince put forth to damn her. Especially after our confrontation earlier.

Something didn't sit quite right. There wasn't any real motivation for Ryleigh to destroy my happiness. Or to rewrite that night. But there were a lot of unanswered questions.

If she had the quill, wouldn't she have used it to stop Duchess Oleander from hating her? Or wouldn't she have used it on her stories to gain wider circulation for her columns?

Why would she hunt the quill so hard only to never use it to advance herself?

Prince Wrath flew past the outpost, his face a mask of pure, untamed fury.

To distract myself from the sounds of battle and to feed that growing hunger to solve the mystery, I kept going over everything Axton had revealed.

It was a solid trail, yet Ryleigh denied the accusation. In front of the whole court.

More secrets and lies? I didn't think so.

A hunter shouted from directly below where I remained hidden within the magical ward. Axton appeared from almost out of thin air, putting himself between the dragon and the hunter.

I screamed as the mad creature lunged for his throat, racing to peer over the stone wall. I'd crossed out of the magical barrier and was exposed to the dragon circling above.

A moment later I was hauled back, an immovable wall of muscle locking me in place as I thrashed. "Let go! He's hurt!"

"He will heal. You won't." Lust wrangled me back into the safety of the ward. "He'll also kill me if you die. So do the realm a favor and remain *here*."

He was right, I knew that logically, but my heart…my cursed heart was pounding so hard it felt as if it would break out of my chest.

I wanted to launch myself over the wall, make sure the stupid, idiotic rake was indeed breathing. So I could throttle him myself when this was over.

Lust gave me a knowing smirk. "Thinking of hitting him? Don't worry, we all do."

I paced around the room, feeling like a caged animal. The sounds of battle raged on, driving me to the brink of madness myself. I couldn't stay here and do nothing.

"You're keeping him from pain," Lust said, reading my thoughts. "He won't admit it, but it's partly why he took so long to heal after the last incident."

I thought back to the kissing competition. To the pain that had flashed in his face. One day I would dunk his head under water.

"Has anyone found the damned paper Ryleigh wrote on yet?" I asked, still needing to do something. Standing around so the prince and I weren't in pain wasn't ideal.

Lust shook his head. "They're tearing the flat apart and looking in other known locations she frequents. It's only a matter of time before they find it."

Time our circle and realm didn't have. Nor did the dragons. A shrill cry rent the air followed by the most mournful noise I'd ever heard. My blood ran cold.

"Does that mean…" I couldn't put my fears into words.

Lust's expression turned morose. "A dragon was killed."

"This is a nightmare."

And it needed to end. *Now.*

I paced more, mind spinning. If they hadn't already located the journal or parchment Ryleigh used to rewrite the All-Sinners Ball, it stood to reason she wasn't the suspect.

My intuition seemed to buzz harder at that, making me think I was correct.

If not Ryleigh, then who? Who would have motive and intent to—

I stopped pacing as a series of clues and comments fell into place.

"Dear gods. Axton got it wrong."

My father's ledger mentioned a quill.

I glanced sharply at my companion, but he wasn't listening.

Lust was on the terrace, muscles taut. He'd been tasked with guarding the outpost and looked ready to immerse himself in the action.

I inwardly scrambled to think before I plotted my next move. I had to be very, very certain I was correct before I flung out such a serious accusation.

No matter how I tried to spin it, I believed I knew exactly who had ruined our lives.

Sophie Everhart. The demon obsessed with material wealth. And the very same demon who hated losing to a commoner above all else.

The clues had been there all along and I hadn't wanted to see them. But now I couldn't seem to stop fitting puzzle pieces together.

My stepmother's knowing smile when Eden was chosen as a suitor. I'd guessed she'd used a spell; she never confirmed my suspicion.

My stepmother had been at the All-Sinners Ball that night. She'd not been pleased with the outcome...but that wasn't quite true, was it?

The longer I forced myself to recall details, the more confused I became about the sequence of events. *Had* Sophie been strangely excited when we'd left the All-Sinners Ball?

Even though I hadn't secured a good match and that was all she claimed my worth to be?

Eden had only been a child at the time, but foggy memories emerged.

Even then Sophie had said her daughter was worthy of becoming a princess, that she'd be eligible for welcoming suitors in less than a decade.

That my failure would still be our family's gain, mark her words. She'd worn a ridiculous feather in her hair that night.

A feather I'd recently seen with my father's ledger. Ryleigh had tucked it back into the little book the day she was in our home collecting recipes. It *had* to be the Hexed Quill.

The world around me came to a crashing halt. That was it. My father's ledger. The one item she continued to threaten to sell but never actually followed through with it. That had to be the place she wrote out our new fate, damning us all, intentionally or not.

"Prince Lust!" I shouted, racing to the walled terrace. "I know where the—"

Lust was battling a dragon in the sky, his attention wholly fixed on the beast who'd been about to storm our shelter. I swallowed hard, gaze darting around at the scene below.

It was chaos unleashed. And no one could escort me to my home without leaving a hole in our defenses. Wrath and Gluttony, Envy and Lust—each prince was a force on the battlefield, a force our realm desperately needed to hold the line.

I couldn't stand here, waiting for a break in the fight that might never come. I needed to act.

I said a silent prayer that Axton wouldn't be harmed as I bolted for the stairs. I raced past the wounded, jumping over bodies slumped in the corridor, shoving the images and fear from my mind. I burst out the door, finding a hell horse and rider slowing to a walk.

That was my ride.

I ran over to the hunter as he dismounted and staggered to the ground, grabbed his mount, and launched myself into the saddle.

With a shout of apology, I kicked my heels into the horse's flank, and we took off. I silently thanked Axton for his horseback riding lesson. Instead of being scared out of my wits, I rode with confidence.

The hell horse raced like his life depended on it, which it did. All our lives came down to this moment, and I prayed my intuition hadn't failed me.

We ran hard and fast, the horse swallowing up the northern terrain as if sparked by magic. Soon we clambered across the cobbled streets of our circle, streets that were eerily silent.

Buildings were shuttered, the normal hustle and bustle gone. Everyone was hiding from the dragons. Pain began in my chest, winding itself around my heart until it squeezed.

Everything in me wanted to turn back to make it end. I hoped Axton wasn't feeling it as strongly. He didn't need any distractions right now.

Instead of giving in to the agony, I didn't let up on the horse until we skidded to a halt in front of my building. I nearly toppled out of the saddle; as my feet hit the ground I took off up the stairs. Each breath felt strained as the magical bond tugged me back.

My front door was unlocked, but there was no time to stop to consider why.

I rushed over to my father's things, frantically flipping through his ledger.

It slipped from my hands, and I forced myself to pause, to breathe. I was shaking far more than I thought.

Once I pulled myself together, I snatched it back up and scanned every page. I'd never realized just how many notes he'd made. It felt like time was ticking faster, that the fate of our circle came down to these moments. That if I failed here, I'd fail us all.

My pulse had never thrashed as hard or as fast, my lungs working so quickly I felt faint. All the while the pain ratcheted up, never relinquishing its power over me. I prayed Axton wouldn't fall in battle. We were so close. If only I could just find it!

"Come on. Come on."

I read faster than I ever have before, my body growing more tense by the second. There was no note. No rewritten event. I had been so sure...

If I was wrong, then all I'd accomplished by leaving Merciless Reach and coming here was weakening Axton when he most needed his strength.

I flipped to the next page, and it nearly fell out.

I paused, glancing down at the sheet of paper that had been hastily glued into the ledger.

"It can't be."

I scanned the note, which wasn't penned in my father's familiar scrawl. Tears flowed hot down my cheeks. I'd been correct: *this* was the evidence we'd been searching for.

Sophie had—

"Oh, my gods. No."

A wave of icy dread swept through me as the initial sense of elation passed. The note wasn't written in Sophie's hand. Nor Ryleigh's. And it certainly wasn't my father's doing. The scrawled note had been written in a child's hand.

"Eden. What have you done?"

As if my whispered plea summoned her, my sister stepped into the room, a candle held in her shaking hands. The flame danced wildly as her tearstained face came into view.

"I didn't mean for any of this to happen, Ad. You must know that. I swear, I didn't know—"

Her voice broke as she wept.

I held my hand out, my voice taking on the authoritative note of the eldest sibling.

"Give me the candle, Edie. We must destroy this at once."

There would be plenty of time for teary confessions later.

For a taut moment that stretched uncomfortably into the next, I thought my sister would blow the candle out, damning us all. But she carefully made her way to me, a hand shielding the little flame, and handed the taper over.

I didn't hesitate to set the parchment ablaze, watching as it slowly caught fire.

In theory the hex should break the moment it turned to ash. If only the damned paper would ignite.

"Cursed thing. Hurry!"

I'd never known patience as I had in that moment, watching the fire slowly lick at the parchment before deciding to swallow it down. It was only moments, but it felt like an interminable wait. Every second that ticked by could mean another death.

Once the flames flickered over my fingertips, I dropped the burning fragment into a little bowl Eden had fetched, watching until nothing but ash remained.

The embers faded from red to orange, then winked out.

I supposed we would find out soon enough if it was over, or if we'd failed. As if that worry manifested my darkest fears, I heard the shrill cry of dragons approaching.

I swore and rushed over to the window, yanking the curtain back. In the distance, I saw the unmistakable silhouettes of beasts flying through the clouds.

The dragons escaped Merciless Reach.

The cries carrying in on the storm indicated the battle was coming south to the heart of Gluttony's circle. The hex might have burned, but until the magic receded, we were all still very much in danger as the sound of attack drew closer.

Unholy gods below. They were heading our way.

"Eden!"

I grabbed my sister and raced to the other end of the room, clutching her to me as a giant shadow from above suddenly darkened the street.

FIFTY-THREE
Prince Gluttony

A BLAST OF PURE white fire sent me reeling backward through the sky, nearly colliding with Wrath. My brother paid me no mind. He flung himself into his battle again, a ferocious look in his eyes as he attacked his dragon with the full might of a demon of war.

I spun around in midair, flying full speed at my dragon, forcing him to retreat. A sudden, violent pain ripped through my chest. I glanced down. There was no blood.

I cursed. Adriana must have left the fortress.

Another blast of dragon fire narrowly missed me.

I gritted my teeth and shoved the pain out of my mind.

Even with Sloth and Greed bringing our numbers to six Princes of Sin versus seven dragons, we had barely driven them north of Merciless Reach.

The more my brothers and I pushed them back, the more fiercely they fought to regain ground, unwilling to retreat.

I threw myself into my dragon's path again, blade arcing through the storm.

Ice made the hilt slick, along with blood.

The stubborn dragon held his ground, his wings pumping the air around him as he hovered. When I neared again, intent on cutting him deeper, his talons struck my chest, shredding my shirt. I hadn't had time to put leathers on, and it wouldn't matter if I had.

Silvanus wasn't holding back like he did in skirmishes.

He was out for blood and glory.

I circled him, then feinted to the left, catching his flank on the right.

He bared his teeth, diving for my throat.

I was slower than I should be because of the damned blood oath and the unrelenting pain, but I deflected what would have been a direct hit with my blade. He nicked my skin but didn't rip my throat out fully. Thank the old gods for that.

Suddenly there was a shift in the dragons. Like some primal instinct yanked on a magical tether, drawing them up short. My brothers noticed too.

The atmosphere itself seemed to inhale deeply and hold its breath.

My shoulders ached as my wings furiously pumped. This wouldn't be good.

I launched myself back at Sil, using the moment of his distraction to land a solid blow. The ice dragon's head whipped from side to side, his nostrils flaring as he scented the air.

He dodged my next hit, lurching up into the storm clouds with one brutally efficient pump of his mighty wings.

Silvanus was on the hunt, and he was about to go capture his prey.

I knew exactly what he'd scented: Adriana.

I aimed for his middle as he careened past me, maneuvering his serpentine body up and around. My fingers grazed his flank, finding no purchase as his scales coated over with protective ice. Slick bastard. "Stop them!"

"That *has* been the goal," Lust quipped, barely avoiding a talon to the chest. Served his smart ass right. "Or we were supposed to be courting them?"

"They're heading for the city!" I shouted to my brothers. "Take them down!"

Envy's dagger-like feathers struck out like the secret blades they were as he unleashed himself on his dragon. The gods-damned creature took the hit, then tucked his wings close, diving hard and fast away.

A sound like two great mountains clashing rumbled the air and earth.

It was hard to tell if it was thunder from the storm or Wrath's anger as he chased down the dragon that slipped past his defenses.

Every time it seemed like we gained an inch, the damned creatures bested us.

They truly were the fiercest fighters we'd ever faced. It was normally thrilling, a way to feed my sin. Now it felt like a curse. We needed to take them down. Now.

I turned my attention to the fleeing pack, flying as hard as I could to catch them. I had a sneaking suspicion I knew exactly where they were heading. They moved with purpose as they unleashed themselves, flying impossibly fast across the stormy sky.

I refused to fall back and chased them, giving everything I had, my brothers flanking my sides. Soon, the tiled rooftops and familiar cobbled streets came into view. My chest ached with a new sort of pain that had nothing to do with the oath Adriana and I had sworn.

The dragons had gone directly to printers' row.

Adriana's house wasn't far from here. A few streets.

Judging by the lessening pain in my chest, she was close by. And Silvanus's war cry indicated he sensed she was near.

When I caught up to him, my world stilled. He was hovering above the building next to hers. If the mood struck, he could unleash his lethal fire on her home and end everyone inside.

My House dagger glowed fiercely, craving a taste of blood.

I would kill him before I let him near her.

"Thought you might need some help, Prince."

The shout came from the street below.

I glanced down, taken off guard by what I was seeing. A line of vampires, led by none other than Blade, marched along the street, breaking off in small groups at some silent command.

It took only a moment to understand what he'd done. He'd placed his vampire fighters in front of businesses, keeping the demons inside safe. Their fangs gleamed, on full display.

They'd always wanted to sink their teeth into ice dragons. It was also a clever reminder that he'd one day need my help, too. As if I'd forget my vow.

"Keep my court safe, Blade!"

"With pleasure." The vampire prince jerked his chin and the rest of his team dispersed.

As I watched them go, my attention landed on Sascha. The witch was standing in the middle of the street, her eyes glowing as her mouth moved in a silent chant. She was warding the neighborhood. I *knew* it had been a good bet to aid her.

Between her and the vampires guarding the streets, I could focus my efforts on the sky.

I turned my attention back on Sil. He'd been scenting the air, circling. Now he flew with renewed purpose. He passed over Adriana's house, then doubled back, his shrill cry echoing through the streets. He was calling in his pack.

Thankful for the unexpected help on the streets, I resumed my chase, blade at the ready. I reached Sil's side in seconds, my dagger aimed directly for his heart.

With as much power as I could put behind the action, I flew for the dragon I'd raised. He was entirely too close to the woman I loved, and my instincts were sharper than ever. He was a threat to Adriana's safety, and I would remove him through any means necessary.

A deep sense of victory fueled me to fly harder than I thought possible. I knew with dark certainty I would take him down this time; my aim was true and he'd been distracted.

Silvanus must have finally sensed danger; he wrenched his attention from the house below and stared at me. But it was too late for mercy.

He slowly blinked as if coming out of a dream. His eyes shone iridescent, not red. They latched onto my glowing blade, and I swore I saw a flicker of sorrow and acceptance.

I was too close and he was too large to dodge the hit.

I cursed—there was no way to avoid a blow; I'd been aiming to kill.

In seconds it would be over. My dragon would fall at my own hand.

The very hand that bottle-fed him, that taught him to flap his wings when his feathers had finally sprouted. Laughing while he'd hopped around like the little sassy fledgling he was.

Unless…

At the last possible moment, I turned the blade on myself, taking the hit meant to end my dragon. The impact stole my breath, the pain unlike anything I'd ever felt as the dagger pierced my heart. I thought I heard Silvanus cry, but it was drowned out by the roar coming from below.

Cheers and whoops rang out from the air and ground. Victory.

The hex was broken. Adriana was safe. My court and our realm were both unharmed.

I hovered there, soaking in the moment for as long as I could.

Sil blinked at me, at the dagger protruding from my chest. Ichor dripped along the hilt, faster and more frequently. My wings slowed, then stopped.

Heroes were gods-damned idiots. But I felt strangely at peace.

The ice dragon let out a cry that would raise the dead and dove at me.

And everything went dark.

FIFTY-FOUR
Adriana

THE SOUND OF victory rang through the thin walls of our home. I let my sister go and went to see for myself that the curse was truly broken. The princes flew through the night district, the joy palpable as they swooped down to help citizens who'd been caught outside during the attack.

I squinted down at the crowd—vampires were helping demons, and Sascha was leaning against Val. She looked like she'd been working spells for hours.

My attention swept across the street; it seemed like only a few buildings had been damaged. We'd avoided what could have—and *should* have been—a great disaster, probably because of the protective spells the witch had cast.

Warmth spread through me. It was really over. Our circle might be overindulgent sinners, our realm filled with the morally corrupt, but we came together when we needed to.

"Is the hex broken?" Eden asked, a hopeful note in her voice.

"It certainly seems to be."

I watched everyone celebrating in the street below for another few moments, searching for a familiar form. I didn't see Axton, but he was probably back at the castle, checking on his court. I should have expected it, but a twinge of unease worked its way in. He was a prince. It made sense for him to tend to his court first, especially since it had been attacked.

And I had my own pressing matters to address.

The hex was broken, but I couldn't ignore the fact there were still questions I needed answers to. I couldn't fathom how my sister could betray me.

I exhaled and sat down. I needed to understand *why*.

Eden dropped onto the settee next to me, silent.

I wasn't sure how to broach the subject gently, but keeping secrets wasn't doing either of us any favors. We needed to sort it out head-on. Then heal. Together.

"How did you come to have the Hexed Quill?"

Eden sniffled, then glanced up.

"Ryleigh brought it over the night of the All-Sinners Ball, telling us stories of impossible magic. When you came home, flushed with excitement, and Mamma said you were to be a princess, I—panicked. I wasn't ready to lose you, so I wrote down a different story. I made sure Ryleigh wouldn't remember. To keep it secret, I rewrote her memory too."

Poor Ryleigh...She'd been publicly condemned for a crime she didn't commit. And I'd lost faith in our friendship. I ached for her and knew how it felt to be the subject of gossip and scandal. I needed to set that right for my friend as soon as I could.

Axton would have to offer a full apology from the Crown. Then maybe he could offer her the position as his official royal reporter. But those were possible solutions for another day and I still had more questions.

"You were so young. How did you even come up with the new history?"

Eden flushed. "I was bored and snuck one of Mamma's novels while you were both at the ball. The scandal in that book made quite an impression. A prince was caught with a viscountess, right after he'd declared himself to another...it was a case of mistaken identity, though."

I took a few moments to gather myself, not wanting to speak out of hurt or anger. My heart ached at the truth. My sister. The one person in the entire world I'd never intentionally hurt had unwittingly caused me the greatest heartbreak of my life. All because she'd read a similar scandal in a book. It was so innocent, the mistake of a child. And yet it caused so much pain.

"I never would have left you, Edie. Surely you must know that. I would have moved you and Sophie into the castle with us. Why didn't you ever tell me?"

"I was afraid. At first it seemed like you were happier, that maybe the quill was a good thing. You hid your feelings for so long, I had no idea how hurt you've been."

"Hid my feelings?" I scoffed. "I tried to destroy Axton's reputation in the paper for the last ten years. Did you ever consider confiding in me?"

She dropped her gaze and nodded slowly.

"When the competition began, I wanted to confess everything. Especially after Axton sent all those gifts. You can say whatever you like about his motivation for doing it, but it was clear to me that he cared deeply for you."

I sighed. "You are far too sweet and innocent. He did it to uncover my identity."

"Ad. I adore you, but you cannot truly believe that all those items were necessary. Did he need to send food, or parchment or oil for our lanterns to accomplish that?"

She smiled softly as I pressed my lips together.

My little sister had somehow pieced together truths I'd overlooked.

"It was obvious how much he liked you and I wanted you to see it too. But I ran out of time. When I was chosen as his suitor, I thought it was the best way to get you close to the prince. I hoped that maybe I could devise a way for you to fall in love as you once had. I'm terribly bad at plotting and scheming. But I swear the competition was always a way to get you and Prince Gluttony together again."

"Your mother would have had your hide if she discovered what you were doing."

A tentative smile crossed her face. "I think she did know. Deep down. Which was why she was so adamant about keeping you and the prince apart."

"Where is Sophie?"

"She was in our private suite with guards when I snuck out to come back here. Axton warded the rooms so the dragons couldn't enter."

Thank the gods for that. Sophie was not the kindest demon in the realm, but that didn't mean I wished to see any harm come to her. She would live to see another scheming day. At least she'd keep us all on our toes, wondering what nefarious plot she was working on next.

I looked my sister over, seeing for the first time the young woman she was.

Eden had been forced to tread carefully between me and Sophie, and while we always wanted to ensure her happiness, we never gave her room to fall and pick herself back up.

"Do you wish to be better at scheming?"

She snorted. "Gods, no. I want a simple life without court politics. I'm perfectly content with cooking and tending to a home. Maybe one day opening my own bakery."

"And your secret lover?" I asked, wanting all the truth out between us. "Do you see your future with them?"

Her face flushed scarlet. "How do you know about Vanity?"

My brows rose.

I hadn't known who her lover was. "You're involved with the House Pride suitor?"

Eden bit her lower lip, blushing. "We spent a lot of time together while the prince was otherwise preoccupied. We formed an attachment."

I gently took her hands in mine and gave them a squeeze.

"I'm happy for you. You deserve all the love and affection in the world." I smiled. "The prince will undoubtedly take full credit for introducing you."

She gave me a hug then drew back. "He loves you, Ad. I hope you give him a chance to redeem himself. It wasn't his fault I used the quill."

I settled back onto the threadbare cushion. "I don't blame him for the quill, but I'm afraid it's a bit more complicated than that now."

"Complicated is a mild term for what happened tonight. He asked you to marry him, Adriana. You refused him in front of his court."

"I didn't *refuse* him. We were interrupted. In case you've forgotten, there was the little matter of a dragon attack."

Eden shook her head. "Everyone could tell you were about to deny him. You don't have to tell me why, but you do need to sort it out for yourself before you speak to him. No matter what you decide, you don't want to have any regrets."

"I know." It wasn't the hex or dark magic. Now I needed to really think about how Axton and I fit together, if we even truly did match on enough levels.

I didn't care for him leaving me out of his plans or simply being too royal to understand when he was overstepping. The truth was—we were from very different worlds.

I wasn't sure we would ever end up on equal footing.

That didn't make him bad or to blame; it was something worth considering for a partnership, though. Just because we worked on a physical level, didn't mean we suited everywhere else. If Axton and I were to truly accept each other, we needed to accept all aspects.

Eden leaned over and kissed my cheek. "When isn't love complicated, though?"

Indeed. I peered at her. "When did you get so wise?"

"After I made a terrible mistake." She pushed to her feet. "Let's promise to never keep secrets from each other again. No matter how terrible we think they are."

"I think that sounds like another wise plan, dear sister. Let's also swear to never play with another hexed object. Where *is* the quill?"

The levity vanished from Eden's face. "I...can't remember."

I didn't need to possess a Prince of Sin's ability to sense lies to know she was being honest. "What do you mean?"

Her brows drew together as she considered.

"Sometimes I think a prince came and took the quill, rewriting my memory of it. Other times I think I might have given it away to a dark market dealer."

My intuition picked its head up at that. It sounded like an investigative story worth pursuing...a hexed object in the hands of the very princes they were meant to bind.

I shook myself from the idea. One adventure with a dark prince was enough for now.

"I truly am so sorry, Ad. If I'd known what the outcome would be, I never would have meddled. I acted out of fear."

"I know." I gave her a tight smile and decided to put the past where it belonged. In the past. "One thing I've learned is decisions based in fear or anxiety or worry will always come back to haunt you. Love is what strengthens us all, though. Familial love, friendship, romantic love, platonic love. Promise me from now on, you'll act from a place of love, not fear."

"I swear it."

"Good. Then I think a proper apology and acceptance of said apology should come with freshly baked frostberry pastries. And yours are the best."

Eden's eyes watered as she jumped to her feet and headed for the kitchen.

"Then I shall get to work now. I still have supplies from when the prince sent over those nefarious gifts to further his plot." Her eyes sparkled. "Do you think you'll see him again soon?"

"Axton is like a bad rash," I teased. "You rid yourself of it for a little while, but eventually it comes back with a vengeance."

"Mm-hmm." Eden gave me a knowing look and went about making the sweet dough for the dessert.

I *wanted* to accept his proposal, but just because the magic was no longer tearing us apart, that didn't negate everything we needed to sort out before I said yes.

If we had a future, I wanted to consider what that truly meant, how it looked. Would I keep my position as Miss Match? Would I be a pauper princess? I had no use for courtly games, and I wasn't sure how I felt about my new column, but it had grown on me.

However, today was not the time to worry about that.

Today was about burning the past and setting my sights on a new dawn, and for now, I was content with that.

FIFTY-FIVE
Prince Gluttony

DRIANA SLANTED A look in my direction, then glanced back up at the Ox & Raven's sign. A small furrow formed between her brows. "Your favorite place to dine is a tavern?"

"Don't use that tone in front of Shirlee; she'll spit in your potpie."

I held the thick wooden door open, and Adriana gave me a filthy hand gesture before slipping inside. My mouth curved. It was the first time I'd seen my sweet nemesis since the attack days ago, and I fought the urge to wrap her in my arms.

After taking my dagger to the chest, I'd fallen unconscious for a few hours. Regenerating a heart was no small task, especially since I'd been so drained.

While I was healing, Val hadn't bothered to send word to Adriana that I was indisposed, not because she disapproved of our relationship, but because she'd been occupied with her own new romance. She and Sascha had grown close after the attack.

Witches and demons *could* bond without bloodshed. I was happy for my second.

The moment I came to, I sent a letter to Adriana, requesting an audience with her at once. We had a very serious matter to settle and if she wanted to negotiate, I was ready to accept her terms. She'd replied within the hour, thanking me, but declined. She said she was pleased I was healing but needed time to think without my *insufferable charm getting in the way.*

I swore the female would drive me to the brink of madness and I'd happily hand her the reins. I wrote her back immediately, unwilling to accept defeat.

It had taken days of constant persistence, but she finally agreed to meet me to talk.

I would use every moment of our time to show her who I truly was behind all the secrets and masks. Starting with my favorite meal.

The scent of savory delights hit us along with a burst of warmth.

Patrons were already deep into their cups of winter ale and barely paid us any attention as I placed a palm to Adriana's lower back and guided her to my favorite booth in the corner.

Adriana scooted onto the bench, uncaring that the scarred table was still littered with bowls and empty mugs from the patrons who'd vacated before us.

A server came over and hurriedly cleaned. "The usual for you and your date, Axton?"

"Yes. Please tell Shirlee to add extra garlic rosemary butter to the crust."

"Will do!"

Adriana watched the encounter with interest. Once our first round of winter ale was set before us and she'd taken a few sips, she leaned back and surveyed me.

"You seem more relaxed here."

I gave her a sly grin. "I'm relaxed in most situations, darling. But I really enjoy the simplicity of eating a good meal in a casual setting."

"It's not very gluttonous of you, Prince *Gluttony*."

"On the contrary. I'm feasting like a king on this fare. I'm indulging in your company, *and* I couldn't be more satisfied. My sin isn't about the most lavish or rich; it's about indulging in things that give pleasure. The simple things are what bring me the greatest amount of pleasure. Good food, good drink, good conversation. A good companion. Those are the things that mark a good life. So, yes, I'm feeling rather full on my power at the moment."

"Hmm."

She sipped her ale. "This is so delicious. I think it's my favorite drink."

"It's mine too." It was such a small, insignificant detail, but pleasure rocked through me. I liked that she enjoyed it as much as I did. "How are things between you and Ryleigh?"

A hopeful smile crossed her face. "We're meeting for tea tomorrow. We've been friends for far too long to let secrets and misunderstandings come between us."

"I'm glad to hear it." I wanted everything in her life to bring her joy. I truly was turning into a lovesick fool like my siblings. I prayed to the old gods that Lust would be struck down next—that meddling bastard had it coming. "I've considered your request." She glanced up. "Ryleigh will be the new royal reporter. She accepted the offer this morning."

Shirlee came out from the back, a tray laden with our food and next round of ales raised high above the tables as she made her way to us.

"Got any other requests concerning my cooking, you royal pain in my ass?" she said by way of greeting.

Adriana snorted and clapped a hand over her mouth.

I stared at her, fighting my own laughter. "That was the most undignified sound I've ever heard. Do it again and I'll fall in love harder."

Shirlee looked over at my companion, a smile flickering across her stern face. "Seems like you finally found someone who doesn't worship the ground you walk upon. I like her."

Adriana stopped laughing long enough to straighten. "I'm Adriana Saint Lucent. I've heard wonderful things about your food."

"*The* Adriana Saint Lucent?" Shirlee surprised me by wiping her hands on her apron and taking Adriana in a hug. "I hear you're the one who broke the hex. You come here whenever you like. Take this pain in my ass with you."

"You flatter me with compliments, Shirlee," I drawled. "Don't let it go to my head."

She rolled her eyes and gave Adriana one more gentle squeeze. "I'll have some of my special chocolate frostberry mousse sent out."

Once Shirlee left, I pulled the item I'd been holding on to for the last decade from my suit and laid it on the table before Adriana.

"Open it," I said, nodding to the little velvet pouch.

My heart pounded as if I was on an intense hunt. I'd hoped it would be a nice surprise. A way to prove I wanted to be more than the rake I'd been. At least when it came to her. Adriana's gaze narrowed in suspicion and I did a better job of schooling my features.

She gingerly loosened the string and dumped the contents into her palm. The bracelet sparkled in the low light of the tavern.

Adriana's throat moved as she swallowed down her emotions. "You knew this was mine."

It wasn't a question, so I didn't treat it as such.

I gave a slight nod, allowing her to sort out her feelings on the matter. She searched my face, and I saw a myriad of emotions play across her features.

"Why?"

I took a long pull of my ale.

"Because I love you," I said simply.

I watched hope and disbelief war across her face.

I'd said the words before, but it felt different now. This time we had no threat looming, no hex interfering. We were not lost to passion. Or performing for a crowd of courtiers and reporters. Or any other excuse she might dream up in that wildly creative mind of hers. It was just me sitting before her, confessing the truth of my heart.

Today I was not her prince, only the male who loved her fiercely.

"I've adored you from nearly the first moment I saw you. I loved you when I didn't like you. I loved you when you bested me. And when I bested you. I love your smart mouth, your clever mind, your darkest fantasies. Your brightest joy. I love that you never let me win, that any victory I have is fleeting but earned. And I will live out the rest of eternity loving you."

She dropped her gaze. And I would have paid an obscene sum to know what she was thinking. I waited, watching her absorb my confession.

"I thought my mother's bracelet was lost forever." She picked it up gingerly, tears gleaming in her eyes. "How do you have it?"

"I've been holding on to it since the All-Sinners Ball. I couldn't quite remember how I came to have it—with our memories restored, I now recall vividly that it broke while we were in the garden." I gave her a shy smile. "I'd put it in my pocket, wanting to have it repaired." But then that event was rewritten, and I found a mystery bracelet. "For the sake of complete honesty, it reminded me of you. Your eyes, your hair. I couldn't part with it."

"I didn't think I'd ever see it again. Thank you. It means more than you know."

"Here. Allow me." I gently turned her wrist over, draping the bracelet around it and fastening it in place. Adriana was so fixated on her mother's jewelry that she hadn't noticed the small velvet box I'd set before her. I cleared my throat. "There is one other matter."

I popped the box open, revealing a wildly extravagant ring.

A diamond nestled with a sapphire and aquamarine.

Adriana went perfectly still.

"Marry me, Adriana Marianna Saint Lucent. Fight with me, vex me, love me for the rest of our days. Just as I vow to do to you."

My heart thudded painfully as she slowly shook her head.

Just when I thought she'd deny me once more, she gave me a tentative smile.

"You truly are abysmal with declarations of love, Axton. But yes. I wish to marry you and irk you for eternity. Because I love you just as foolishly and fiercely."

I leapt across the table and gathered her into my arms, taking her mouth in a kiss that was both punishing and promising of all the wicked delights to come.

The crowd slammed their mugs of winter ale on their tables, cheering. And I kissed her harder, deeper, until all I heard were her soft exhales.

❄ ❄ ❄

"I've never petted a dragon before."

I glanced down at my fiancée, smirking as I guided us behind the stables of House Gluttony to where Silvanus waited. "Untrue. You know that's what I call my cock."

"Heathen." Adriana lightly punched my arm, and I tugged her close.

Silvanus emerged from the woods, snuffing the air, and I swore he rolled his eyes. Warmth spread through my chest at seeing my favorite dragon restored.

His eyes shone with the familiar iridescent gleam as they flicked to Adriana.

I'd had Sascha spell us so we could communicate, and when Sil let loose his thoughts, I rather wished I hadn't.

She's far too good for you.

Adriana laughed, the best sound in the world, and strode over to the dragon. "I adore him! He's clearly wise."

And handsome.

"Let's not forget I took a dagger for you," I interjected.

Sil huffed, but I saw a slight sheen in his eye. If I didn't know better, I'd think the sassy bastard was getting emotional over my injury.

Adriana held out a gloved hand. "May I?"

The dragon nodded, then sank down, granting her access to his giant head. Adriana lightly stroked his scales, then drew her hand back. "You really are ice-cold."

I can warm my scales should you like to take a ride, milady.

I scoffed. "Are you serious? You've never offered *me* a ride and I raised your sorry scaled bottom. And, need I remind you once more, took a dagger to the heart for you."

Perhaps if you minded your tongue, Prince. Though I suppose you ought to make sure your princess doesn't lose her seat.

"Will wonders never cease. The great Silvanus is playing the role of royal horse."

Sil scowled the only way an ice dragon could, by growling and spewing flames at my favorite boots. I flipped him off, then helped Adriana up.

I was about to hop up behind her when a frantic bleating drew my attention back.

Vex, the little baby dragon, launched himself into my arms.

Apparently, he was coming along for the ride.

Adriana held her hands out. "Isn't that the cutest thing? What's its name?"

Sil and I both huffed at her calling the baby the cutest thing.

"This is Vex. He's been vexing me almost as much as you, sweet nemesis." I gently placed him in her arms, monitoring her shiver. "If you bite my intended," I warned him, "I will bite you back harder, Vex. Understood?"

The little dragon nudged me with its head. Charmer.

Is our fine lady secure?

Adriana nodded, then nestled into my chest, the little dragon cooing from where he snuggled in her lap. Both Val and Envy would be incredulous when I told them the little deviant dragon didn't bite Adriana.

I held her tightly to me. "I've got her."

Good, try not to let go.

"That, dear dragon, is a vow I intend to keep forever."

You're finally using that upper head; the pack wasn't sure it worked. Prick.

In a show of great power, Silvanus launched us into the sky, and Adriana's excited shriek echoed through the air along with the excited bleating of the baby as we soared toward the mountains, feeling the wind whipping at us as snow began to fall.

This next journey was sure to be the most thrilling adventure of my existence.

And I'd make sure that every gossip columnist in the realm knew this rake was indeed reformed and my heart belonged solely to my rival, my love, my match.

Though I was sure we'd find plenty of fun ways to *stay scandalous*.

As Silvanus banked around and raced toward the city, flying dangerously low across the rooftops in the night district, I felt the moment Adriana realized where our destination was.

She twisted to look at me over her shoulder, a grin twitching at the corners of her lips.

"The Seven Sins?"

"As the secret owner of that fine establishment, I fully intend to bring you as often as you'd like." I nipped playfully at her ear. "I seem to recall a few fantasies we'd like to indulge. If you're bold enough to play, Lady Frost."

"Perhaps I'll bring you to your knees tonight, Your Highness."

I'd never heard a more seductive threat and welcomed my demise.

"You can try, but don't think I'll make it easy just because you're to be my wife."

Adriana's gaze darkened with the challenge, and I knew tonight would be one to remember. "May the best heathen win, darling."

Dear Miss Match,

How do you know when it's time to stop staying scandalous and enjoy your happily-ever-after?

Yours,
Secretly Scandalous

Dear Secret,

When you find the one who drives you to the brink of insanity and tests your patience (and who tests your will to not commit a bloody, vengeful murder), then you know it's time to settle down and settle into your eternal bliss.

Humor aside, when your heart flutters madly each time you see them, when they love and respect you without limits or rules, when you find your idea of a perfect match for you, that's when you know it's time for your happily-ever-after. Even if he or she is a reformed rake.

Until next time, sweet sinners, stay scandalous.
Miss Match

ACKNOWLEDGMENTS

Writing a book starts out as a solitary venture, but quickly turns into the most wonderful team experience. I am forever grateful to my agent, Barbara Poelle, who is the best advocate and friend this side of the Seven Circles. Huge thank you to my team at Word One Literary, Heather Baror-Shapiro at Baror Intl, and Sean Berard at Grand View.

Helen O'Hare, I cannot thank you enough for your wonderful eye and willingness to keep rolling up your editorial sleeves or hop on a call to make sure we land on the story of our dreams.

To my whole Little, Brown team, thank you for all the hard work and magic you put into these books. Your early excitement is one of my favorite parts of the journey. Thank you for cheering me on and for loving these sinful demon princes: Ben Allen, Linda Arends, Katie Blatt, Eileen Chetti, Danielle Finnegan, Elece Green, Sally Kim, Gregg Kulick, Gabrielle Leporati, Allison Merchant, Taylor Navis, Bruce Nichols, Gianella Rojas, Liv Ryan, Stacy Schuck, Mary Tondorf-Dick, and a heartfelt thanks to Shane East and Marisa Calin for their stellar voice performances. Virginia Allyn, special thanks for the amazing maps of the Seven Circles—I am obsessed with each one!

To my brilliant UK team at Hodderscape, I could not be more grateful for everything you do to make these books so sinfully beautiful. Molly Powell, editor extraordinaire, thank you for your wickedly smart notes. Kate Keehan, Natasha Qureshi, Sophie Judge, Laura Bartholomew and the whole team, I seriously can't thank you enough.

Mom, Dad, Kelli, Ben—love you all beyond mere mortal words.

To all the booksellers, librarians, and to every reader who shouts from the social media rooftops about these books, I hope you know how amazing you are and how thankful I am to have you adventuring with me. On to the next House of Sin!

ABOUT THE AUTHOR

Kerri Maniscalco is the #1 *New York Times* bestselling author of the Stalking Jack the Ripper series, the Kingdom of the Wicked series and her adult fantasy romance *Throne of the Fallen,* the start of her Prince of Sin series. Kerri grew up in a semi-haunted house outside NYC, where her fascination with Gothic settings began. To date her books have been translated into more than twenty languages and have been viewed on TikTok a few hundred million times.

Gluttony

THE NIGHT DISTRICT

SEVEN SINS CLUB

THE SEVEN SINS

GENOASE

CONFECTIONS

MILLINERY

ETERNAL REST

ADRIANA'S HOUSE

THE WICKED DAILY

LE BLANC

WICKED DAILY

PRINTER'S ROW